GENERATIONS

my little PONY

GENERATIONS

Licensed By:

IDW @IDWpublishing
IDWpublishing.com

COVER ARTIST:
Amy Mebberson

SERIES EDITOR:
Megan Brown

COLLECTION EDITORS:
Alonzo Simon and Zac Boone

COLLECTION DESIGNER:
Neil Uyetake

978-1-68405-794-8   25 24 23 22   1 2 3 4

MY LITTLE PONY: GENERATIONS. AUGUST 2022. FIRST PRINTING. MY LITTLE PONY
and HASBRO and all related trademarks and logos are trademarks of Hasbro, Inc. ©
2022 Hasbro. The IDW Logo is registered in the U.S. Patent and Trademark Office. IDW
Publishing, a division of Idea and Design Works, LLC. Editorial offices: 2355 Northside
Drive, Suite 140, San Diego, CA 92108. Any similarities to persons living or dead are
purely coincidental. With the exception of artwork used for review purposes, none
of the contents of this publication may be reprinted without permission of Idea and
Design Works, LLC. IDW Publishing does not read or accept unsolicited submissions of
ideas, stories, or artwork. Printed in Canada.

Originally published as MY LITTLE PONY: GENERATIONS issues #1–5.

Nachie Marsham, Publisher
Blake Kobashigawa, SVP Sales, Marketing & Strategy
Tara McCrillis, VP Publishing Operations
Anna Morrow, VP Marketing & Publicity
Alex Hargett, VP Sales
Jamie S. Rich, Executive Editorial Director
Scott Dunbier, Director, Special Projects
Greg Gustin, Sr. Director, Content Strategy
Lauren LePera, Sr. Managing Editor
Keith Davidsen, Director, Marketing & PR
Topher Alford, Sr. Digital Marketing Manager
Patrick O'Connell, Sr. Manager, Direct Market Sales
Shauna Monteforte, Sr. Director of Manufacturing Operations
Greg Foreman, Director DTC Sales & Operations
Nathan Widick, Director of Design
Neil Uyetake, Sr. Art Director, Design & Production
Shawn Lee, Art Director, Design & Production
Jack Rivera, Art Director, Marketing

Ted Adams and Robbie Robbins, IDW Founders

Special thanks to Tayla Reo, Ed Lane, Beth Artale, and Michael Kelly for their
invaluable assistance.

For international rights, contact licensing@idwpublishing.com.

www.IDWpublishing.com

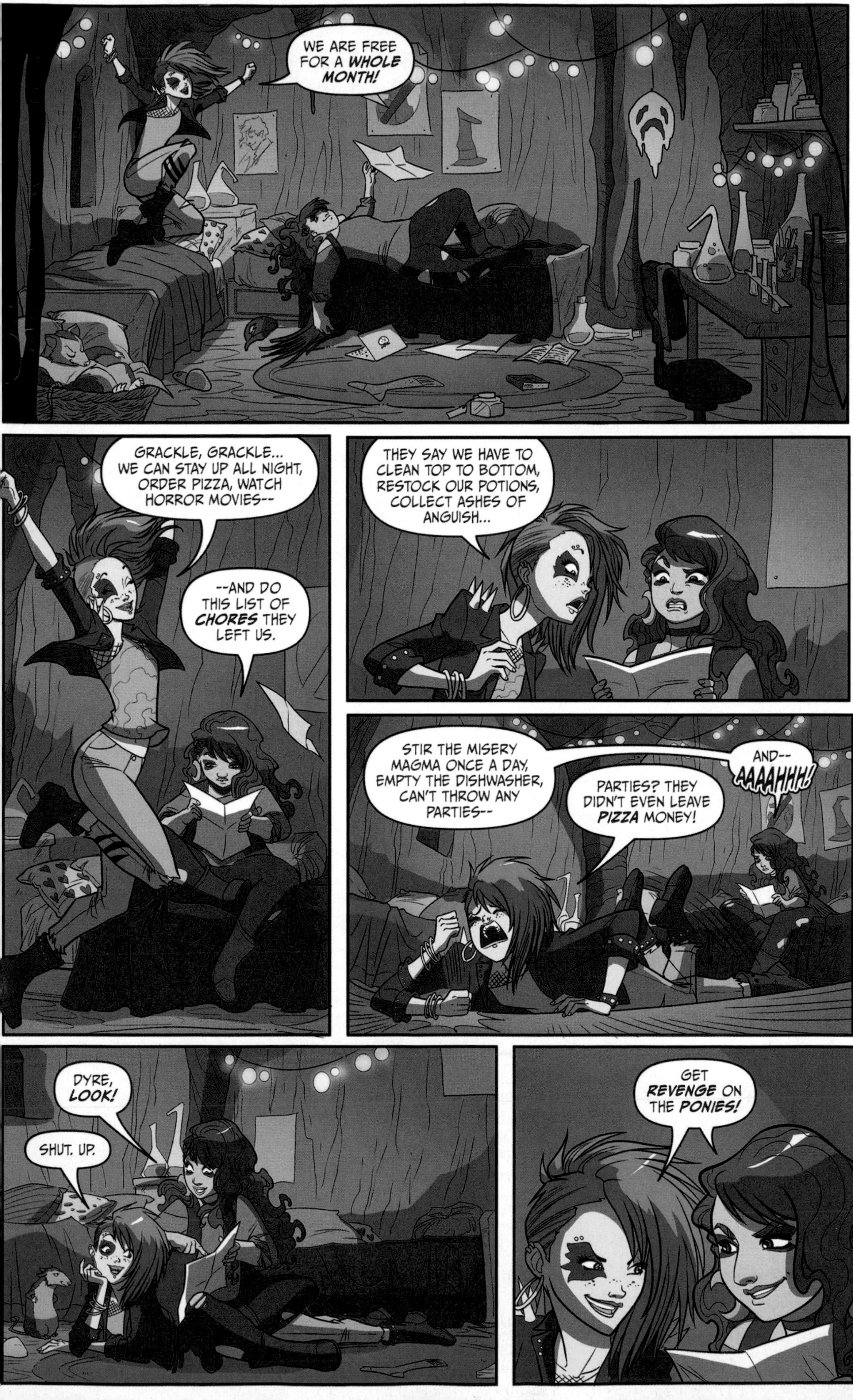
WE ARE FREE FOR A *WHOLE MONTH!*
GRACKLE, GRACKLE... WE CAN STAY UP ALL NIGHT, ORDER PIZZA, WATCH HORROR MOVIES--
--AND DO THIS LIST OF *CHORES* THEY LEFT US.
THEY SAY WE HAVE TO CLEAN TOP TO BOTTOM, RESTOCK OUR POTIONS, COLLECT ASHES OF ANGUISH...
STIR THE MISERY MAGMA ONCE A DAY, EMPTY THE DISHWASHER, CAN'T THROW ANY PARTIES--
AND--
AAAAHHH!
PARTIES? THEY DIDN'T EVEN LEAVE *PIZZA* MONEY!
DYRE, *LOOK!*
SHUT. UP.
GET *REVENGE* ON THE *PONIES!*

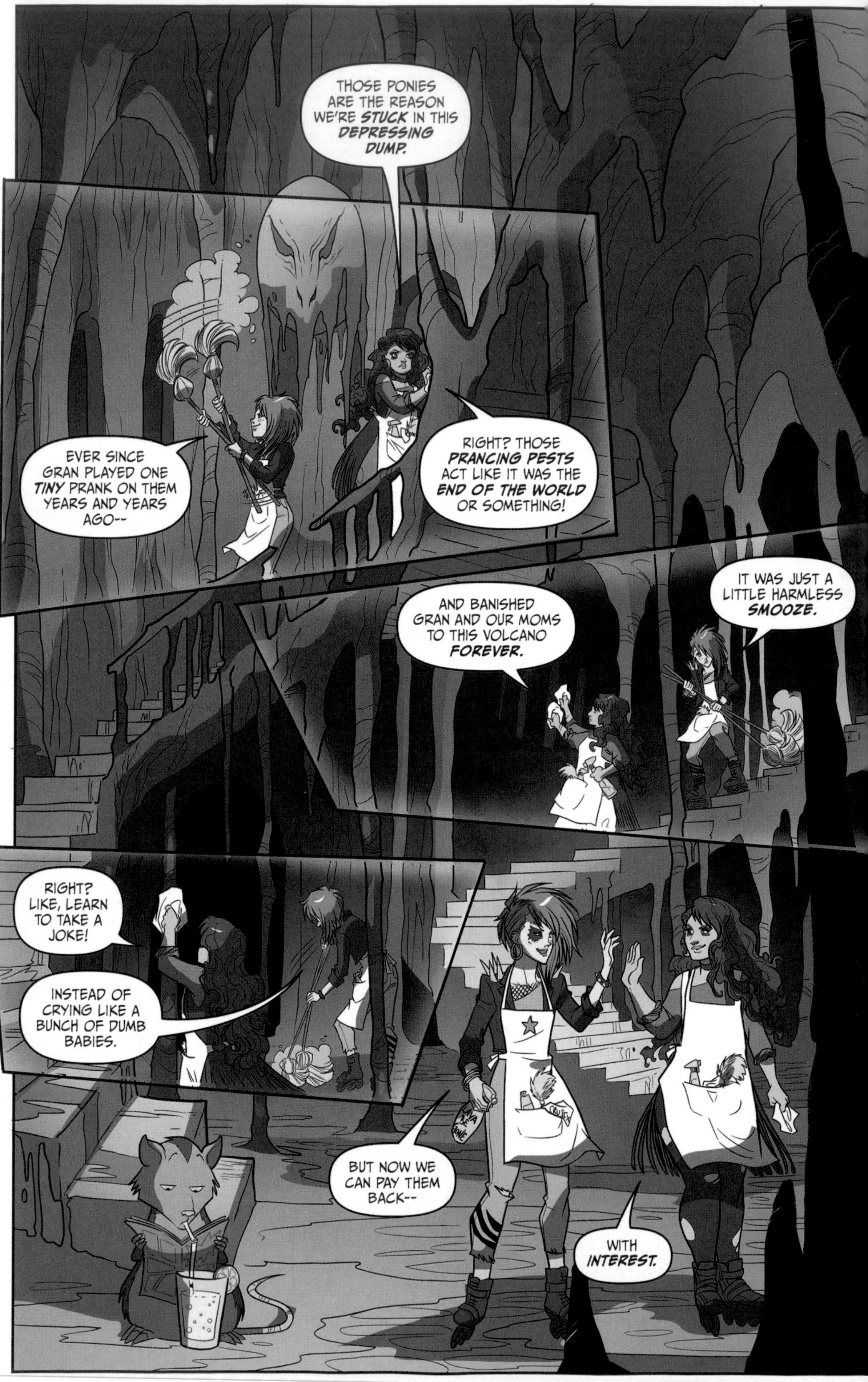
THOSE PONIES ARE THE REASON WE'RE *STUCK* IN THIS *DEPRESSING DUMP.*
EVER SINCE GRAN PLAYED ONE *TINY* PRANK ON THEM YEARS AND YEARS AGO--
RIGHT? THOSE *PRANCING PESTS* ACT LIKE IT WAS THE *END OF THE WORLD* OR SOMETHING!
AND BANISHED GRAN AND OUR MOMS TO THIS VOLCANO *FOREVER.*
IT WAS JUST A LITTLE HARMLESS *SMOOZE.*
RIGHT? LIKE, LEARN TO TAKE A JOKE!
INSTEAD OF CRYING LIKE A BUNCH OF DUMB BABIES.
BUT NOW WE CAN PAY THEM BACK--
WITH *INTEREST.*

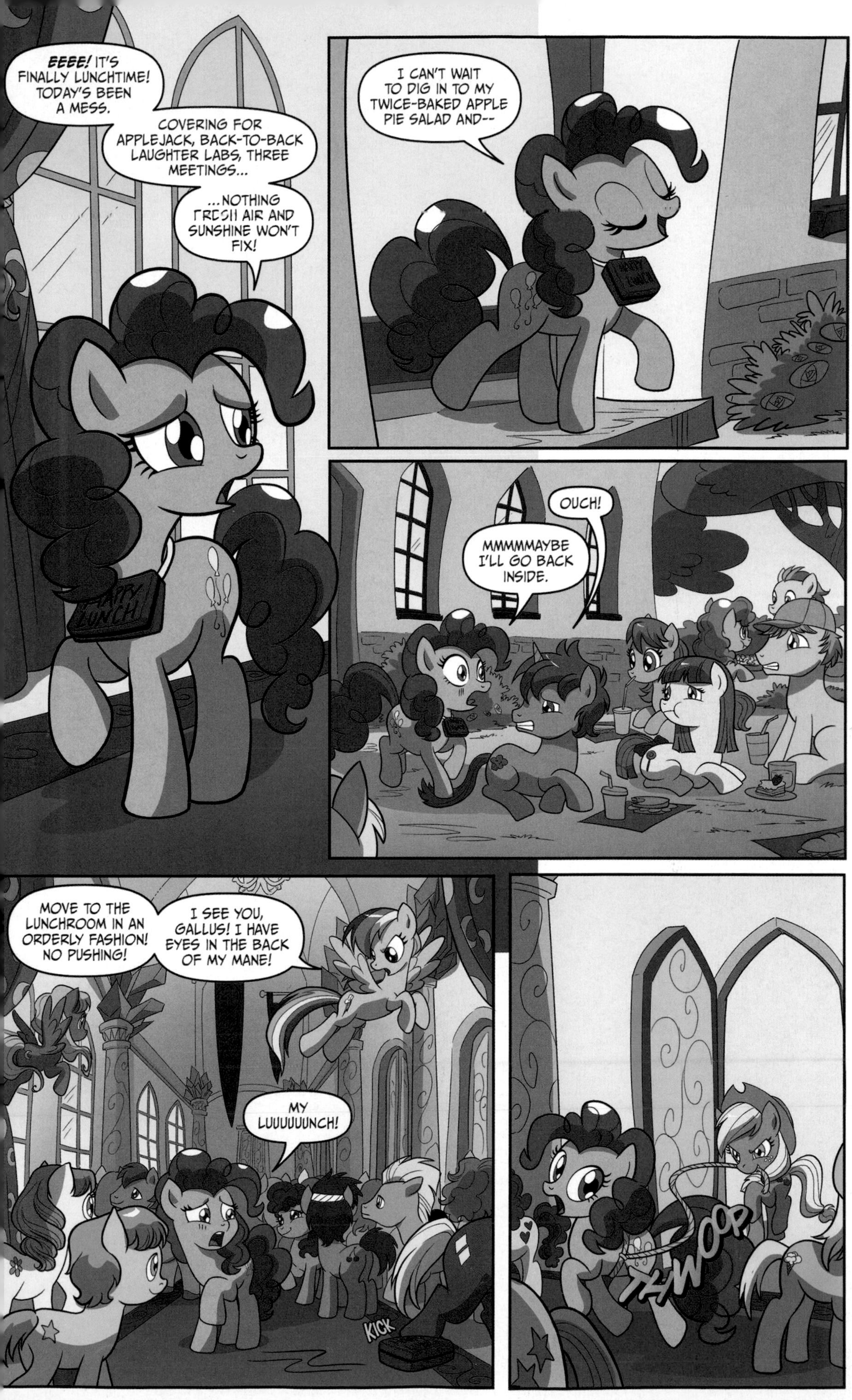

EEEE! IT'S FINALLY LUNCHTIME! TODAY'S BEEN A MESS.
COVERING FOR APPLEJACK, BACK-TO-BACK LAUGHTER LABS, THREE MEETINGS...
...NOTHING FRESH AIR AND SUNSHINE WON'T FIX!
HAPPY LUNCH!
I CAN'T WAIT TO DIG IN TO MY TWICE-BAKED APPLE PIE SALAD AND--
OUCH!
MMMMMAYBE I'LL GO BACK INSIDE.
MOVE TO THE LUNCHROOM IN AN ORDERLY FASHION! NO PUSHING!
I SEE YOU, GALLUS! I HAVE EYES IN THE BACK OF MY MANE!
MY LUUUUUUNCH!
KICK
THWOOP

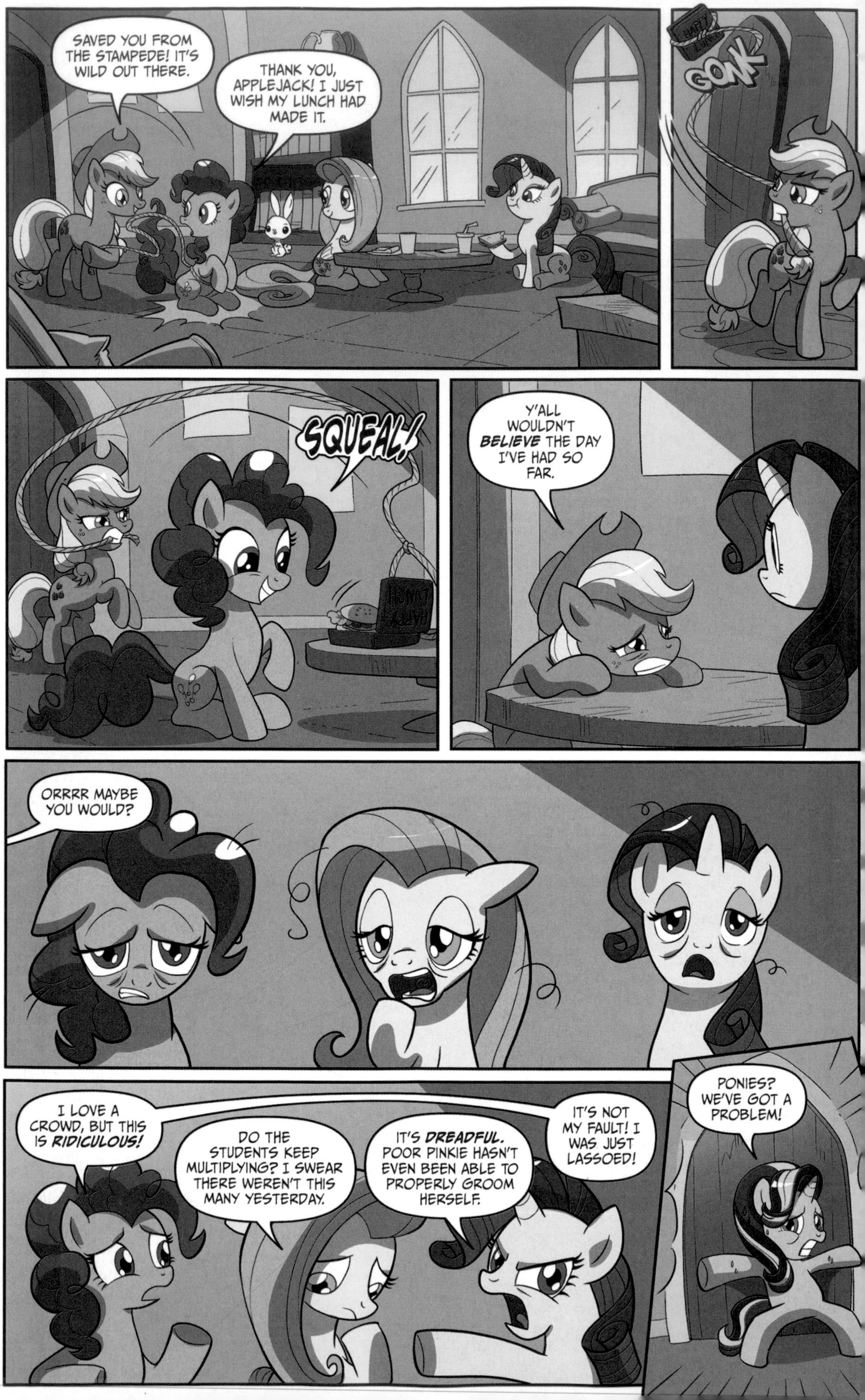
SAVED YOU FROM THE STAMPEDE! IT'S WILD OUT THERE.
THANK YOU, APPLEJACK! I JUST WISH MY LUNCH HAD MADE IT.
GONK
SQUEAL!
Y'ALL WOULDN'T **BELIEVE** THE DAY I'VE HAD SO FAR.
ORRRR MAYBE YOU WOULD?
I LOVE A CROWD, BUT THIS IS ***RIDICULOUS!***
DO THE STUDENTS KEEP MULTIPLYING? I SWEAR THERE WEREN'T THIS MANY YESTERDAY.
IT'S ***DREADFUL.*** POOR PINKIE HASN'T EVEN BEEN ABLE TO PROPERLY GROOM HERSELF.
IT'S NOT MY FAULT! I WAS JUST LASSOED!
PONIES? WE'VE GOT A PROBLEM!

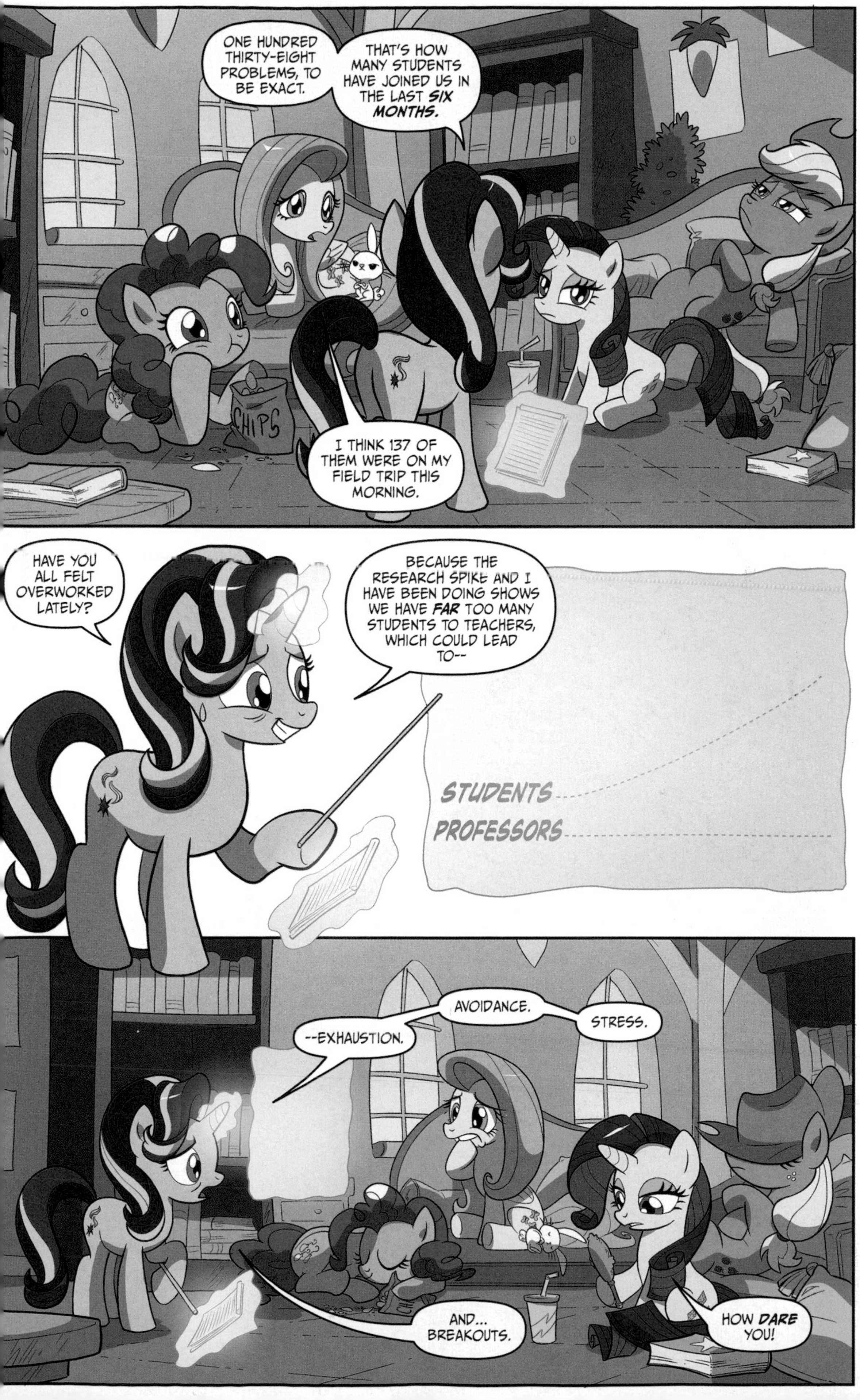
ONE HUNDRED THIRTY-EIGHT PROBLEMS, TO BE EXACT.
THAT'S HOW MANY STUDENTS HAVE JOINED US IN THE LAST *SIX MONTHS.*
I THINK 137 OF THEM WERE ON MY FIELD TRIP THIS MORNING.
HAVE YOU ALL FELT OVERWORKED LATELY?
BECAUSE THE RESEARCH SPIKE AND I HAVE BEEN DOING SHOWS WE HAVE *FAR* TOO MANY STUDENTS TO TEACHERS, WHICH COULD LEAD TO--
STUDENTS
PROFESSORS
--EXHAUSTION.
AVOIDANCE.
STRESS.
AND... BREAKOUTS.
HOW *DARE* YOU!

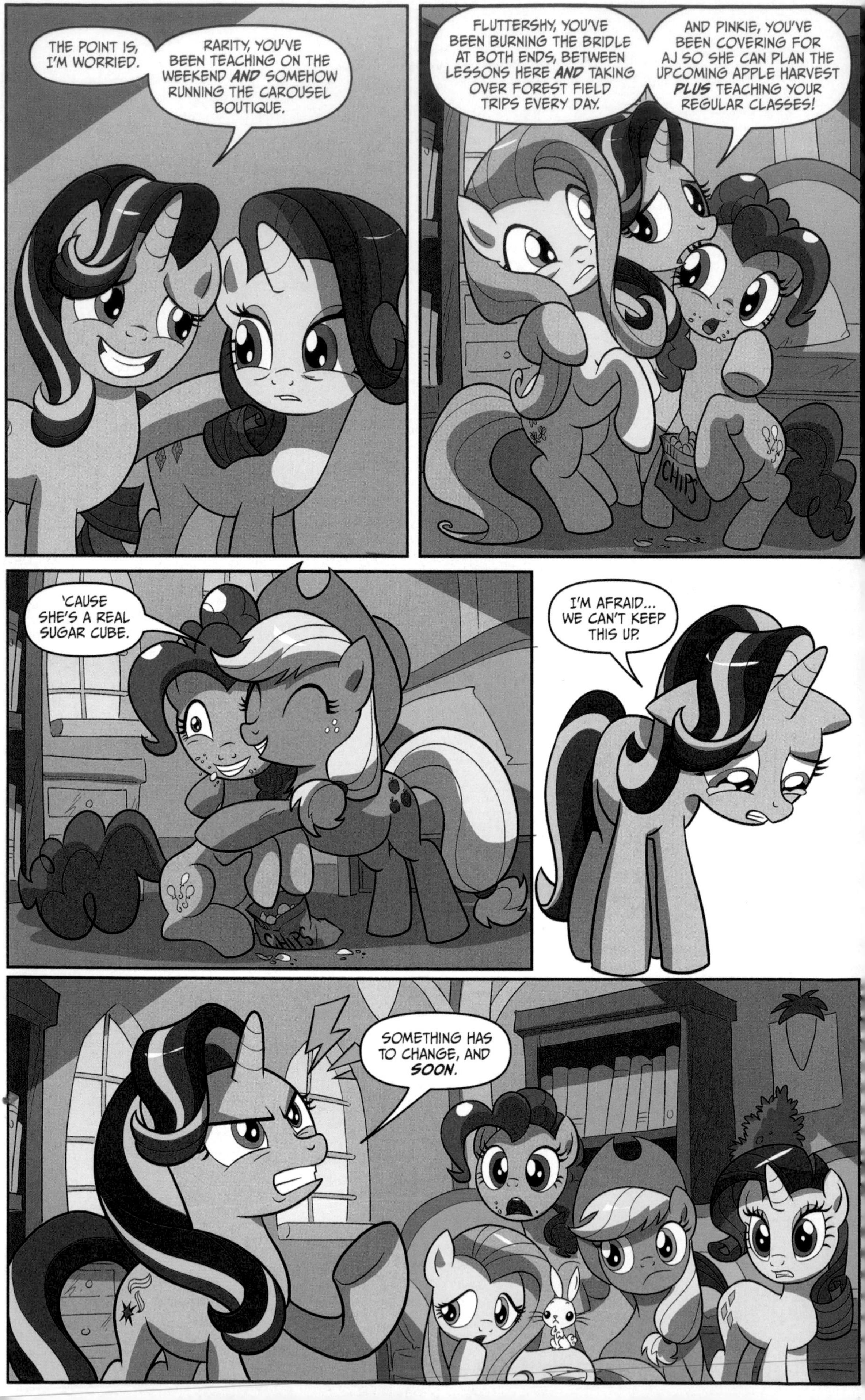

THE POINT IS, I'M WORRIED.
RARITY, YOU'VE BEEN TEACHING ON THE WEEKEND AND SOMEHOW RUNNING THE CAROUSEL BOUTIQUE.
FLUTTERSHY, YOU'VE BEEN BURNING THE BRIDLE AT BOTH ENDS, BETWEEN LESSONS HERE AND TAKING OVER FOREST FIELD TRIPS EVERY DAY.
AND PINKIE, YOU'VE BEEN COVERING FOR AJ SO SHE CAN PLAN THE UPCOMING APPLE HARVEST PLUS TEACHING YOUR REGULAR CLASSES!
CHIPS
'CAUSE SHE'S A REAL SUGAR CUBE.
CHIPS
I'M AFRAID... WE CAN'T KEEP THIS UP.
SOMETHING HAS TO CHANGE, AND SOON.

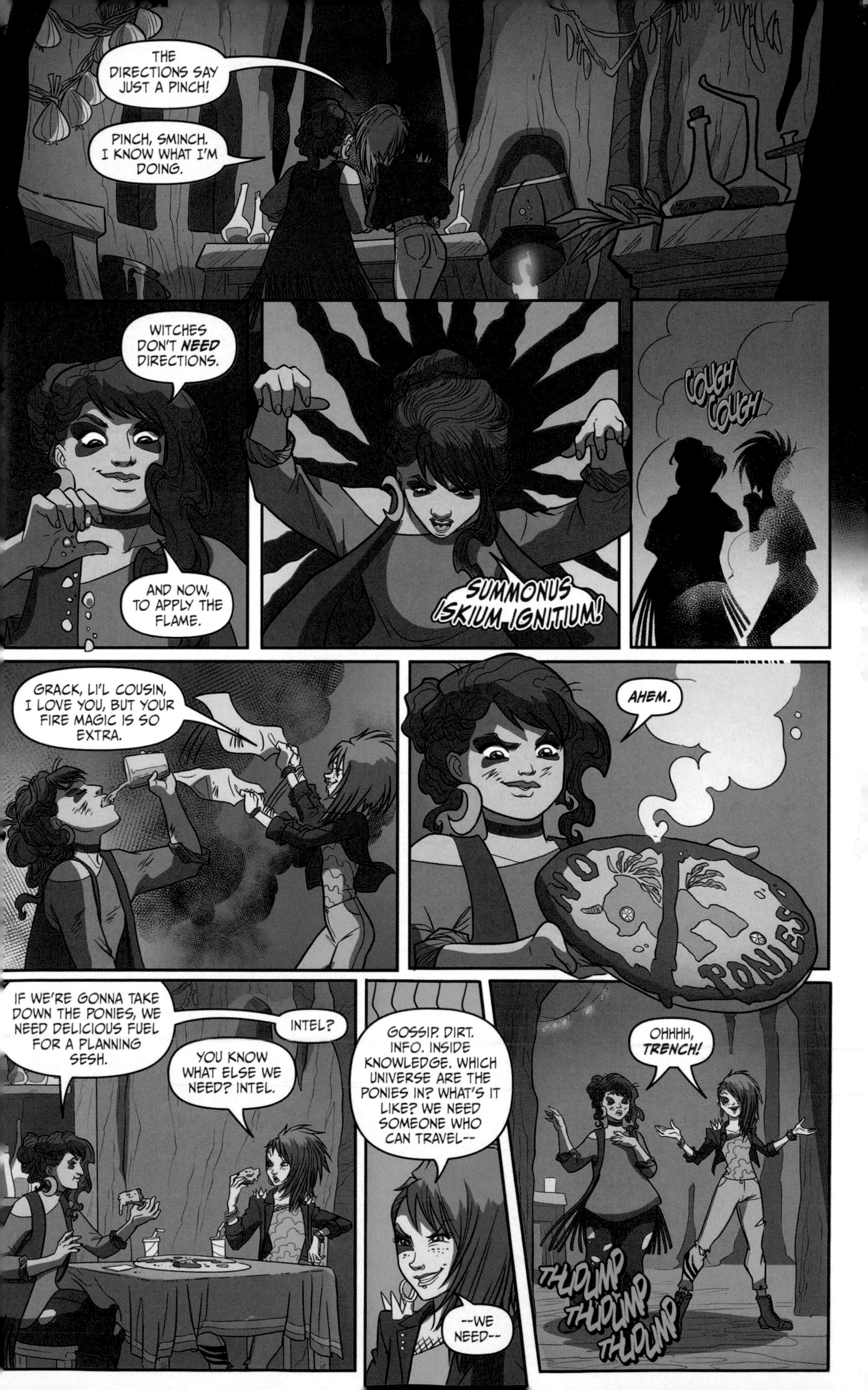
THE DIRECTIONS SAY JUST A PINCH!
PINCH, SMINCH. I KNOW WHAT I'M DOING.
WITCHES DON'T **NEED** DIRECTIONS.
AND NOW, TO APPLY THE FLAME.
SUMMONUS ISKIUM IGNITIUM!
COUGH COUGH
GRACK, LI'L COUSIN, I LOVE YOU, BUT YOUR FIRE MAGIC IS SO EXTRA.
AHEM.
NO PONIES
IF WE'RE GONNA TAKE DOWN THE PONIES, WE NEED DELICIOUS FUEL FOR A PLANNING SESH.
YOU KNOW WHAT ELSE WE NEED? INTEL.
INTEL?
GOSSIP. DIRT. INFO. INSIDE KNOWLEDGE. WHICH UNIVERSE ARE THE PONIES IN? WHAT'S IT LIKE? WE NEED SOMEONE WHO CAN TRAVEL--
--WE NEED--
OHHHH, **TRENCH!**
THUDUMP THUDUMP THUDUMP

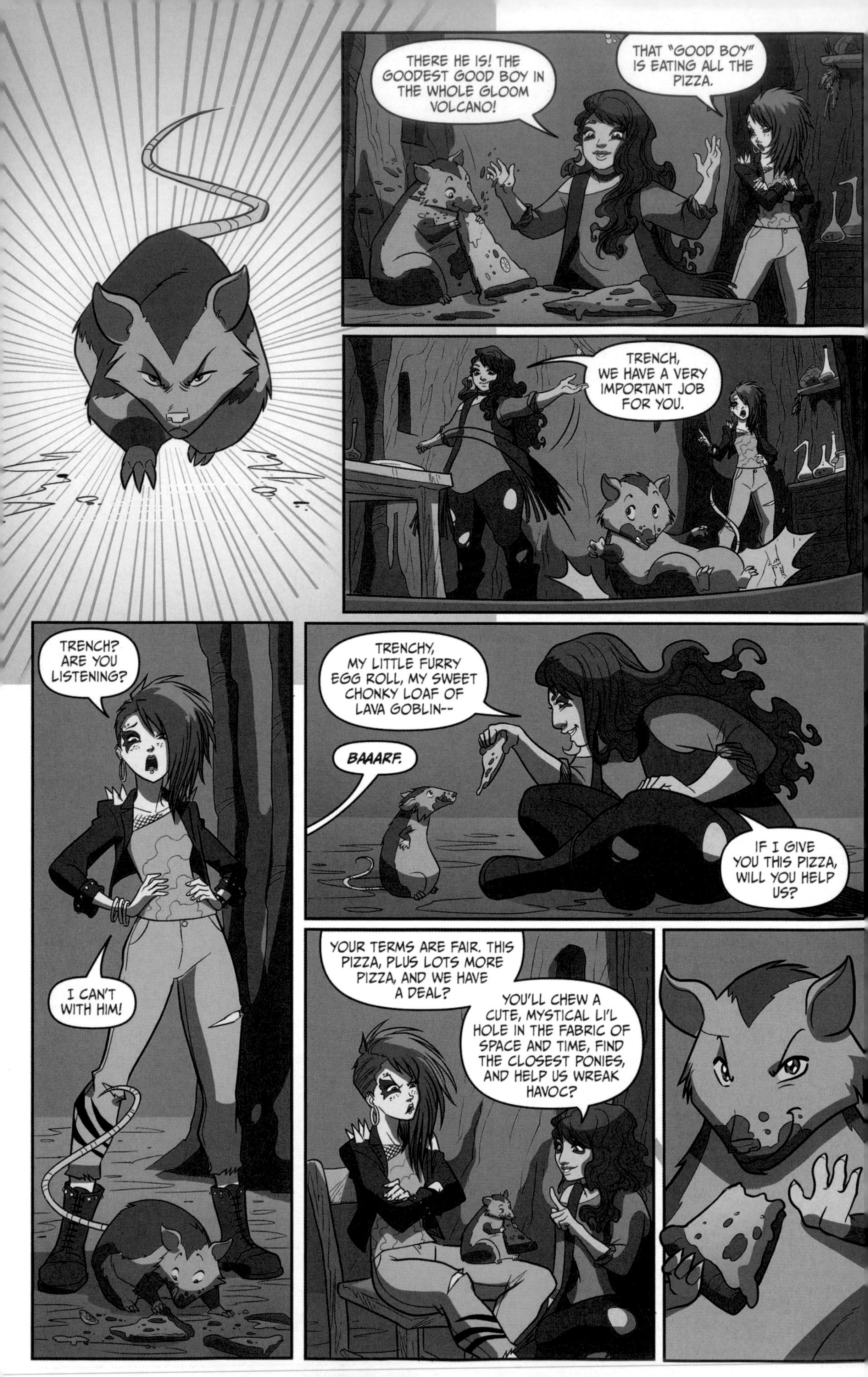
THERE HE IS! THE GOODEST GOOD BOY IN THE WHOLE GLOOM VOLCANO!
THAT "GOOD BOY" IS EATING ALL THE PIZZA.
TRENCH, WE HAVE A VERY IMPORTANT JOB FOR YOU.
TRENCH? ARE YOU LISTENING?
I CAN'T WITH HIM!
TRENCHY, MY LITTLE FURRY EGG ROLL, MY SWEET CHONKY LOAF OF LAVA GOBLIN--
BAAARF.
IF I GIVE YOU THIS PIZZA, WILL YOU HELP US?
YOU'LL CHEW A CUTE, MYSTICAL LI'L HOLE IN THE FABRIC OF SPACE AND TIME, FIND THE CLOSEST PONIES, AND HELP US WREAK HAVOC?
YOUR TERMS ARE FAIR. THIS PIZZA, PLUS LOTS MORE PIZZA, AND WE HAVE A DEAL?

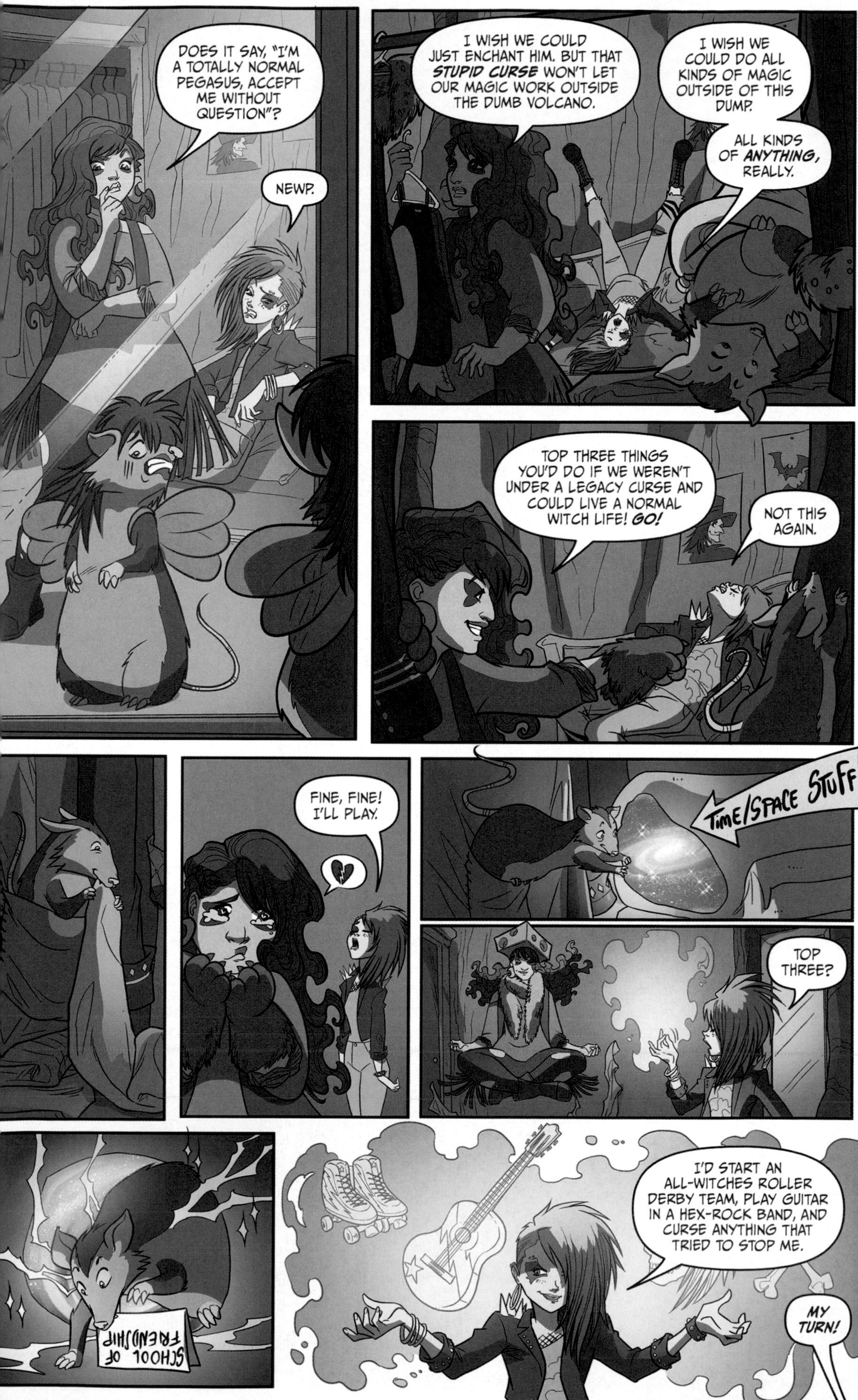
DOES IT SAY, "I'M A TOTALLY NORMAL PEGASUS, ACCEPT ME WITHOUT QUESTION"?
NEWP.
I WISH WE COULD JUST ENCHANT HIM. BUT THAT STUPID CURSE WON'T LET OUR MAGIC WORK OUTSIDE THE DUMB VOLCANO.
I WISH WE COULD DO ALL KINDS OF MAGIC OUTSIDE OF THIS DUMP.
ALL KINDS OF ANYTHING, REALLY.
TOP THREE THINGS YOU'D DO IF WE WEREN'T UNDER A LEGACY CURSE AND COULD LIVE A NORMAL WITCH LIFE! GO!
NOT THIS AGAIN.
FINE, FINE! I'LL PLAY.
TIME/SPACE STUFF
TOP THREE?
SCHOOL OF FRIENDSHIP
I'D START AN ALL-WITCHES ROLLER DERBY TEAM, PLAY GUITAR IN A HEX-ROCK BAND, AND CURSE ANYTHING THAT TRIED TO STOP ME.
MY TURN!

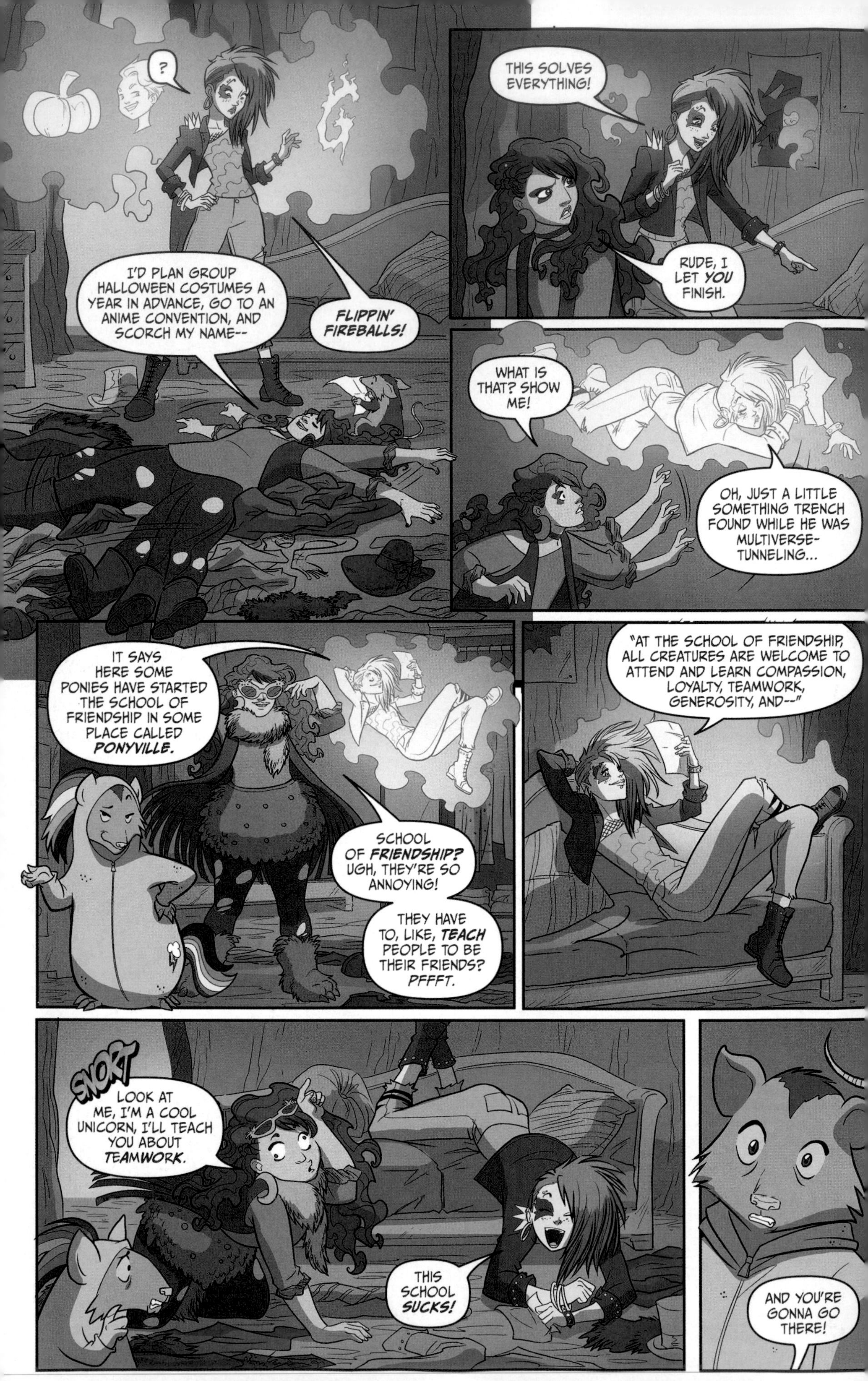
?
I'D PLAN GROUP HALLOWEEN COSTUMES A YEAR IN ADVANCE, GO TO AN ANIME CONVENTION, AND SCORCH MY NAME--
FLIPPIN' FIREBALLS!
THIS SOLVES EVERYTHING!
RUDE, I LET YOU FINISH.
WHAT IS THAT? SHOW ME!
OH, JUST A LITTLE SOMETHING TRENCH FOUND WHILE HE WAS MULTIVERSE-TUNNELING...
IT SAYS HERE SOME PONIES HAVE STARTED THE SCHOOL OF FRIENDSHIP IN SOME PLACE CALLED PONYVILLE.
SCHOOL OF FRIENDSHIP? UGH, THEY'RE SO ANNOYING!
THEY HAVE TO, LIKE, TEACH PEOPLE TO BE THEIR FRIENDS? PFFFT.
"AT THE SCHOOL OF FRIENDSHIP, ALL CREATURES ARE WELCOME TO ATTEND AND LEARN COMPASSION, LOYALTY, TEAMWORK, GENEROSITY, AND--"
SNORT
LOOK AT ME, I'M A COOL UNICORN, I'LL TEACH YOU ABOUT TEAMWORK.
THIS SCHOOL SUCKS!
AND YOU'RE GONNA GO THERE!

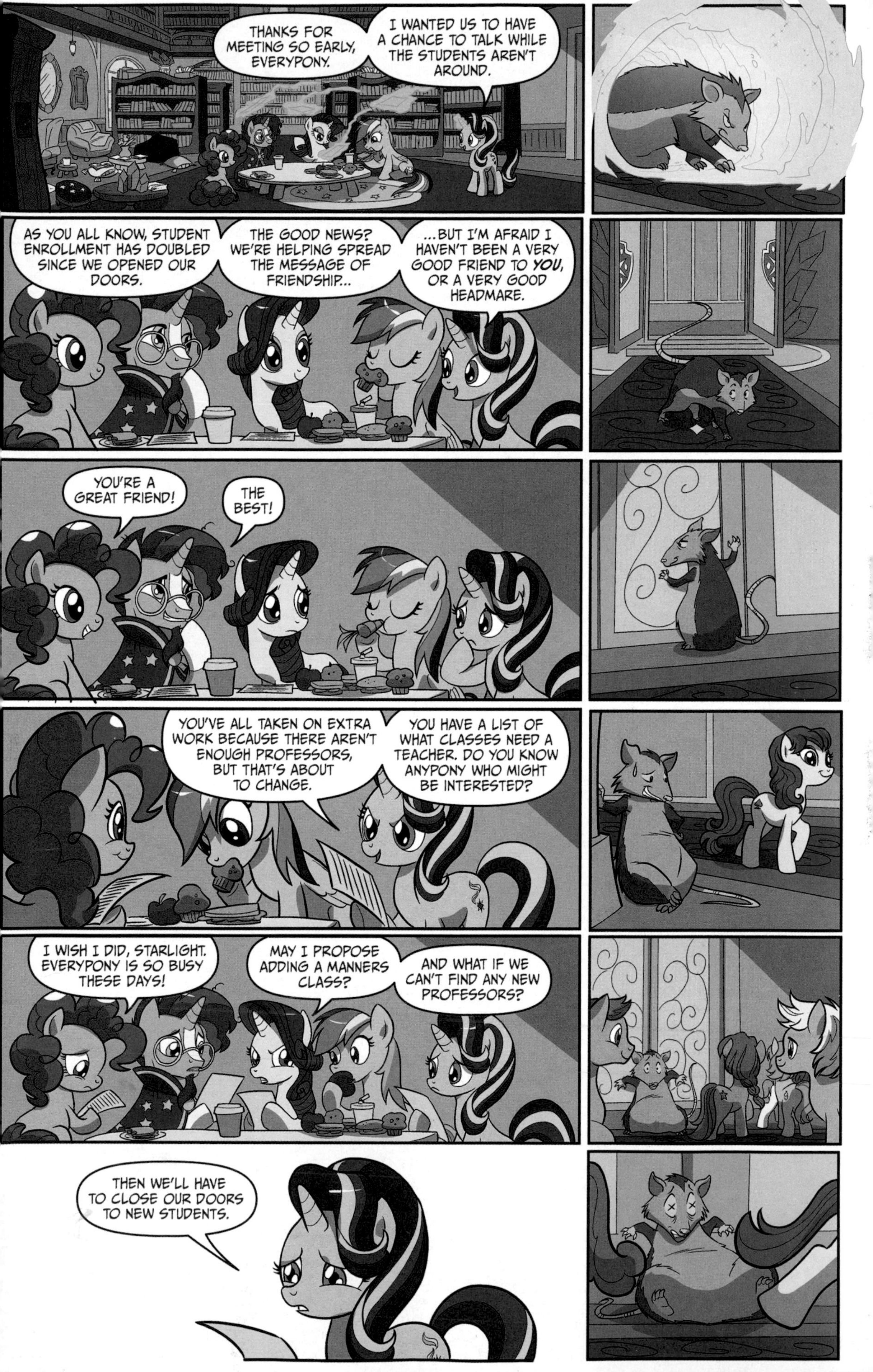
THANKS FOR MEETING SO EARLY, EVERYPONY.
I WANTED US TO HAVE A CHANCE TO TALK WHILE THE STUDENTS AREN'T AROUND.
AS YOU ALL KNOW, STUDENT ENROLLMENT HAS DOUBLED SINCE WE OPENED OUR DOORS.
THE GOOD NEWS? WE'RE HELPING SPREAD THE MESSAGE OF FRIENDSHIP...
...BUT I'M AFRAID I HAVEN'T BEEN A VERY GOOD FRIEND TO *YOU*, OR A VERY GOOD HEADMARE.
YOU'RE A GREAT FRIEND!
THE BEST!
YOU'VE ALL TAKEN ON EXTRA WORK BECAUSE THERE AREN'T ENOUGH PROFESSORS, BUT THAT'S ABOUT TO CHANGE.
YOU HAVE A LIST OF WHAT CLASSES NEED A TEACHER. DO YOU KNOW ANYPONY WHO MIGHT BE INTERESTED?
I WISH I DID, STARLIGHT. EVERYPONY IS SO BUSY THESE DAYS!
MAY I PROPOSE ADDING A MANNERS CLASS?
AND WHAT IF WE CAN'T FIND ANY NEW PROFESSORS?
THEN WE'LL HAVE TO CLOSE OUR DOORS TO NEW STUDENTS.

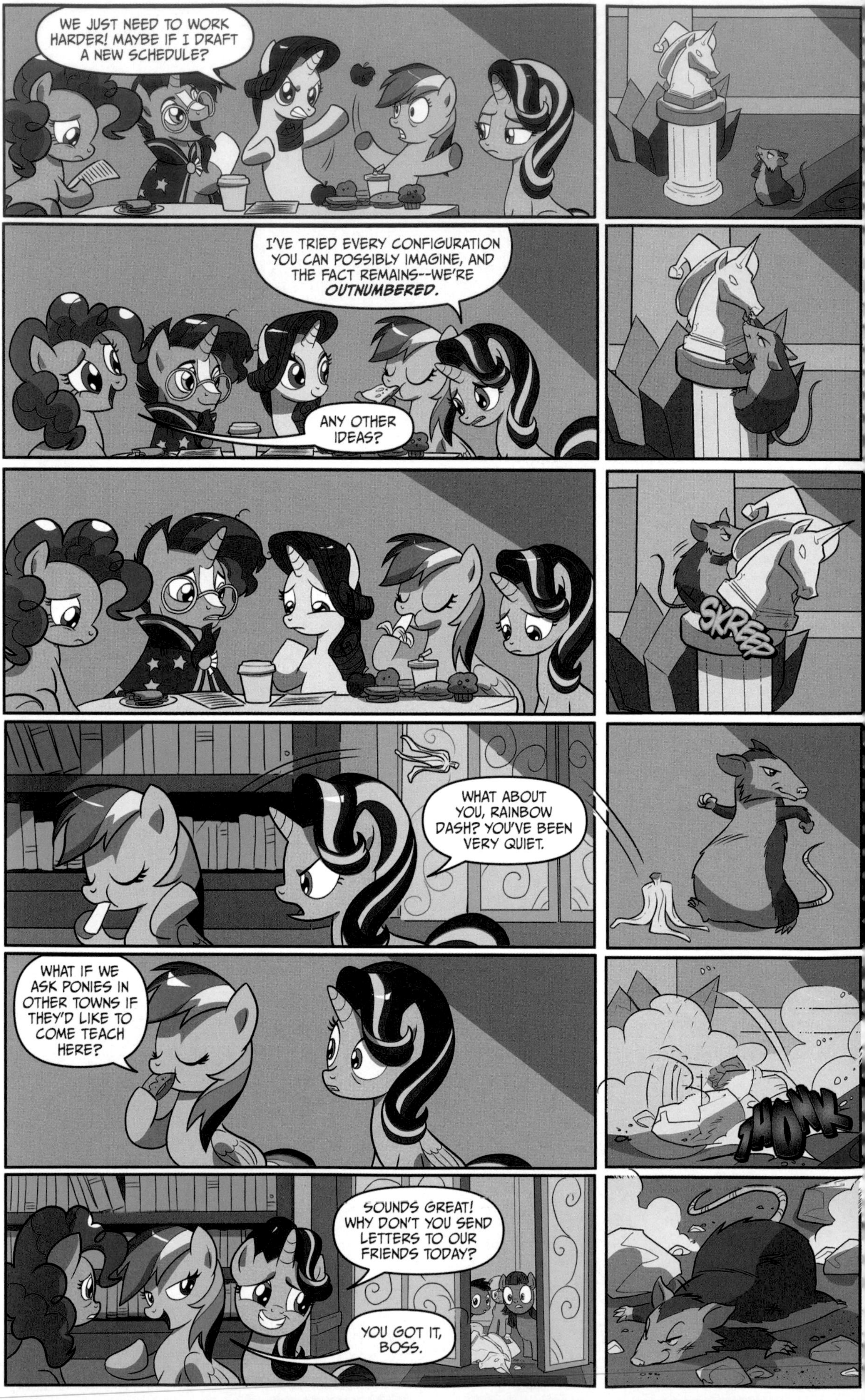
WE JUST NEED TO WORK HARDER! MAYBE IF I DRAFT A NEW SCHEDULE?
I'VE TRIED EVERY CONFIGURATION YOU CAN POSSIBLY IMAGINE, AND THE FACT REMAINS--WE'RE *OUTNUMBERED.*
ANY OTHER IDEAS?
SKREEP
WHAT ABOUT YOU, RAINBOW DASH? YOU'VE BEEN VERY QUIET.
WHAT IF WE ASK PONIES IN OTHER TOWNS IF THEY'D LIKE TO COME TEACH HERE?
THONK
SOUNDS GREAT! WHY DON'T YOU SEND LETTERS TO OUR FRIENDS TODAY?
YOU GOT IT, BOSS.

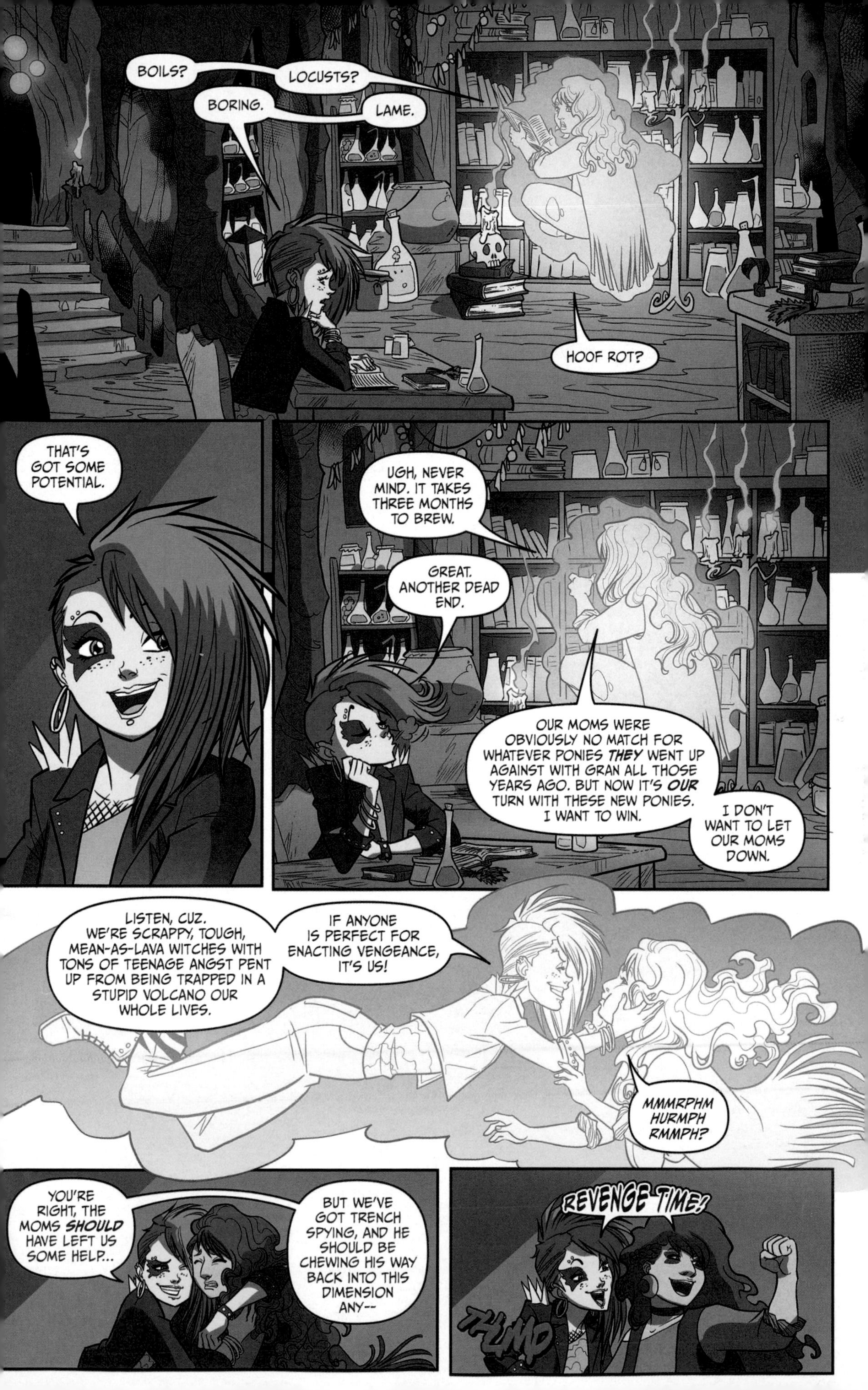
BOILS?
LOCUSTS?
BORING.
LAME.
HOOF ROT?
THAT'S GOT SOME POTENTIAL.
UGH, NEVER MIND. IT TAKES THREE MONTHS TO BREW.
GREAT. ANOTHER DEAD END.
OUR MOMS WERE OBVIOUSLY NO MATCH FOR WHATEVER PONIES *THEY* WENT UP AGAINST WITH GRAN ALL THOSE YEARS AGO. BUT NOW IT'S *OUR* TURN WITH THESE NEW PONIES. I WANT TO WIN.
I DON'T WANT TO LET OUR MOMS DOWN.
LISTEN, CUZ. WE'RE SCRAPPY, TOUGH, MEAN-AS-LAVA WITCHES WITH TONS OF TEENAGE ANGST PENT UP FROM BEING TRAPPED IN A STUPID VOLCANO OUR WHOLE LIVES.
IF ANYONE IS PERFECT FOR ENACTING VENGEANCE, IT'S US!
MMMRPHM HURMPH RMMPH?
YOU'RE RIGHT, THE MOMS *SHOULD* HAVE LEFT US SOME HELP...
BUT WE'VE GOT TRENCH SPYING, AND HE SHOULD BE CHEWING HIS WAY BACK INTO THIS DIMENSION ANY--
REVENGE TIME!
THUMP

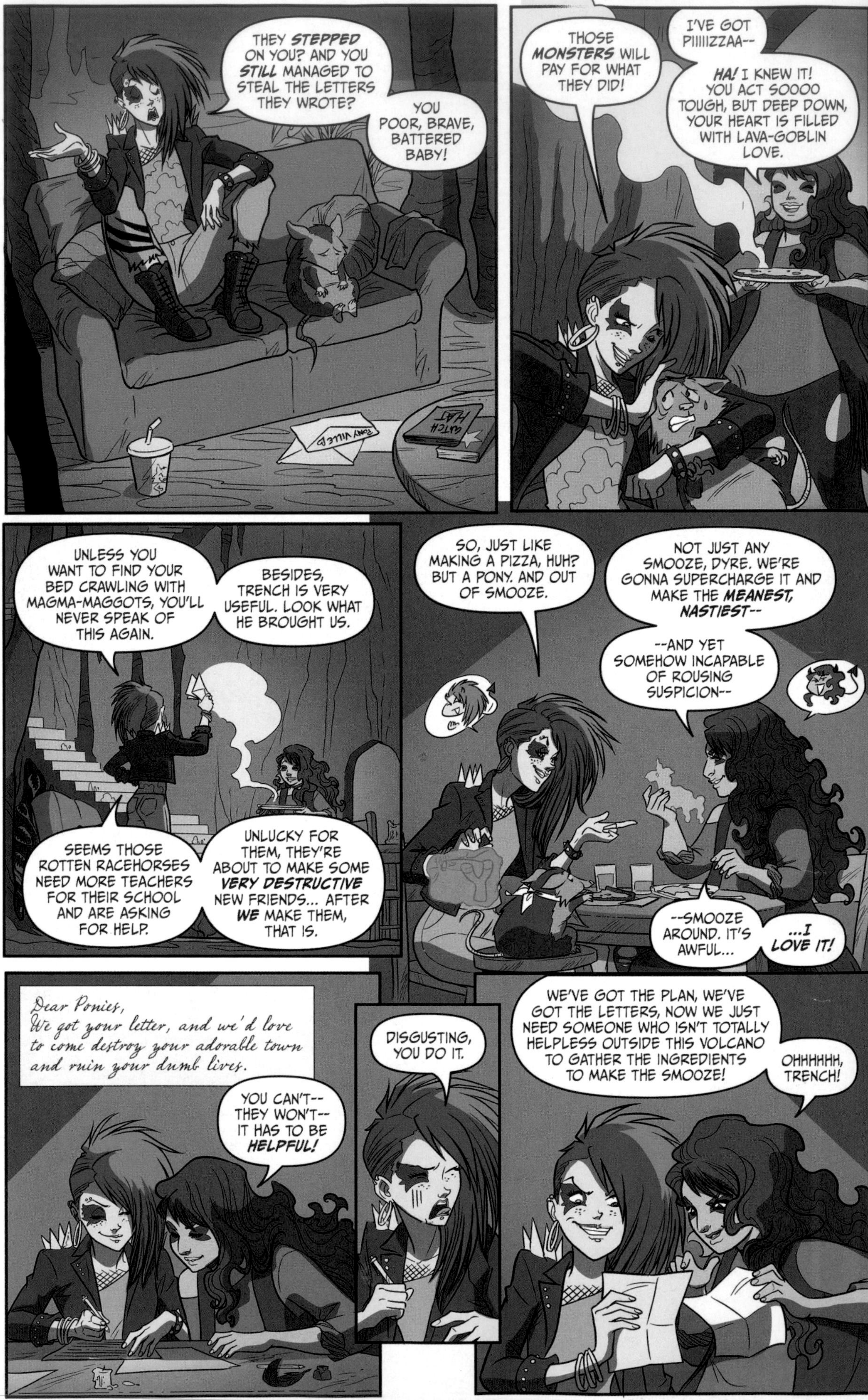

THEY *STEPPED* ON YOU? AND YOU *STILL* MANAGED TO STEAL THE LETTERS THEY WROTE?
YOU POOR, BRAVE, BATTERED BABY!
THOSE *MONSTERS* WILL PAY FOR WHAT THEY DID!
I'VE GOT PIIIIIZZAA--
HA! I KNEW IT! YOU ACT SOOOO TOUGH, BUT DEEP DOWN, YOUR HEART IS FILLED WITH LAVA-GOBLIN LOVE.
UNLESS YOU WANT TO FIND YOUR BED CRAWLING WITH MAGMA-MAGGOTS, YOU'LL NEVER SPEAK OF THIS AGAIN.
BESIDES, TRENCH IS VERY USEFUL. LOOK WHAT HE BROUGHT US.
SEEMS THOSE ROTTEN RACEHORSES NEED MORE TEACHERS FOR THEIR SCHOOL AND ARE ASKING FOR HELP.
UNLUCKY FOR THEM, THEY'RE ABOUT TO MAKE SOME *VERY DESTRUCTIVE* NEW FRIENDS... AFTER *WE* MAKE THEM, THAT IS.
SO, JUST LIKE MAKING A PIZZA, HUH? BUT A PONY. AND OUT OF SMOOZE.
NOT JUST ANY SMOOZE, DYRE. WE'RE GONNA SUPERCHARGE IT AND MAKE THE *MEANEST, NASTIEST*--
--AND YET SOMEHOW INCAPABLE OF ROUSING SUSPICION--
--SMOOZE AROUND. IT'S AWFUL...
...I LOVE IT!
Dear Ponies,
We got your letter, and we'd love to come destroy your adorable town and ruin your dumb lives.
YOU CAN'T-- THEY WON'T-- IT HAS TO BE *HELPFUL!*
DISGUSTING, YOU DO IT.
WE'VE GOT THE PLAN, WE'VE GOT THE LETTERS, NOW WE JUST NEED SOMEONE WHO ISN'T TOTALLY HELPLESS OUTSIDE THIS VOLCANO TO GATHER THE INGREDIENTS TO MAKE THE SMOOZE!
OHHHHHH, TRENCH!

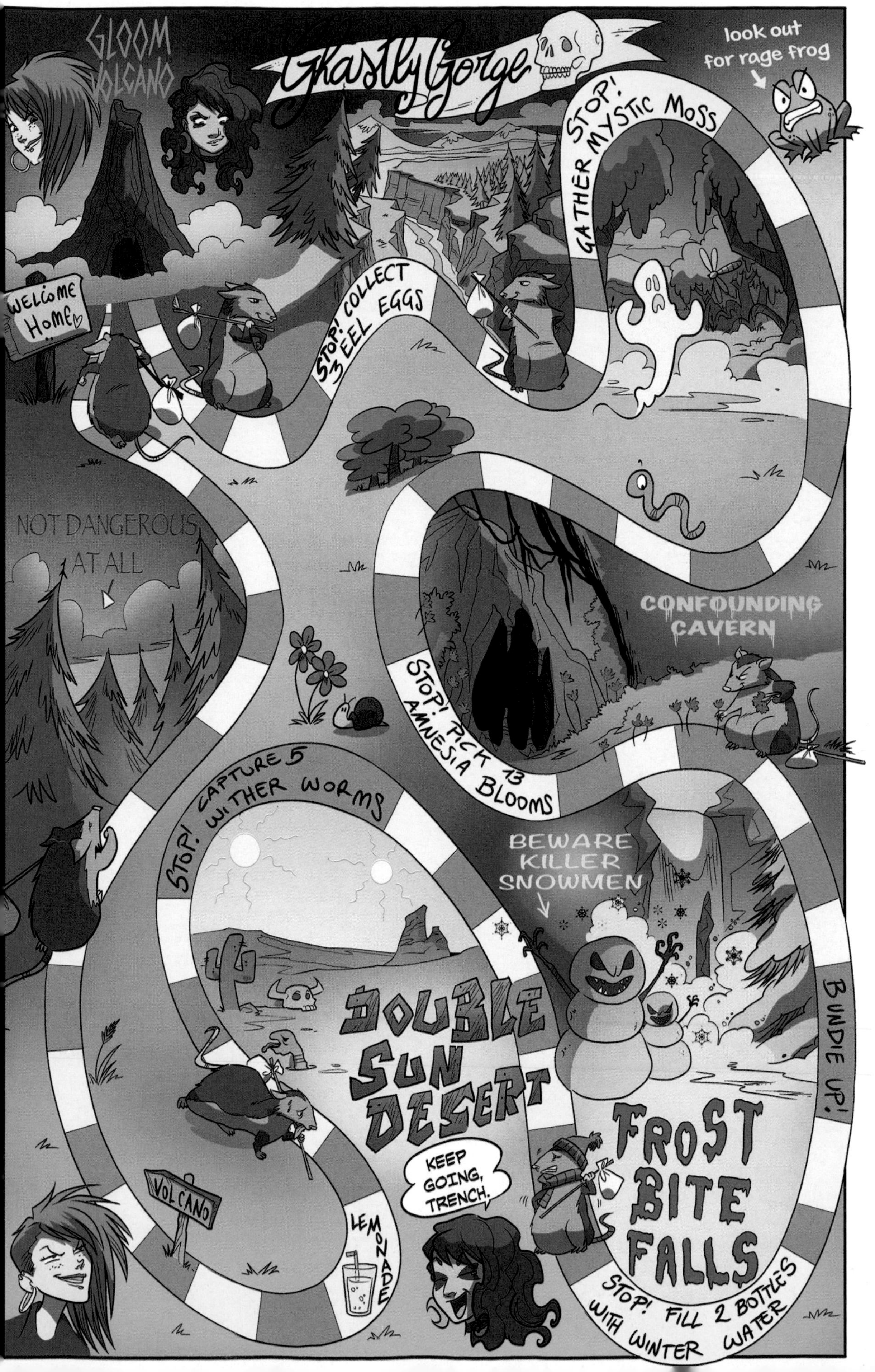

GLOOM VOLCANO
Ghastly Gorge
look out for rage frog
WELCOME HOME
STOP! COLLECT 3 EEL EGGS
STOP! GATHER MYSTIC MOSS
NOT DANGEROUS AT ALL
CONFOUNDING CAVERN
STOP! PICK 13 AMNESIA BLOOMS
STOP! CAPTURE 5 WITHER WORMS
BEWARE KILLER SNOWMEN
DOUBLE SUN DESERT
BUNDLE UP!
FROST BITE FALLS
KEEP GOING, TRENCH.
VOLCANO
LEMONADE
STOP! FILL 2 BOTTLES WITH WINTER WATER

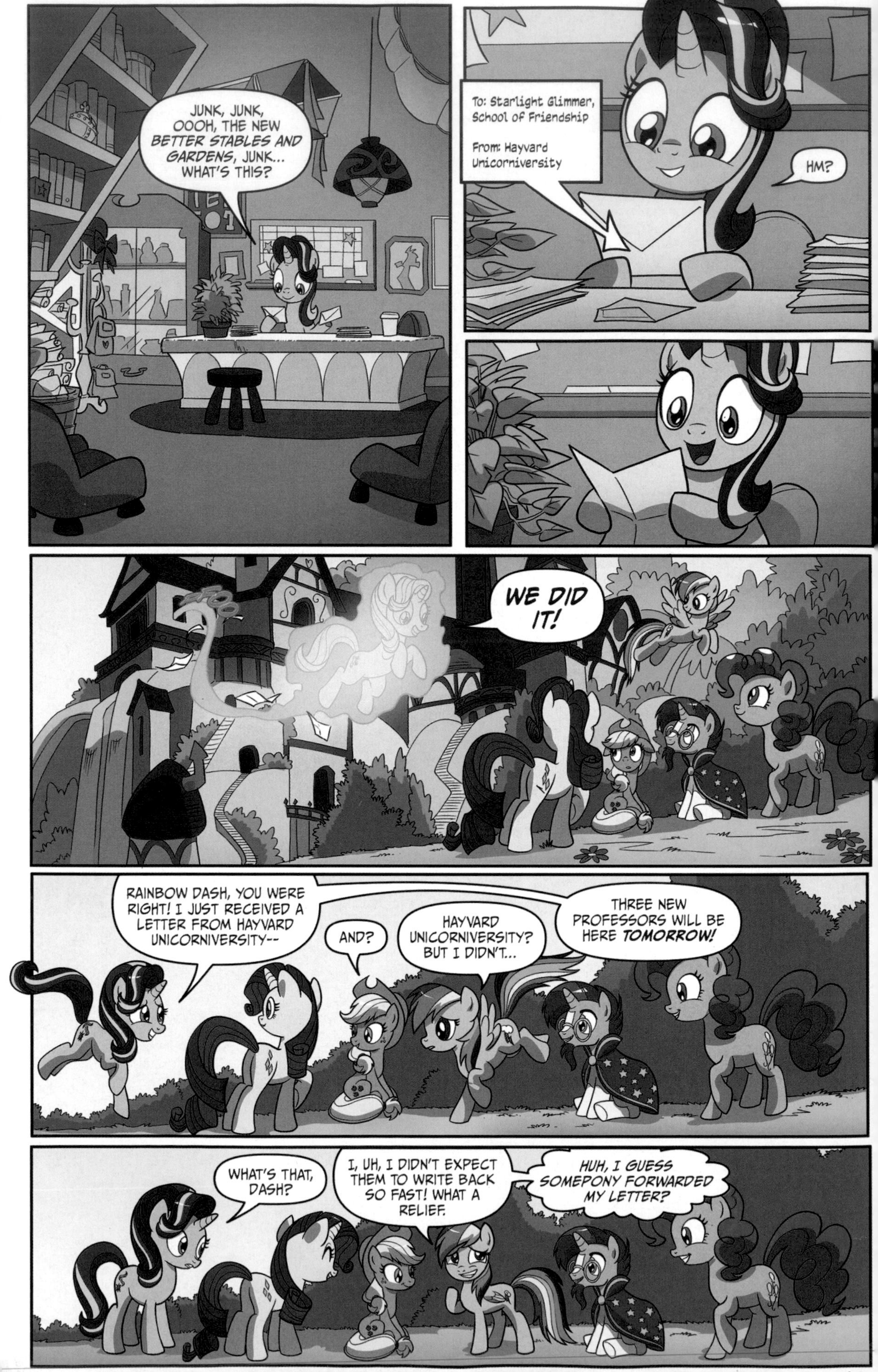
JUNK, JUNK, OOOH, THE NEW BETTER STABLES AND GARDENS, JUNK... WHAT'S THIS?
To: Starlight Glimmer, School of Friendship
From: Hayvard Unicorniversity
HM?
WE DID IT!
RAINBOW DASH, YOU WERE RIGHT! I JUST RECEIVED A LETTER FROM HAYVARD UNICORNIVERSITY--
THREE NEW PROFESSORS WILL BE HERE TOMORROW!
AND?
HAYVARD UNICORNIVERSITY? BUT I DIDN'T...
WHAT'S THAT, DASH?
I, UH, I DIDN'T EXPECT THEM TO WRITE BACK SO FAST! WHAT A RELIEF.
HUH, I GUESS SOMEPONY FORWARDED MY LETTER?

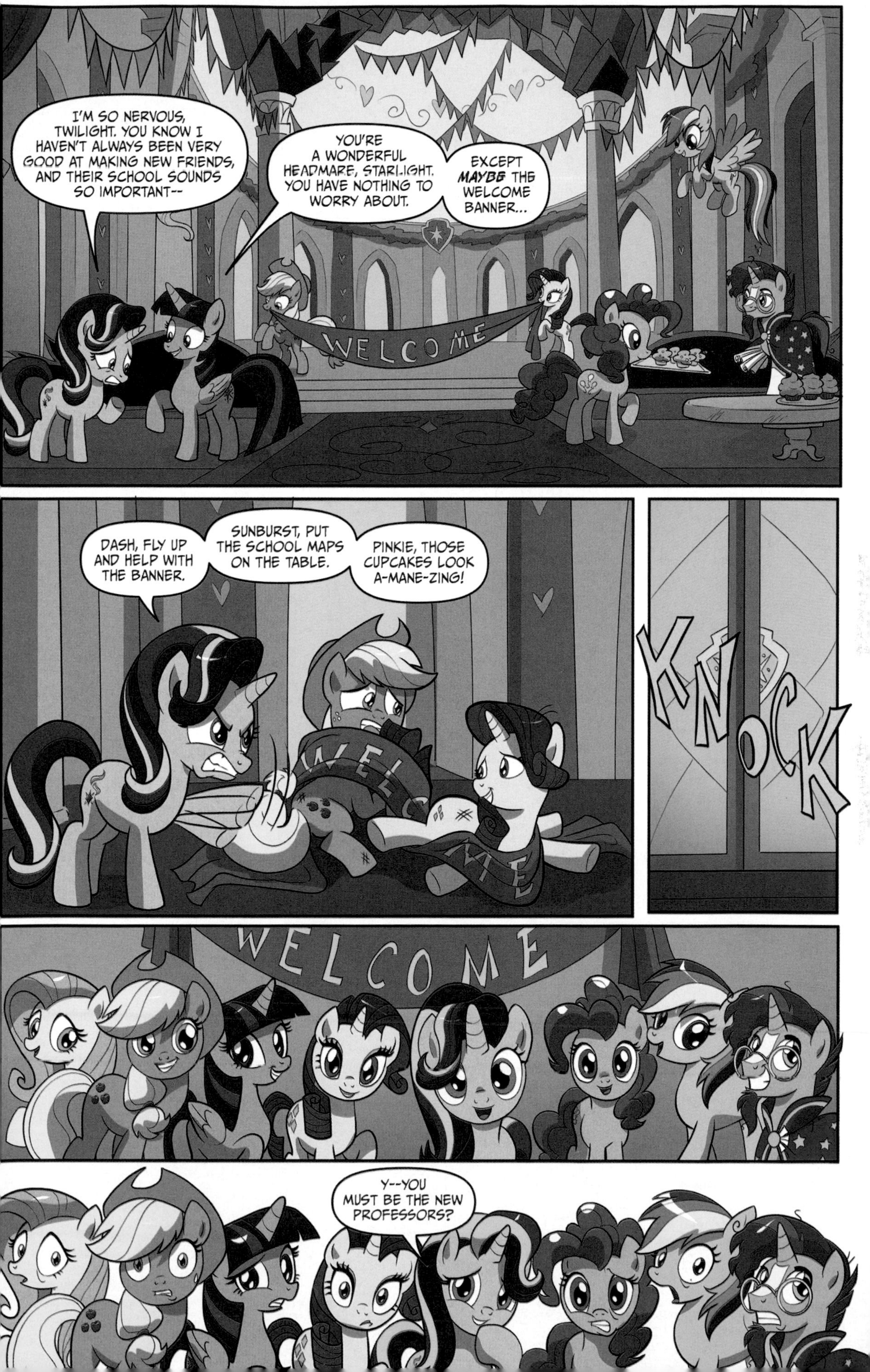
I'M SO NERVOUS, TWILIGHT. YOU KNOW I HAVEN'T ALWAYS BEEN VERY GOOD AT MAKING NEW FRIENDS, AND THEIR SCHOOL SOUNDS SO IMPORTANT--
YOU'RE A WONDERFUL HEADMARE, STARLIGHT. YOU HAVE NOTHING TO WORRY ABOUT.
EXCEPT *MAYBE* THE WELCOME BANNER...
WELCOME
DASH, FLY UP AND HELP WITH THE BANNER.
SUNBURST, PUT THE SCHOOL MAPS ON THE TABLE.
PINKIE, THOSE CUPCAKES LOOK A-MANE-ZING!
KNOCK
WELCOME
Y--YOU MUST BE THE NEW PROFESSORS?

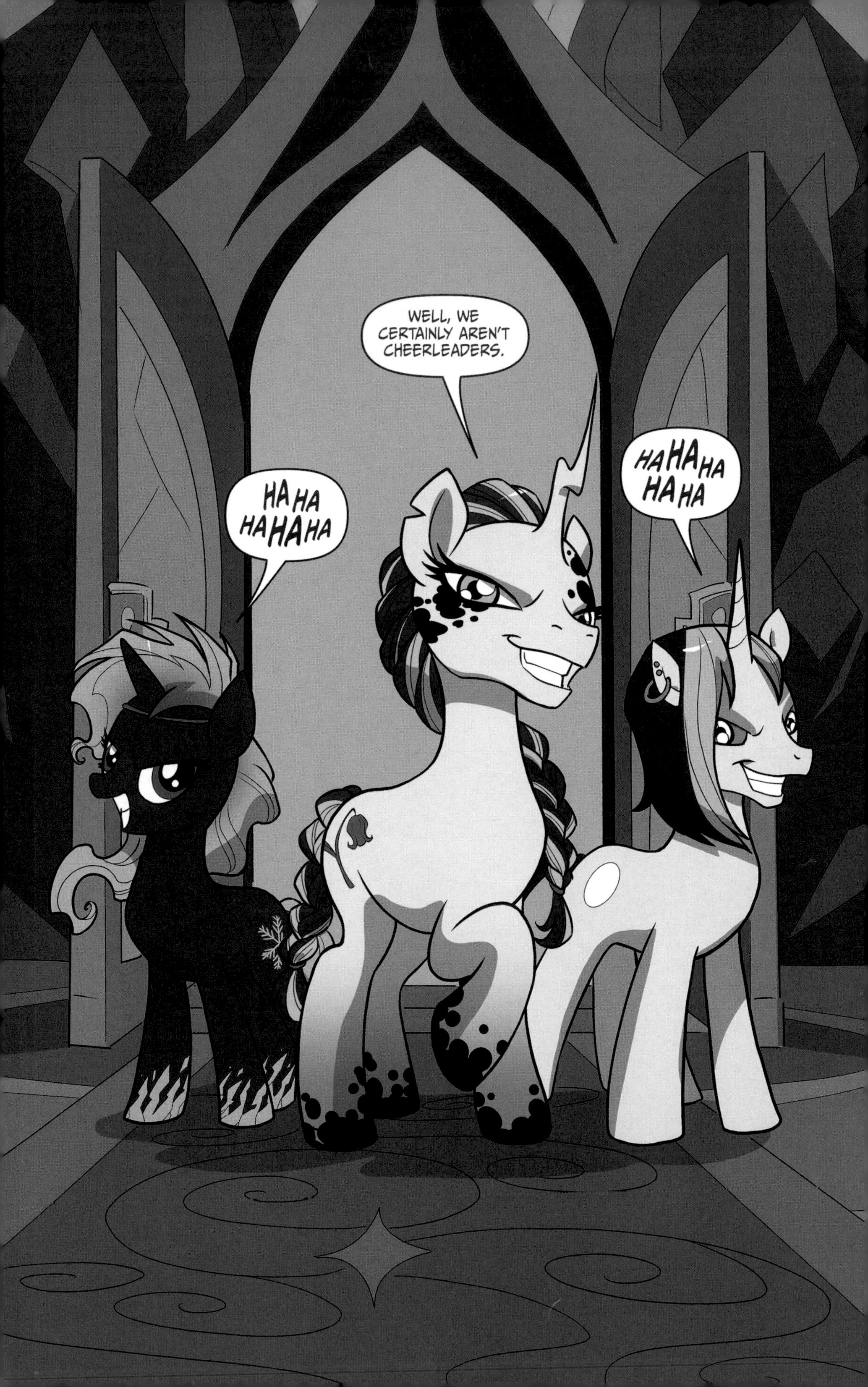
WELL, WE CERTAINLY AREN'T CHEERLEADERS.
HA HA HA HA HA HA
HA HA HA HA HA HA

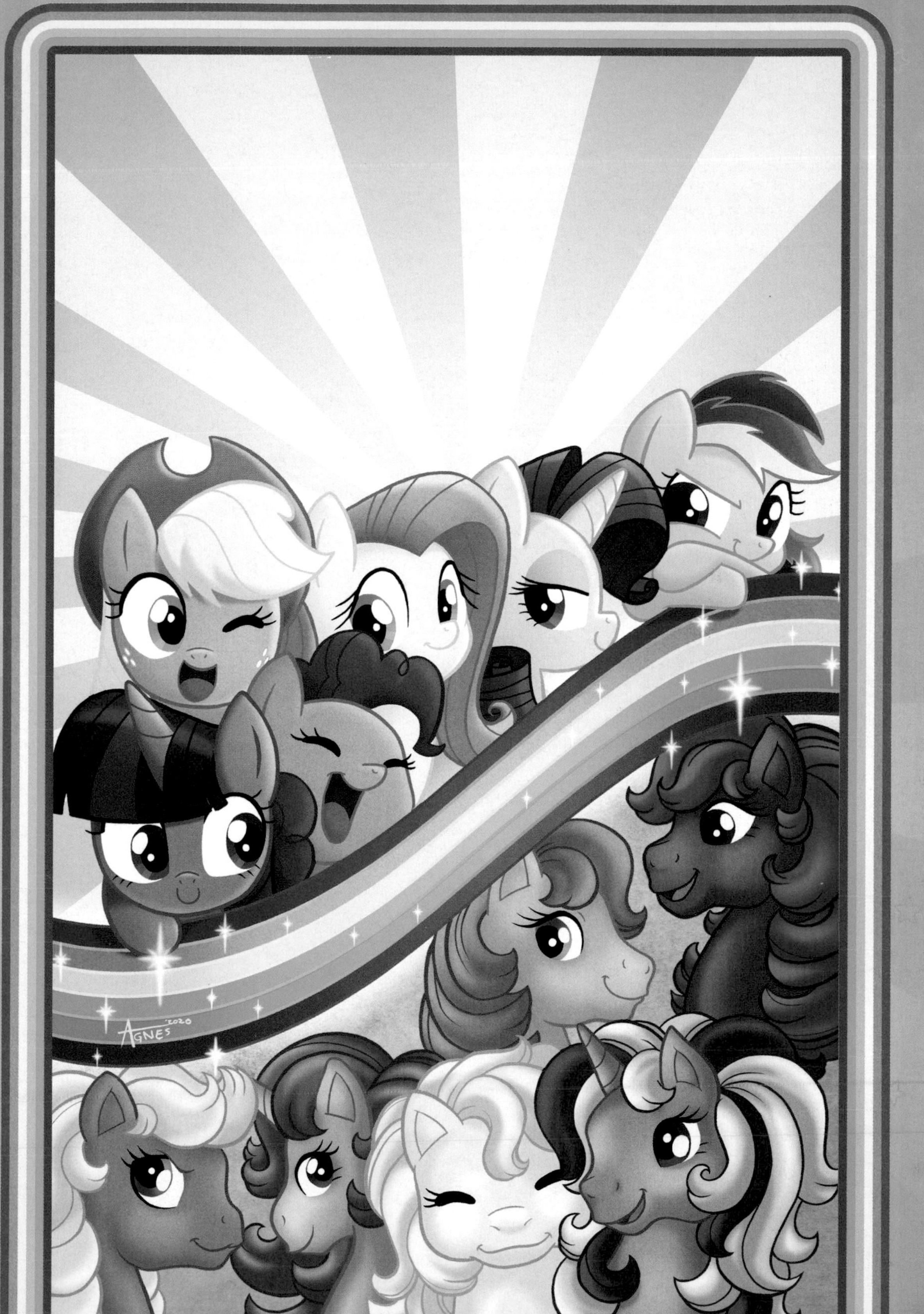
AGNES '2020

Art by **Agnes Garbowska**

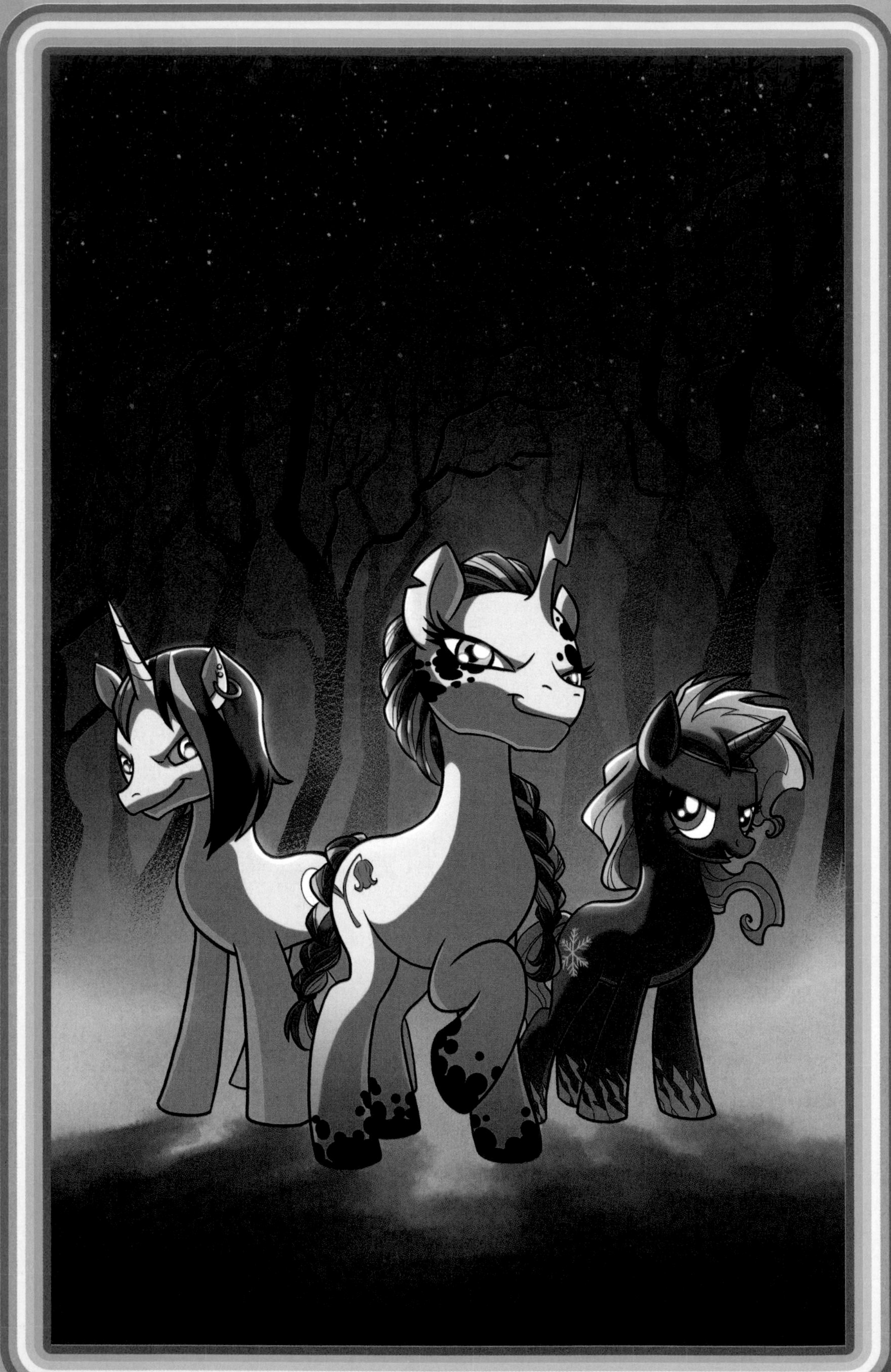

Art by **Michela Cacciatore**

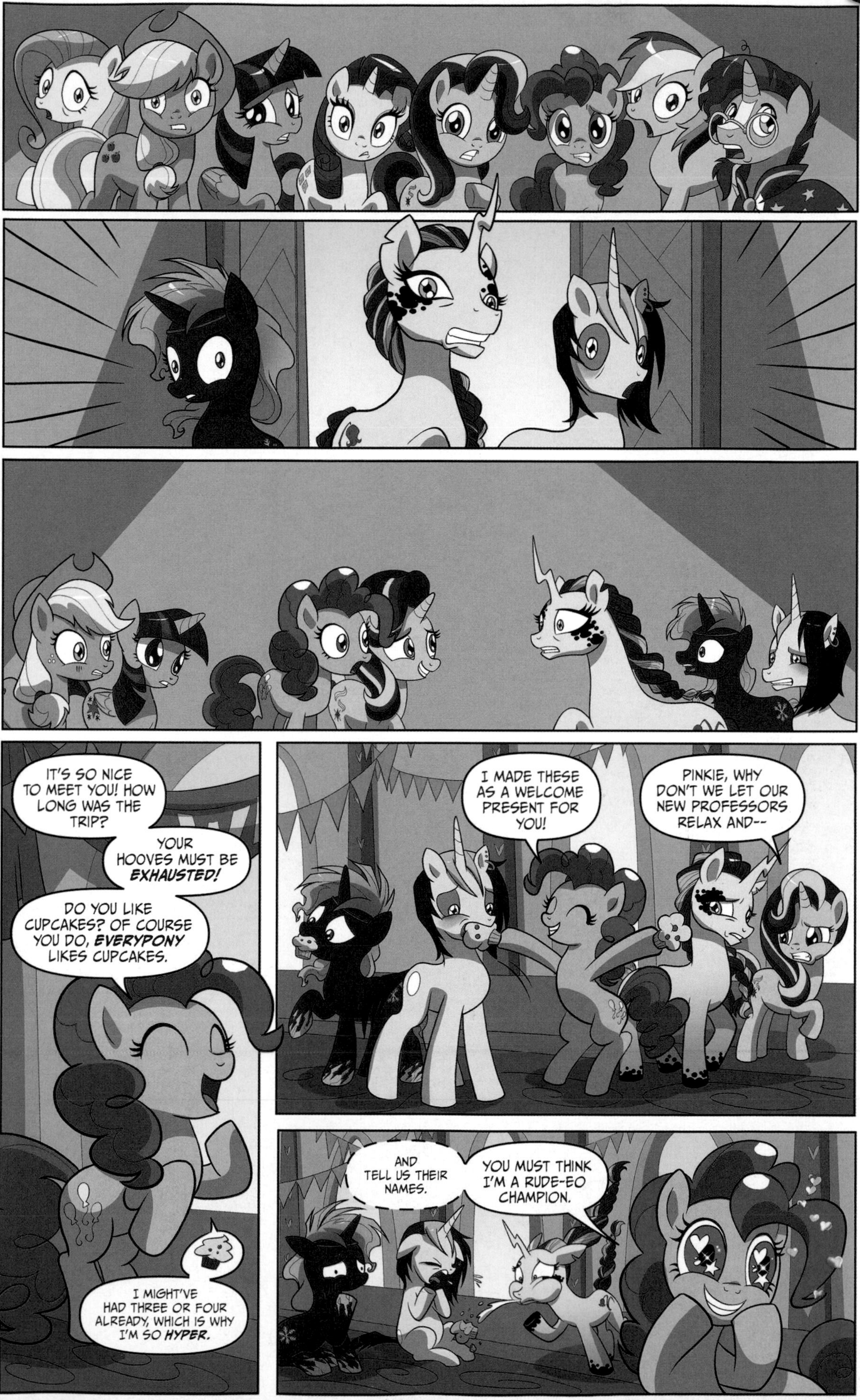

IT'S SO NICE TO MEET YOU! HOW LONG WAS THE TRIP?
YOUR HOOVES MUST BE ***EXHAUSTED!***
DO YOU LIKE CUPCAKES? OF COURSE YOU DO, ***EVERYPONY*** LIKES CUPCAKES.
I MIGHT'VE HAD THREE OR FOUR ALREADY, WHICH IS WHY I'M SO ***HYPER.***
I MADE THESE AS A WELCOME PRESENT FOR YOU!
PINKIE, WHY DON'T WE LET OUR NEW PROFESSORS RELAX AND--
AND TELL US THEIR NAMES.
YOU MUST THINK I'M A RUDE-EO CHAMPION.

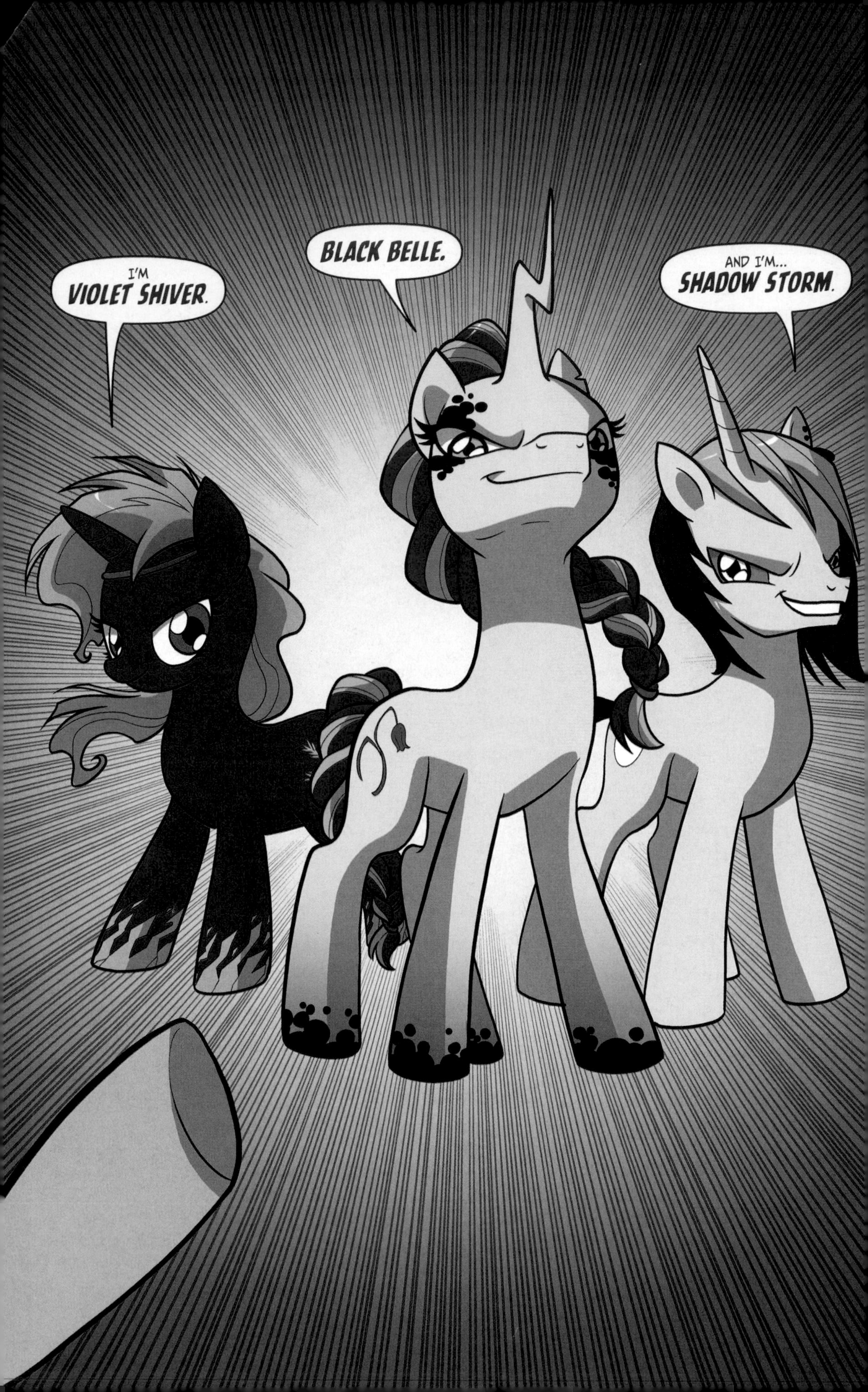
I'M VIOLET SHIVER.
BLACK BELLE.
AND I'M... SHADOW STORM.

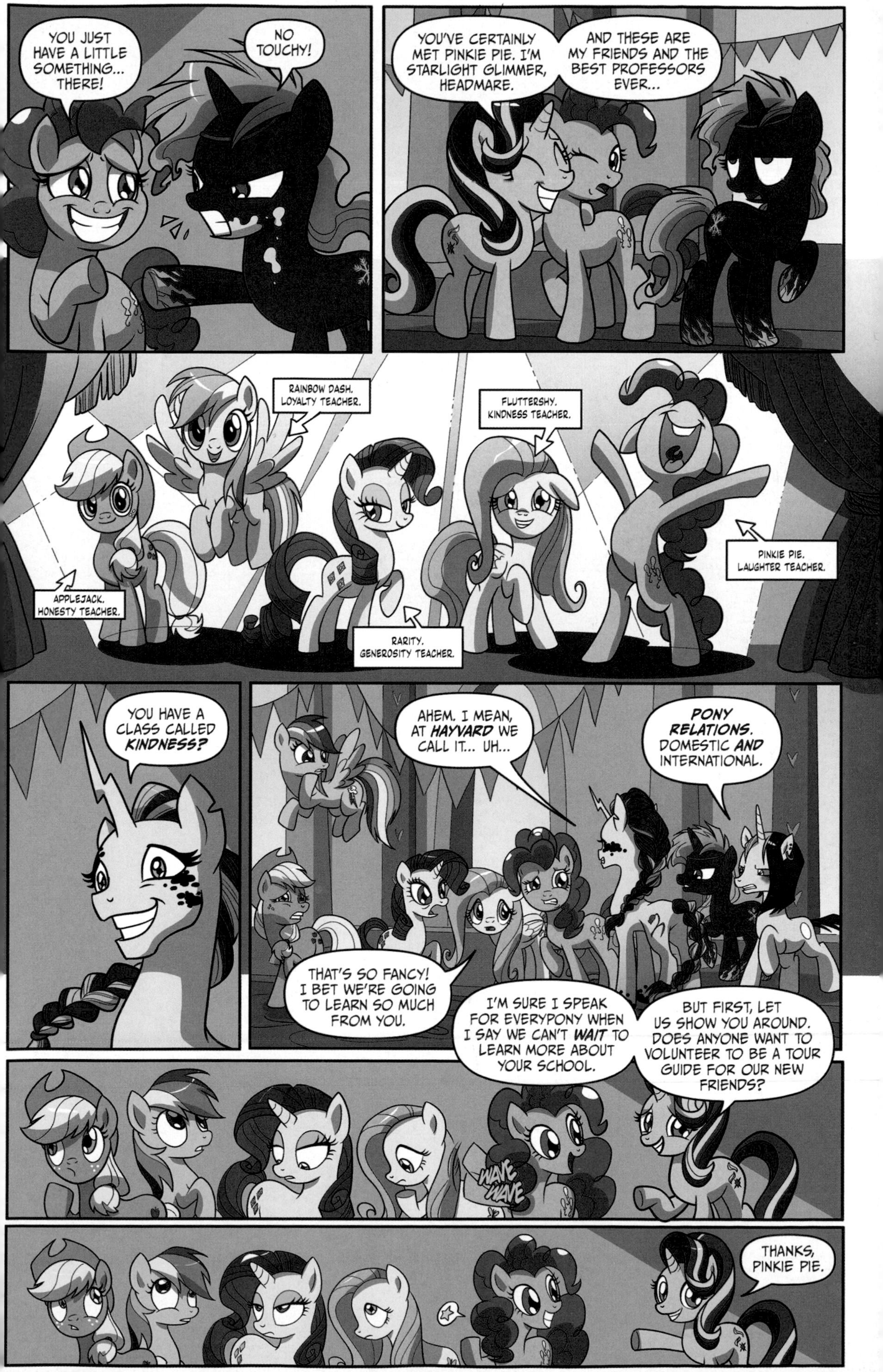
YOU JUST HAVE A LITTLE SOMETHING... THERE!
NO TOUCHY!
YOU'VE CERTAINLY MET PINKIE PIE. I'M STARLIGHT GLIMMER, HEADMARE.
AND THESE ARE MY FRIENDS AND THE BEST PROFESSORS EVER...
RAINBOW DASH. LOYALTY TEACHER.
FLUTTERSHY. KINDNESS TEACHER.
PINKIE PIE. LAUGHTER TEACHER.
APPLEJACK. HONESTY TEACHER.
RARITY. GENEROSITY TEACHER.
YOU HAVE A CLASS CALLED *KINDNESS?*
AHEM. I MEAN, AT *HAYVARD* WE CALL IT... UH...
PONY RELATIONS. DOMESTIC ***AND*** INTERNATIONAL.
THAT'S SO FANCY! I BET WE'RE GOING TO LEARN SO MUCH FROM YOU.
I'M SURE I SPEAK FOR EVERYPONY WHEN I SAY WE CAN'T ***WAIT*** TO LEARN MORE ABOUT YOUR SCHOOL.
BUT FIRST, LET US SHOW YOU AROUND. DOES ANYONE WANT TO VOLUNTEER TO BE A TOUR GUIDE FOR OUR NEW FRIENDS?
WAVE WAVE
THANKS, PINKIE PIE.

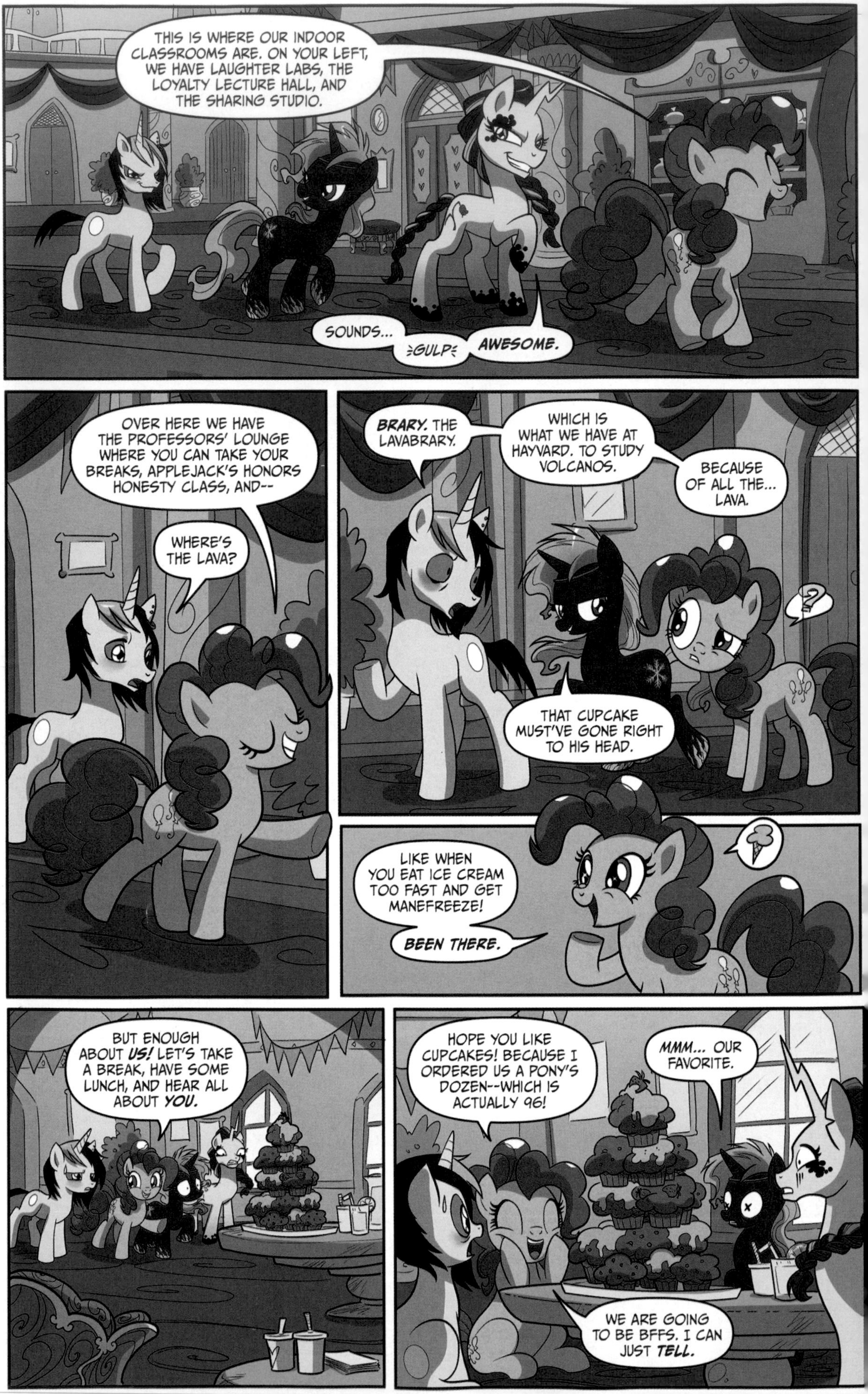

THIS IS WHERE OUR INDOOR CLASSROOMS ARE. ON YOUR LEFT, WE HAVE LAUGHTER LABS, THE LOYALTY LECTURE HALL, AND THE SHARING STUDIO.
SOUNDS...
GULP
AWESOME.
OVER HERE WE HAVE THE PROFESSORS' LOUNGE WHERE YOU CAN TAKE YOUR BREAKS, APPLEJACK'S HONORS HONESTY CLASS, AND--
WHERE'S THE LAVA?
BRARY. THE LAVABRARY.
WHICH IS WHAT WE HAVE AT HAYVARD. TO STUDY VOLCANOS.
BECAUSE OF ALL THE... LAVA.
THAT CUPCAKE MUST'VE GONE RIGHT TO HIS HEAD.
LIKE WHEN YOU EAT ICE CREAM TOO FAST AND GET MANEFREEZE!
BEEN THERE.
BUT ENOUGH ABOUT US! LET'S TAKE A BREAK, HAVE SOME LUNCH, AND HEAR ALL ABOUT YOU.
HOPE YOU LIKE CUPCAKES! BECAUSE I ORDERED US A PONY'S DOZEN--WHICH IS ACTUALLY 96!
MMM... OUR FAVORITE.
WE ARE GOING TO BE BFFS. I CAN JUST TELL.

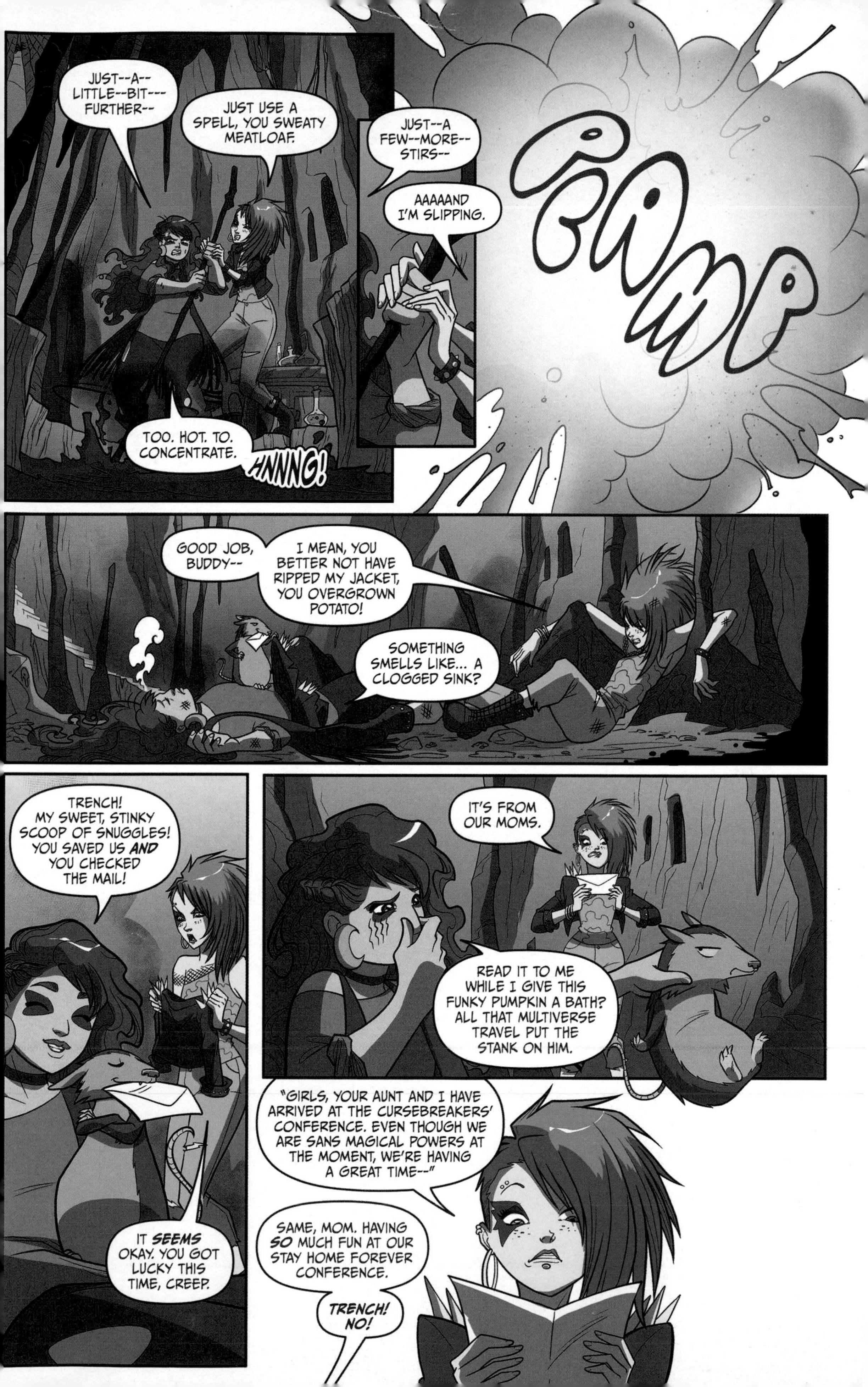
JUST--A--
LITTLE--BIT---
FURTHER--
JUST USE A SPELL, YOU SWEATY MEATLOAF.
TOO. HOT. TO. CONCENTRATE.
HNNNG!
JUST--A FEW--MORE--STIRS--
AAAAAND I'M SLIPPING.
BLAMP
GOOD JOB, BUDDY--
I MEAN, YOU BETTER NOT HAVE RIPPED MY JACKET, YOU OVERGROWN POTATO!
SOMETHING SMELLS LIKE... A CLOGGED SINK?
TRENCH! MY SWEET, STINKY SCOOP OF SNUGGLES! YOU SAVED US **AND** YOU CHECKED THE MAIL!
IT **SEEMS** OKAY. YOU GOT LUCKY THIS TIME, CREEP.
IT'S FROM OUR MOMS.
READ IT TO ME WHILE I GIVE THIS FUNKY PUMPKIN A BATH? ALL THAT MULTIVERSE TRAVEL PUT THE STANK ON HIM.
"GIRLS, YOUR AUNT AND I HAVE ARRIVED AT THE CURSEBREAKERS' CONFERENCE. EVEN THOUGH WE ARE SANS MAGICAL POWERS AT THE MOMENT, WE'RE HAVING A GREAT TIME--"
SAME, MOM. HAVING **SO** MUCH FUN AT OUR STAY HOME FOREVER CONFERENCE.
TRENCH! NO!

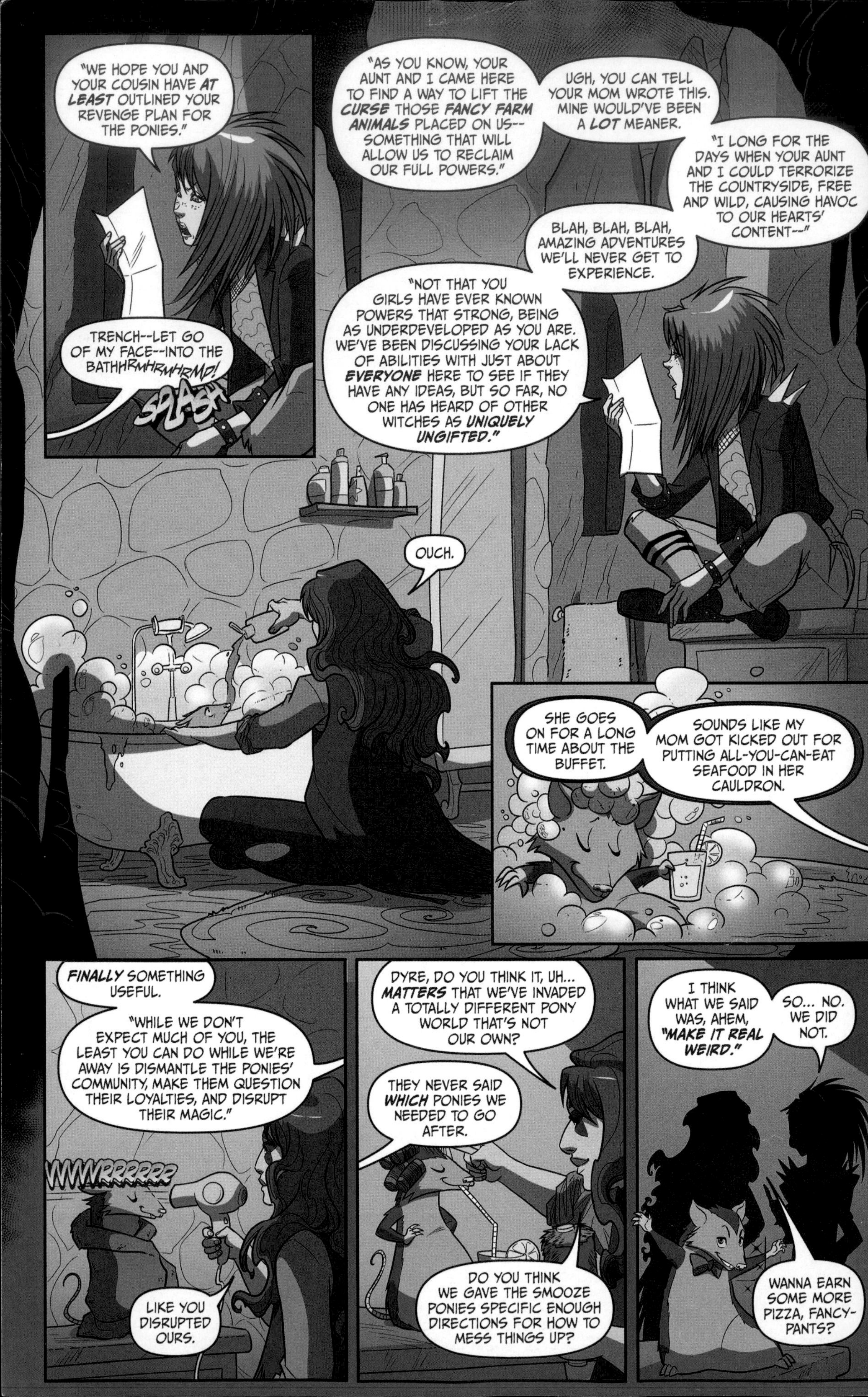
"WE HOPE YOU AND YOUR COUSIN HAVE AT LEAST OUTLINED YOUR REVENGE PLAN FOR THE PONIES."
TRENCH--LET GO OF MY FACE--INTO THE BATHHRMHRMHRMD!
SPLASH
"AS YOU KNOW, YOUR AUNT AND I CAME HERE TO FIND A WAY TO LIFT THE CURSE THOSE FANCY FARM ANIMALS PLACED ON US-- SOMETHING THAT WILL ALLOW US TO RECLAIM OUR FULL POWERS."
UGH, YOU CAN TELL YOUR MOM WROTE THIS. MINE WOULD'VE BEEN A LOT MEANER.
"I LONG FOR THE DAYS WHEN YOUR AUNT AND I COULD TERRORIZE THE COUNTRYSIDE, FREE AND WILD, CAUSING HAVOC TO OUR HEARTS' CONTENT--"
BLAH, BLAH, BLAH, AMAZING ADVENTURES WE'LL NEVER GET TO EXPERIENCE.
"NOT THAT YOU GIRLS HAVE EVER KNOWN POWERS THAT STRONG, BEING AS UNDERDEVELOPED AS YOU ARE. WE'VE BEEN DISCUSSING YOUR LACK OF ABILITIES WITH JUST ABOUT EVERYONE HERE TO SEE IF THEY HAVE ANY IDEAS, BUT SO FAR, NO ONE HAS HEARD OF OTHER WITCHES AS UNIQUELY UNGIFTED."
OUCH.
SHE GOES ON FOR A LONG TIME ABOUT THE BUFFET.
SOUNDS LIKE MY MOM GOT KICKED OUT FOR PUTTING ALL-YOU-CAN-EAT SEAFOOD IN HER CAULDRON.
FINALLY SOMETHING USEFUL.
"WHILE WE DON'T EXPECT MUCH OF YOU, THE LEAST YOU CAN DO WHILE WE'RE AWAY IS DISMANTLE THE PONIES' COMMUNITY, MAKE THEM QUESTION THEIR LOYALTIES, AND DISRUPT THEIR MAGIC."
WWWRRRRRR
LIKE YOU DISRUPTED OURS.
DYRE, DO YOU THINK IT, UH... MATTERS THAT WE'VE INVADED A TOTALLY DIFFERENT PONY WORLD THAT'S NOT OUR OWN?
THEY NEVER SAID WHICH PONIES WE NEEDED TO GO AFTER.
DO YOU THINK WE GAVE THE SMOOZE PONIES SPECIFIC ENOUGH DIRECTIONS FOR HOW TO MESS THINGS UP?
I THINK WHAT WE SAID WAS, AHEM, "MAKE IT REAL WEIRD."
SO... NO. WE DID NOT.
WANNA EARN SOME MORE PIZZA, FANCY-PANTS?

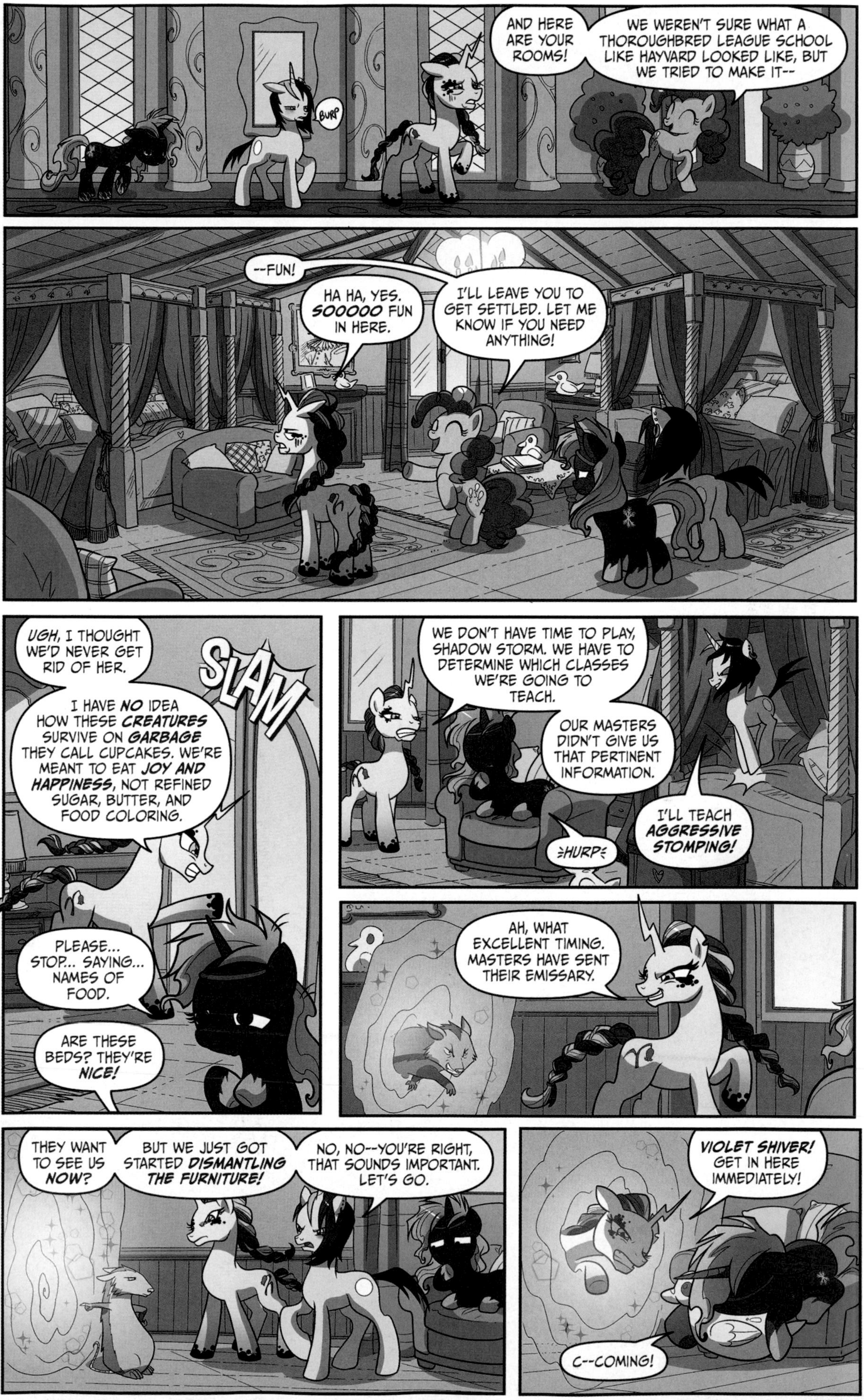
BURP
AND HERE ARE YOUR ROOMS!
WE WEREN'T SURE WHAT A THOROUGHBRED LEAGUE SCHOOL LIKE HAYVARD LOOKED LIKE, BUT WE TRIED TO MAKE IT--
--FUN!
HA HA, YES. SOOOOO FUN IN HERE.
I'LL LEAVE YOU TO GET SETTLED. LET ME KNOW IF YOU NEED ANYTHING!
UGH, I THOUGHT WE'D NEVER GET RID OF HER.
SLAM
I HAVE NO IDEA HOW THESE CREATURES SURVIVE ON GARBAGE THEY CALL CUPCAKES. WE'RE MEANT TO EAT JOY AND HAPPINESS, NOT REFINED SUGAR, BUTTER, AND FOOD COLORING.
PLEASE... STOP... SAYING... NAMES OF FOOD.
ARE THESE BEDS? THEY'RE NICE!
WE DON'T HAVE TIME TO PLAY, SHADOW STORM. WE HAVE TO DETERMINE WHICH CLASSES WE'RE GOING TO TEACH.
OUR MASTERS DIDN'T GIVE US THAT PERTINENT INFORMATION.
I'LL TEACH AGGRESSIVE STOMPING!
HURP
AH, WHAT EXCELLENT TIMING. MASTERS HAVE SENT THEIR EMISSARY.
THEY WANT TO SEE US NOW?
BUT WE JUST GOT STARTED DISMANTLING THE FURNITURE!
NO, NO--YOU'RE RIGHT, THAT SOUNDS IMPORTANT. LET'S GO.
VIOLET SHIVER! GET IN HERE IMMEDIATELY!
C--COMING!

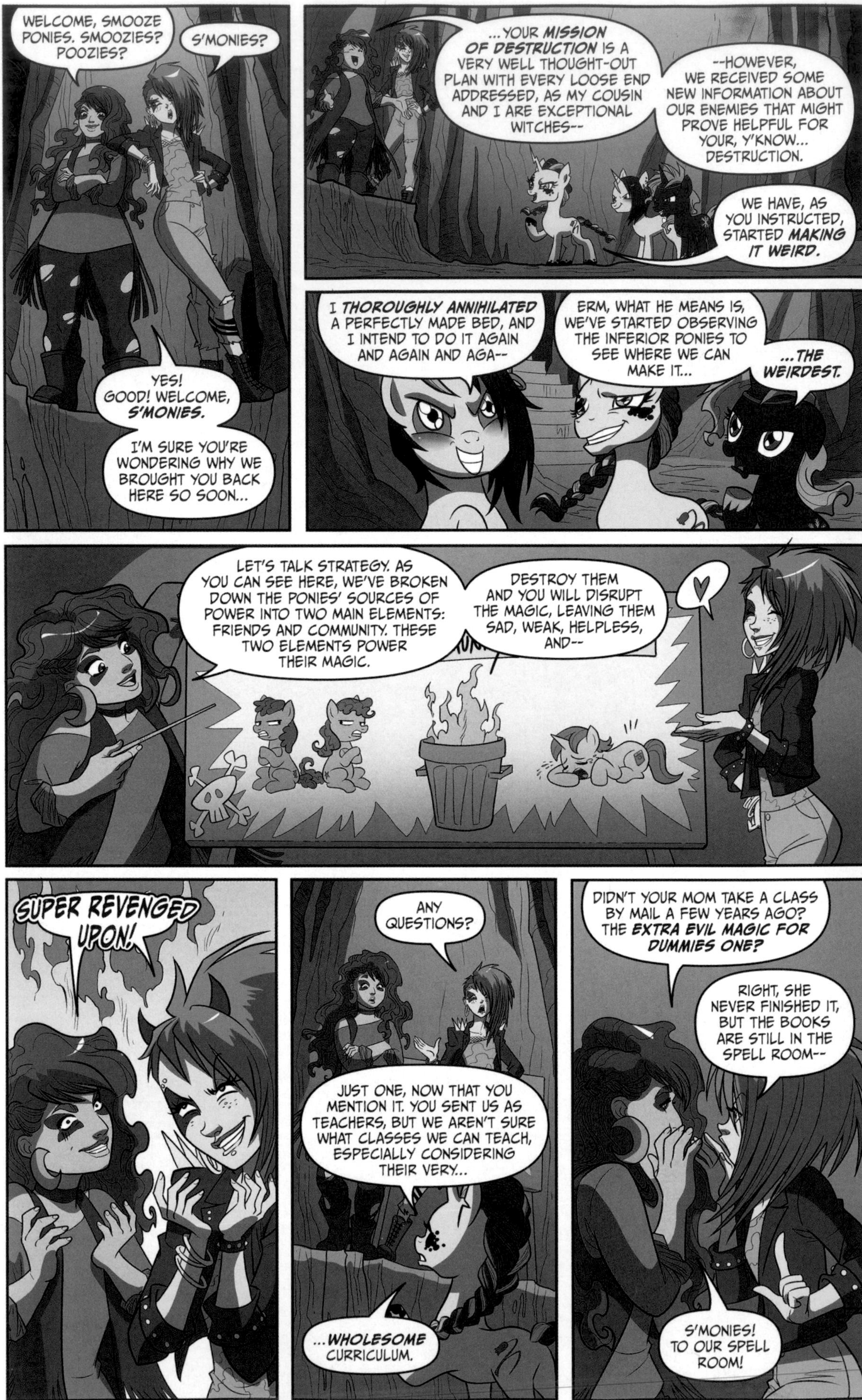

WELCOME, SMOOZE PONIES. SMOOZIES? POOZIES?
S'MONIES?
YES! GOOD! WELCOME, S'MONIES.
I'M SURE YOU'RE WONDERING WHY WE BROUGHT YOU BACK HERE SO SOON...
...YOUR MISSION OF DESTRUCTION IS A VERY WELL THOUGHT-OUT PLAN WITH EVERY LOOSE END ADDRESSED, AS MY COUSIN AND I ARE EXCEPTIONAL WITCHES--
--HOWEVER, WE RECEIVED SOME NEW INFORMATION ABOUT OUR ENEMIES THAT MIGHT PROVE HELPFUL FOR YOUR, Y'KNOW... DESTRUCTION.
WE HAVE, AS YOU INSTRUCTED, STARTED MAKING IT WEIRD.
I THOROUGHLY ANNIHILATED A PERFECTLY MADE BED, AND I INTEND TO DO IT AGAIN AND AGAIN AND AGA--
ERM, WHAT HE MEANS IS, WE'VE STARTED OBSERVING THE INFERIOR PONIES TO SEE WHERE WE CAN MAKE IT...
...THE WEIRDEST.
LET'S TALK STRATEGY. AS YOU CAN SEE HERE, WE'VE BROKEN DOWN THE PONIES' SOURCES OF POWER INTO TWO MAIN ELEMENTS: FRIENDS AND COMMUNITY. THESE TWO ELEMENTS POWER THEIR MAGIC.
DESTROY THEM AND YOU WILL DISRUPT THE MAGIC, LEAVING THEM SAD, WEAK, HELPLESS, AND--
♥
SUPER REVENGED UPON!
ANY QUESTIONS?
JUST ONE, NOW THAT YOU MENTION IT. YOU SENT US AS TEACHERS, BUT WE AREN'T SURE WHAT CLASSES WE CAN TEACH, ESPECIALLY CONSIDERING THEIR VERY...
...WHOLESOME CURRICULUM.
DIDN'T YOUR MOM TAKE A CLASS BY MAIL A FEW YEARS AGO? THE EXTRA EVIL MAGIC FOR DUMMIES ONE?
RIGHT, SHE NEVER FINISHED IT, BUT THE BOOKS ARE STILL IN THE SPELL ROOM--
S'MONIES! TO OUR SPELL ROOM!

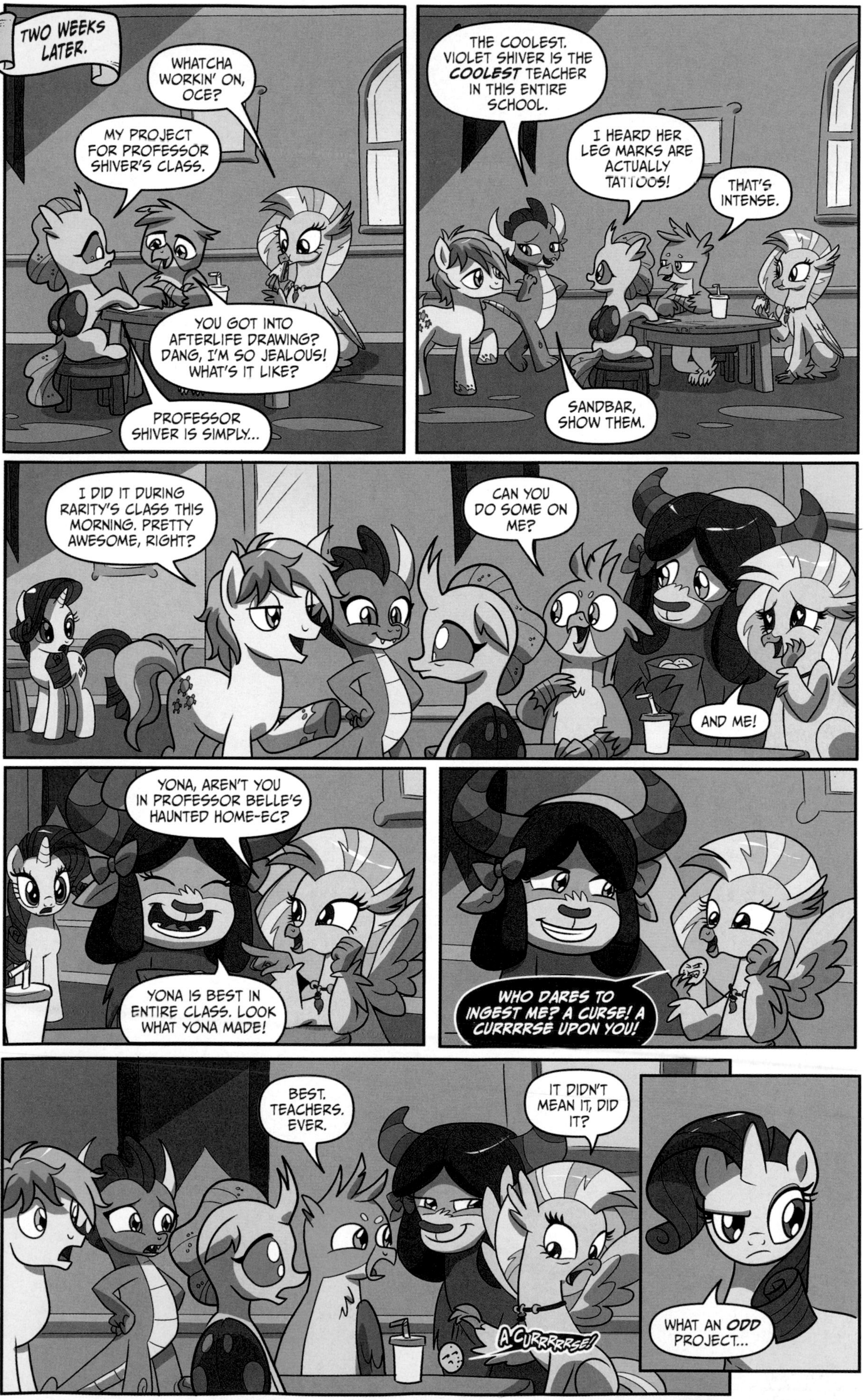
TWO WEEKS LATER.
WHATCHA WORKIN' ON, OCE?
MY PROJECT FOR PROFESSOR SHIVER'S CLASS.
YOU GOT INTO AFTERLIFE DRAWING? DANG, I'M SO JEALOUS! WHAT'S IT LIKE?
PROFESSOR SHIVER IS SIMPLY...
THE COOLEST. VIOLET SHIVER IS THE COOLEST TEACHER IN THIS ENTIRE SCHOOL.
I HEARD HER LEG MARKS ARE ACTUALLY TATTOOS!
THAT'S INTENSE.
SANDBAR, SHOW THEM.
I DID IT DURING RARITY'S CLASS THIS MORNING. PRETTY AWESOME, RIGHT?
CAN YOU DO SOME ON ME?
AND ME!
YONA, AREN'T YOU IN PROFESSOR BELLE'S HAUNTED HOME-EC?
YONA IS BEST IN ENTIRE CLASS. LOOK WHAT YONA MADE!
WHO DARES TO INGEST ME? A CURSE! A CURRRRSE UPON YOU!
BEST. TEACHERS. EVER.
IT DIDN'T MEAN IT, DID IT?
A CURRRRRSE!
WHAT AN ODD PROJECT...

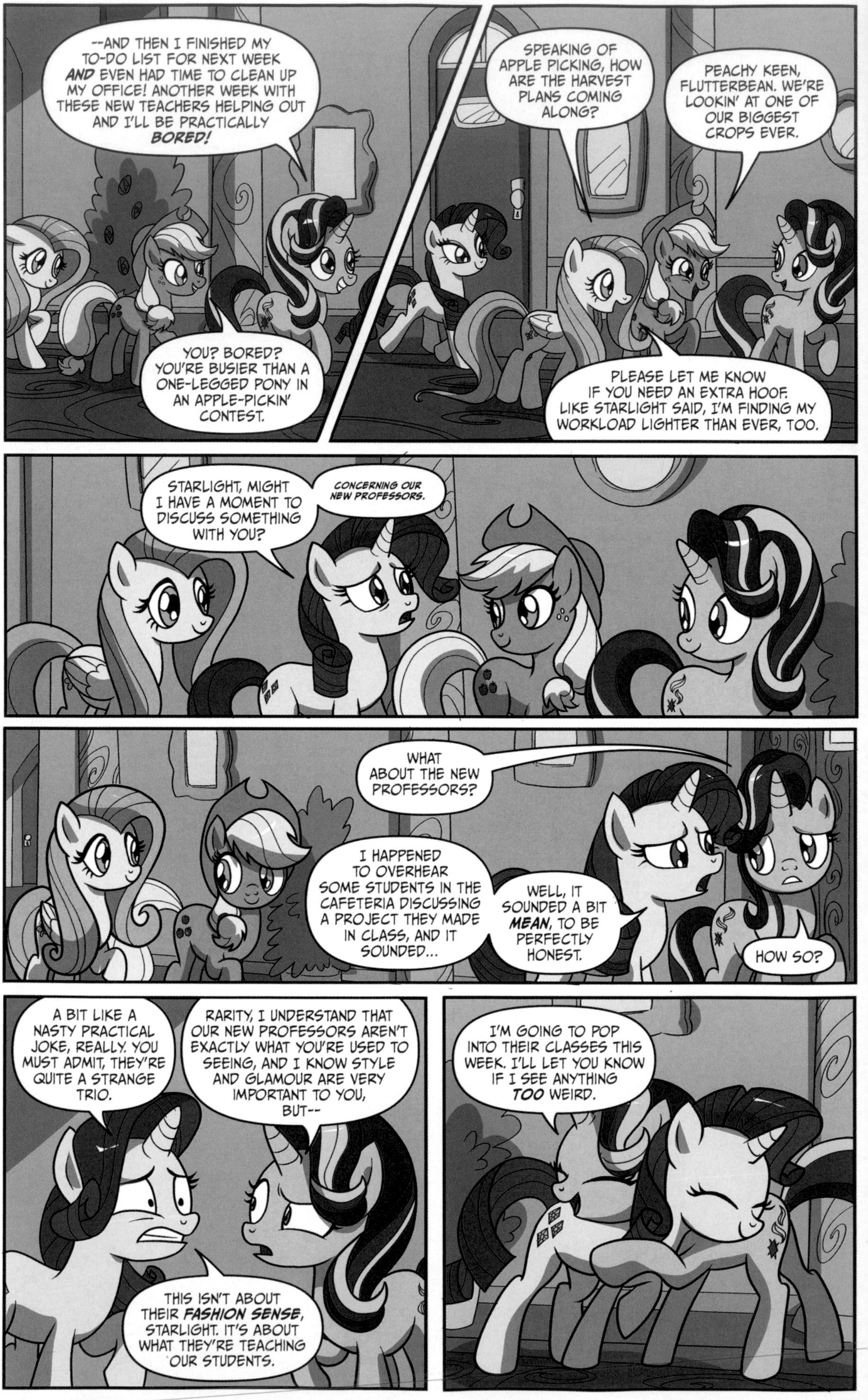
--AND THEN I FINISHED MY TO-DO LIST FOR NEXT WEEK AND EVEN HAD TIME TO CLEAN UP MY OFFICE! ANOTHER WEEK WITH THESE NEW TEACHERS HELPING OUT AND I'LL BE PRACTICALLY BORED!
YOU? BORED? YOU'RE BUSIER THAN A ONE-LEGGED PONY IN AN APPLE-PICKIN' CONTEST.
SPEAKING OF APPLE PICKING, HOW ARE THE HARVEST PLANS COMING ALONG?
PEACHY KEEN, FLUTTERBEAN. WE'RE LOOKIN' AT ONE OF OUR BIGGEST CROPS EVER.
PLEASE LET ME KNOW IF YOU NEED AN EXTRA HOOF. LIKE STARLIGHT SAID, I'M FINDING MY WORKLOAD LIGHTER THAN EVER, TOO.
STARLIGHT, MIGHT I HAVE A MOMENT TO DISCUSS SOMETHING WITH YOU?
CONCERNING OUR NEW PROFESSORS.
WHAT ABOUT THE NEW PROFESSORS?
I HAPPENED TO OVERHEAR SOME STUDENTS IN THE CAFETERIA DISCUSSING A PROJECT THEY MADE IN CLASS, AND IT SOUNDED...
WELL, IT SOUNDED A BIT MEAN, TO BE PERFECTLY HONEST.
HOW SO?
A BIT LIKE A NASTY PRACTICAL JOKE, REALLY. YOU MUST ADMIT, THEY'RE QUITE A STRANGE TRIO.
RARITY, I UNDERSTAND THAT OUR NEW PROFESSORS AREN'T EXACTLY WHAT YOU'RE USED TO SEEING, AND I KNOW STYLE AND GLAMOUR ARE VERY IMPORTANT TO YOU, BUT--
THIS ISN'T ABOUT THEIR FASHION SENSE, STARLIGHT. IT'S ABOUT WHAT THEY'RE TEACHING OUR STUDENTS.
I'M GOING TO POP INTO THEIR CLASSES THIS WEEK. I'LL LET YOU KNOW IF I SEE ANYTHING TOO WEIRD.

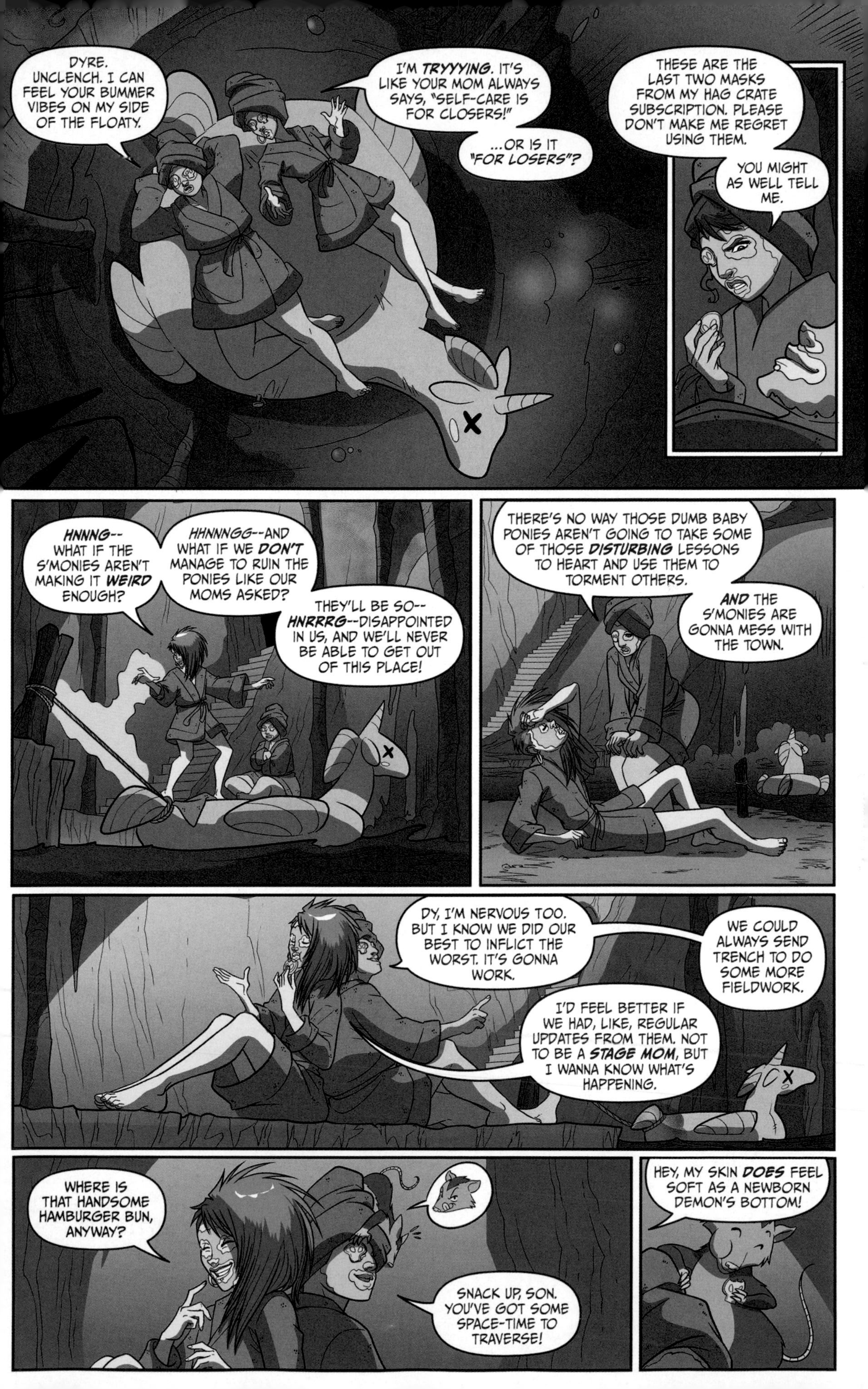
DYRE. UNCLENCH. I CAN FEEL YOUR BUMMER VIBES ON MY SIDE OF THE FLOATY.
I'M TRYYYING. IT'S LIKE YOUR MOM ALWAYS SAYS, "SELF-CARE IS FOR CLOSERS!"
...OR IS IT "FOR LOSERS"?
THESE ARE THE LAST TWO MASKS FROM MY HAG CRATE SUBSCRIPTION. PLEASE DON'T MAKE ME REGRET USING THEM.
YOU MIGHT AS WELL TELL ME.
HNNNG-- WHAT IF THE S'MONIES AREN'T MAKING IT WEIRD ENOUGH?
HHNNNGG--AND WHAT IF WE DON'T MANAGE TO RUIN THE PONIES LIKE OUR MOMS ASKED?
THEY'LL BE SO-- HNRRRG--DISAPPOINTED IN US, AND WE'LL NEVER BE ABLE TO GET OUT OF THIS PLACE!
THERE'S NO WAY THOSE DUMB BABY PONIES AREN'T GOING TO TAKE SOME OF THOSE DISTURBING LESSONS TO HEART AND USE THEM TO TORMENT OTHERS.
AND THE S'MONIES ARE GONNA MESS WITH THE TOWN.
DY, I'M NERVOUS TOO. BUT I KNOW WE DID OUR BEST TO INFLICT THE WORST. IT'S GONNA WORK.
WE COULD ALWAYS SEND TRENCH TO DO SOME MORE FIELDWORK.
I'D FEEL BETTER IF WE HAD, LIKE, REGULAR UPDATES FROM THEM. NOT TO BE A STAGE MOM, BUT I WANNA KNOW WHAT'S HAPPENING.
WHERE IS THAT HANDSOME HAMBURGER BUN, ANYWAY?
SNACK UP, SON. YOU'VE GOT SOME SPACE-TIME TO TRAVERSE!
HEY, MY SKIN DOES FEEL SOFT AS A NEWBORN DEMON'S BOTTOM!

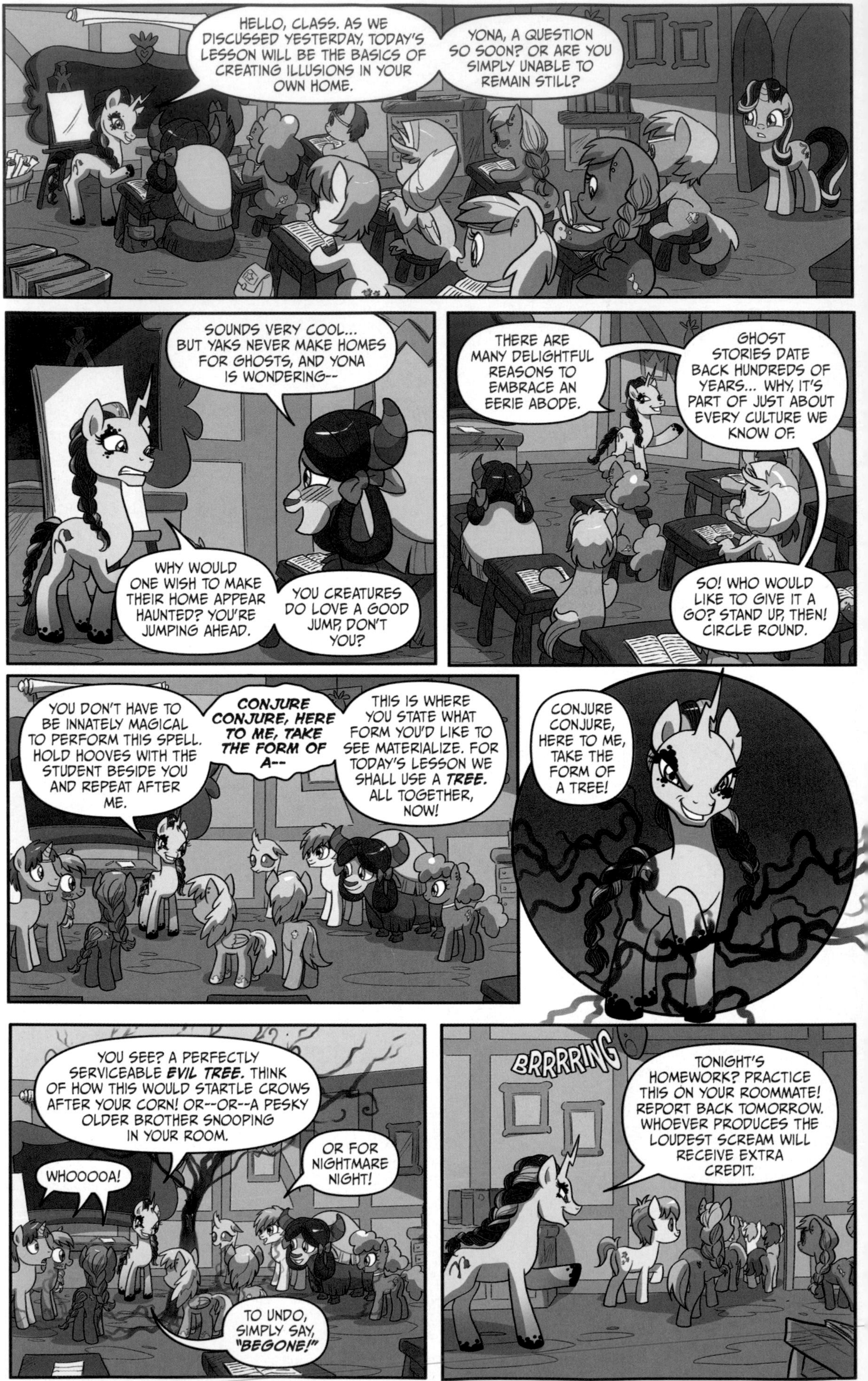
HELLO, CLASS. AS WE DISCUSSED YESTERDAY, TODAY'S LESSON WILL BE THE BASICS OF CREATING ILLUSIONS IN YOUR OWN HOME.
YONA, A QUESTION SO SOON? OR ARE YOU SIMPLY UNABLE TO REMAIN STILL?
SOUNDS VERY COOL... BUT YAKS NEVER MAKE HOMES FOR GHOSTS, AND YONA IS WONDERING--
WHY WOULD ONE WISH TO MAKE THEIR HOME APPEAR HAUNTED? YOU'RE JUMPING AHEAD.
YOU CREATURES DO LOVE A GOOD JUMP, DON'T YOU?
THERE ARE MANY DELIGHTFUL REASONS TO EMBRACE AN EERIE ABODE.
GHOST STORIES DATE BACK HUNDREDS OF YEARS... WHY, IT'S PART OF JUST ABOUT EVERY CULTURE WE KNOW OF.
SO! WHO WOULD LIKE TO GIVE IT A GO? STAND UP, THEN! CIRCLE ROUND.
YOU DON'T HAVE TO BE INNATELY MAGICAL TO PERFORM THIS SPELL. HOLD HOOVES WITH THE STUDENT BESIDE YOU AND REPEAT AFTER ME.
CONJURE CONJURE, HERE TO ME, TAKE THE FORM OF A--
THIS IS WHERE YOU STATE WHAT FORM YOU'D LIKE TO SEE MATERIALIZE. FOR TODAY'S LESSON WE SHALL USE A *TREE.* ALL TOGETHER, NOW!
CONJURE CONJURE, HERE TO ME, TAKE THE FORM OF A TREE!
YOU SEE? A PERFECTLY SERVICEABLE *EVIL TREE.* THINK OF HOW THIS WOULD STARTLE CROWS AFTER YOUR CORN! OR--OR--A PESKY OLDER BROTHER SNOOPING IN YOUR ROOM.
WHOOOOA!
OR FOR NIGHTMARE NIGHT!
TO UNDO, SIMPLY SAY, *"BEGONE!"*
BRRRRING
TONIGHT'S HOMEWORK? PRACTICE THIS ON YOUR ROOMMATE! REPORT BACK TOMORROW. WHOEVER PRODUCES THE LOUDEST SCREAM WILL RECEIVE EXTRA CREDIT.

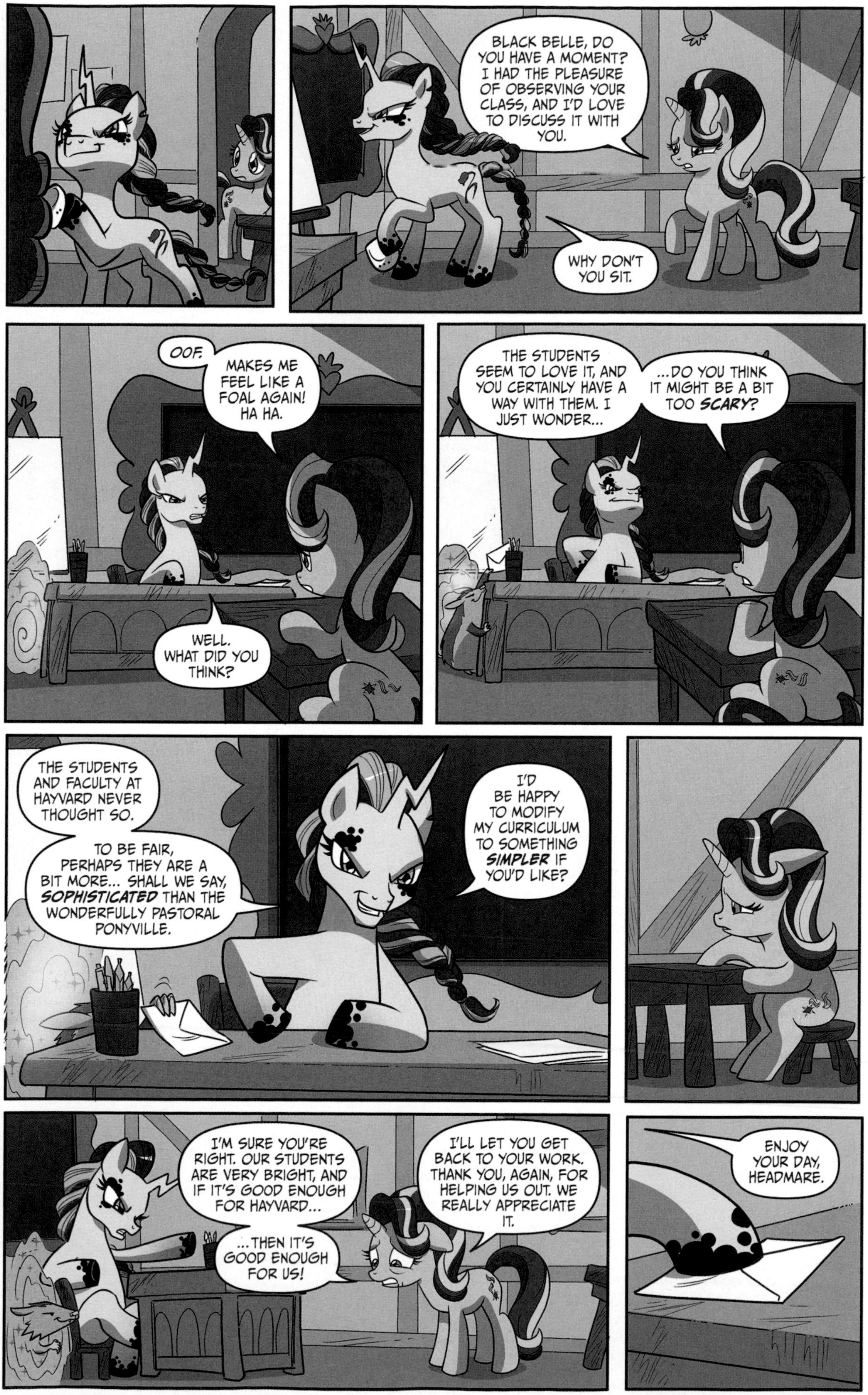
BLACK BELLE, DO YOU HAVE A MOMENT? I HAD THE PLEASURE OF OBSERVING YOUR CLASS, AND I'D LOVE TO DISCUSS IT WITH YOU.
WHY DON'T YOU SIT.
OOF.
MAKES ME FEEL LIKE A FOAL AGAIN! HA HA.
WELL. WHAT DID YOU THINK?
THE STUDENTS SEEM TO LOVE IT, AND YOU CERTAINLY HAVE A WAY WITH THEM. I JUST WONDER...
...DO YOU THINK IT MIGHT BE A BIT TOO SCARY?
THE STUDENTS AND FACULTY AT HAYVARD NEVER THOUGHT SO.
TO BE FAIR, PERHAPS THEY ARE A BIT MORE... SHALL WE SAY, SOPHISTICATED THAN THE WONDERFULLY PASTORAL PONYVILLE.
I'D BE HAPPY TO MODIFY MY CURRICULUM TO SOMETHING SIMPLER IF YOU'D LIKE?
I'M SURE YOU'RE RIGHT. OUR STUDENTS ARE VERY BRIGHT, AND IF IT'S GOOD ENOUGH FOR HAYVARD...
...THEN IT'S GOOD ENOUGH FOR US!
I'LL LET YOU GET BACK TO YOUR WORK. THANK YOU, AGAIN, FOR HELPING US OUT. WE REALLY APPRECIATE IT.
ENJOY YOUR DAY, HEADMARE.

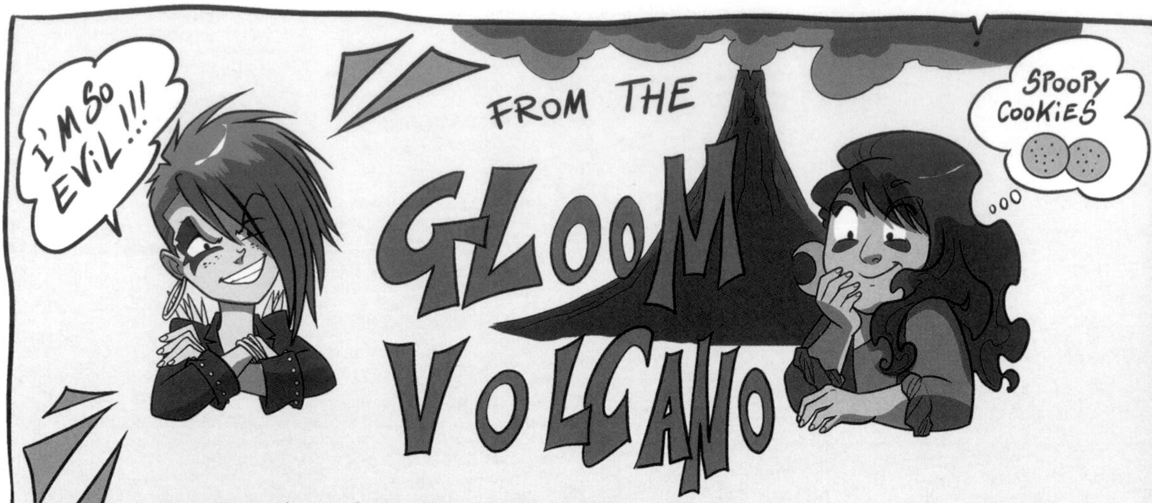
I'M SO EVIL!!!
FROM THE
GLOOM VOLCANO
SPOOPY COOKIES

Dear Violet Shiver, Shadow Storm, and Black Belle,

Our instructions were clear: destroy the ponies' friendships and community. So far, you've just taught them to make spoopy cookies (which did look good, btw) and terrorize their roommates. We created you with the most VICIOUS Smooze any witch has ever concocted, armed you with destructive powers, and this is what you do with them?! Perhaps you are just UNIQUELY UNGIFTED.

Is it time for us to take back what we've given you? Or can you try harder? It goes without saying we don't expect much of you. It's only a simple takedown of some ANNOYING, GLITTERY NAGS who are no match for S'Monies!

Step it up, or we'll turn this volcano into a GLUE FACTORY!
You Know You Love Us,

Grackle and Dyre

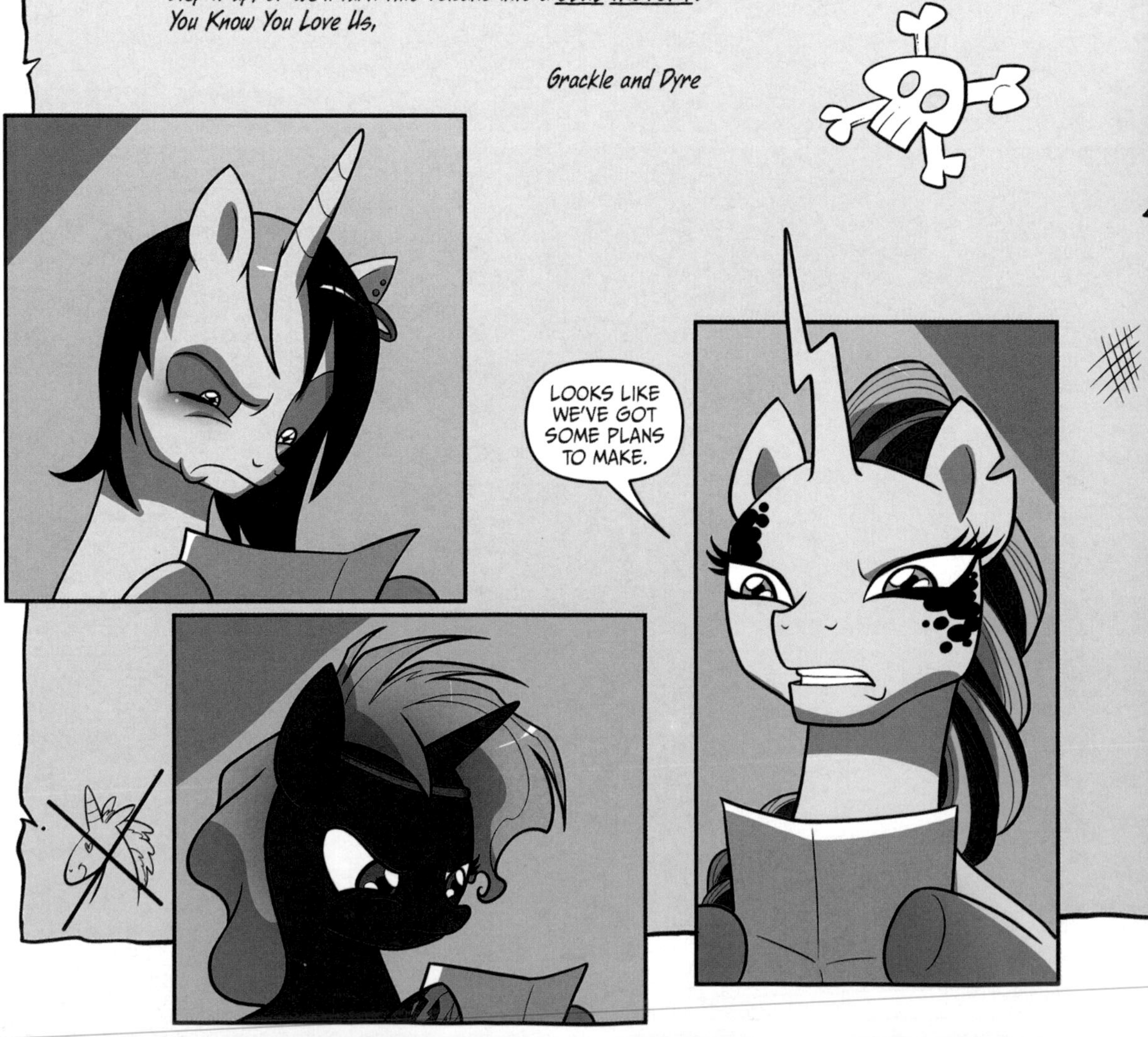
LOOKS LIKE WE'VE GOT SOME PLANS TO MAKE.

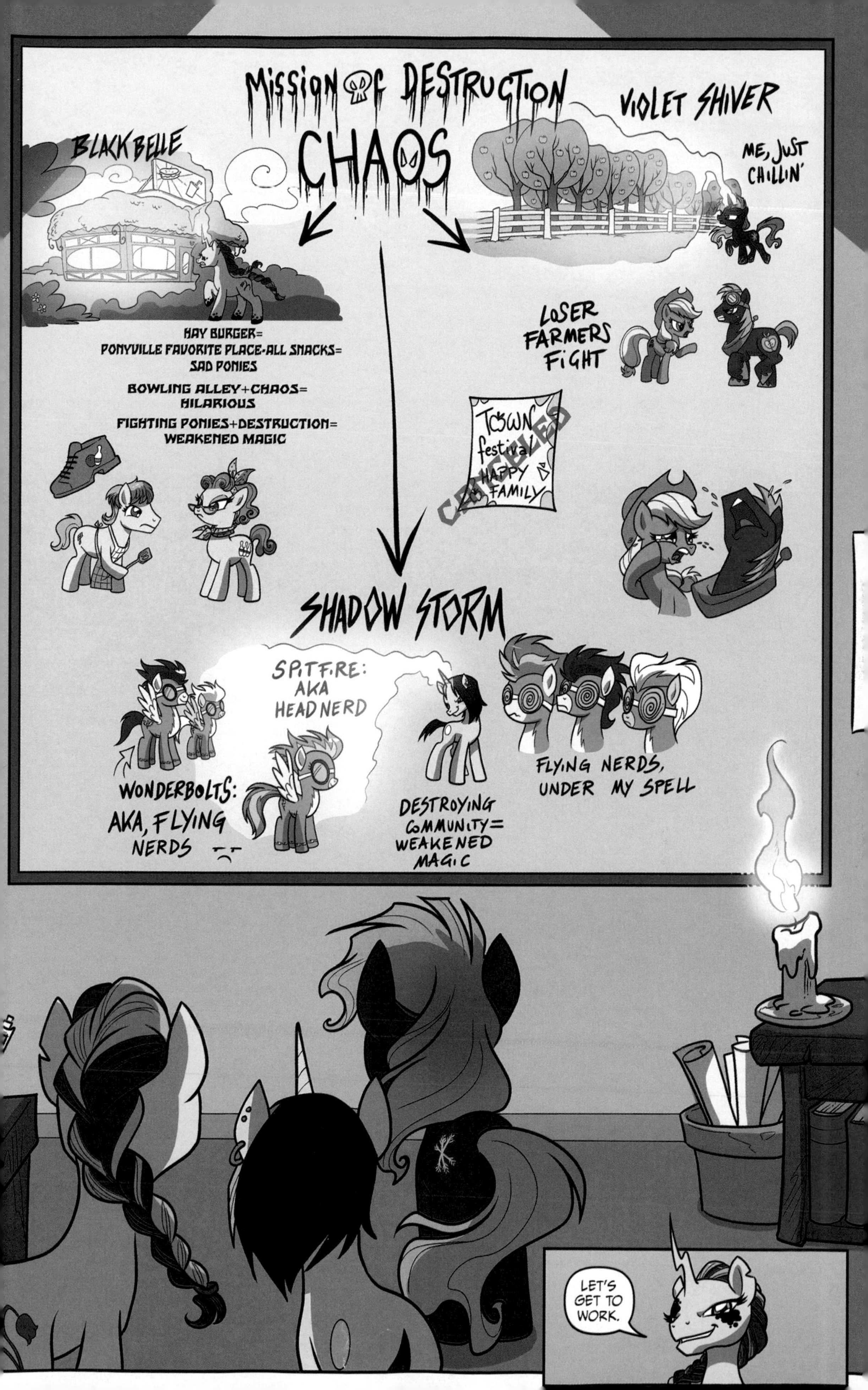

MISSION OF DESTRUCTION
CHAOS
BLACKBELLE
VIOLET SHIVER
ME, JUST CHILLIN'
HAY BURGER=
PONYVILLE FAVORITE PLACE-ALL SNACKS=
SAD PONIES
BOWLING ALLEY+CHAOS=
HILARIOUS
FIGHTING PONIES+DESTRUCTION=
WEAKENED MAGIC
LOSER FARMERS FIGHT
TOWN festival HAPPY FAMILY
CANCELED
SHADOW STORM
SPITFIRE: AKA HEADNERD
WONDERBOLTS: AKA, FLYING NERDS
DESTROYING COMMUNITY= WEAKENED MAGIC
FLYING NERDS, UNDER MY SPELL
LET'S GET TO WORK.

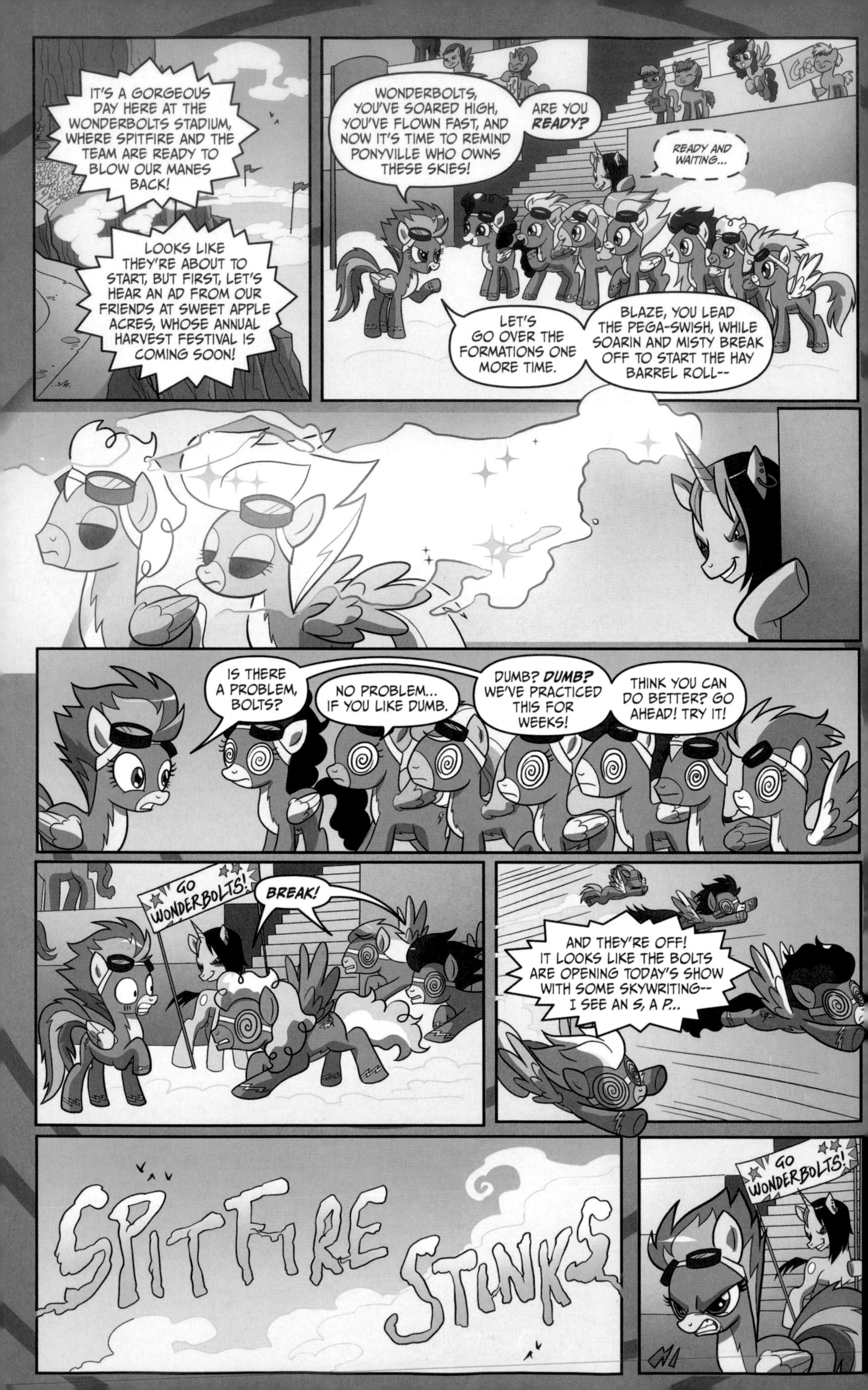
IT'S A GORGEOUS DAY HERE AT THE WONDERBOLTS STADIUM, WHERE SPITFIRE AND THE TEAM ARE READY TO BLOW OUR MANES BACK!
LOOKS LIKE THEY'RE ABOUT TO START, BUT FIRST, LET'S HEAR AN AD FROM OUR FRIENDS AT SWEET APPLE ACRES, WHOSE ANNUAL HARVEST FESTIVAL IS COMING SOON!
WONDERBOLTS, YOU'VE SOARED HIGH, YOU'VE FLOWN FAST, AND NOW IT'S TIME TO REMIND PONYVILLE WHO OWNS THESE SKIES!
ARE YOU ***READY?***
READY AND WAITING...
LET'S GO OVER THE FORMATIONS ONE MORE TIME.
BLAZE, YOU LEAD THE PEGA-SWISH, WHILE SOARIN AND MISTY BREAK OFF TO START THE HAY BARREL ROLL--
IS THERE A PROBLEM, BOLTS?
NO PROBLEM... IF YOU LIKE DUMB.
DUMB? ***DUMB?*** WE'VE PRACTICED THIS FOR WEEKS!
THINK YOU CAN DO BETTER? GO AHEAD! TRY IT!
GO WONDERBOLTS!
BREAK!
AND THEY'RE OFF! IT LOOKS LIKE THE BOLTS ARE OPENING TODAY'S SHOW WITH SOME SKYWRITING-- I SEE AN S, A P...
SPITFIRE STINKS
GO WONDERBOLTS!

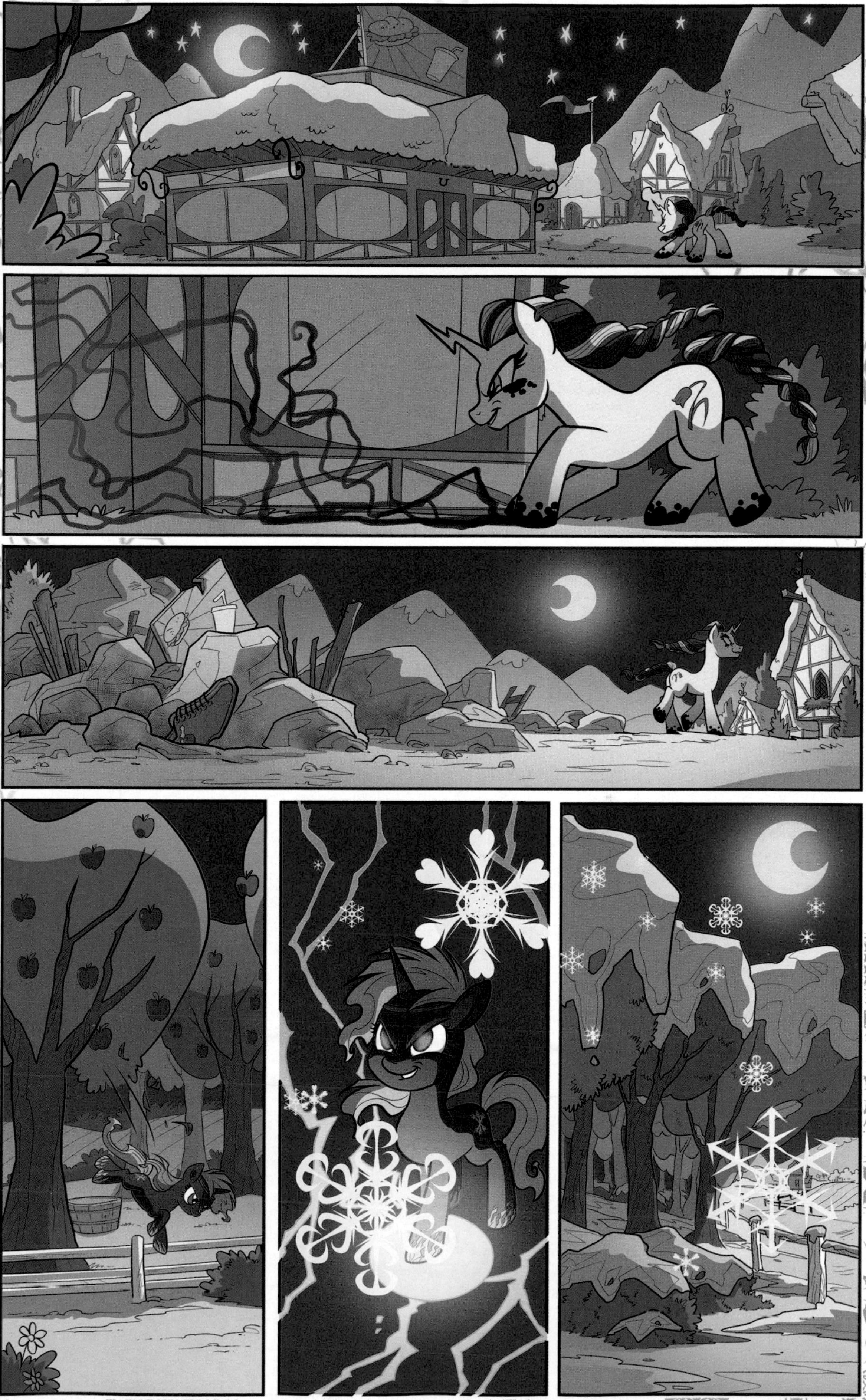

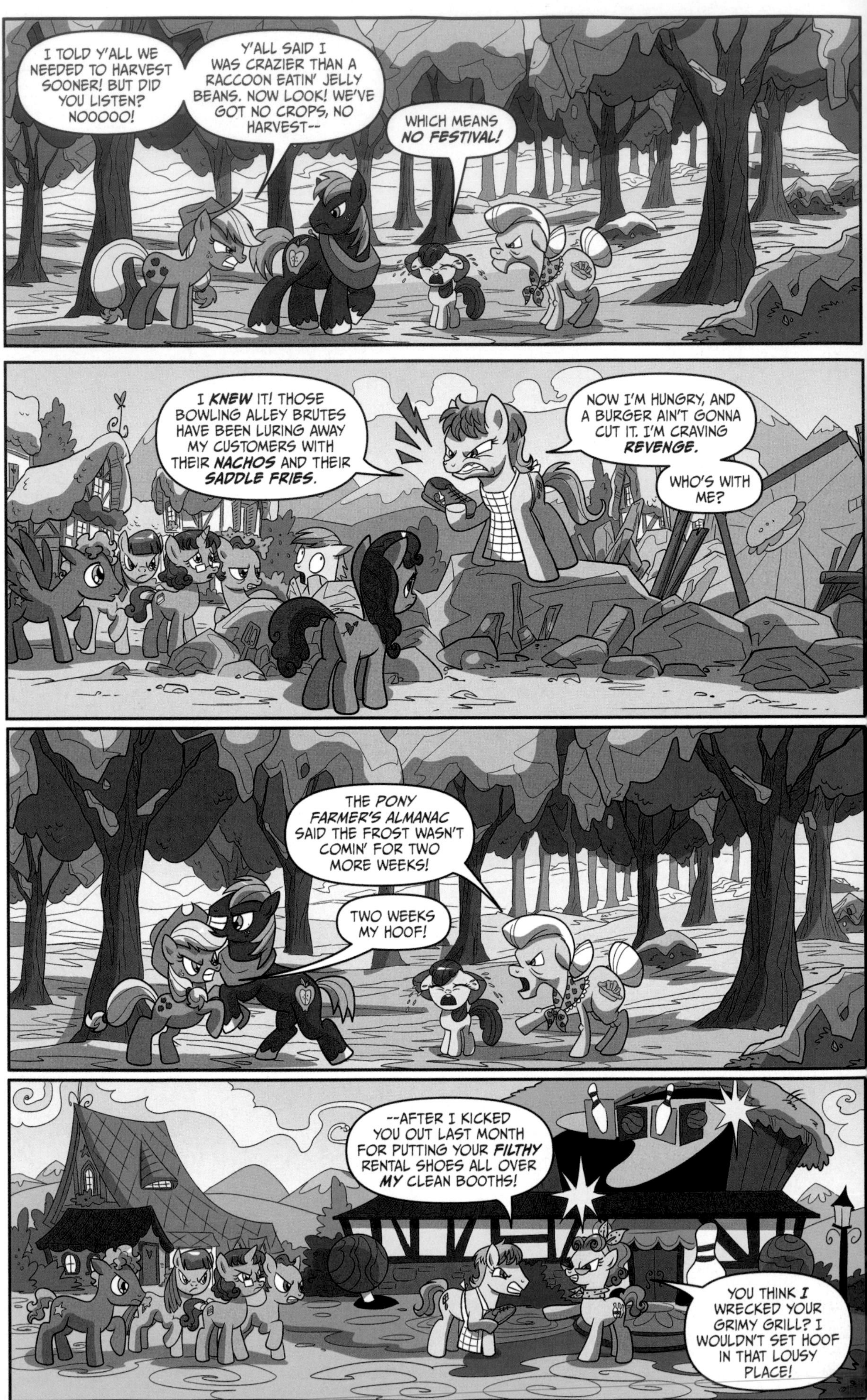
I TOLD Y'ALL WE NEEDED TO HARVEST SOONER! BUT DID YOU LISTEN? NOOOOO!
Y'ALL SAID I WAS CRAZIER THAN A RACCOON EATIN' JELLY BEANS. NOW LOOK! WE'VE GOT NO CROPS, NO HARVEST--
WHICH MEANS NO FESTIVAL!
I KNEW IT! THOSE BOWLING ALLEY BRUTES HAVE BEEN LURING AWAY MY CUSTOMERS WITH THEIR NACHOS AND THEIR SADDLE FRIES.
NOW I'M HUNGRY, AND A BURGER AIN'T GONNA CUT IT. I'M CRAVING REVENGE.
WHO'S WITH ME?
THE PONY FARMER'S ALMANAC SAID THE FROST WASN'T COMIN' FOR TWO MORE WEEKS!
TWO WEEKS MY HOOF!
--AFTER I KICKED YOU OUT LAST MONTH FOR PUTTING YOUR FILTHY RENTAL SHOES ALL OVER MY CLEAN BOOTHS!
YOU THINK I WRECKED YOUR GRIMY GRILL? I WOULDN'T SET HOOF IN THAT LOUSY PLACE!

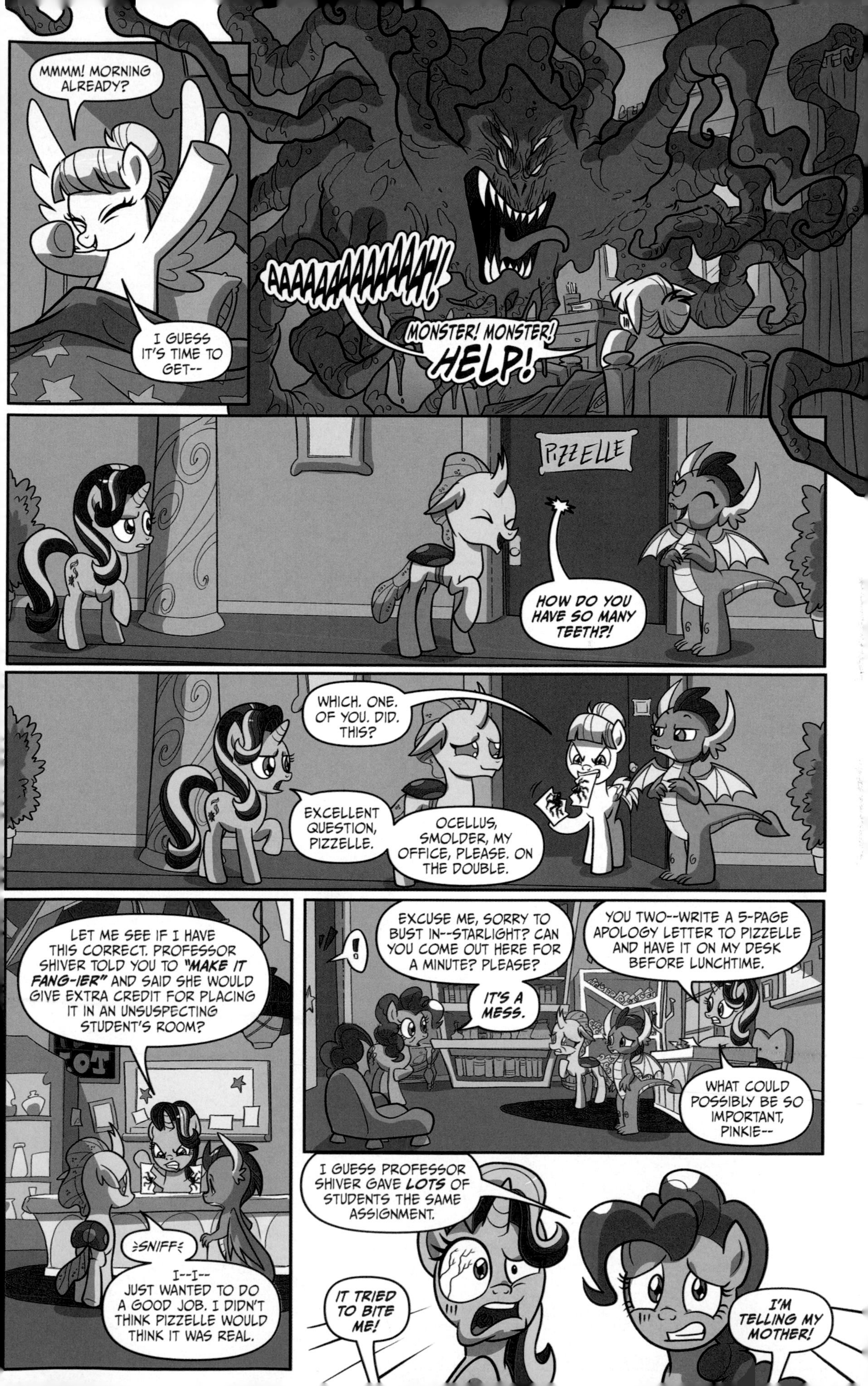
MMMM! MORNING ALREADY?
I GUESS IT'S TIME TO GET--
AAAAAAAAAAAAAH!
MONSTER! MONSTER! HELP!
PIZZELLE
HOW DO YOU HAVE SO MANY TEETH?!
WHICH. ONE. OF YOU. DID. THIS?
EXCELLENT QUESTION, PIZZELLE.
OCELLUS, SMOLDER, MY OFFICE, PLEASE. ON THE DOUBLE.
LET ME SEE IF I HAVE THIS CORRECT. PROFESSOR SHIVER TOLD YOU TO "MAKE IT FANG-IER" AND SAID SHE WOULD GIVE EXTRA CREDIT FOR PLACING IT IN AN UNSUSPECTING STUDENT'S ROOM?
SNIFF
I--I-- JUST WANTED TO DO A GOOD JOB. I DIDN'T THINK PIZZELLE WOULD THINK IT WAS REAL.
!
EXCUSE ME, SORRY TO BUST IN--STARLIGHT? CAN YOU COME OUT HERE FOR A MINUTE? PLEASE?
IT'S A MESS.
YOU TWO--WRITE A 5-PAGE APOLOGY LETTER TO PIZZELLE AND HAVE IT ON MY DESK BEFORE LUNCHTIME.
WHAT COULD POSSIBLY BE SO IMPORTANT, PINKIE--
I GUESS PROFESSOR SHIVER GAVE LOTS OF STUDENTS THE SAME ASSIGNMENT.
IT TRIED TO BITE ME!
I'M TELLING MY MOTHER!

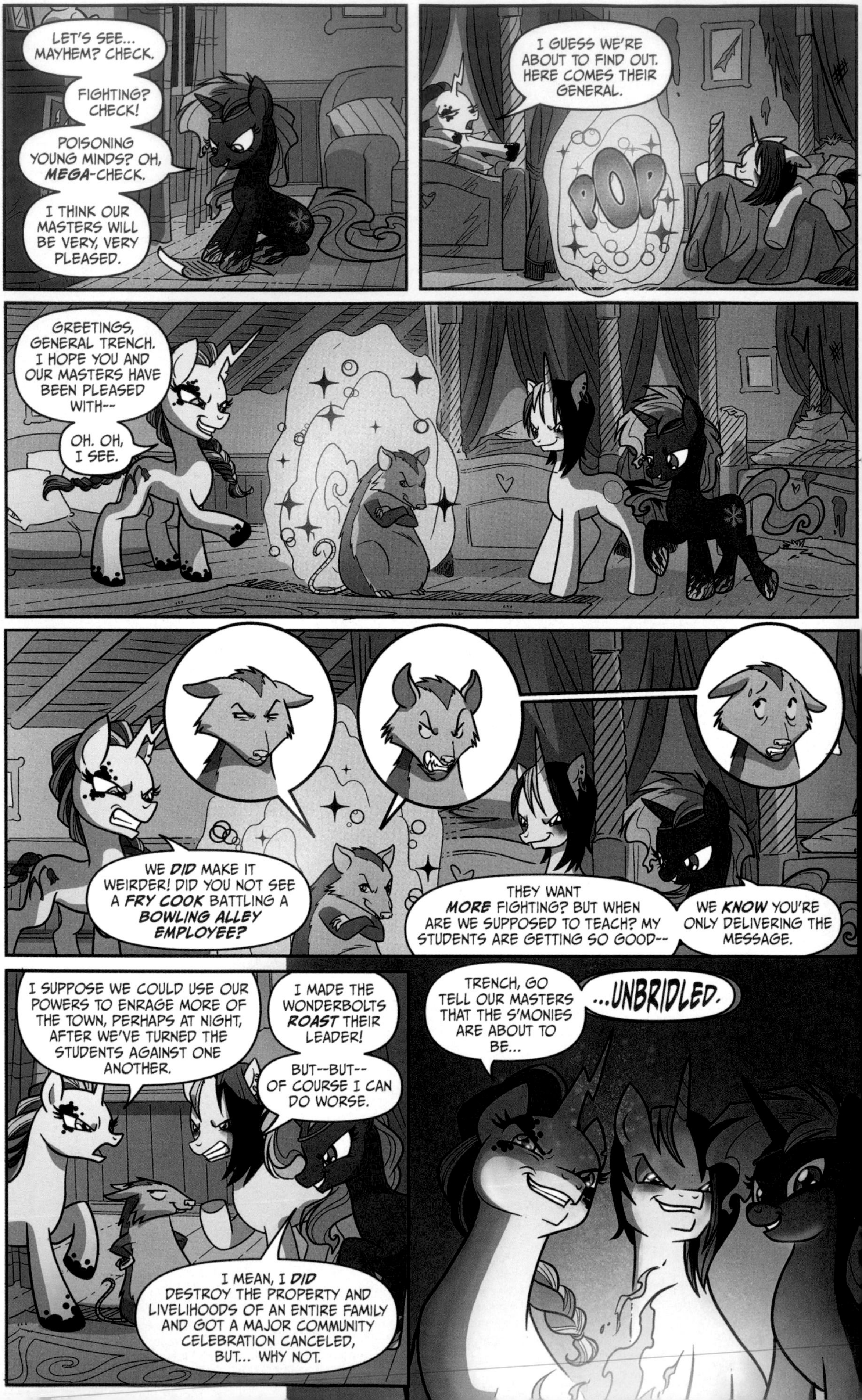
LET'S SEE... MAYHEM? CHECK.
FIGHTING? CHECK!
POISONING YOUNG MINDS? OH, **MEGA**-CHECK.
I THINK OUR MASTERS WILL BE VERY, VERY PLEASED.
I GUESS WE'RE ABOUT TO FIND OUT. HERE COMES THEIR GENERAL.
POP
GREETINGS, GENERAL TRENCH. I HOPE YOU AND OUR MASTERS HAVE BEEN PLEASED WITH--
OH. OH, I SEE.
WE **DID** MAKE IT WEIRDER! DID YOU NOT SEE A **FRY COOK** BATTLING A **BOWLING ALLEY EMPLOYEE?**
THEY WANT **MORE** FIGHTING? BUT WHEN ARE WE SUPPOSED TO TEACH? MY STUDENTS ARE GETTING SO GOOD--
WE **KNOW** YOU'RE ONLY DELIVERING THE MESSAGE.
I SUPPOSE WE COULD USE OUR POWERS TO ENRAGE MORE OF THE TOWN, PERHAPS AT NIGHT, AFTER WE'VE TURNED THE STUDENTS AGAINST ONE ANOTHER.
I MADE THE WONDERBOLTS **ROAST** THEIR LEADER!
BUT--BUT-- OF COURSE I CAN DO WORSE.
I MEAN, I **DID** DESTROY THE PROPERTY AND LIVELIHOODS OF AN ENTIRE FAMILY AND GOT A MAJOR COMMUNITY CELEBRATION CANCELED, BUT... WHY NOT.
TRENCH, GO TELL OUR MASTERS THAT THE S'MONIES ARE ABOUT TO BE...
...UNBRIDLED.

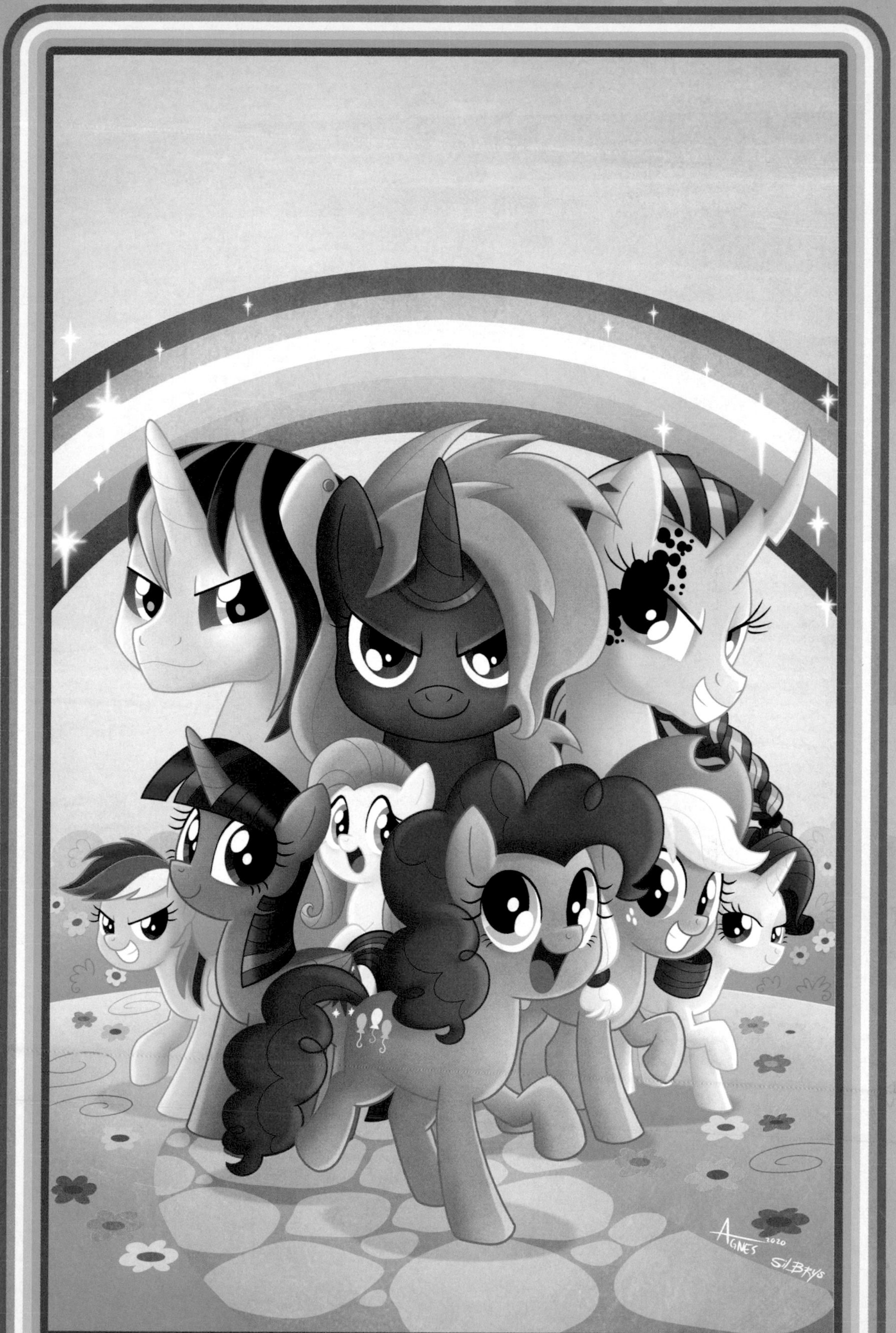

Art by **Agnes Garbowska** Colors by **Silvana Brys**

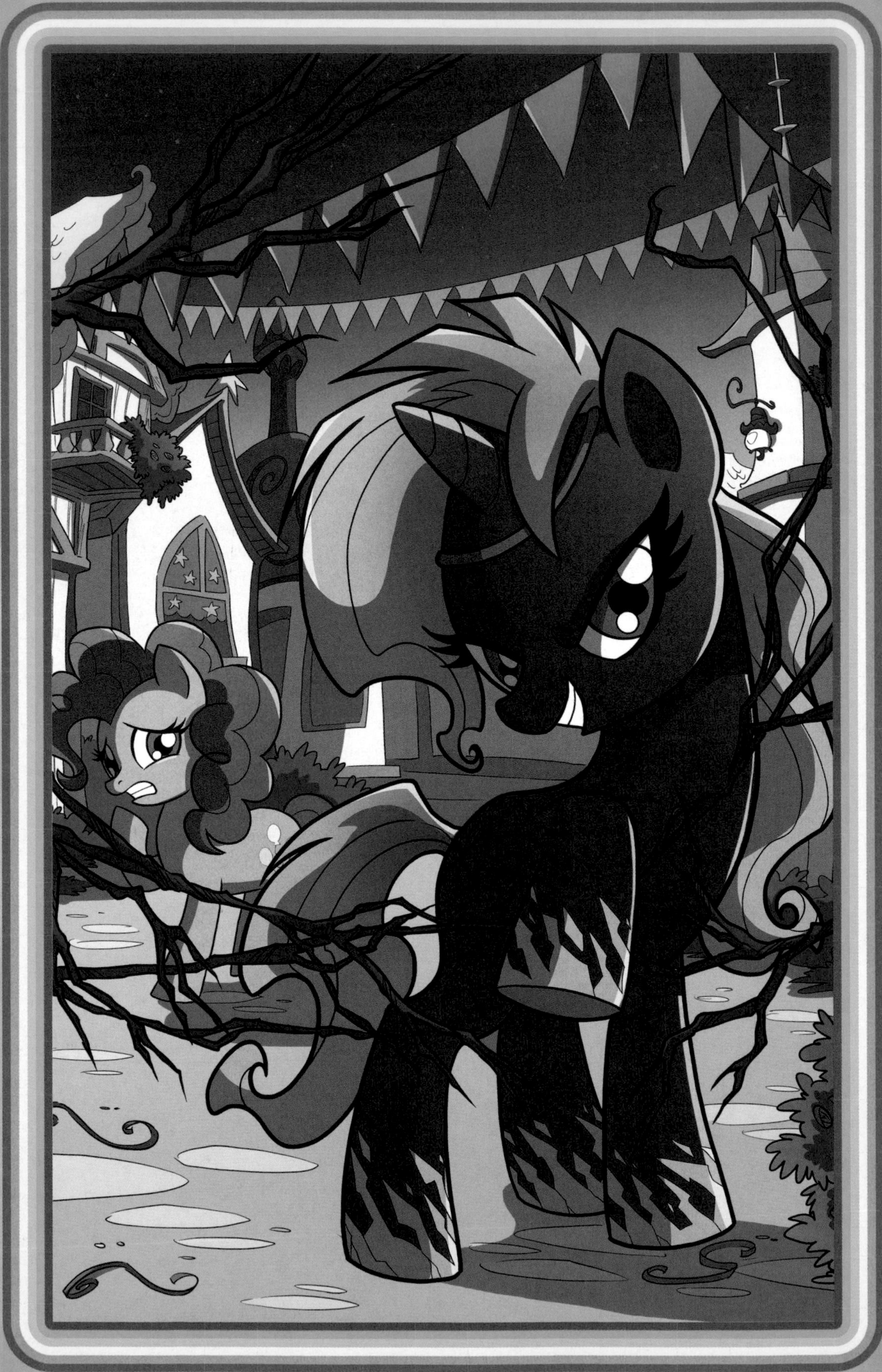

Art by Michela Cacciatore

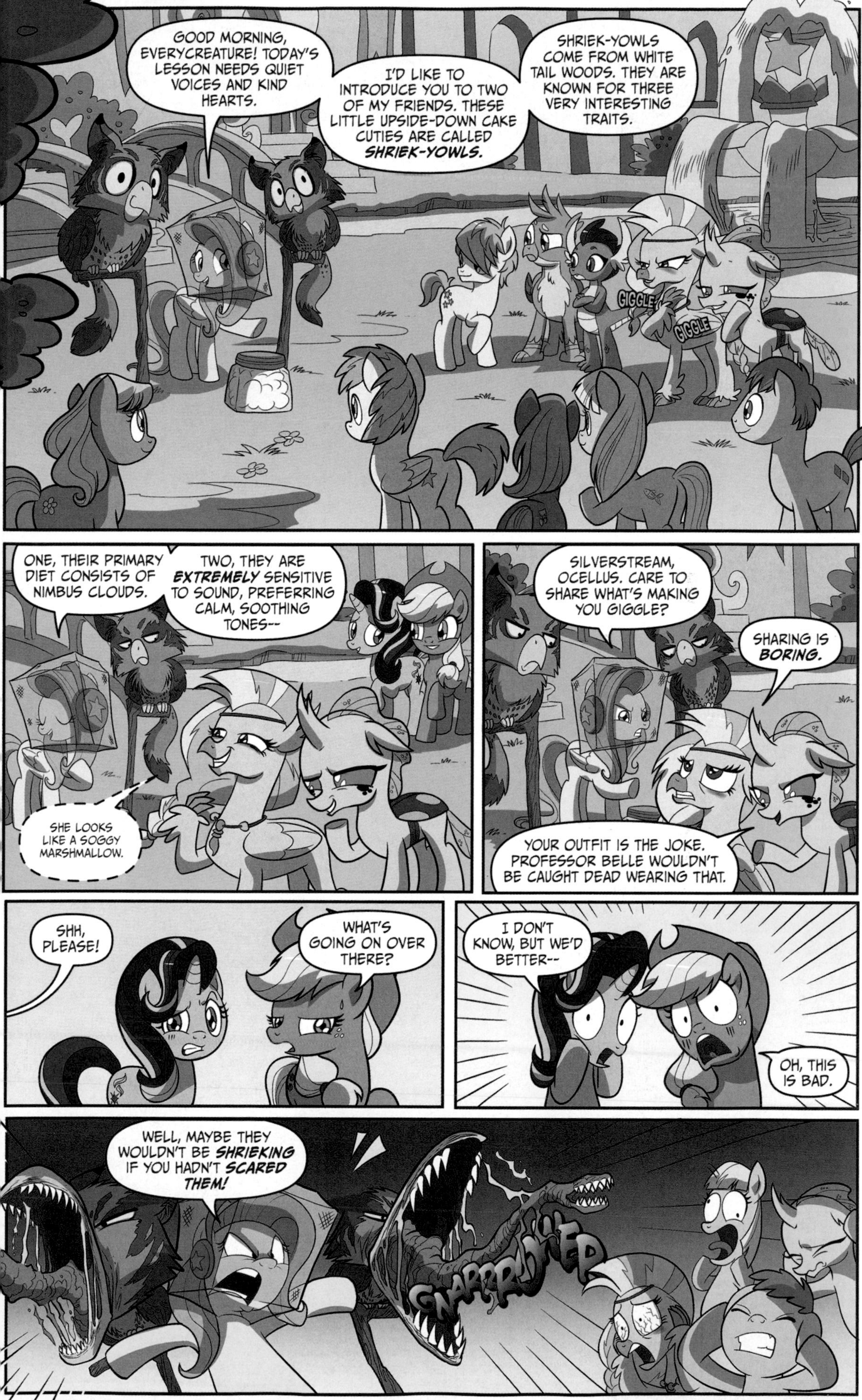
GOOD MORNING, EVERYCREATURE! TODAY'S LESSON NEEDS QUIET VOICES AND KIND HEARTS.
I'D LIKE TO INTRODUCE YOU TO TWO OF MY FRIENDS. THESE LITTLE UPSIDE-DOWN CAKE CUTIES ARE CALLED SHRIEK-YOWLS.
SHRIEK-YOWLS COME FROM WHITE TAIL WOODS. THEY ARE KNOWN FOR THREE VERY INTERESTING TRAITS.
GIGGLE
GIGGLE
ONE, THEIR PRIMARY DIET CONSISTS OF NIMBUS CLOUDS.
TWO, THEY ARE EXTREMELY SENSITIVE TO SOUND, PREFERRING CALM, SOOTHING TONES--
SHE LOOKS LIKE A SOGGY MARSHMALLOW.
SILVERSTREAM, OCELLUS. CARE TO SHARE WHAT'S MAKING YOU GIGGLE?
SHARING IS BORING.
YOUR OUTFIT IS THE JOKE. PROFESSOR BELLE WOULDN'T BE CAUGHT DEAD WEARING THAT.
SHH, PLEASE!
WHAT'S GOING ON OVER THERE?
I DON'T KNOW, BUT WE'D BETTER--
OH, THIS IS BAD.
WELL, MAYBE THEY WOULDN'T BE SHRIEKING IF YOU HADN'T SCARED THEM!
GNARRRHHHEP

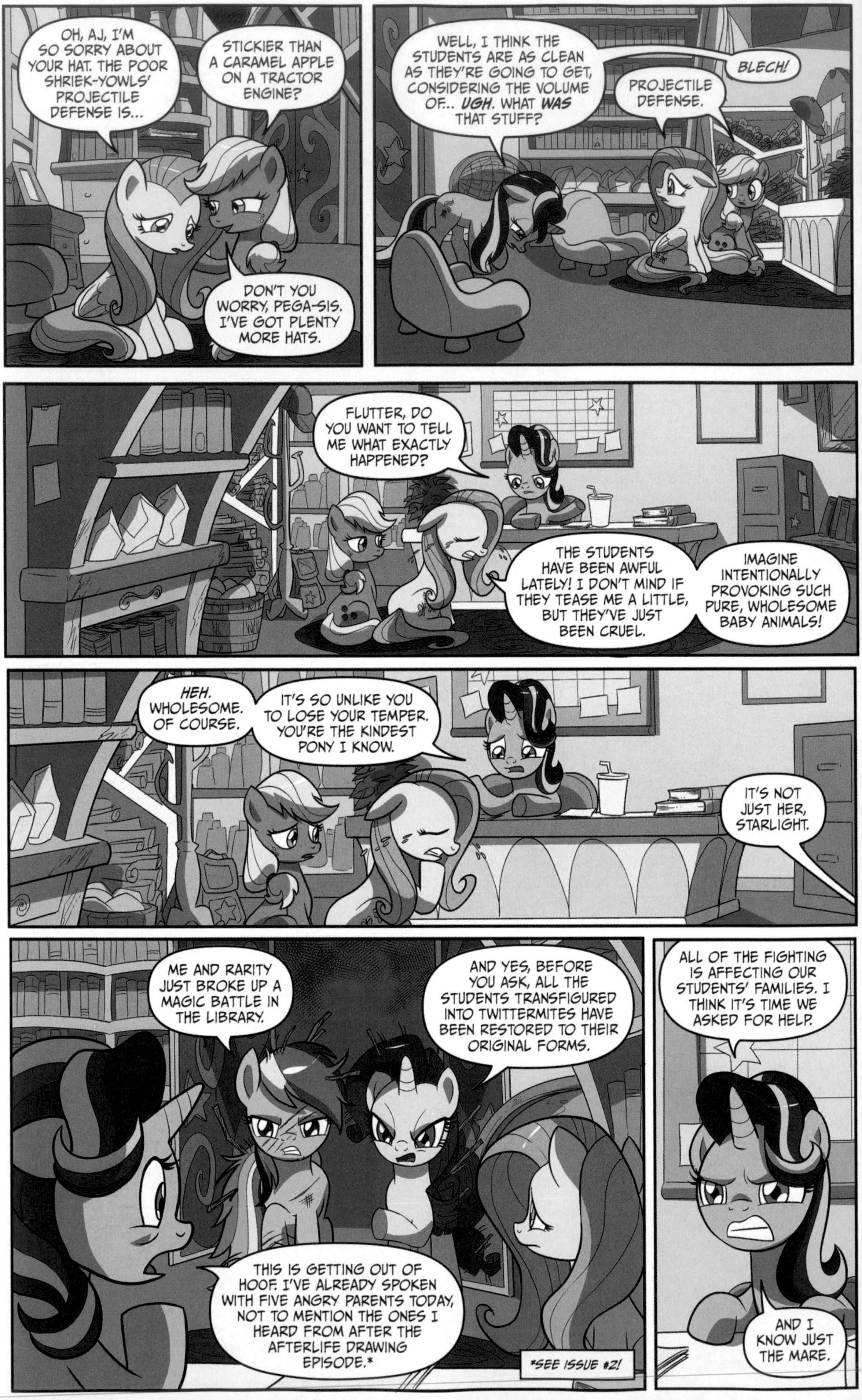
OH, AJ, I'M SO SORRY ABOUT YOUR HAT. THE POOR SHRIEK-YOWLS' PROJECTILE DEFENSE IS...
STICKIER THAN A CARAMEL APPLE ON A TRACTOR ENGINE?
DON'T YOU WORRY, PEGA-SIS. I'VE GOT PLENTY MORE HATS.
WELL, I THINK THE STUDENTS ARE AS CLEAN AS THEY'RE GOING TO GET, CONSIDERING THE VOLUME OF... *UGH*. WHAT *WAS* THAT STUFF?
PROJECTILE DEFENSE.
BLECH!
FLUTTER, DO YOU WANT TO TELL ME WHAT EXACTLY HAPPENED?
THE STUDENTS HAVE BEEN AWFUL LATELY! I DON'T MIND IF THEY TEASE ME A LITTLE, BUT THEY'VE JUST BEEN CRUEL.
IMAGINE INTENTIONALLY PROVOKING SUCH PURE, WHOLESOME BABY ANIMALS!
HEH. WHOLESOME. OF COURSE.
IT'S SO UNLIKE YOU TO LOSE YOUR TEMPER. YOU'RE THE KINDEST PONY I KNOW.
IT'S NOT JUST HER, STARLIGHT.
ME AND RARITY JUST BROKE UP A MAGIC BATTLE IN THE LIBRARY.
AND YES, BEFORE YOU ASK, ALL THE STUDENTS TRANSFIGURED INTO TWITTERMITES HAVE BEEN RESTORED TO THEIR ORIGINAL FORMS.
THIS IS GETTING OUT OF HOOF. I'VE ALREADY SPOKEN WITH FIVE ANGRY PARENTS TODAY, NOT TO MENTION THE ONES I HEARD FROM AFTER THE AFTERLIFE DRAWING EPISODE.*
*SEE ISSUE #2!
ALL OF THE FIGHTING IS AFFECTING OUR STUDENTS' FAMILIES. I THINK IT'S TIME WE ASKED FOR HELP.
AND I KNOW JUST THE MARE.

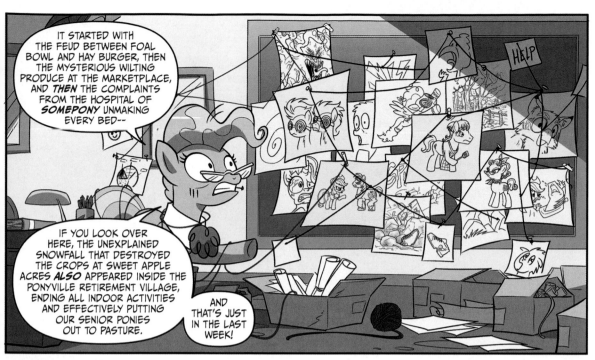

IT STARTED WITH THE FEUD BETWEEN FOAL BOWL AND HAY BURGER, THEN THE MYSTERIOUS WILTING PRODUCE AT THE MARKETPLACE, AND *THEN* THE COMPLAINTS FROM THE HOSPITAL OF *SOMEPONY* UNMAKING EVERY BED--

IF YOU LOOK OVER HERE, THE UNEXPLAINED SNOWFALL THAT DESTROYED THE CROPS AT SWEET APPLE ACRES *ALSO* APPEARED INSIDE THE PONYVILLE RETIREMENT VILLAGE, ENDING ALL INDOOR ACTIVITIES AND EFFECTIVELY PUTTING OUR SENIOR PONIES OUT TO PASTURE.

AND THAT'S JUST IN THE LAST WEEK!

BUT OF *COURSE* I HAVE *PLENTY* OF TIME FOR PONIES WITHOUT AN APPOINTMENT. HOW CAN I HELP YOU?

AFTER HEARING WHAT'S BEEN HEAPED INTO YOUR FEEDBAG, MAYBE WE CAN HELP EACH OTHER? THERE'S SOMETHING *WRONG* IN PONYVILLE.

OH? I'M INTRIGUED.

AS YOU CAN SEE, THINGS AT THE SCHOOL OF FRIENDSHIP *HAVEN'T* BEEN ALL DONUTS AND SPRINKLES.

Get comfortable, it's gonna take the mayor a while to get caught up!

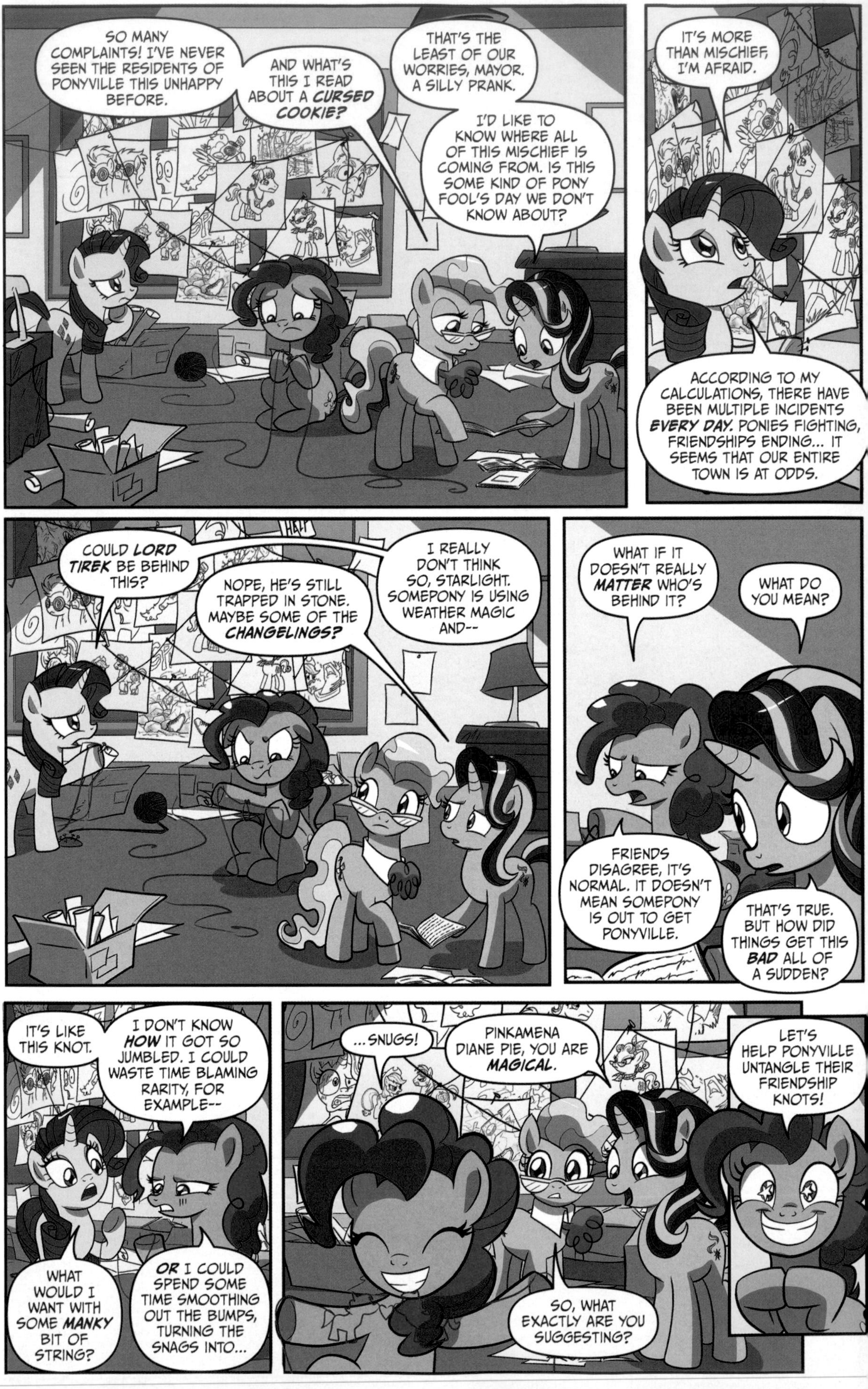
SO MANY COMPLAINTS! I'VE NEVER SEEN THE RESIDENTS OF PONYVILLE THIS UNHAPPY BEFORE.
AND WHAT'S THIS I READ ABOUT A *CURSED COOKIE?*
THAT'S THE LEAST OF OUR WORRIES, MAYOR. A SILLY PRANK.
I'D LIKE TO KNOW WHERE ALL OF THIS MISCHIEF IS COMING FROM. IS THIS SOME KIND OF PONY FOOL'S DAY WE DON'T KNOW ABOUT?
IT'S MORE THAN MISCHIEF, I'M AFRAID.
ACCORDING TO MY CALCULATIONS, THERE HAVE BEEN MULTIPLE INCIDENTS **EVERY DAY.** PONIES FIGHTING, FRIENDSHIPS ENDING... IT SEEMS THAT OUR ENTIRE TOWN IS AT ODDS.
COULD **LORD TIREK** BE BEHIND THIS?
NOPE, HE'S STILL TRAPPED IN STONE. MAYBE SOME OF THE **CHANGELINGS?**
I REALLY DON'T THINK SO, STARLIGHT. SOMEPONY IS USING WEATHER MAGIC AND--
WHAT IF IT DOESN'T REALLY **MATTER** WHO'S BEHIND IT?
WHAT DO YOU MEAN?
FRIENDS DISAGREE, IT'S NORMAL. IT DOESN'T MEAN SOMEPONY IS OUT TO GET PONYVILLE.
THAT'S TRUE. BUT HOW DID THINGS GET THIS **BAD** ALL OF A SUDDEN?
IT'S LIKE THIS KNOT.
I DON'T KNOW **HOW** IT GOT SO JUMBLED. I COULD WASTE TIME BLAMING RARITY, FOR EXAMPLE--
WHAT WOULD I WANT WITH SOME **MANKY** BIT OF STRING?
OR I COULD SPEND SOME TIME SMOOTHING OUT THE BUMPS, TURNING THE SNAGS INTO...
...SNUGS!
PINKAMENA DIANE PIE, YOU ARE **MAGICAL.**
SO, WHAT EXACTLY ARE YOU SUGGESTING?
LET'S HELP PONYVILLE UNTANGLE THEIR FRIENDSHIP KNOTS!

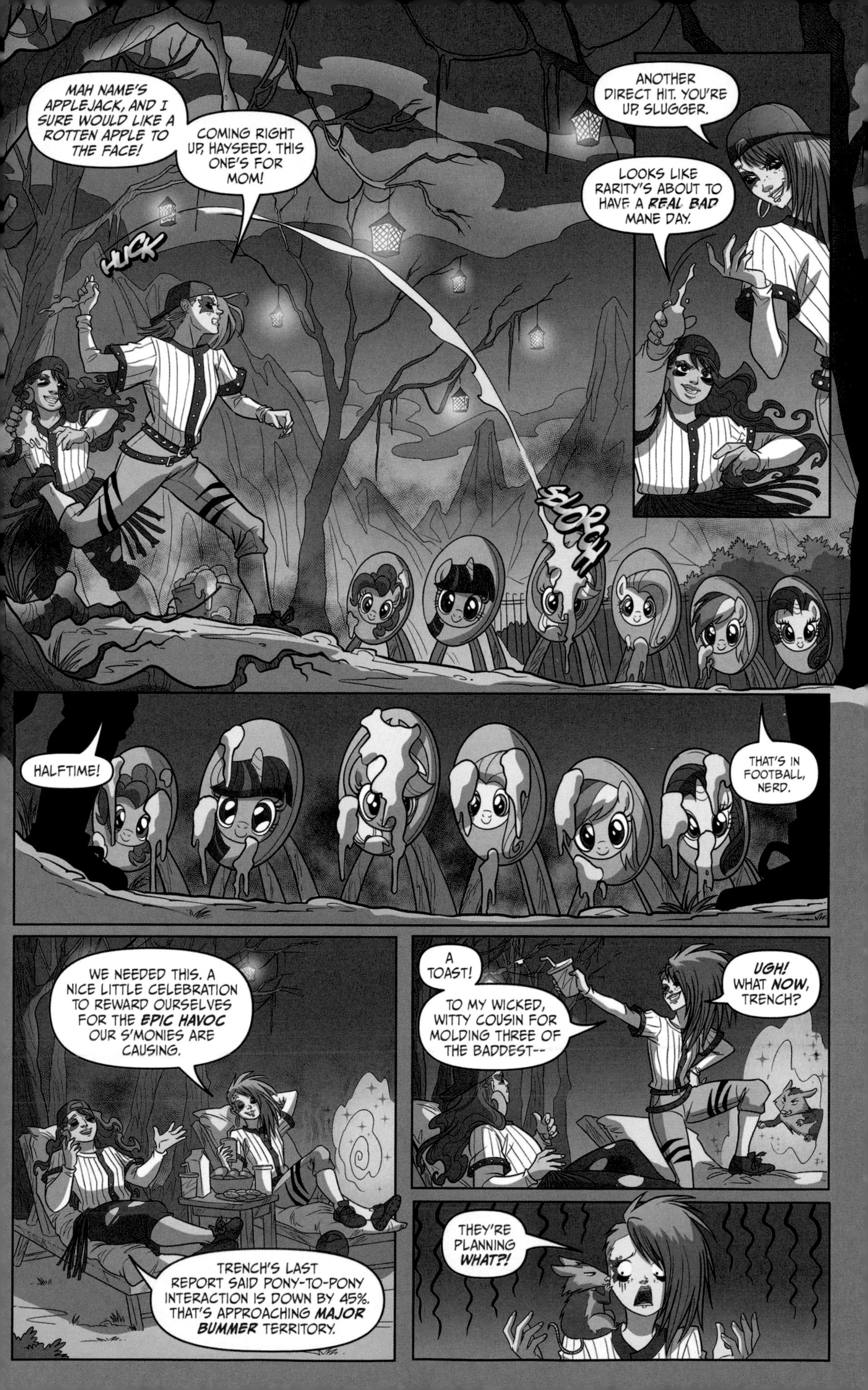
MAH NAME'S APPLEJACK, AND I SURE WOULD LIKE A ROTTEN APPLE TO THE FACE!
COMING RIGHT UP, HAYSEED. THIS ONE'S FOR MOM!
HUCK
SPLORCH
ANOTHER DIRECT HIT. YOU'RE UP, SLUGGER.
LOOKS LIKE RARITY'S ABOUT TO HAVE A REAL BAD MANE DAY.
HALFTIME!
THAT'S IN FOOTBALL, NERD.
WE NEEDED THIS. A NICE LITTLE CELEBRATION TO REWARD OURSELVES FOR THE EPIC HAVOC OUR S'MONIES ARE CAUSING.
TRENCH'S LAST REPORT SAID PONY-TO-PONY INTERACTION IS DOWN BY 45%. THAT'S APPROACHING MAJOR BUMMER TERRITORY.
A TOAST!
TO MY WICKED, WITTY COUSIN FOR MOLDING THREE OF THE BADDEST--
UGH! WHAT NOW, TRENCH?
THEY'RE PLANNING WHAT?!

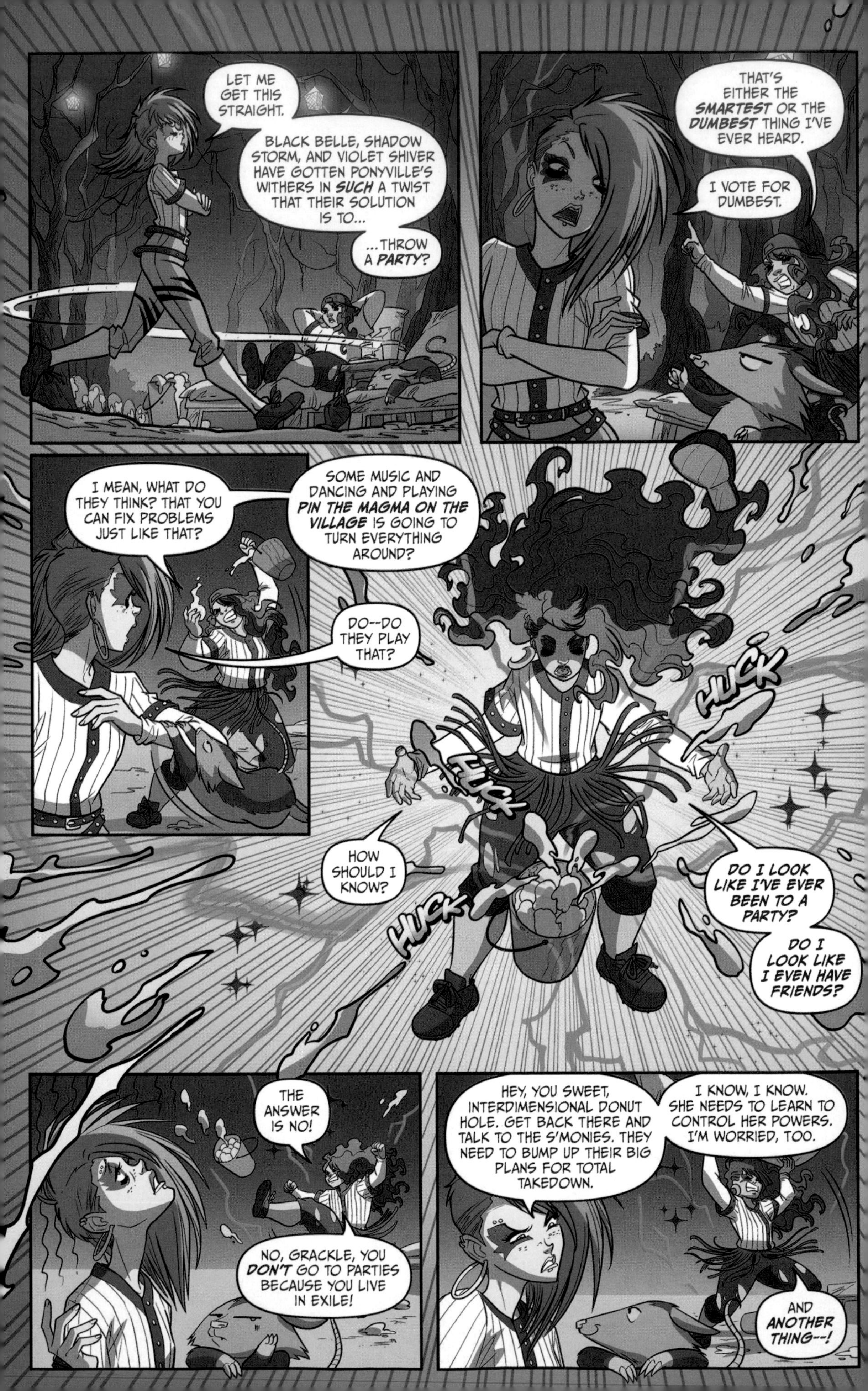
LET ME GET THIS STRAIGHT.
BLACK BELLE, SHADOW STORM, AND VIOLET SHIVER HAVE GOTTEN PONYVILLE'S WITHERS IN SUCH A TWIST THAT THEIR SOLUTION IS TO...
...THROW A PARTY?
THAT'S EITHER THE SMARTEST OR THE DUMBEST THING I'VE EVER HEARD.
I VOTE FOR DUMBEST.
I MEAN, WHAT DO THEY THINK? THAT YOU CAN FIX PROBLEMS JUST LIKE THAT?
SOME MUSIC AND DANCING AND PLAYING PIN THE MAGMA ON THE VILLAGE IS GOING TO TURN EVERYTHING AROUND?
DO--DO THEY PLAY THAT?
HUCK
HUCK
HOW SHOULD I KNOW?
DO I LOOK LIKE I'VE EVER BEEN TO A PARTY?
DO I LOOK LIKE I EVEN HAVE FRIENDS?
HUCK
THE ANSWER IS NO!
NO, GRACKLE, YOU DON'T GO TO PARTIES BECAUSE YOU LIVE IN EXILE!
HEY, YOU SWEET, INTERDIMENSIONAL DONUT HOLE. GET BACK THERE AND TALK TO THE S'MONIES. THEY NEED TO BUMP UP THEIR BIG PLANS FOR TOTAL TAKEDOWN.
I KNOW, I KNOW. SHE NEEDS TO LEARN TO CONTROL HER POWERS. I'M WORRIED, TOO.
AND ANOTHER THING--!

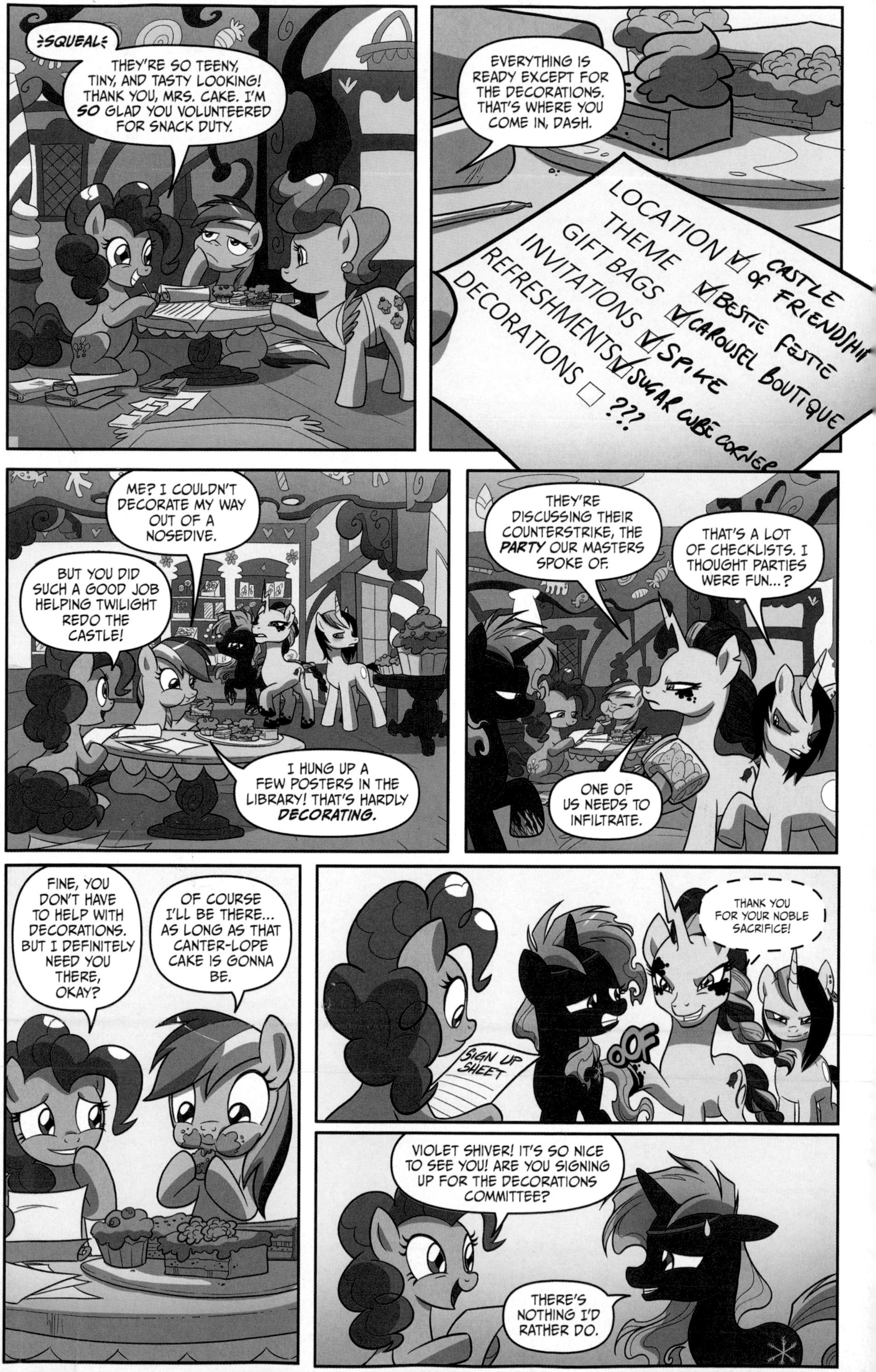

SQUEAL
THEY'RE SO TEENY, TINY, AND TASTY LOOKING! THANK YOU, MRS. CAKE. I'M SO GLAD YOU VOLUNTEERED FOR SNACK DUTY.
EVERYTHING IS READY EXCEPT FOR THE DECORATIONS. THAT'S WHERE YOU COME IN, DASH.
LOCATION ☑ CASTLE OF FRIENDSHI
THEME ☑ BESTIE FESTIE
GIFT BAGS ☑ CAROUSEL BOUTIQUE
INVITATIONS ☑ SPIKE
REFRESHMENTS ☑ SUGAR CUBE CORNER
DECORATIONS ☐ ???
ME? I COULDN'T DECORATE MY WAY OUT OF A NOSEDIVE.
BUT YOU DID SUCH A GOOD JOB HELPING TWILIGHT REDO THE CASTLE!
I HUNG UP A FEW POSTERS IN THE LIBRARY! THAT'S HARDLY DECORATING.
THEY'RE DISCUSSING THEIR COUNTERSTRIKE, THE PARTY OUR MASTERS SPOKE OF.
THAT'S A LOT OF CHECKLISTS. I THOUGHT PARTIES WERE FUN...?
ONE OF US NEEDS TO INFILTRATE.
FINE, YOU DON'T HAVE TO HELP WITH DECORATIONS. BUT I DEFINITELY NEED YOU THERE, OKAY?
OF COURSE I'LL BE THERE... AS LONG AS THAT CANTER-LOPE CAKE IS GONNA BE.
THANK YOU FOR YOUR NOBLE SACRIFICE!
SIGN UP SHEET
OOF
VIOLET SHIVER! IT'S SO NICE TO SEE YOU! ARE YOU SIGNING UP FOR THE DECORATIONS COMMITTEE?
THERE'S NOTHING I'D RATHER DO.

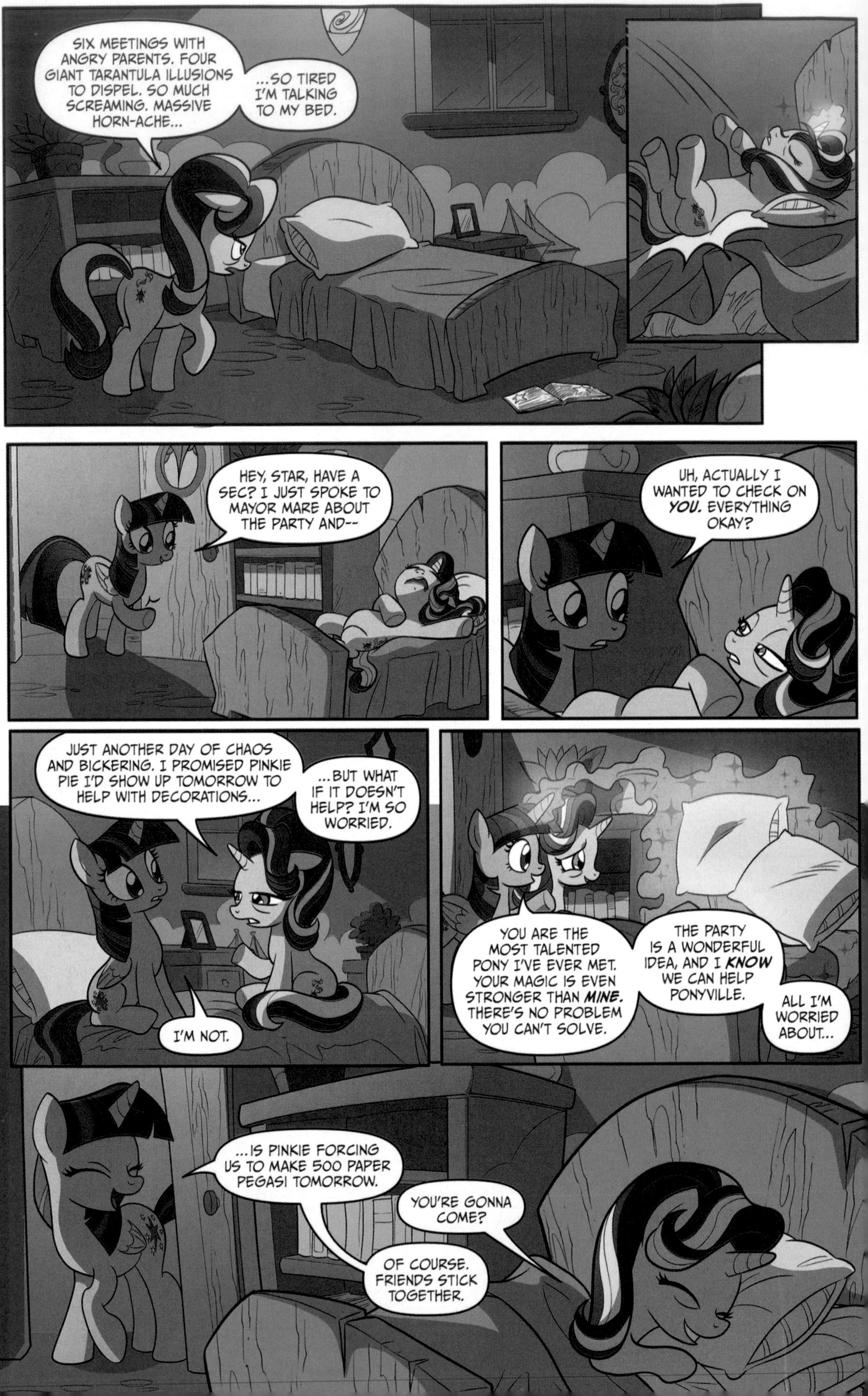
SIX MEETINGS WITH ANGRY PARENTS. FOUR GIANT TARANTULA ILLUSIONS TO DISPEL. SO MUCH SCREAMING. MASSIVE HORN-ACHE...
...SO TIRED I'M TALKING TO MY BED.
HEY, STAR, HAVE A SEC? I JUST SPOKE TO MAYOR MARE ABOUT THE PARTY AND--
UH, ACTUALLY I WANTED TO CHECK ON *YOU.* EVERYTHING OKAY?
JUST ANOTHER DAY OF CHAOS AND BICKERING. I PROMISED PINKIE PIE I'D SHOW UP TOMORROW TO HELP WITH DECORATIONS...
...BUT WHAT IF IT DOESN'T HELP? I'M SO WORRIED.
I'M NOT.
YOU ARE THE MOST TALENTED PONY I'VE EVER MET. YOUR MAGIC IS EVEN STRONGER THAN *MINE.* THERE'S NO PROBLEM YOU CAN'T SOLVE.
THE PARTY IS A WONDERFUL IDEA, AND I *KNOW* WE CAN HELP PONYVILLE.
ALL I'M WORRIED ABOUT...
...IS PINKIE FORCING US TO MAKE 500 PAPER PEGASI TOMORROW.
YOU'RE GONNA COME?
OF COURSE. FRIENDS STICK TOGETHER.

THANK YOU ALL FOR BEING HERE TO HELP!

TWI AND SPIKE, YOU'RE ON LANTERNS. STARLIGHT AND CHEERILEE, YOU'VE GOT GARLANDS.

I'M WITH VIOLET SHIVER ON STREAMERS!

STREAMERS

GARLANDS

LANTERNS

OKAY, DON'T THINK I'M WEIRD, BUT...

...I PAIRED US TOGETHER ON PURPOSE! I'VE BEEN *DYING* TO HANG OUT WITH YOU.

STREAMERS

SO, WHAT COLOR DO YOU THINK THE STREAMERS SHOULD BE?

HEH. SO MANY CHOICES. UM...

YOU'RE BRILLIANT! WHY CHOOSE WHEN WE CAN USE THEM *ALL?*

I BET YOU HAVE LOTS OF PARTIES AT HAYVARD. WHAT'S YOUR FAVORITE KIND?

PARTIES AREN'T REALLY MY *THING.*

OHHHH, I GET IT. HAYVARD IS *SO* SOPHISTICATED, I BET YOU HAVE *SOIRÉES.*

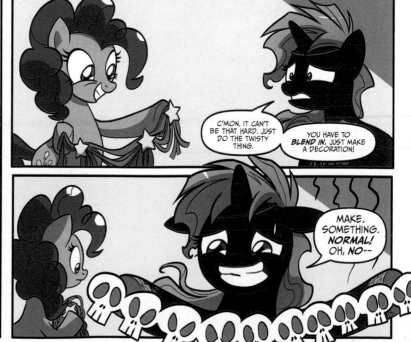

C'MON. IT CAN'T BE THAT HARD. JUST DO THE TWISTY THING.

YOU HAVE TO *BLEND IN.* JUST MAKE A DECORATION!

MAKE. SOMETHING. *NORMAL!* OH, *NO--*

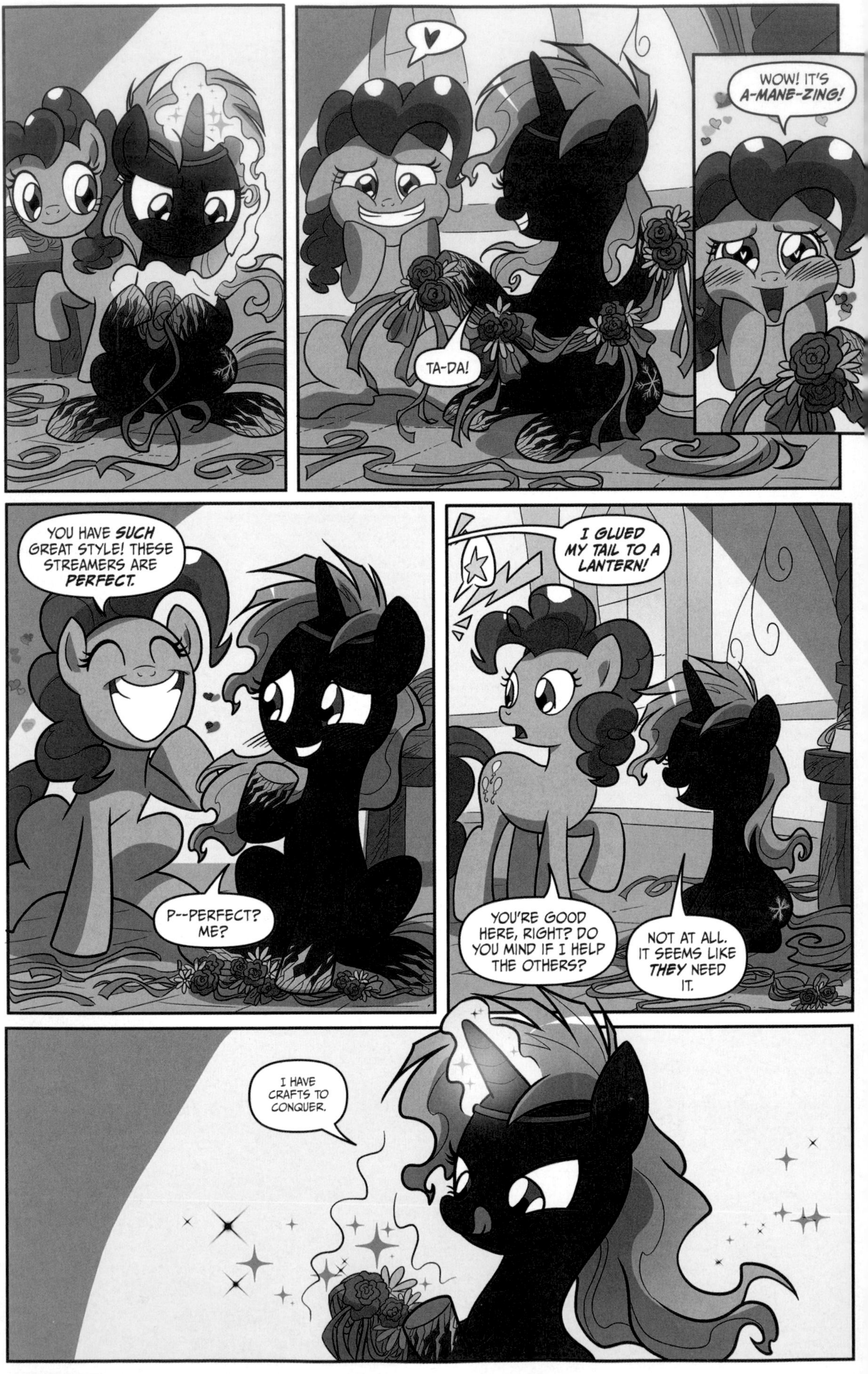
WOW! IT'S A-MANE-ZING!
TA-DA!
YOU HAVE SUCH GREAT STYLE! THESE STREAMERS ARE PERFECT.
P--PERFECT? ME?
I GLUED MY TAIL TO A LANTERN!
YOU'RE GOOD HERE, RIGHT? DO YOU MIND IF I HELP THE OTHERS?
NOT AT ALL. IT SEEMS LIKE THEY NEED IT.
I HAVE CRAFTS TO CONQUER.

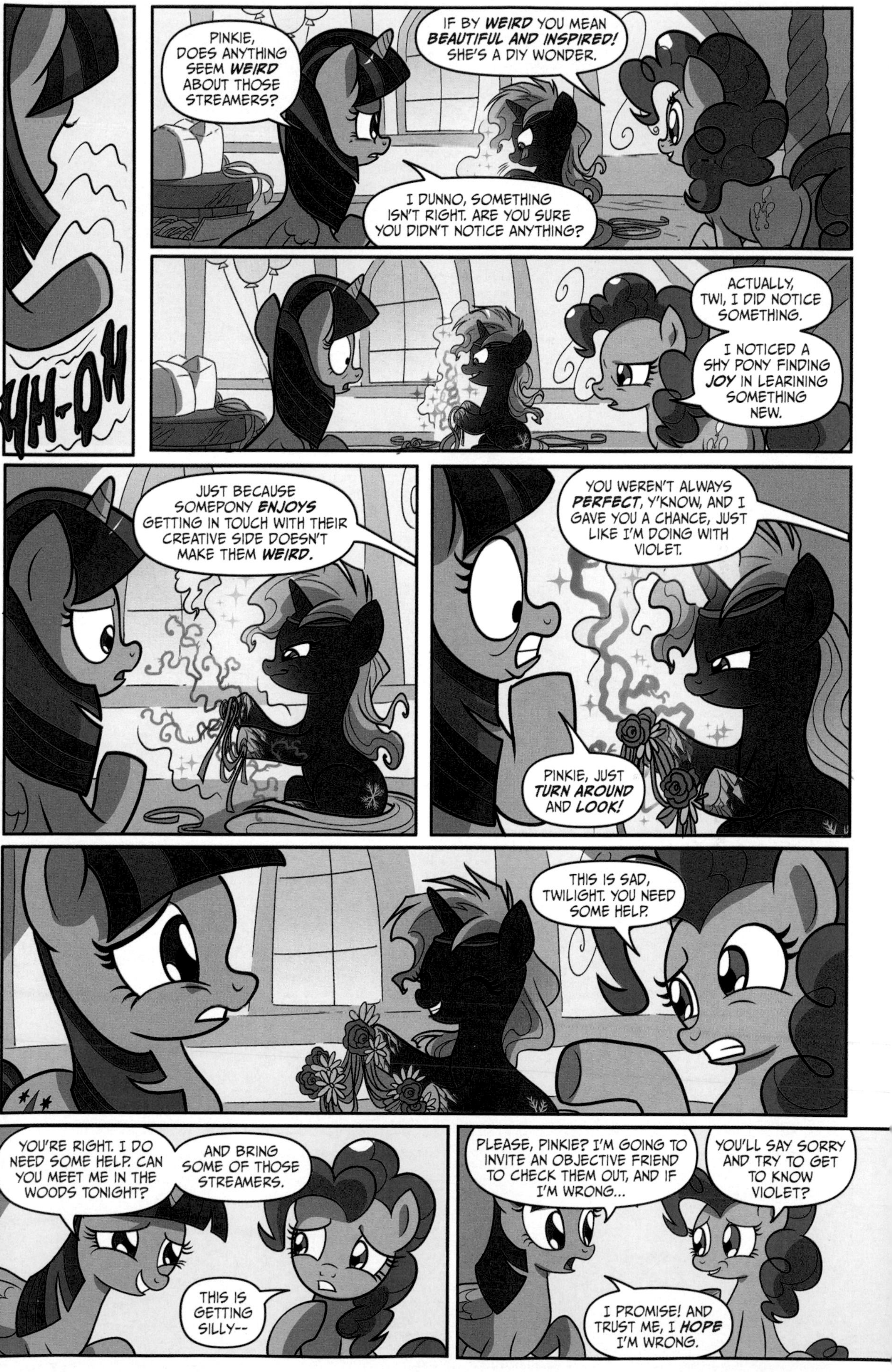
UH-OH
PINKIE, DOES ANYTHING SEEM WEIRD ABOUT THOSE STREAMERS?
IF BY WEIRD YOU MEAN BEAUTIFUL AND INSPIRED! SHE'S A DIY WONDER.
I DUNNO, SOMETHING ISN'T RIGHT. ARE YOU SURE YOU DIDN'T NOTICE ANYTHING?
ACTUALLY, TWI, I DID NOTICE SOMETHING.
I NOTICED A SHY PONY FINDING JOY IN LEARINING SOMETHING NEW.
JUST BECAUSE SOMEPONY ENJOYS GETTING IN TOUCH WITH THEIR CREATIVE SIDE DOESN'T MAKE THEM WEIRD.
YOU WEREN'T ALWAYS PERFECT, Y'KNOW, AND I GAVE YOU A CHANCE, JUST LIKE I'M DOING WITH VIOLET.
PINKIE, JUST TURN AROUND AND LOOK!
THIS IS SAD, TWILIGHT. YOU NEED SOME HELP.
YOU'RE RIGHT. I DO NEED SOME HELP. CAN YOU MEET ME IN THE WOODS TONIGHT?
AND BRING SOME OF THOSE STREAMERS.
THIS IS GETTING SILLY--
PLEASE, PINKIE? I'M GOING TO INVITE AN OBJECTIVE FRIEND TO CHECK THEM OUT, AND IF I'M WRONG...
YOU'LL SAY SORRY AND TRY TO GET TO KNOW VIOLET?
I PROMISE! AND TRUST ME, I HOPE I'M WRONG.

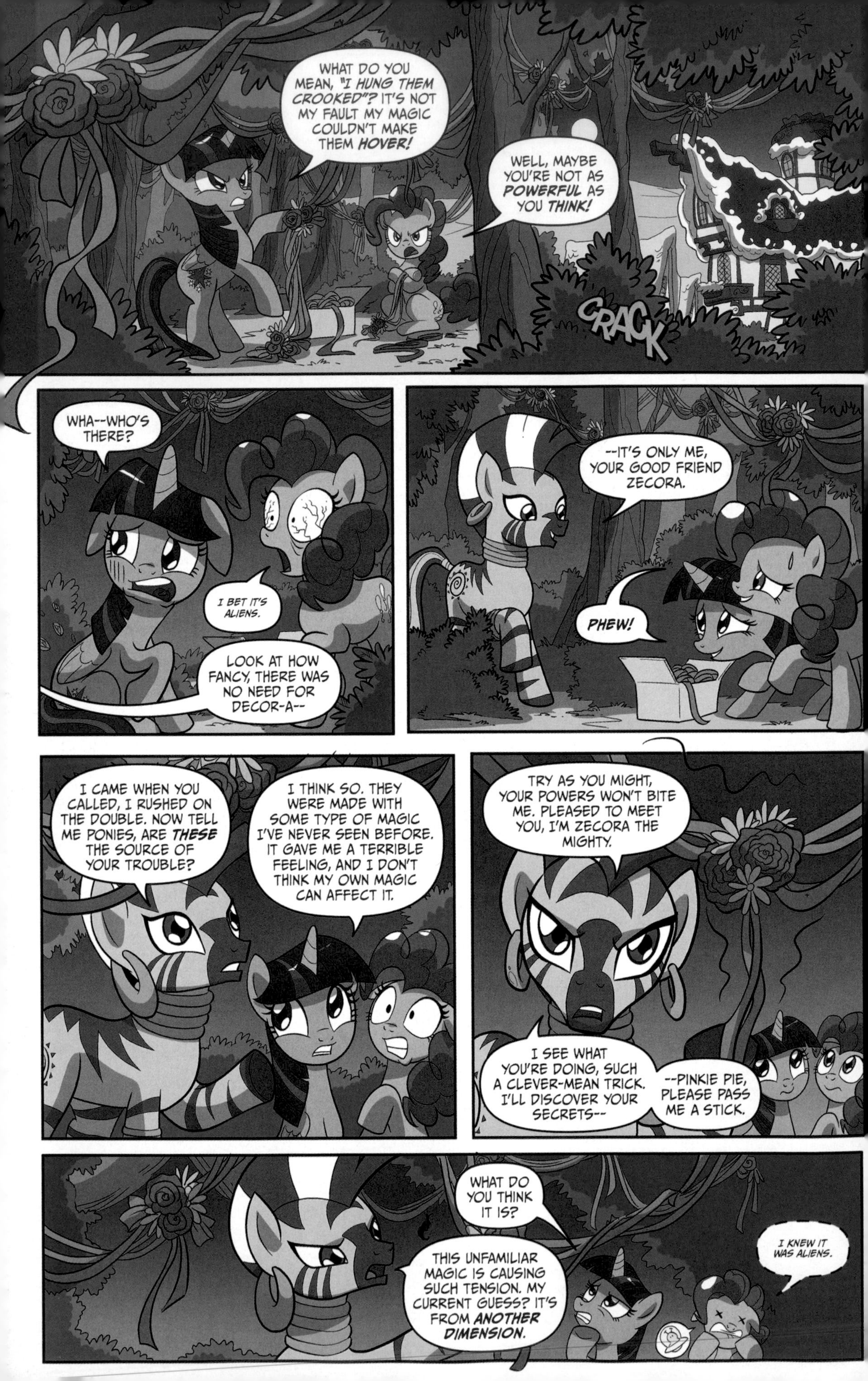
WHAT DO YOU MEAN, *"I HUNG THEM CROOKED"?* IT'S NOT MY FAULT MY MAGIC COULDN'T MAKE THEM ***HOVER!***
WELL, MAYBE YOU'RE NOT AS ***POWERFUL*** AS YOU ***THINK!***
CRACK
WHA--WHO'S THERE?
I BET IT'S ALIENS.
LOOK AT HOW FANCY, THERE WAS NO NEED FOR DECOR-A--
--IT'S ONLY ME, YOUR GOOD FRIEND ZECORA.
PHEW!
I CAME WHEN YOU CALLED, I RUSHED ON THE DOUBLE. NOW TELL ME PONIES, ARE ***THESE*** THE SOURCE OF YOUR TROUBLE?
I THINK SO. THEY WERE MADE WITH SOME TYPE OF MAGIC I'VE NEVER SEEN BEFORE. IT GAVE ME A TERRIBLE FEELING, AND I DON'T THINK MY OWN MAGIC CAN AFFECT IT.
TRY AS YOU MIGHT, YOUR POWERS WON'T BITE ME. PLEASED TO MEET YOU, I'M ZECORA THE MIGHTY.
I SEE WHAT YOU'RE DOING, SUCH A CLEVER-MEAN TRICK. I'LL DISCOVER YOUR SECRETS--
--PINKIE PIE, PLEASE PASS ME A STICK.
WHAT DO YOU THINK IT IS?
THIS UNFAMILIAR MAGIC IS CAUSING SUCH TENSION. MY CURRENT GUESS? IT'S FROM ***ANOTHER DIMENSION.***
I KNEW IT WAS ALIENS.

LET'S RUN SOME TESTS TO SEE HOW THIS IS CURSED--BUT BEFORE WE DO, SAFETY COMES FIRST.

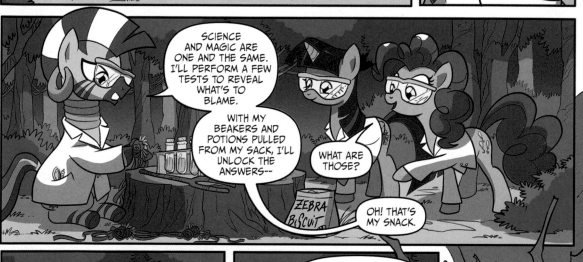

SCIENCE AND MAGIC ARE ONE AND THE SAME. I'LL PERFORM A FEW TESTS TO REVEAL WHAT'S TO BLAME.

WITH MY BEAKERS AND POTIONS PULLED FROM MY SACK, I'LL UNLOCK THE ANSWERS--

WHAT ARE THOSE?

OH! THAT'S MY SNACK.

ZEBRA BISCUIT

HMM. THAT'S TWO DOWN WITH ONE LEFT TO GO. HOOVES CROSSED THAT IT DOESN'T--

--BLOW.

COUGH COUGH

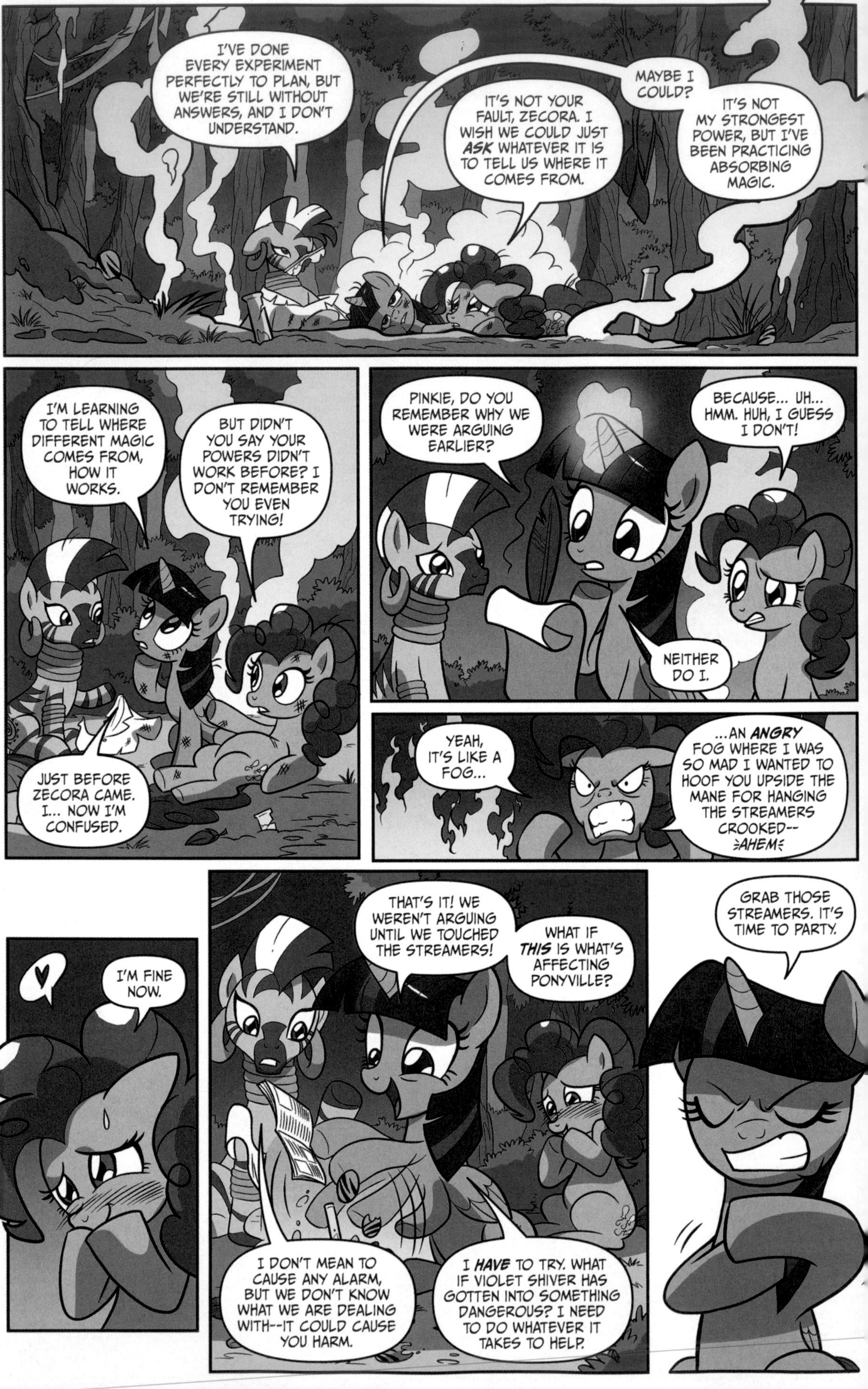
I'VE DONE EVERY EXPERIMENT PERFECTLY TO PLAN, BUT WE'RE STILL WITHOUT ANSWERS, AND I DON'T UNDERSTAND.
IT'S NOT YOUR FAULT, ZECORA. I WISH WE COULD JUST ASK WHATEVER IT IS TO TELL US WHERE IT COMES FROM.
MAYBE I COULD?
IT'S NOT MY STRONGEST POWER, BUT I'VE BEEN PRACTICING ABSORBING MAGIC.
I'M LEARNING TO TELL WHERE DIFFERENT MAGIC COMES FROM, HOW IT WORKS.
BUT DIDN'T YOU SAY YOUR POWERS DIDN'T WORK BEFORE? I DON'T REMEMBER YOU EVEN TRYING!
JUST BEFORE ZECORA CAME. I... NOW I'M CONFUSED.
PINKIE, DO YOU REMEMBER WHY WE WERE ARGUING EARLIER?
BECAUSE... UH... HMM. HUH, I GUESS I DON'T!
NEITHER DO I.
YEAH, IT'S LIKE A FOG...
...AN ANGRY FOG WHERE I WAS SO MAD I WANTED TO HOOF YOU UPSIDE THE MANE FOR HANGING THE STREAMERS CROOKED--
AHEM
I'M FINE NOW.
THAT'S IT! WE WEREN'T ARGUING UNTIL WE TOUCHED THE STREAMERS!
WHAT IF THIS IS WHAT'S AFFECTING PONYVILLE?
I DON'T MEAN TO CAUSE ANY ALARM, BUT WE DON'T KNOW WHAT WE ARE DEALING WITH--IT COULD CAUSE YOU HARM.
I HAVE TO TRY. WHAT IF VIOLET SHIVER HAS GOTTEN INTO SOMETHING DANGEROUS? I NEED TO DO WHATEVER IT TAKES TO HELP.
GRAB THOSE STREAMERS. IT'S TIME TO PARTY.

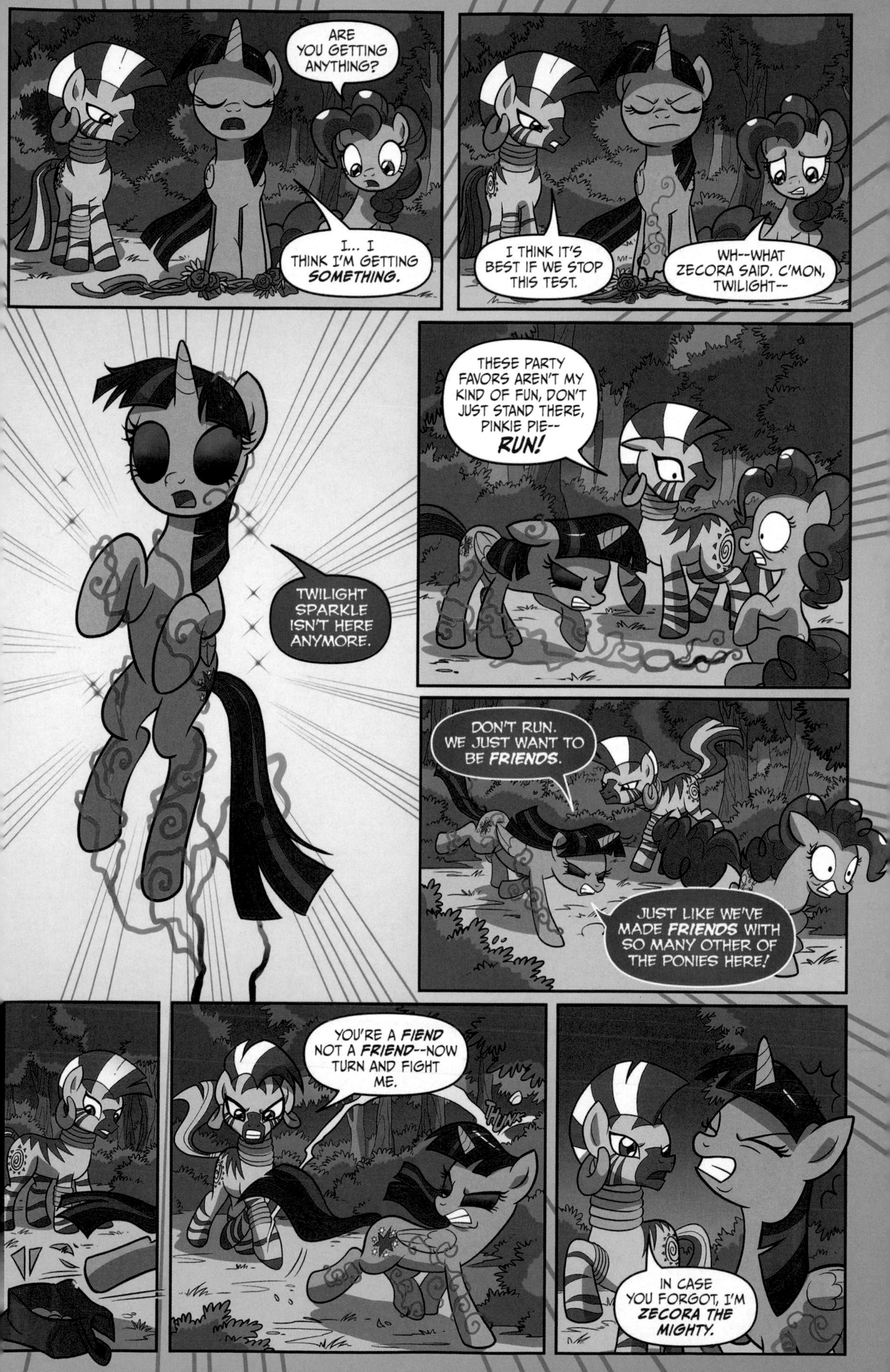
ARE YOU GETTING ANYTHING?
I... I THINK I'M GETTING SOMETHING.
I THINK IT'S BEST IF WE STOP THIS TEST.
WH--WHAT ZECORA SAID. C'MON, TWILIGHT--
TWILIGHT SPARKLE ISN'T HERE ANYMORE.
THESE PARTY FAVORS AREN'T MY KIND OF FUN, DON'T JUST STAND THERE, PINKIE PIE-- RUN!
DON'T RUN. WE JUST WANT TO BE FRIENDS.
JUST LIKE WE'VE MADE FRIENDS WITH SO MANY OTHER OF THE PONIES HERE!
YOU'RE A FIEND NOT A FRIEND--NOW TURN AND FIGHT ME.
THUNK
IN CASE YOU FORGOT, I'M ZECORA THE MIGHTY.

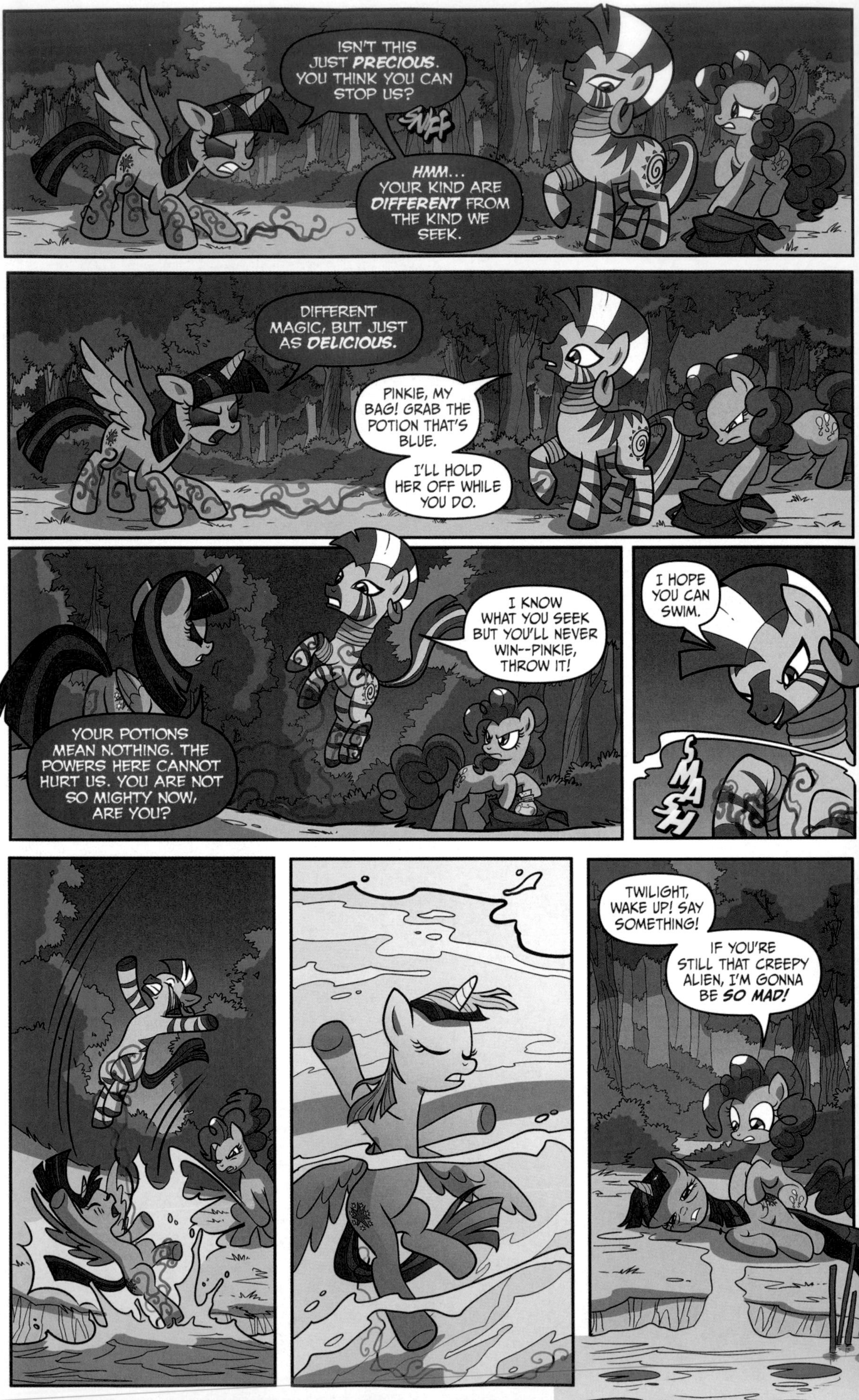
ISN'T THIS JUST **PRECIOUS**. YOU THINK YOU CAN STOP US?
SNIFF
HMM... YOUR KIND ARE **DIFFERENT** FROM THE KIND WE SEEK.
DIFFERENT MAGIC, BUT JUST AS **DELICIOUS.**
PINKIE, MY BAG! GRAB THE POTION THAT'S BLUE.
I'LL HOLD HER OFF WHILE YOU DO.
I KNOW WHAT YOU SEEK BUT YOU'LL NEVER WIN--PINKIE, THROW IT!
YOUR POTIONS MEAN NOTHING. THE POWERS HERE CANNOT HURT US. YOU ARE NOT SO MIGHTY NOW, ARE YOU?
I HOPE YOU CAN SWIM.
SMASH
TWILIGHT, WAKE UP! SAY SOMETHING!
IF YOU'RE STILL THAT CREEPY ALIEN, I'M GONNA BE **SO MAD!**

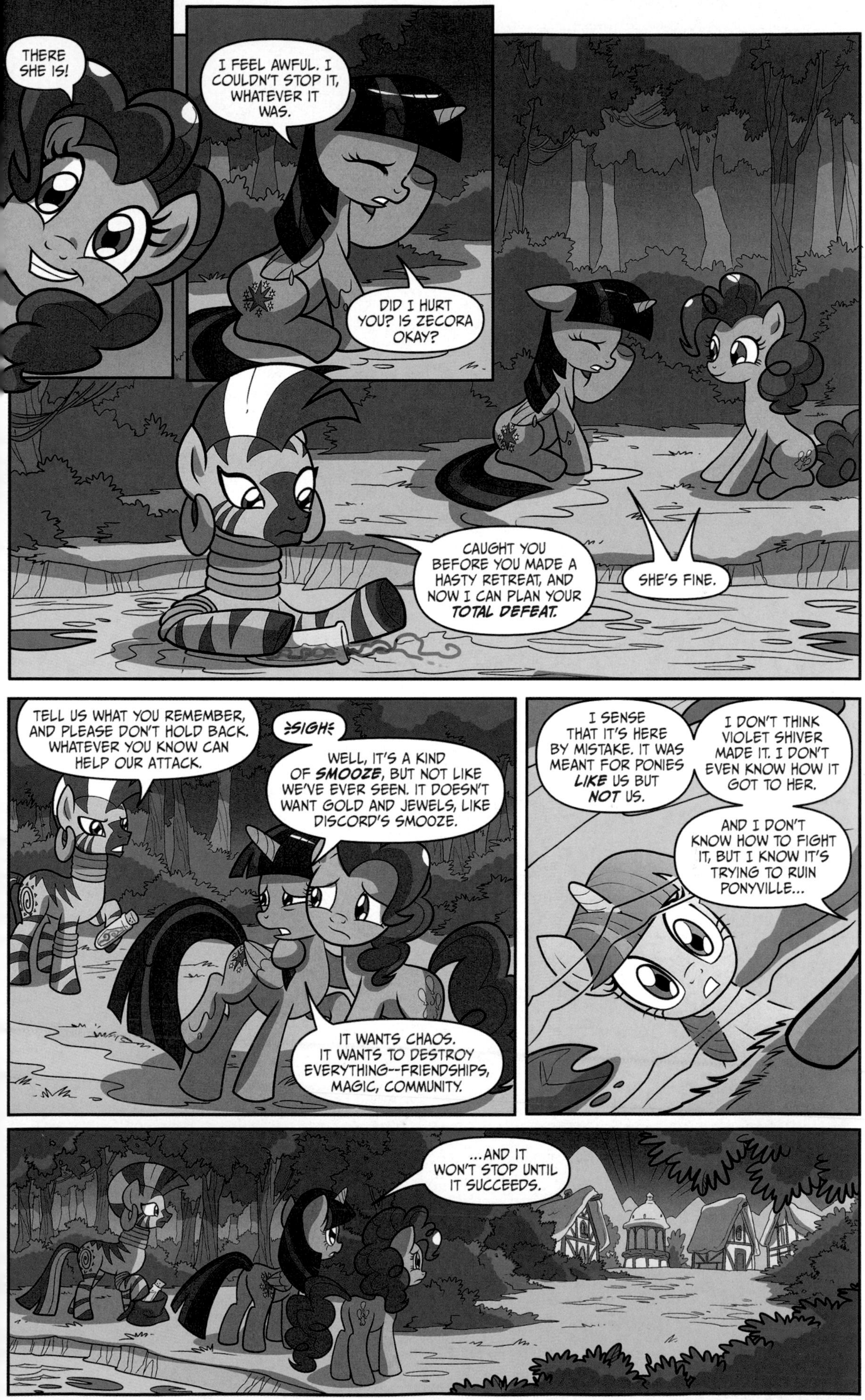

THERE SHE IS!
I FEEL AWFUL. I COULDN'T STOP IT, WHATEVER IT WAS.
DID I HURT YOU? IS ZECORA OKAY?
SHE'S FINE.
CAUGHT YOU BEFORE YOU MADE A HASTY RETREAT, AND NOW I CAN PLAN YOUR TOTAL DEFEAT.
TELL US WHAT YOU REMEMBER, AND PLEASE DON'T HOLD BACK. WHATEVER YOU KNOW CAN HELP OUR ATTACK.
SIGH
WELL, IT'S A KIND OF SMOOZE, BUT NOT LIKE WE'VE EVER SEEN. IT DOESN'T WANT GOLD AND JEWELS, LIKE DISCORD'S SMOOZE.
IT WANTS CHAOS. IT WANTS TO DESTROY EVERYTHING--FRIENDSHIPS, MAGIC, COMMUNITY.
I SENSE THAT IT'S HERE BY MISTAKE. IT WAS MEANT FOR PONIES LIKE US BUT NOT US.
I DON'T THINK VIOLET SHIVER MADE IT. I DON'T EVEN KNOW HOW IT GOT TO HER.
AND I DON'T KNOW HOW TO FIGHT IT, BUT I KNOW IT'S TRYING TO RUIN PONYVILLE...
...AND IT WON'T STOP UNTIL IT SUCCEEDS.

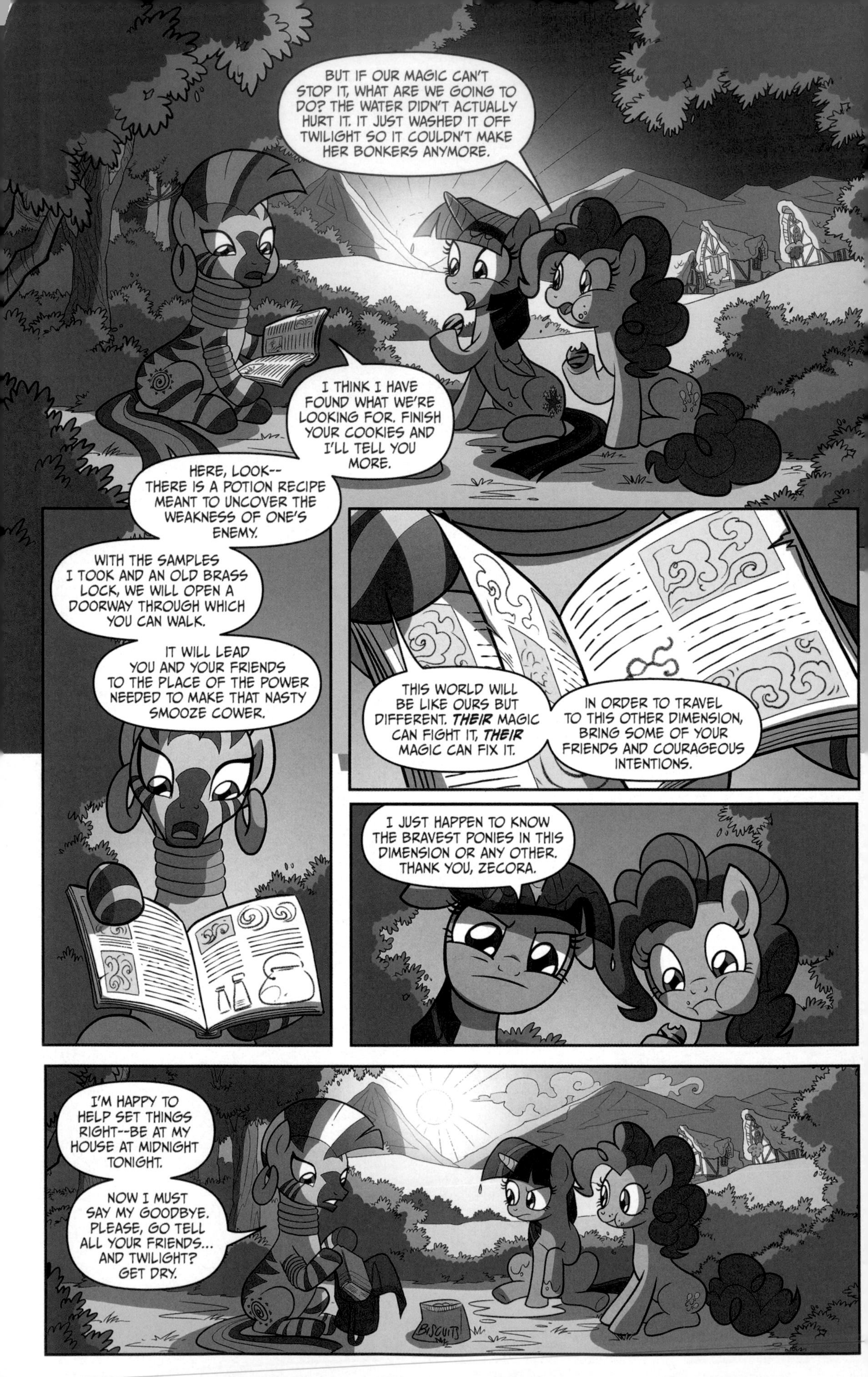

BUT IF OUR MAGIC CAN'T STOP IT, WHAT ARE WE GOING TO DO? THE WATER DIDN'T ACTUALLY HURT IT. IT JUST WASHED IT OFF TWILIGHT SO IT COULDN'T MAKE HER BONKERS ANYMORE.
I THINK I HAVE FOUND WHAT WE'RE LOOKING FOR. FINISH YOUR COOKIES AND I'LL TELL YOU MORE.
HERE, LOOK-- THERE IS A POTION RECIPE MEANT TO UNCOVER THE WEAKNESS OF ONE'S ENEMY.
WITH THE SAMPLES I TOOK AND AN OLD BRASS LOCK, WE WILL OPEN A DOORWAY THROUGH WHICH YOU CAN WALK.
IT WILL LEAD YOU AND YOUR FRIENDS TO THE PLACE OF THE POWER NEEDED TO MAKE THAT NASTY SMOOZE COWER.
THIS WORLD WILL BE LIKE OURS BUT DIFFERENT. ***THEIR*** MAGIC CAN FIGHT IT, ***THEIR*** MAGIC CAN FIX IT.
IN ORDER TO TRAVEL TO THIS OTHER DIMENSION, BRING SOME OF YOUR FRIENDS AND COURAGEOUS INTENTIONS.
I JUST HAPPEN TO KNOW THE BRAVEST PONIES IN THIS DIMENSION OR ANY OTHER. THANK YOU, ZECORA.
I'M HAPPY TO HELP SET THINGS RIGHT--BE AT MY HOUSE AT MIDNIGHT TONIGHT.
NOW I MUST SAY MY GOODBYE. PLEASE, GO TELL ALL YOUR FRIENDS... AND TWILIGHT? GET DRY.
BISCUITS

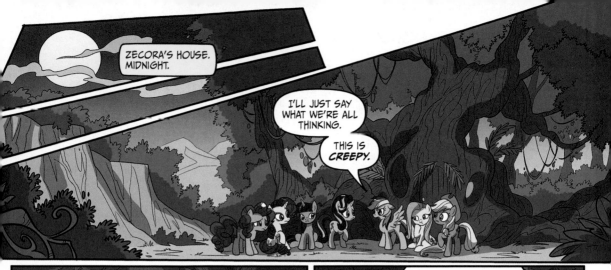

ZECORA'S HOUSE. MIDNIGHT.

I'LL JUST SAY WHAT WE'RE ALL THINKING.

THIS IS *CREEPY*.

ZECORA IS HELPING US, AND FROM WHAT I'VE HEARD, IF YOU THINK *THIS* IS CREEPY, MAYBE YOU AREN'T UP FOR WHAT COMES NEXT.

I'M UP FOR *ANYTHING*.

RAINBOW DASH, I HOPE THAT IS TRUE, FOR NOW WE HAVE A POTION TO BREW.

GATHER ROUND, THE POTION IS JUST ABOUT READY. DASH, HANG THIS LOCK ON THE TREE AND BE STEADY.

NOW RARITY, CAST THIS VIAL AROUND ALL OF THE ROOTS TOUCHING THE GROUND.

I'M ADDING SOME SMOOZE, JUST A DROP OR THREE, AND WITH A BIT OF LUCK...

HEY. LOOK! THERE'S A KEY!

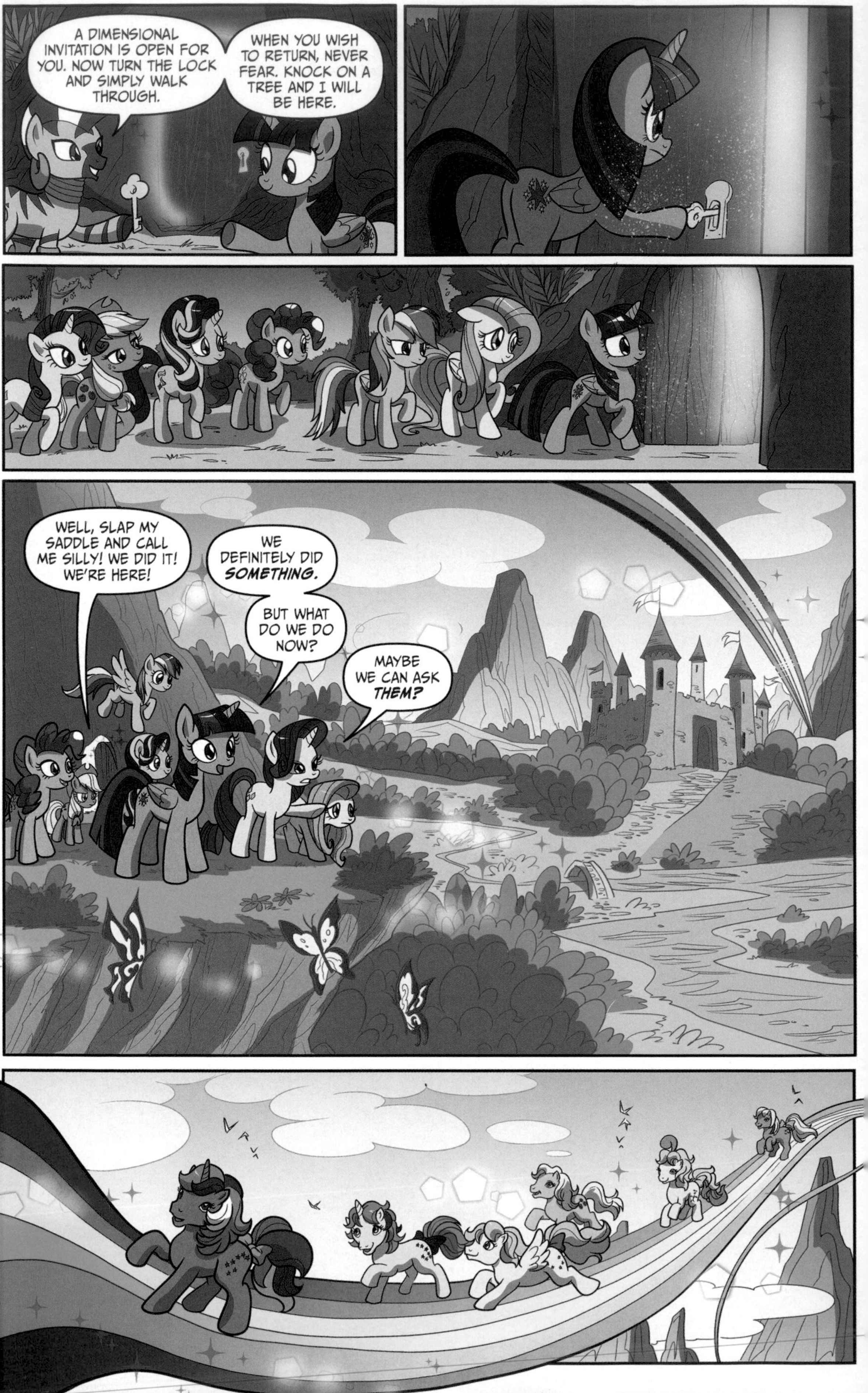
A DIMENSIONAL INVITATION IS OPEN FOR YOU. NOW TURN THE LOCK AND SIMPLY WALK THROUGH.
WHEN YOU WISH TO RETURN, NEVER FEAR. KNOCK ON A TREE AND I WILL BE HERE.
WELL, SLAP MY SADDLE AND CALL ME SILLY! WE DID IT! WE'RE HERE!
WE DEFINITELY DID *SOMETHING.*
BUT WHAT DO WE DO NOW?
MAYBE WE CAN ASK *THEM?*

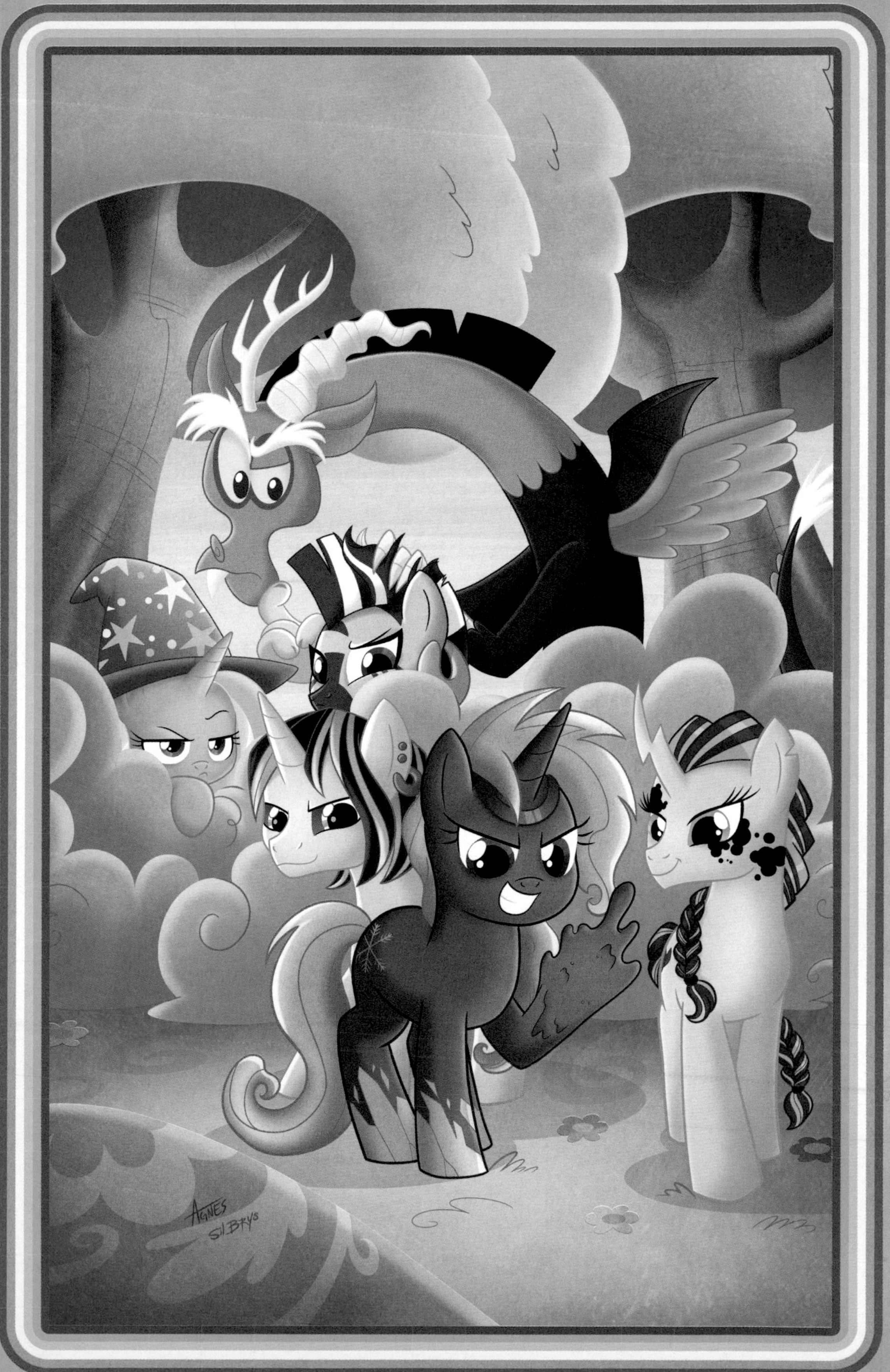

Art by **Agnes Garbowska** | Colors by **Silvana Brys**

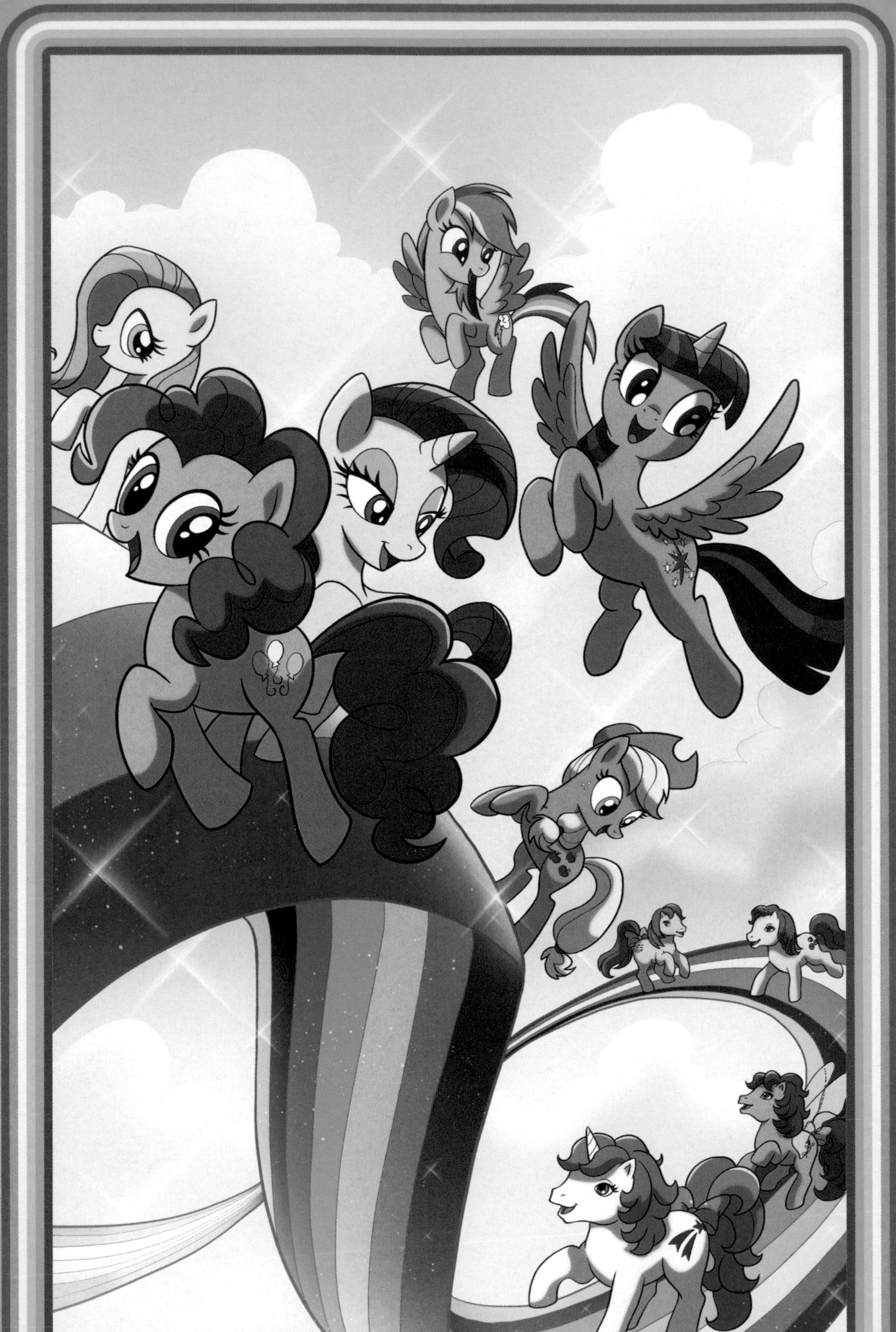

Art by **Michela Cacciatore**

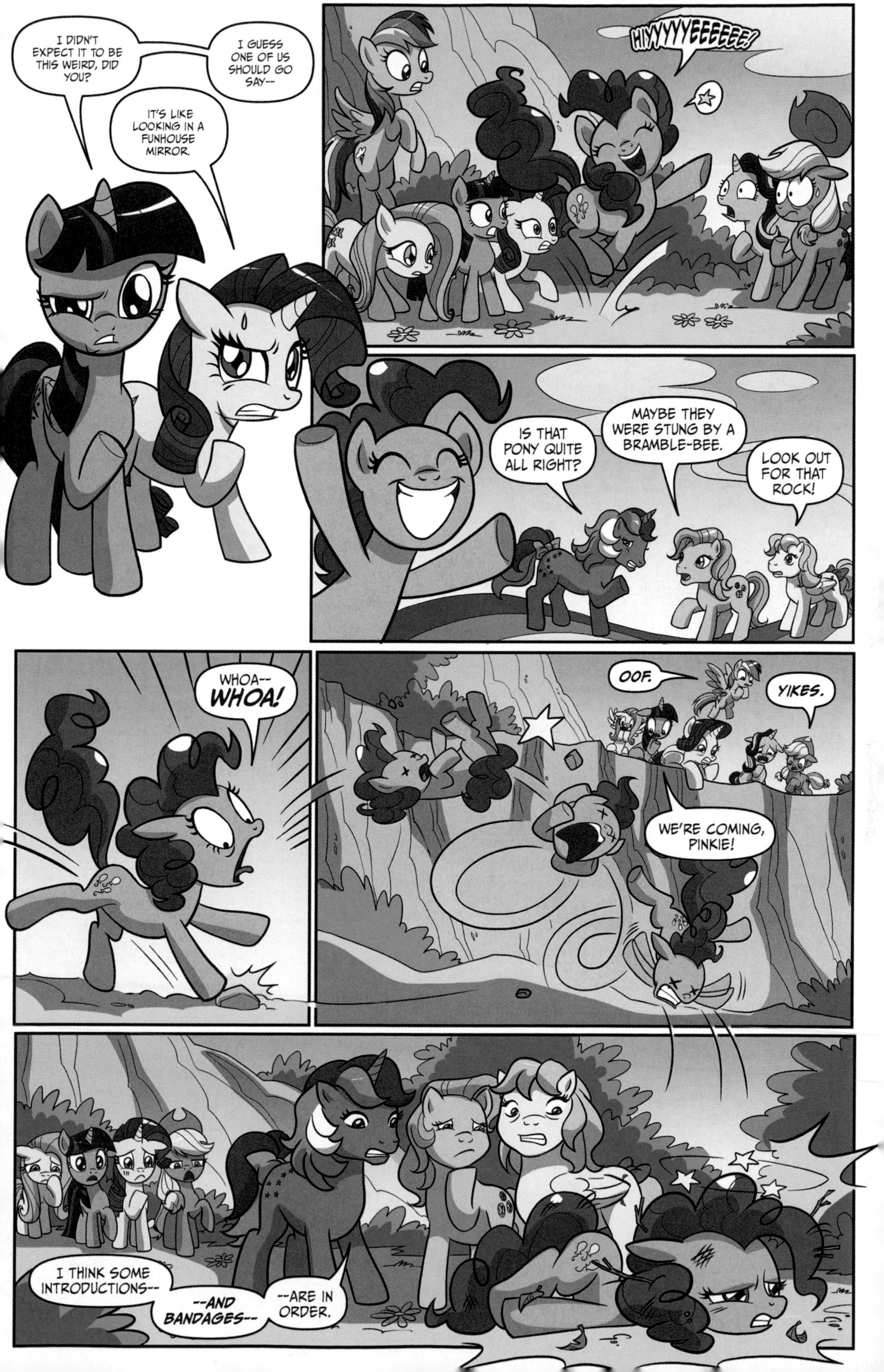
I DIDN'T EXPECT IT TO BE THIS WEIRD, DID YOU?
I GUESS ONE OF US SHOULD GO SAY--
IT'S LIKE LOOKING IN A FUNHOUSE MIRROR.
HIYYYYYEEEEEE!
IS THAT PONY QUITE ALL RIGHT?
MAYBE THEY WERE STUNG BY A BRAMBLE-BEE.
LOOK OUT FOR THAT ROCK!
WHOA-- WHOA!
OOF.
YIKES.
WE'RE COMING, PINKIE!
I THINK SOME INTRODUCTIONS--
--AND BANDAGES--
--ARE IN ORDER.

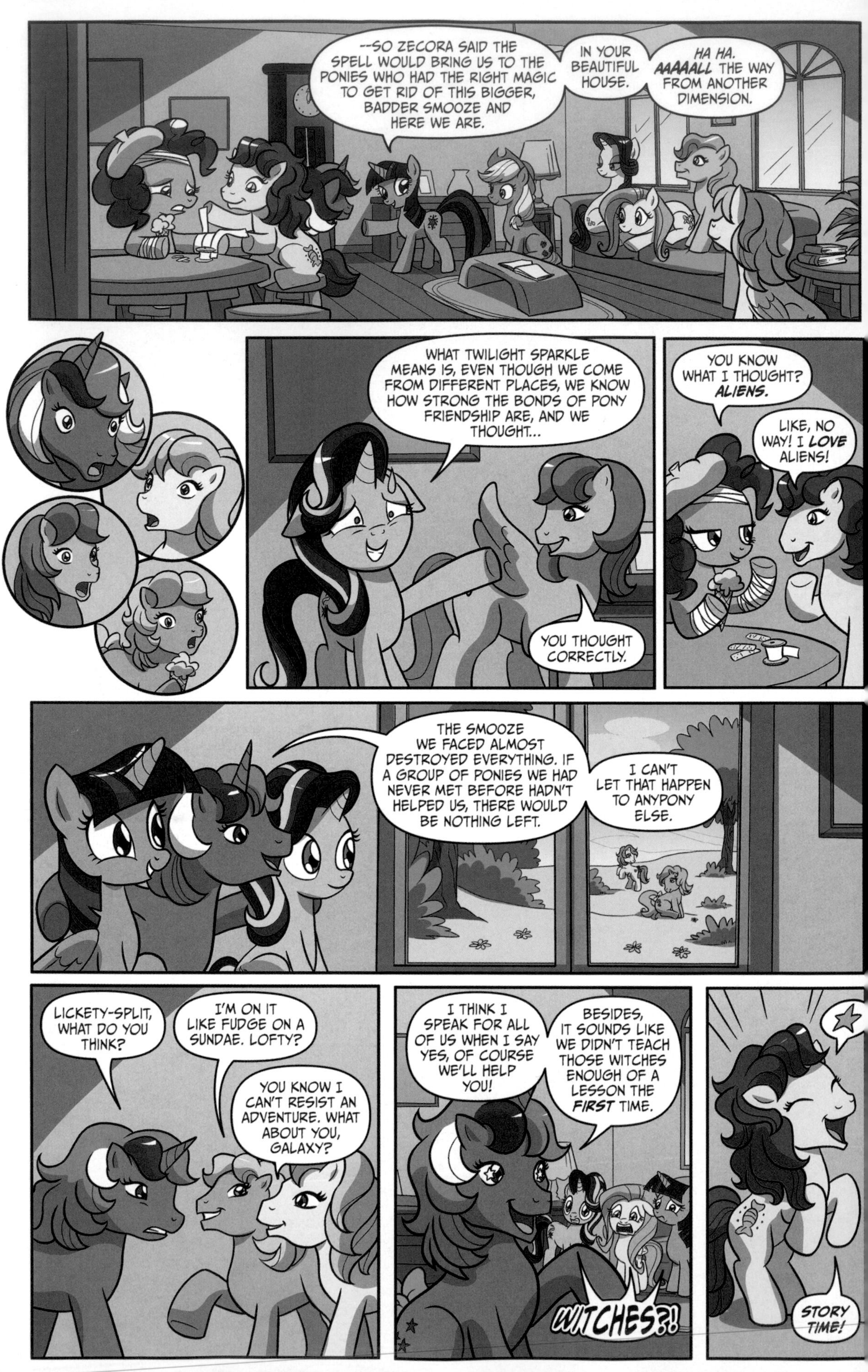
--SO ZECORA SAID THE SPELL WOULD BRING US TO THE PONIES WHO HAD THE RIGHT MAGIC TO GET RID OF THIS BIGGER, BADDER SMOOZE AND HERE WE ARE.
IN YOUR BEAUTIFUL HOUSE.
HA HA. AAAAALL THE WAY FROM ANOTHER DIMENSION.
WHAT TWILIGHT SPARKLE MEANS IS, EVEN THOUGH WE COME FROM DIFFERENT PLACES, WE KNOW HOW STRONG THE BONDS OF PONY FRIENDSHIP ARE, AND WE THOUGHT...
YOU THOUGHT CORRECTLY.
YOU KNOW WHAT I THOUGHT? ALIENS.
LIKE, NO WAY! I LOVE ALIENS!
THE SMOOZE WE FACED ALMOST DESTROYED EVERYTHING. IF A GROUP OF PONIES WE HAD NEVER MET BEFORE HADN'T HELPED US, THERE WOULD BE NOTHING LEFT.
I CAN'T LET THAT HAPPEN TO ANYPONY ELSE.
LICKETY-SPLIT, WHAT DO YOU THINK?
I'M ON IT LIKE FUDGE ON A SUNDAE. LOFTY?
YOU KNOW I CAN'T RESIST AN ADVENTURE. WHAT ABOUT YOU, GALAXY?
I THINK I SPEAK FOR ALL OF US WHEN I SAY YES, OF COURSE WE'LL HELP YOU!
BESIDES, IT SOUNDS LIKE WE DIDN'T TEACH THOSE WITCHES ENOUGH OF A LESSON THE FIRST TIME.
WITCHES?!
STORY TIME!

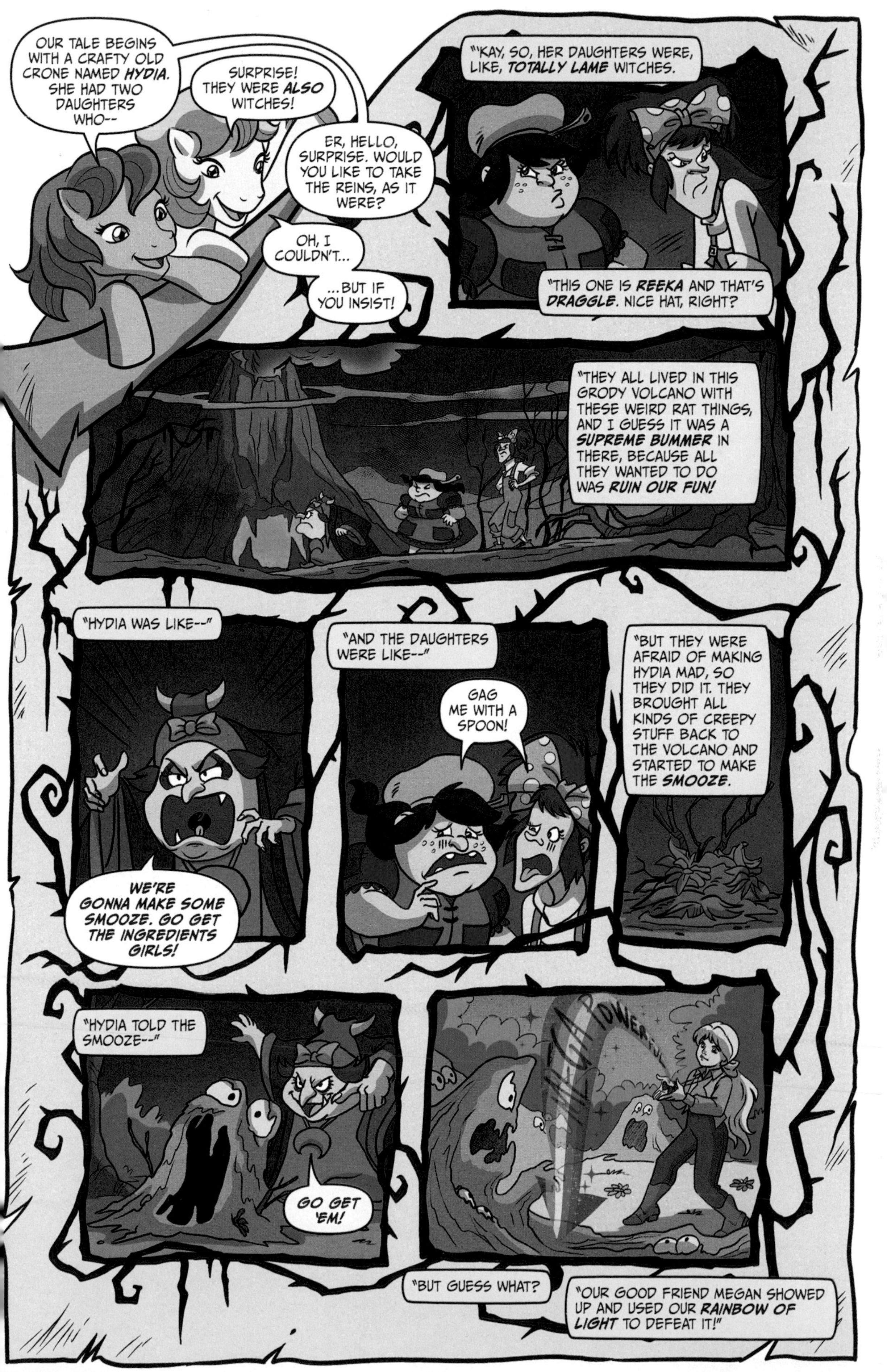
OUR TALE BEGINS WITH A CRAFTY OLD CRONE NAMED HYDIA. SHE HAD TWO DAUGHTERS WHO--
SURPRISE! THEY WERE ALSO WITCHES!
ER, HELLO, SURPRISE. WOULD YOU LIKE TO TAKE THE REINS, AS IT WERE?
OH, I COULDN'T...
...BUT IF YOU INSIST!
"KAY, SO, HER DAUGHTERS WERE, LIKE, TOTALLY LAME WITCHES.
"THIS ONE IS REEKA AND THAT'S DRAGGLE. NICE HAT, RIGHT?
"THEY ALL LIVED IN THIS GRODY VOLCANO WITH THESE WEIRD RAT THINGS, AND I GUESS IT WAS A SUPREME BUMMER IN THERE, BECAUSE ALL THEY WANTED TO DO WAS RUIN OUR FUN!
"HYDIA WAS LIKE--"
WE'RE GONNA MAKE SOME SMOOZE. GO GET THE INGREDIENTS GIRLS!
"AND THE DAUGHTERS WERE LIKE--"
GAG ME WITH A SPOON!
"BUT THEY WERE AFRAID OF MAKING HYDIA MAD, SO THEY DID IT. THEY BROUGHT ALL KINDS OF CREEPY STUFF BACK TO THE VOLCANO AND STARTED TO MAKE THE SMOOZE.
"HYDIA TOLD THE SMOOZE--"
GO GET 'EM!
"BUT GUESS WHAT?
"OUR GOOD FRIEND MEGAN SHOWED UP AND USED OUR RAINBOW OF LIGHT TO DEFEAT IT!"

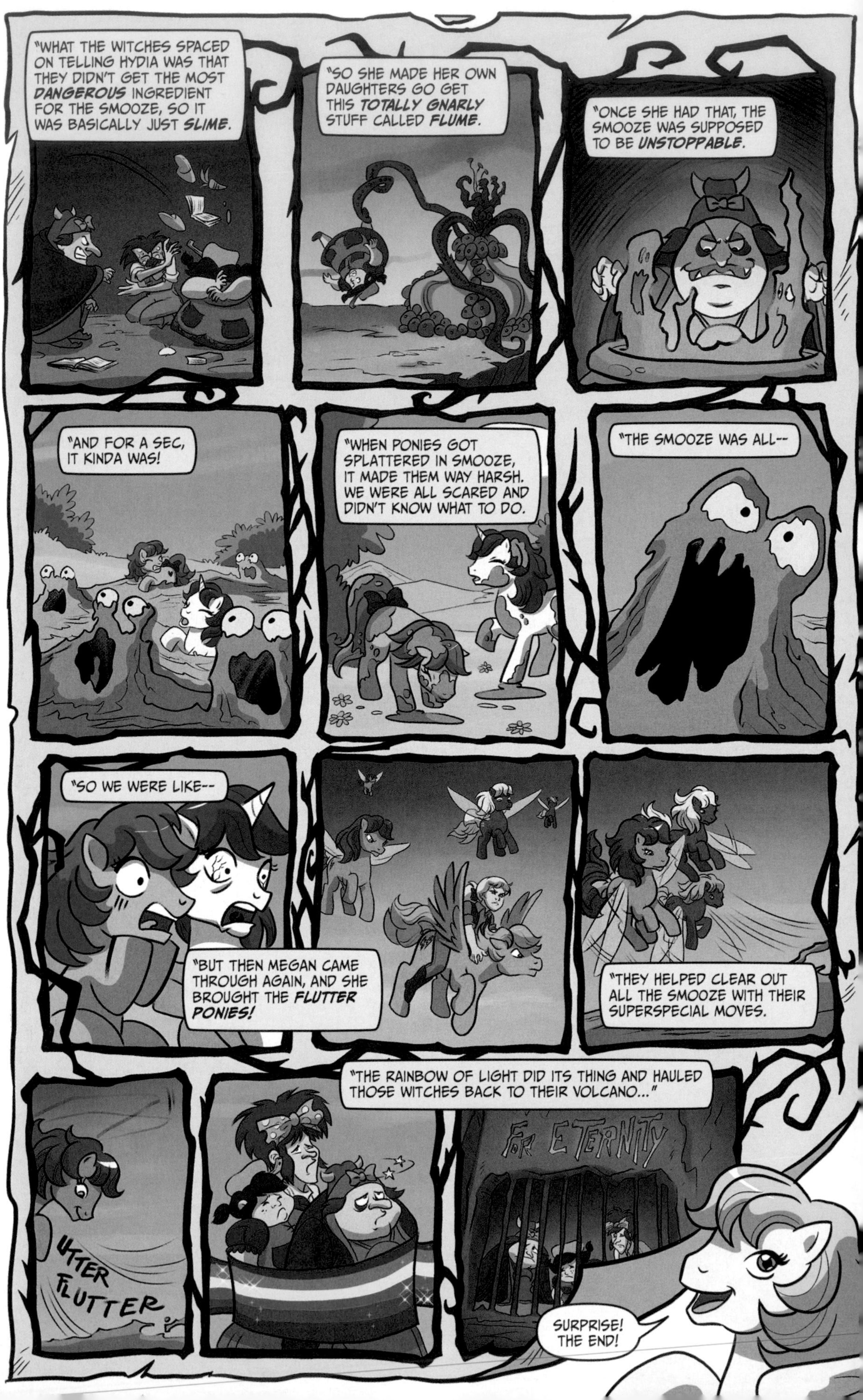
"WHAT THE WITCHES SPACED ON TELLING HYDIA WAS THAT THEY DIDN'T GET THE MOST *DANGEROUS* INGREDIENT FOR THE SMOOZE, SO IT WAS BASICALLY JUST *SLIME*.
"SO SHE MADE HER OWN DAUGHTERS GO GET THIS *TOTALLY GNARLY* STUFF CALLED *FLUME*.
"ONCE SHE HAD THAT, THE SMOOZE WAS SUPPOSED TO BE *UNSTOPPABLE*.
"AND FOR A SEC, IT KINDA WAS!
"WHEN PONIES GOT SPLATTERED IN SMOOZE, IT MADE THEM WAY HARSH. WE WERE ALL SCARED AND DIDN'T KNOW WHAT TO DO.
"THE SMOOZE WAS ALL--
"SO WE WERE LIKE--
"BUT THEN MEGAN CAME THROUGH AGAIN, AND SHE BROUGHT THE *FLUTTER PONIES!*
"THEY HELPED CLEAR OUT ALL THE SMOOZE WITH THEIR SUPERSPECIAL MOVES.
UTTER FLUTTER
"THE RAINBOW OF LIGHT DID ITS THING AND HAULED THOSE WITCHES BACK TO THEIR VOLCANO..."
FOR ETERNITY
SURPRISE! THE END!

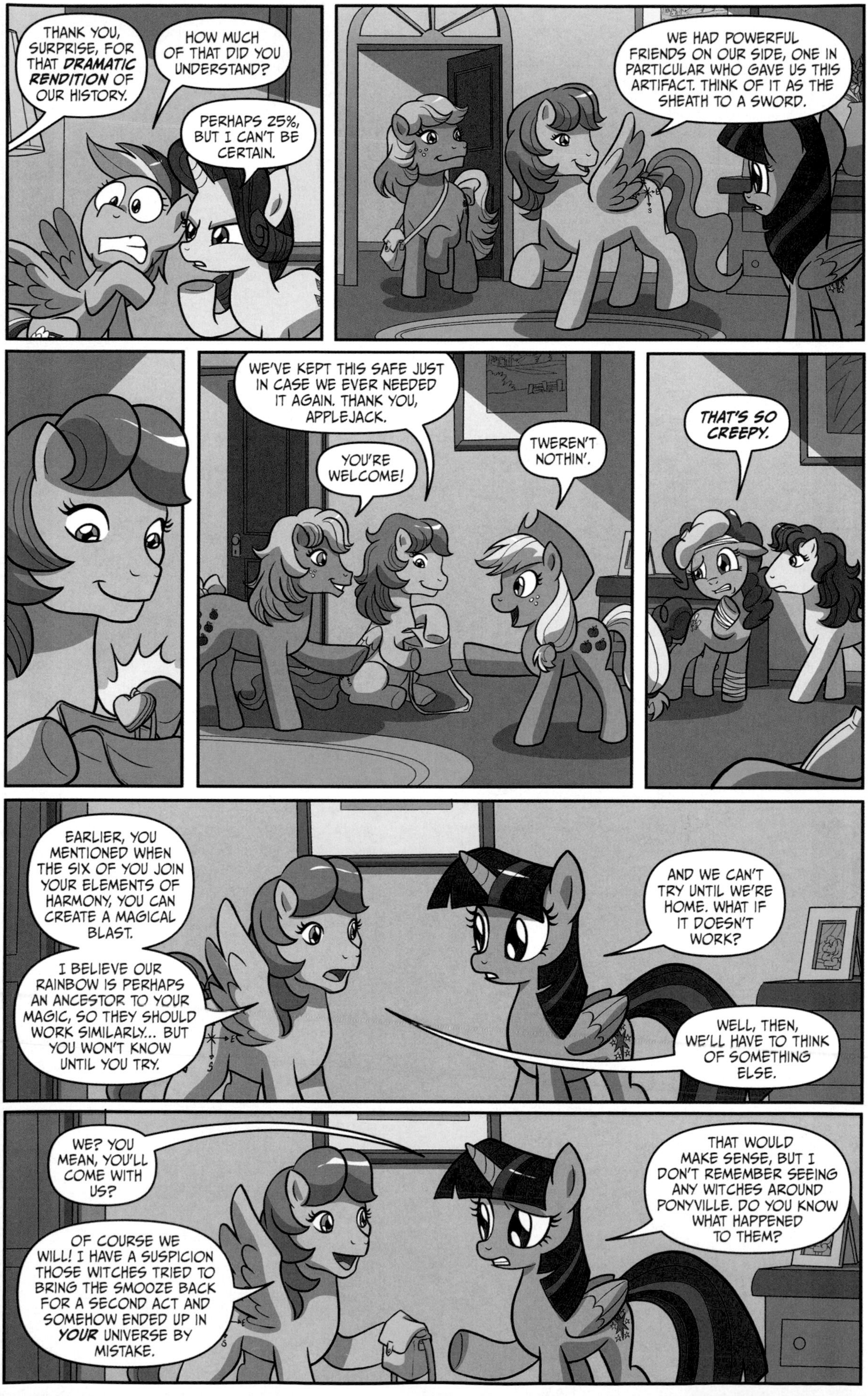
THANK YOU, SURPRISE, FOR THAT *DRAMATIC RENDITION* OF OUR HISTORY.
HOW MUCH OF THAT DID YOU UNDERSTAND?
PERHAPS 25%, BUT I CAN'T BE CERTAIN.
WE HAD POWERFUL FRIENDS ON OUR SIDE, ONE IN PARTICULAR WHO GAVE US THIS ARTIFACT. THINK OF IT AS THE SHEATH TO A SWORD.
WE'VE KEPT THIS SAFE JUST IN CASE WE EVER NEEDED IT AGAIN. THANK YOU, APPLEJACK.
YOU'RE WELCOME!
TWEREN'T NOTHIN'.
THAT'S SO CREEPY.
EARLIER, YOU MENTIONED WHEN THE SIX OF YOU JOIN YOUR ELEMENTS OF HARMONY, YOU CAN CREATE A MAGICAL BLAST.
I BELIEVE OUR RAINBOW IS PERHAPS AN ANCESTOR TO YOUR MAGIC, SO THEY SHOULD WORK SIMILARLY... BUT YOU WON'T KNOW UNTIL YOU TRY.
AND WE CAN'T TRY UNTIL WE'RE HOME. WHAT IF IT DOESN'T WORK?
WELL, THEN, WE'LL HAVE TO THINK OF SOMETHING ELSE.
WE? YOU MEAN, YOU'LL COME WITH US?
OF COURSE WE WILL! I HAVE A SUSPICION THOSE WITCHES TRIED TO BRING THE SMOOZE BACK FOR A SECOND ACT AND SOMEHOW ENDED UP IN *YOUR* UNIVERSE BY MISTAKE.
THAT WOULD MAKE SENSE, BUT I DON'T REMEMBER SEEING ANY WITCHES AROUND PONYVILLE. DO YOU KNOW WHAT HAPPENED TO THEM?

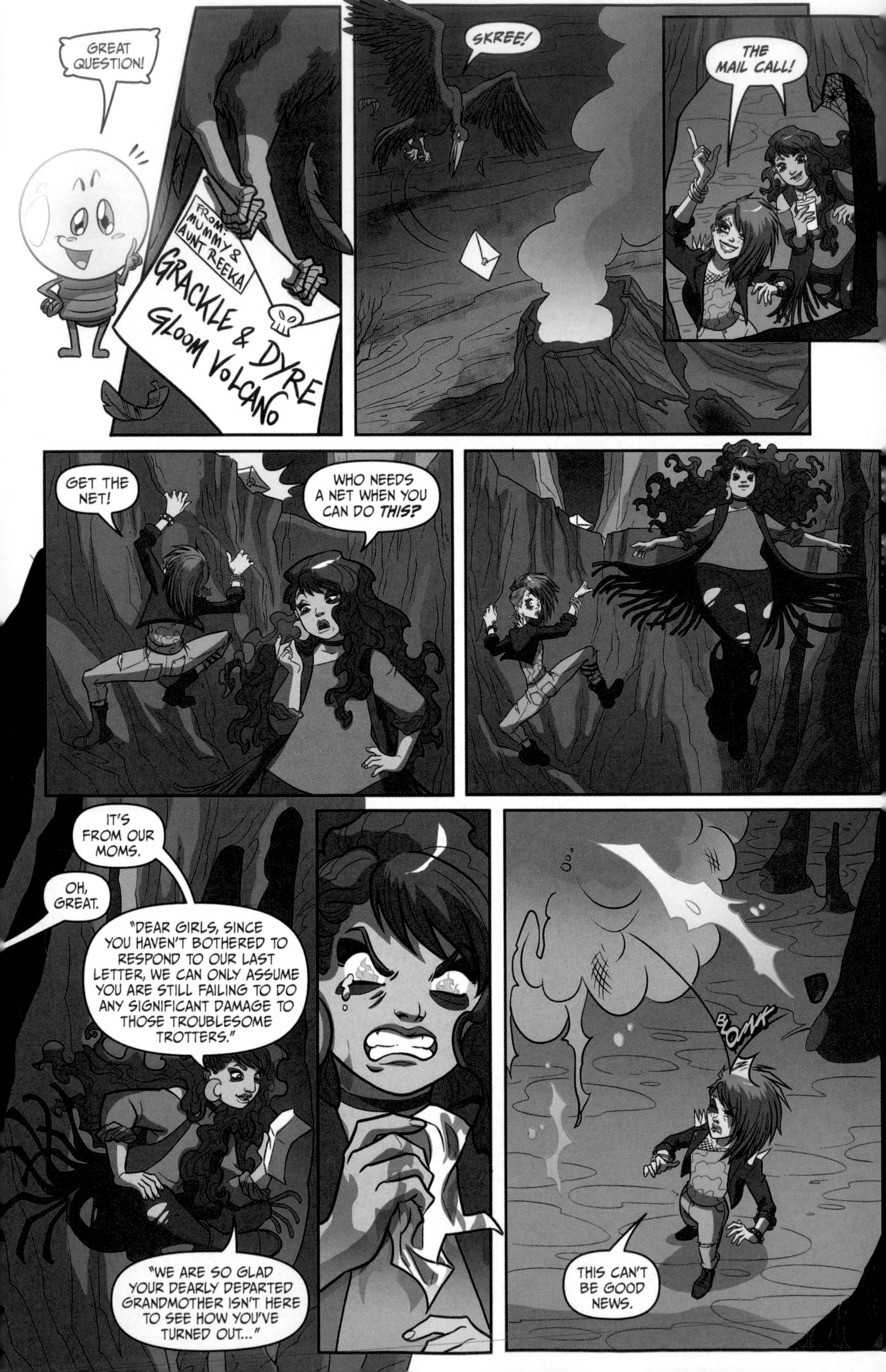
GREAT QUESTION!
FROM: MUMMY & AUNT REEKA
GRACKLE & DYRE
GLOOM VOLCANO
SKREE!
THE MAIL CALL!
GET THE NET!
WHO NEEDS A NET WHEN YOU CAN DO THIS?
IT'S FROM OUR MOMS.
OH, GREAT.
"DEAR GIRLS, SINCE YOU HAVEN'T BOTHERED TO RESPOND TO OUR LAST LETTER, WE CAN ONLY ASSUME YOU ARE STILL FAILING TO DO ANY SIGNIFICANT DAMAGE TO THOSE TROUBLESOME TROTTERS."
"WE ARE SO GLAD YOUR DEARLY DEPARTED GRANDMOTHER ISN'T HERE TO SEE HOW YOU'VE TURNED OUT..."
BLONK
THIS CAN'T BE GOOD NEWS.

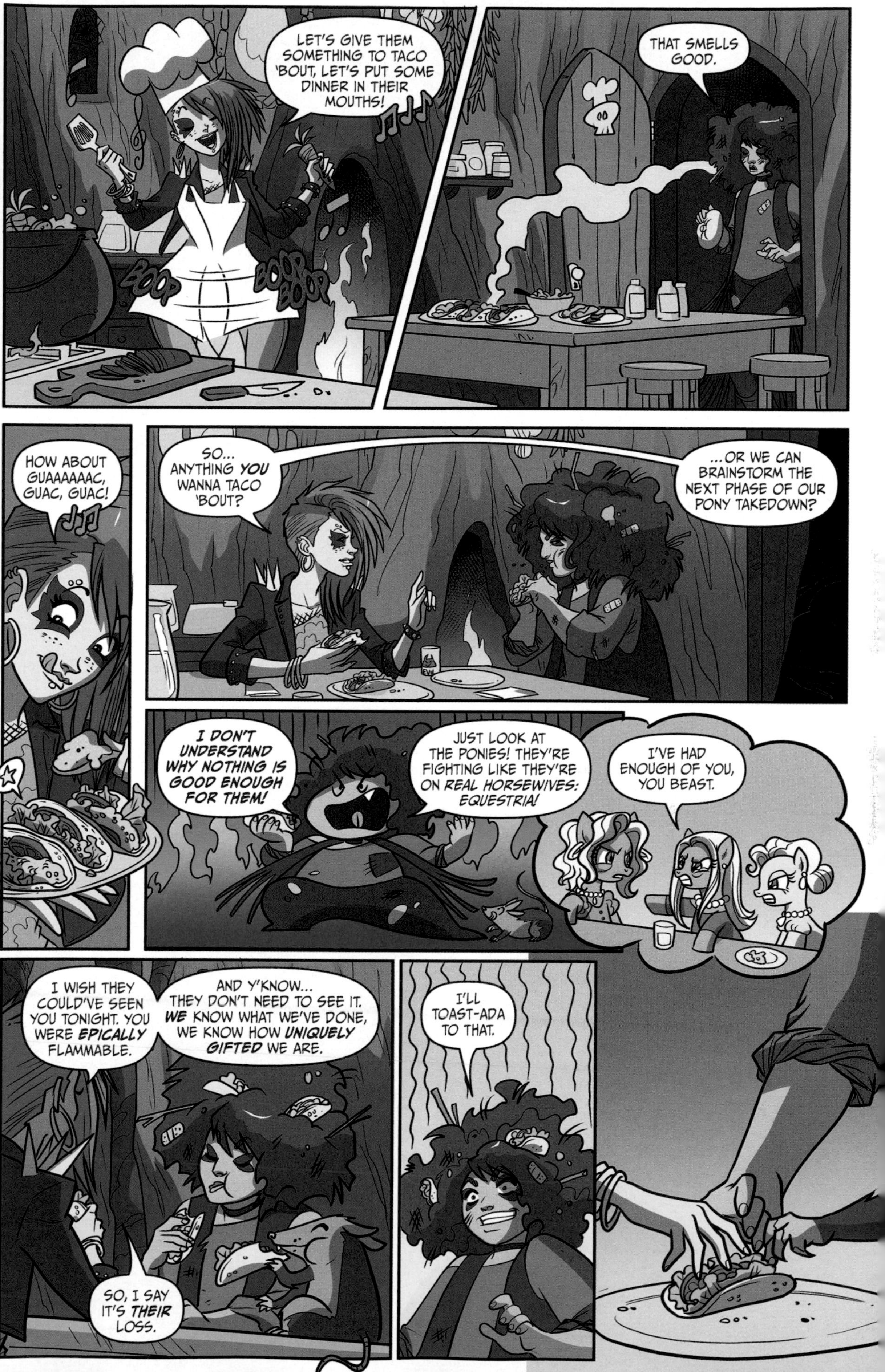
LET'S GIVE THEM SOMETHING TO TACO 'BOUT, LET'S PUT SOME DINNER IN THEIR MOUTHS!
BOOP
BOOP BOOP
THAT SMELLS GOOD.
HOW ABOUT GUAAAAAAC, GUAC, GUAC!
SO... ANYTHING *YOU* WANNA TACO 'BOUT?
...OR WE CAN BRAINSTORM THE NEXT PHASE OF OUR PONY TAKEDOWN?
EVIL
I DON'T UNDERSTAND WHY NOTHING IS GOOD ENOUGH FOR THEM!
JUST LOOK AT THE PONIES! THEY'RE FIGHTING LIKE THEY'RE ON *REAL HORSEWIVES: EQUESTRIA!*
I'VE HAD ENOUGH OF YOU, YOU BEAST.
I WISH THEY COULD'VE SEEN YOU TONIGHT. YOU WERE *EPICALLY* FLAMMABLE.
AND Y'KNOW... THEY DON'T NEED TO SEE IT. *WE* KNOW WHAT WE'VE DONE, WE KNOW HOW *UNIQUELY GIFTED* WE ARE.
SO, I SAY IT'S *THEIR* LOSS.
I'LL TOAST-ADA TO THAT.

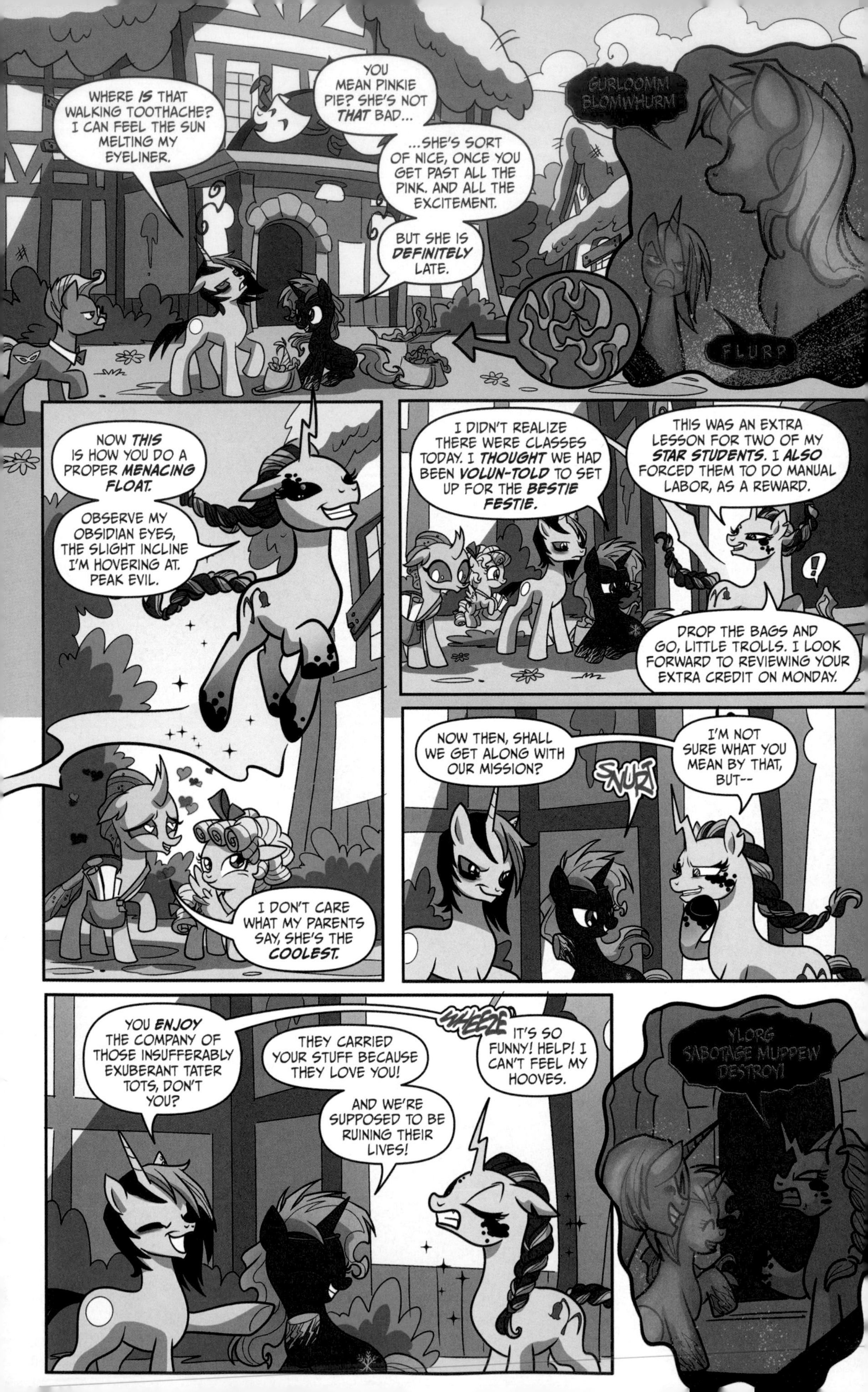

WHERE IS THAT WALKING TOOTHACHE? I CAN FEEL THE SUN MELTING MY EYELINER.
YOU MEAN PINKIE PIE? SHE'S NOT THAT BAD...
...SHE'S SORT OF NICE, ONCE YOU GET PAST ALL THE PINK. AND ALL THE EXCITEMENT.
BUT SHE IS DEFINITELY LATE.
GURLOOMM BLOMWHURM
FLURP
NOW THIS IS HOW YOU DO A PROPER MENACING FLOAT.
OBSERVE MY OBSIDIAN EYES, THE SLIGHT INCLINE I'M HOVERING AT. PEAK EVIL.
I DON'T CARE WHAT MY PARENTS SAY, SHE'S THE COOLEST.
I DIDN'T REALIZE THERE WERE CLASSES TODAY. I THOUGHT WE HAD BEEN VOLUN-TOLD TO SET UP FOR THE BESTIE FESTIE.
THIS WAS AN EXTRA LESSON FOR TWO OF MY STAR STUDENTS. I ALSO FORCED THEM TO DO MANUAL LABOR, AS A REWARD.
!
DROP THE BAGS AND GO, LITTLE TROLLS. I LOOK FORWARD TO REVIEWING YOUR EXTRA CREDIT ON MONDAY.
NOW THEN, SHALL WE GET ALONG WITH OUR MISSION?
SNURT
I'M NOT SURE WHAT YOU MEAN BY THAT, BUT--
YOU ENJOY THE COMPANY OF THOSE INSUFFERABLY EXUBERANT TATER TOTS, DON'T YOU?
WHEEZE
IT'S SO FUNNY! HELP! I CAN'T FEEL MY HOOVES.
THEY CARRIED YOUR STUFF BECAUSE THEY LOVE YOU!
AND WE'RE SUPPOSED TO BE RUINING THEIR LIVES!
YLORG SABOTAGE MUPPEW DESTROY!

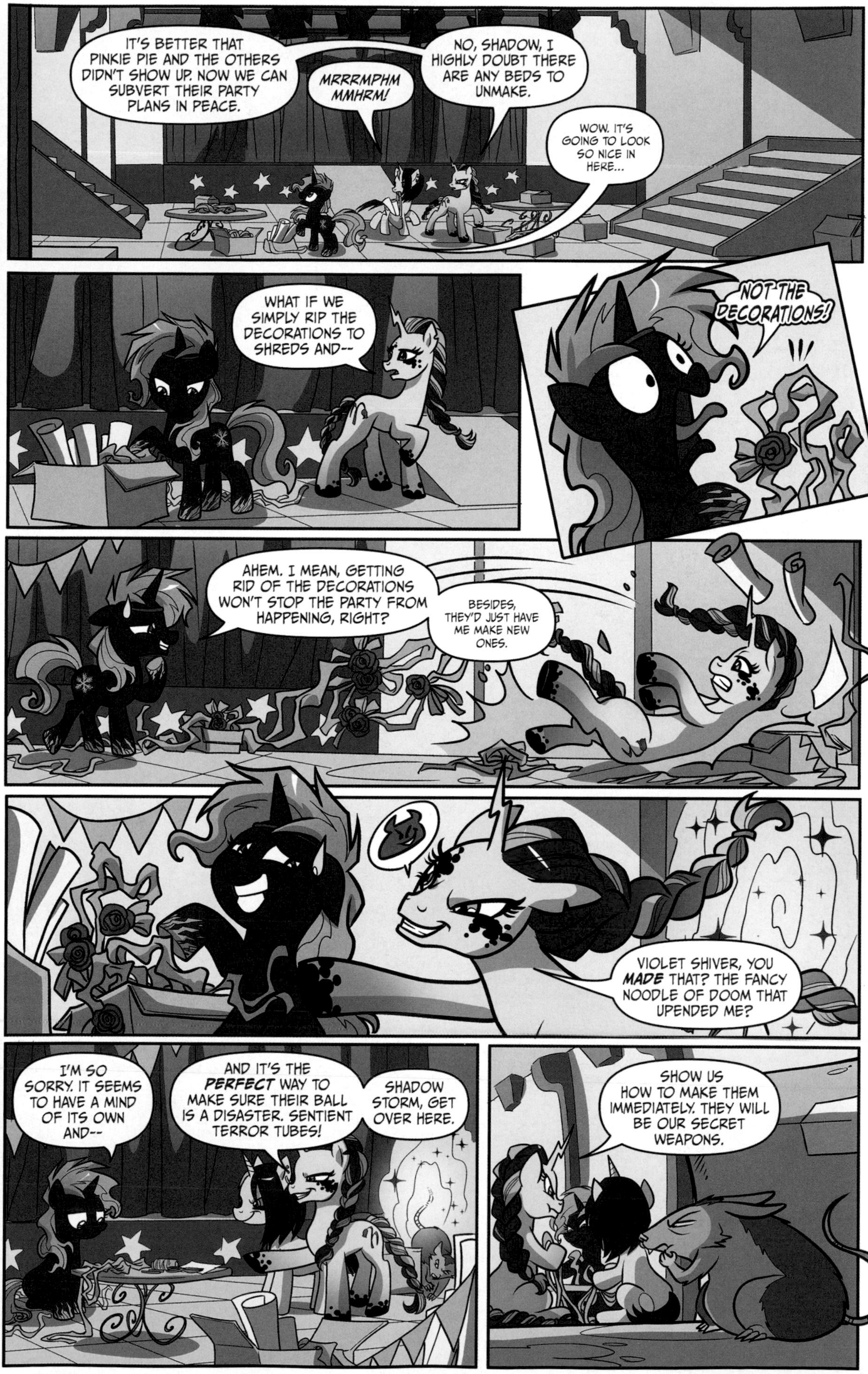
IT'S BETTER THAT PINKIE PIE AND THE OTHERS DIDN'T SHOW UP. NOW WE CAN SUBVERT THEIR PARTY PLANS IN PEACE.
MRRRMPHM MMHRM!
NO, SHADOW, I HIGHLY DOUBT THERE ARE ANY BEDS TO UNMAKE.
WOW. IT'S GOING TO LOOK SO NICE IN HERE...
WHAT IF WE SIMPLY RIP THE DECORATIONS TO SHREDS AND--
NOT THE DECORATIONS!
AHEM. I MEAN, GETTING RID OF THE DECORATIONS WON'T STOP THE PARTY FROM HAPPENING, RIGHT?
BESIDES, THEY'D JUST HAVE ME MAKE NEW ONES.
VIOLET SHIVER, YOU MADE THAT? THE FANCY NOODLE OF DOOM THAT UPENDED ME?
I'M SO SORRY. IT SEEMS TO HAVE A MIND OF ITS OWN AND--
AND IT'S THE PERFECT WAY TO MAKE SURE THEIR BALL IS A DISASTER. SENTIENT TERROR TUBES!
SHADOW STORM, GET OVER HERE.
SHOW US HOW TO MAKE THEM IMMEDIATELY. THEY WILL BE OUR SECRET WEAPONS.

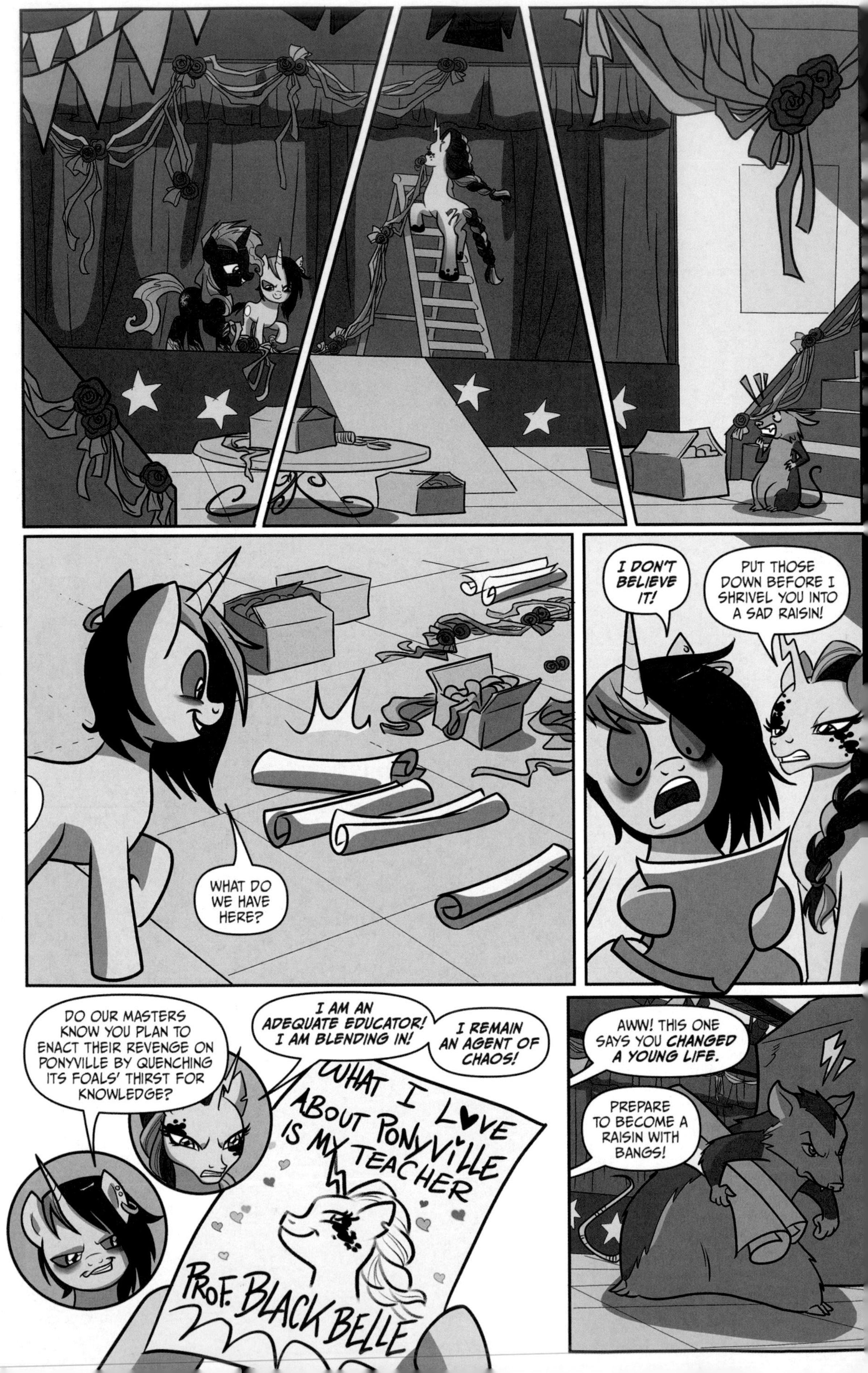
WHAT DO WE HAVE HERE?
I DON'T BELIEVE IT!
PUT THOSE DOWN BEFORE I SHRIVEL YOU INTO A SAD RAISIN!
DO OUR MASTERS KNOW YOU PLAN TO ENACT THEIR REVENGE ON PONYVILLE BY QUENCHING ITS FOALS' THIRST FOR KNOWLEDGE?
I AM AN ADEQUATE EDUCATOR! I AM BLENDING IN!
I REMAIN AN AGENT OF CHAOS!
WHAT I LOVE ABOUT PONYVILLE IS MY TEACHER
PROF. BLACKBELLE
AWW! THIS ONE SAYS YOU CHANGED A YOUNG LIFE.
PREPARE TO BECOME A RAISIN WITH BANGS!

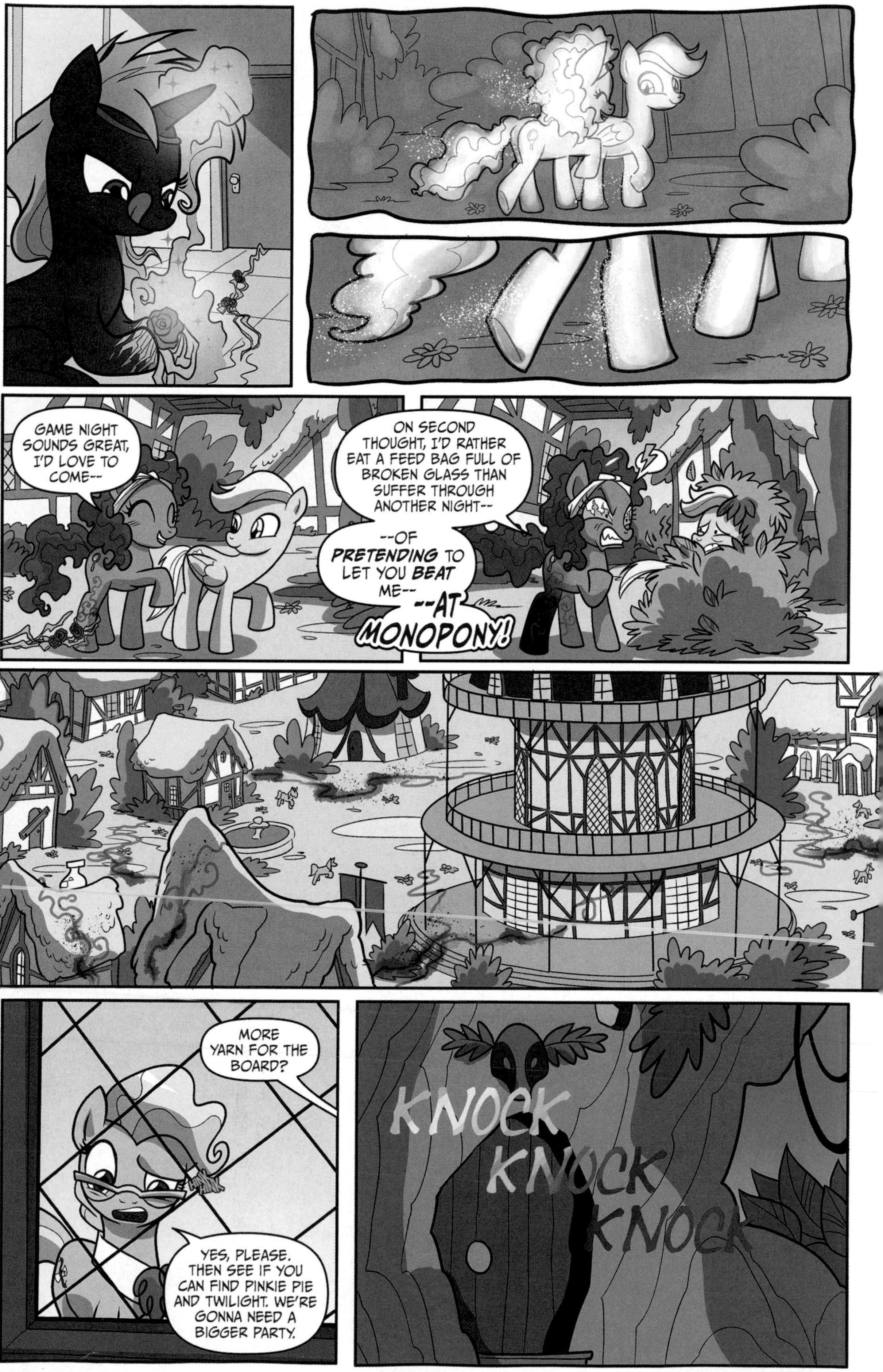
GAME NIGHT SOUNDS GREAT, I'D LOVE TO COME--
ON SECOND THOUGHT, I'D RATHER EAT A FEED BAG FULL OF BROKEN GLASS THAN SUFFER THROUGH ANOTHER NIGHT--
--OF PRETENDING TO LET YOU BEAT ME--
--AT MONOPONY!
MORE YARN FOR THE BOARD?
YES, PLEASE. THEN SEE IF YOU CAN FIND PINKIE PIE AND TWILIGHT. WE'RE GONNA NEED A BIGGER PARTY.
KNOCK
KNOCK
KNOCK

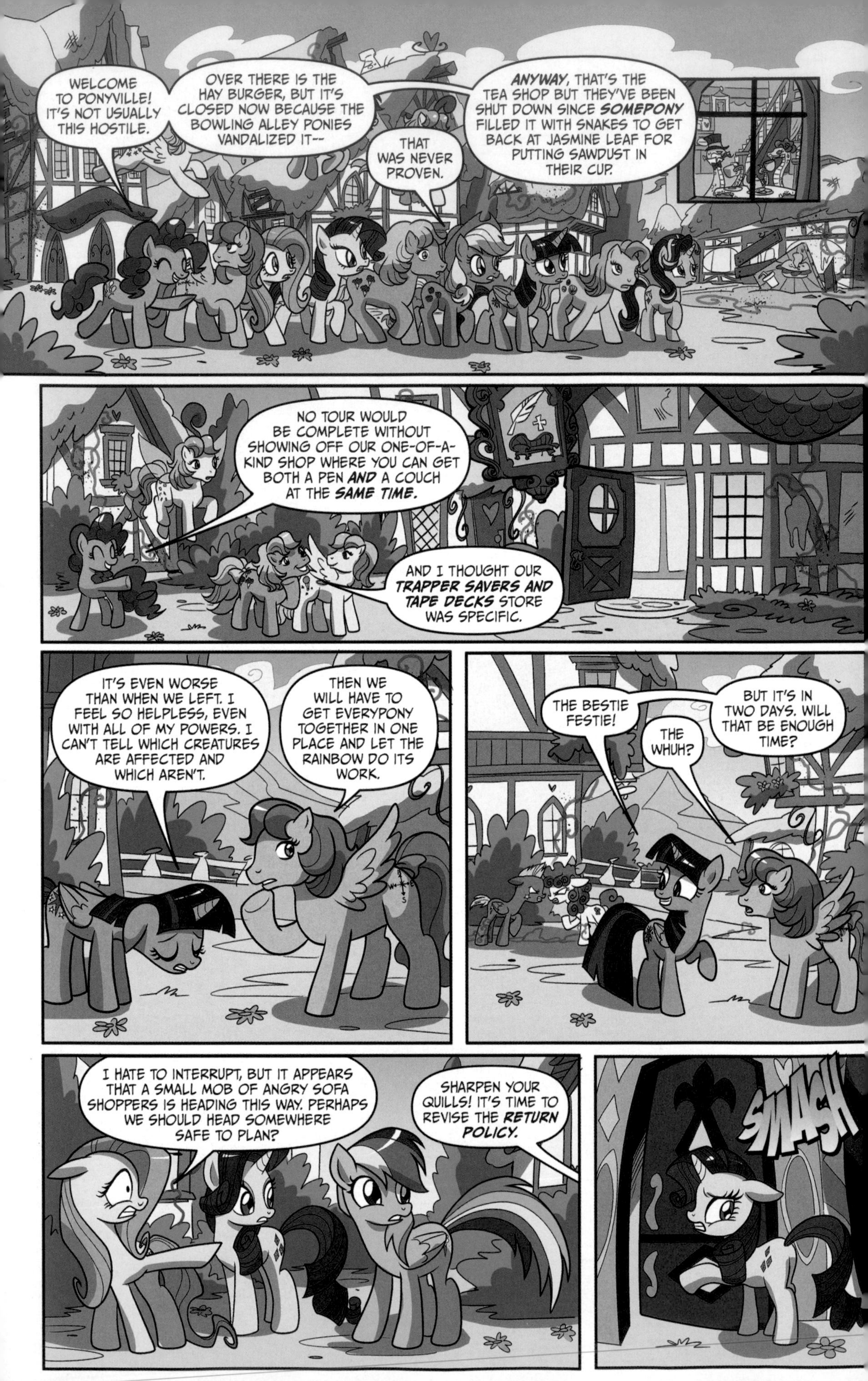

WELCOME TO PONYVILLE! IT'S NOT USUALLY THIS HOSTILE.
OVER THERE IS THE HAY BURGER, BUT IT'S CLOSED NOW BECAUSE THE BOWLING ALLEY PONIES VANDALIZED IT--
THAT WAS NEVER PROVEN.
ANYWAY, THAT'S THE TEA SHOP BUT THEY'VE BEEN SHUT DOWN SINCE SOMEPONY FILLED IT WITH SNAKES TO GET BACK AT JASMINE LEAF FOR PUTTING SAWDUST IN THEIR CUP.
NO TOUR WOULD BE COMPLETE WITHOUT SHOWING OFF OUR ONE-OF-A-KIND SHOP WHERE YOU CAN GET BOTH A PEN AND A COUCH AT THE SAME TIME.
AND I THOUGHT OUR TRAPPER SAVERS AND TAPE DECKS STORE WAS SPECIFIC.
IT'S EVEN WORSE THAN WHEN WE LEFT. I FEEL SO HELPLESS, EVEN WITH ALL OF MY POWERS. I CAN'T TELL WHICH CREATURES ARE AFFECTED AND WHICH AREN'T.
THEN WE WILL HAVE TO GET EVERYPONY TOGETHER IN ONE PLACE AND LET THE RAINBOW DO ITS WORK.
THE BESTIE FESTIE!
THE WHUH?
BUT IT'S IN TWO DAYS. WILL THAT BE ENOUGH TIME?
I HATE TO INTERRUPT, BUT IT APPEARS THAT A SMALL MOB OF ANGRY SOFA SHOPPERS IS HEADING THIS WAY. PERHAPS WE SHOULD HEAD SOMEWHERE SAFE TO PLAN?
SHARPEN YOUR QUILLS! IT'S TIME TO REVISE THE RETURN POLICY.
SMASH

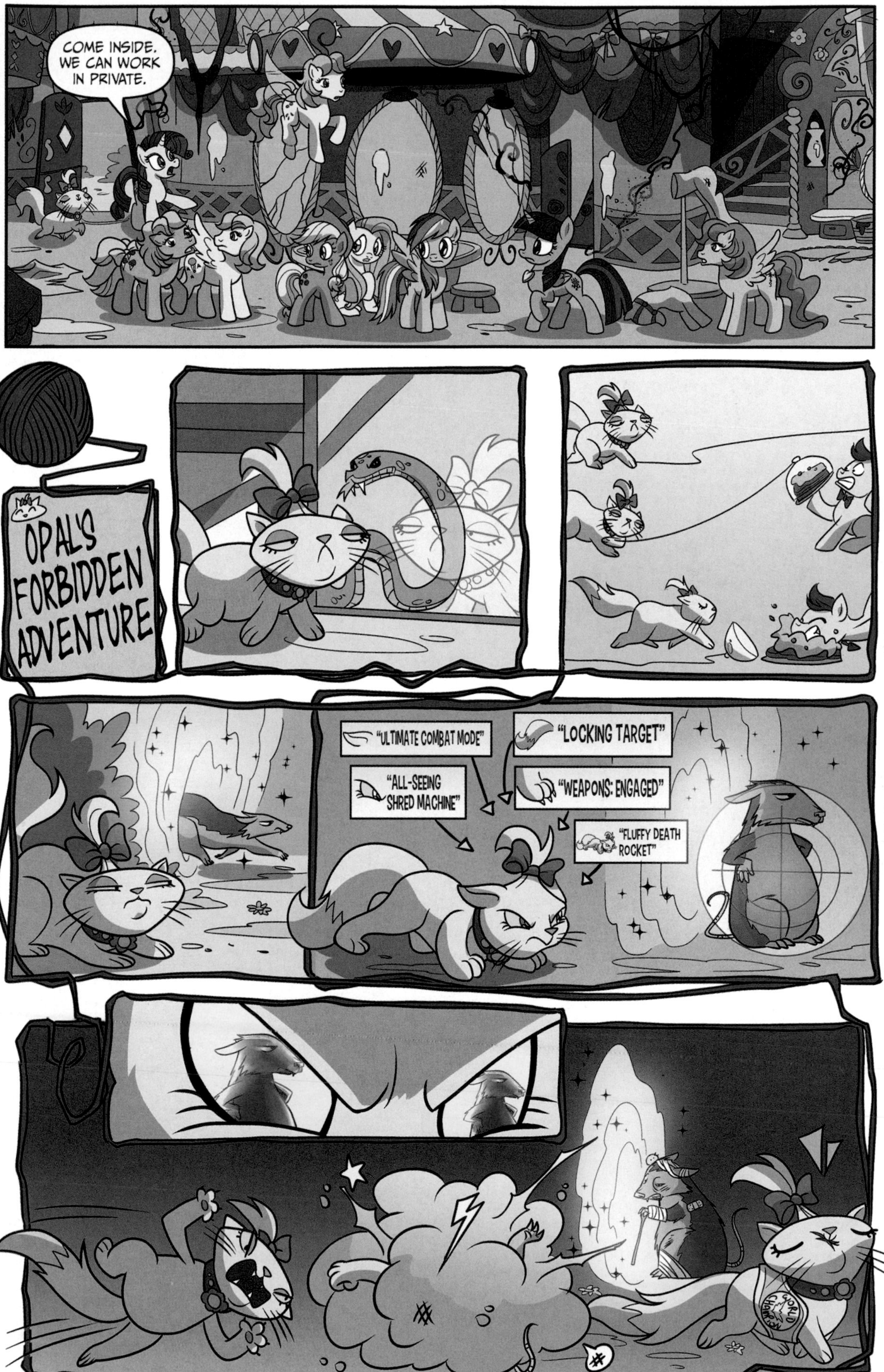

COME INSIDE. WE CAN WORK IN PRIVATE.
OPAL'S FORBIDDEN ADVENTURE
"ULTIMATE COMBAT MODE"
"LOCKING TARGET"
"ALL-SEEING SHRED MACHINE"
"WEAPONS: ENGAGED"
"FLUFFY DEATH ROCKET"
WORLD CHAMPION

IT FEELS LIKE THERE ARE SONIC RAINBOOMS IN MY BRAIN.

YOU MEAN SONIC *BRAINBOOMS*. HEHURHURM.

MY SHOP IS A DISASTER, AND WE *STILL* DON'T KNOW HOW TO GET OUR MAGIC INTO THAT LOCKET.

zzz

LET ME TRY AGAIN. THERE *HAS* TO BE A WAY FOR US TO HARNESS THE ELEMENTS OF HARMONY AND JUST *SHOVE* THEM IN THERE--

IF THAT'S THE SMOOZE, JUST LET IT IN. I'M TOO TIRED TO THINK.

skritch skritch skritch

OPAL! WHERE HAVE YOU BEEN, AND WHAT IS THAT *DISGUSTING* THING IN YOUR MOUTH?

FROWROW ROWROW!

YOU PERFECTLY BEAUTIFUL LITTLE BEAST!

FLUTTERSHY, CAN YOU *PLEASE* SPEAK TO HER?

WHO IS THE BIGGEST, TOUGHEST, MOST VICIOUS VANILLA MILKSHAKE IN ALL OF EQUESTRIA?

LET ME SEE WHAT'S IN YOUR MOUTH, YOU LITTLE ANGORA ASSASSIN.

♥

PRRRRRR

I'VE GOT IT!

UGH! WHAT IS THAT *SMELL?*

THAT, MY FRIEND, IS LAVA GOBLIN FUR.

IT REEKS OF SULFUR.

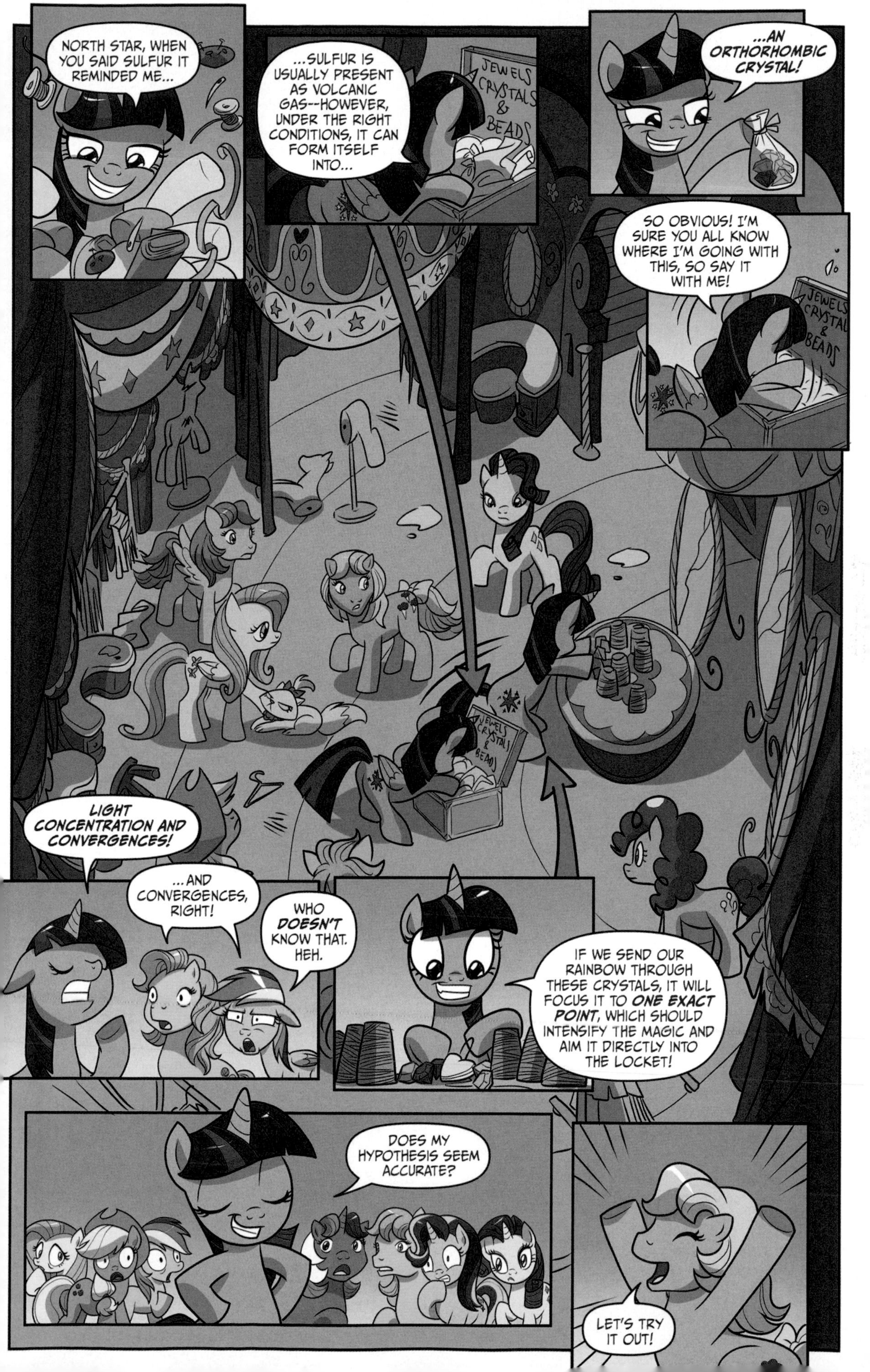

NORTH STAR, WHEN YOU SAID SULFUR IT REMINDED ME...
...SULFUR IS USUALLY PRESENT AS VOLCANIC GAS--HOWEVER, UNDER THE RIGHT CONDITIONS, IT CAN FORM ITSELF INTO...
JEWELS CRYSTALS & BEADS
...AN ORTHORHOMBIC CRYSTAL!
SO OBVIOUS! I'M SURE YOU ALL KNOW WHERE I'M GOING WITH THIS, SO SAY IT WITH ME!
JEWELS CRYSTALS & BEADS
JEWELS CRYSTALS & BEADS
LIGHT CONCENTRATION AND CONVERGENCES!
...AND CONVERGENCES, RIGHT!
WHO DOESN'T KNOW THAT. HEH.
IF WE SEND OUR RAINBOW THROUGH THESE CRYSTALS, IT WILL FOCUS IT TO ONE EXACT POINT, WHICH SHOULD INTENSIFY THE MAGIC AND AIM IT DIRECTLY INTO THE LOCKET!
DOES MY HYPOTHESIS SEEM ACCURATE?
LET'S TRY IT OUT!

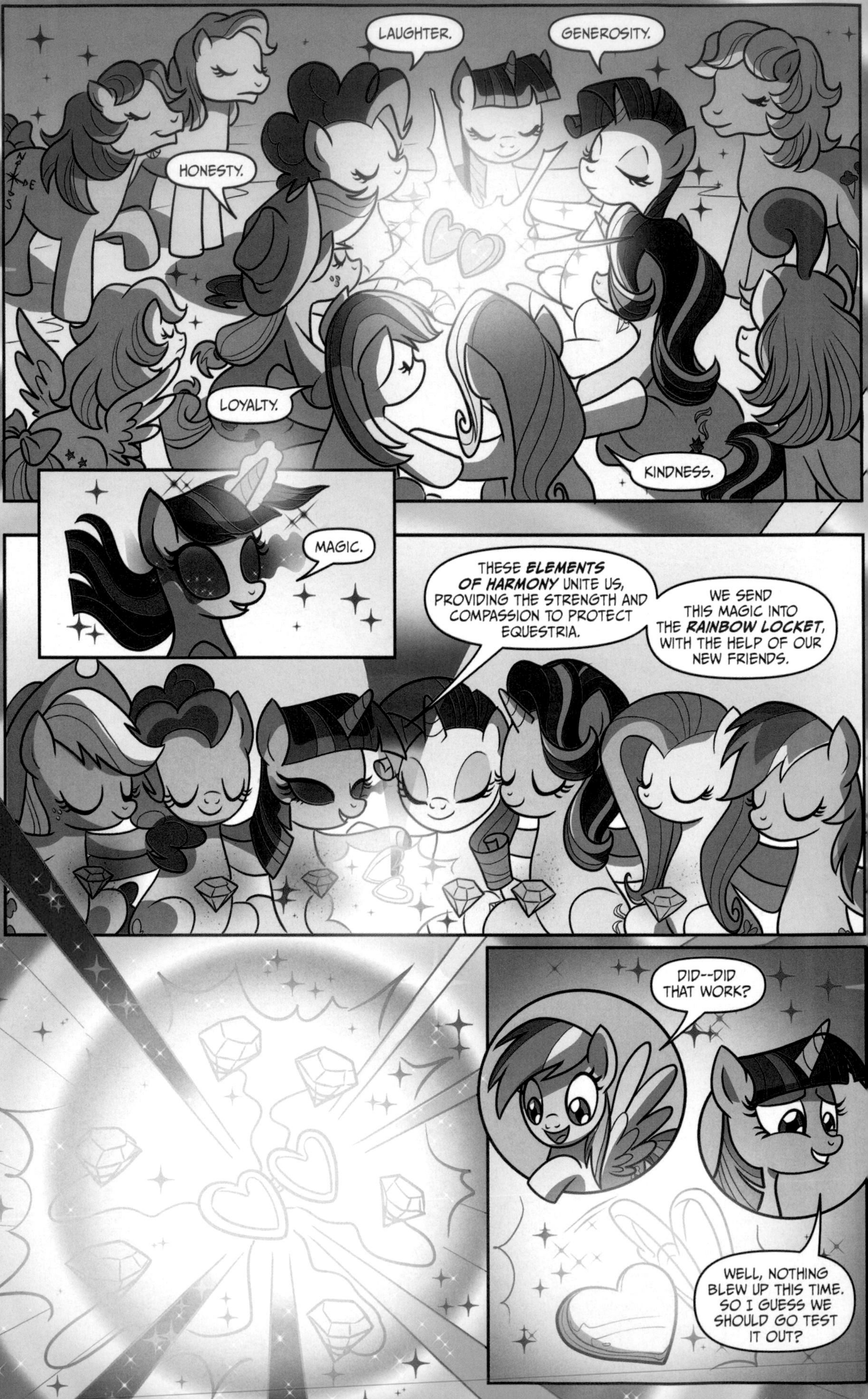

LAUGHTER.
GENEROSITY.
HONESTY.
LOYALTY.
KINDNESS.
MAGIC.
THESE **ELEMENTS OF HARMONY** UNITE US, PROVIDING THE STRENGTH AND COMPASSION TO PROTECT EQUESTRIA.
WE SEND THIS MAGIC INTO THE **RAINBOW LOCKET**, WITH THE HELP OF OUR NEW FRIENDS.
DID--DID THAT WORK?
WELL, NOTHING BLEW UP THIS TIME. SO I GUESS WE SHOULD GO TEST IT OUT?

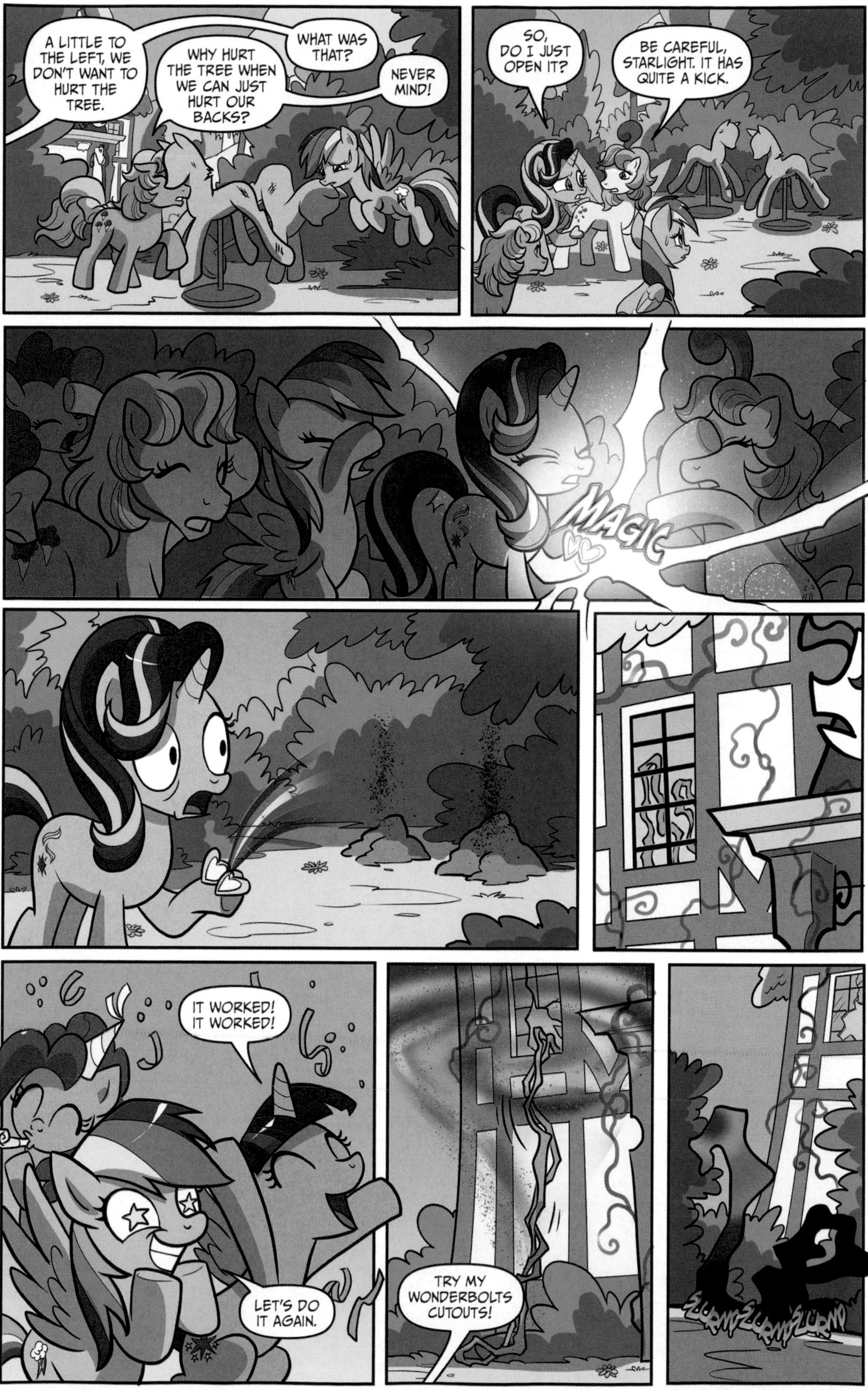
A LITTLE TO THE LEFT, WE DON'T WANT TO HURT THE TREE.
WHY HURT THE TREE WHEN WE CAN JUST HURT OUR BACKS?
WHAT WAS THAT?
NEVER MIND!
SO, DO I JUST OPEN IT?
BE CAREFUL, STARLIGHT. IT HAS QUITE A KICK.
MAGIC
IT WORKED! IT WORKED!
LET'S DO IT AGAIN.
TRY MY WONDERBOLTS CUTOUTS!
SLURMP SLURMP SLURMP

I'M SORRY, DYRE, BUT I CAN'T THINK OF A WAY TO UPGRADE THE S'MONIES TO BE ABLE TO *SPRAY ACTUAL LAVA OUT OF THEIR ACTUAL EYEBALLS.* WHAT ELSE YOU GOT?

I HAVE TO BE HONEST, NOT FEELING SUPER INSPIRED AFTER BEING SHUT DOWN SO HARD.

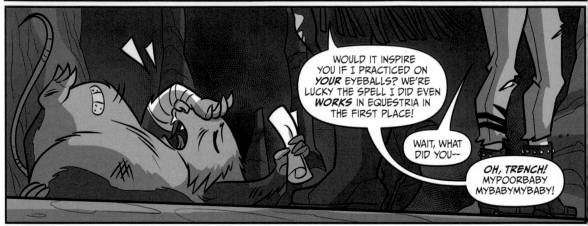

WOULD IT INSPIRE YOU IF I PRACTICED ON *YOUR* EYEBALLS? WE'RE LUCKY THE SPELL I DID EVEN *WORKS* IN EQUESTRIA IN THE FIRST PLACE!

WAIT, WHAT DID YOU--

OH, TRENCH! MYPOORBABY MYBABYMYBABY!

YOU BRAVE, BROKEN BUTTERCUP. WHO DID THIS TO YOU?

NO, DON'T TRY TO TALK. SAVE YOUR STRENGTH!

UH, GRACK? YOU SHOULD TAKE A LOOK AT THESE.

BUT MAYBE BACK AWAY FROM THE SHARP MEDICAL SUPPLIES FIRST.

LET ME KNOW WHEN YOU WANT TRENCH TO TELL YOU HOW THEY WERE ALSO DECORATING FOR THE PARTY THING.

THIS IS HOW THEY REPAY ME? BY HELPING PUT TOGETHER A--A--

--A PONY PROM?

BY BEING TEACHER OF THE YEAR?

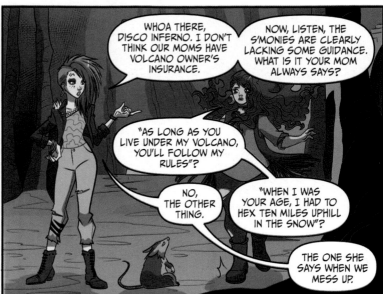

WHOA THERE, DISCO INFERNO. I DON'T THINK OUR MOMS HAVE VOLCANO OWNER'S INSURANCE.

NOW, LISTEN, THE S'MONIES ARE CLEARLY LACKING SOME GUIDANCE. WHAT IS IT YOUR MOM ALWAYS SAYS?

"AS LONG AS YOU LIVE UNDER MY VOLCANO, YOU'LL FOLLOW MY RULES"?

NO, THE OTHER THING.

"WHEN I WAS YOUR AGE, I HAD TO HEX TEN MILES UPHILL IN THE SNOW"?

THE ONE SHE SAYS WHEN WE MESS UP.

"IF YOU WANT SOMETHING CURSED, YOU BETTER DO IT YOURSELF."

BUT HOW ARE WE GOING TO DO IT OURSELVES?

IT'S NOT LIKE WE CAN USE OUR MAGIC OUT THERE.

I'VE BEEN THINKING ABOUT THAT. THE S'MONIES HAVE POWERS, RIGHT?

PFF, MORE THAN THEY CAN USE, APPARENTLY.

AND DO YOU REMEMBER WHAT THE S'MONIES ARE MADE OUT OF?

PIZZA DOUGH AND SMOOZE, DYRE. DUH.

THERE'S ONE MORE INGREDIENT.

M--MAGIC.

AND WHOSE MAGIC WOULD THAT BE?

FLIPPIN' FIREBALLS...

IT'S MINE!

AND IT WORKS OUTSIDE OF OUR REALM!

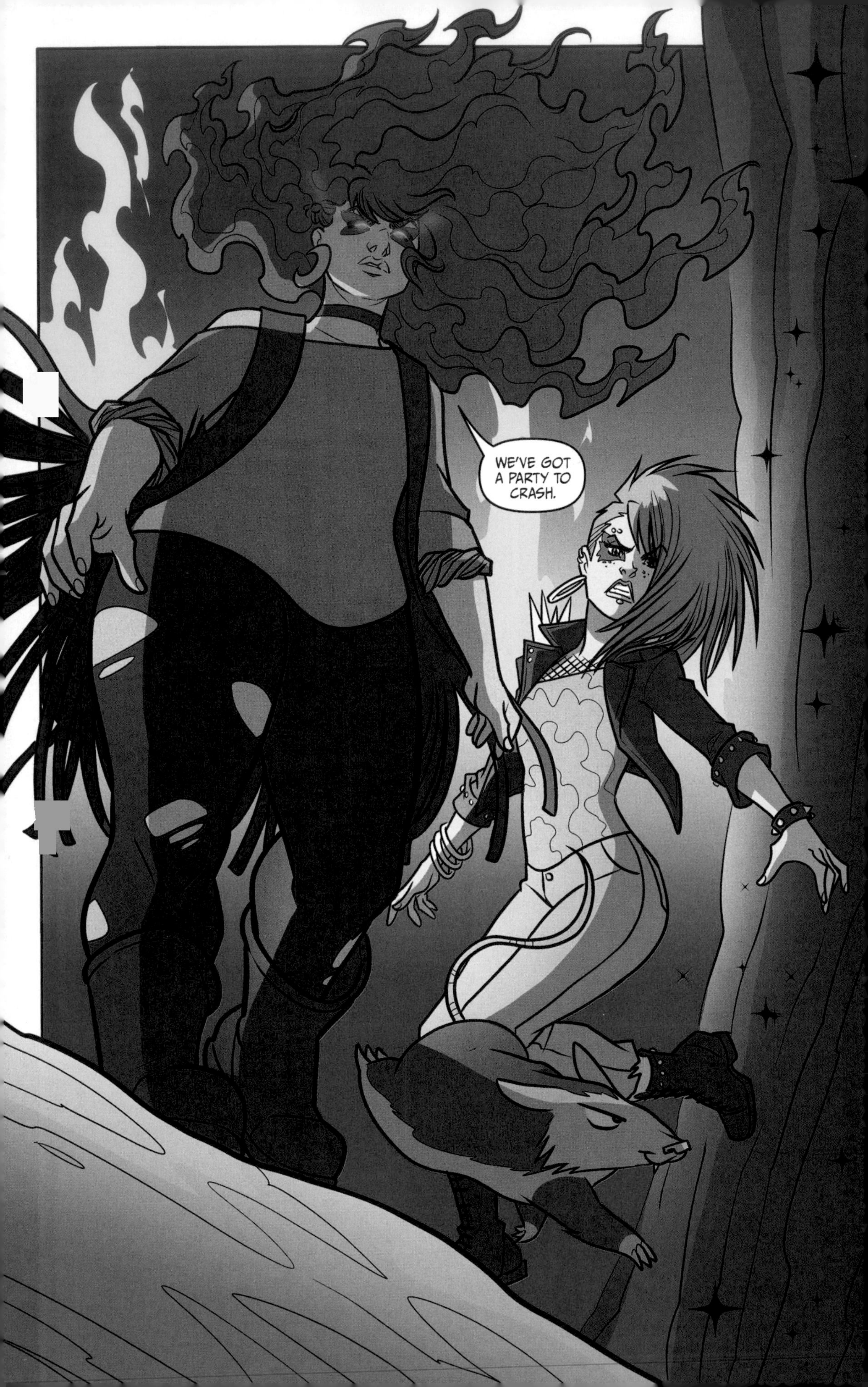
WE'VE GOT A PARTY TO CRASH.

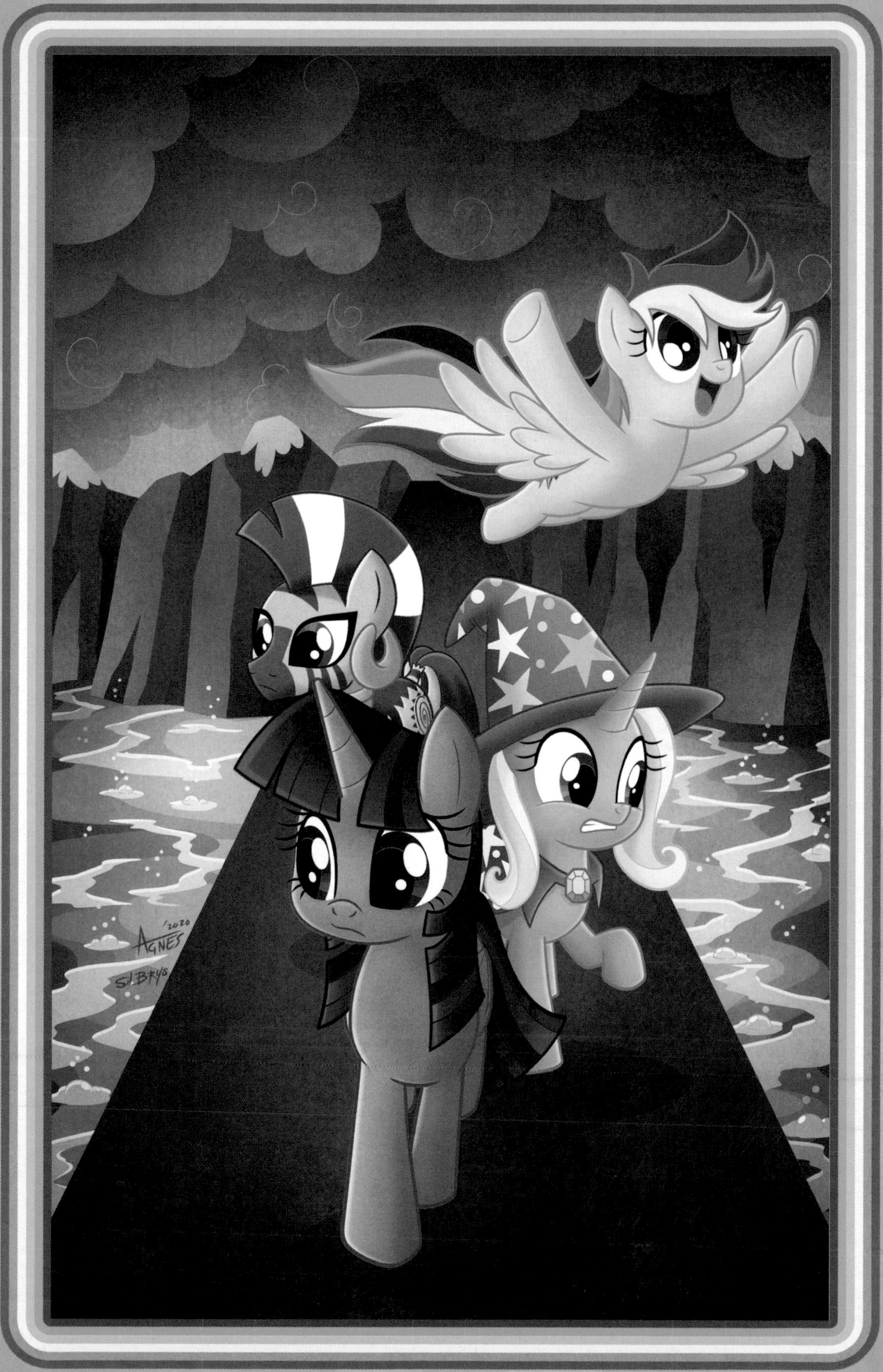
'2020
AGNES
SilBRYS

Art by Agnes Garbowska Colors by Silvana Brys

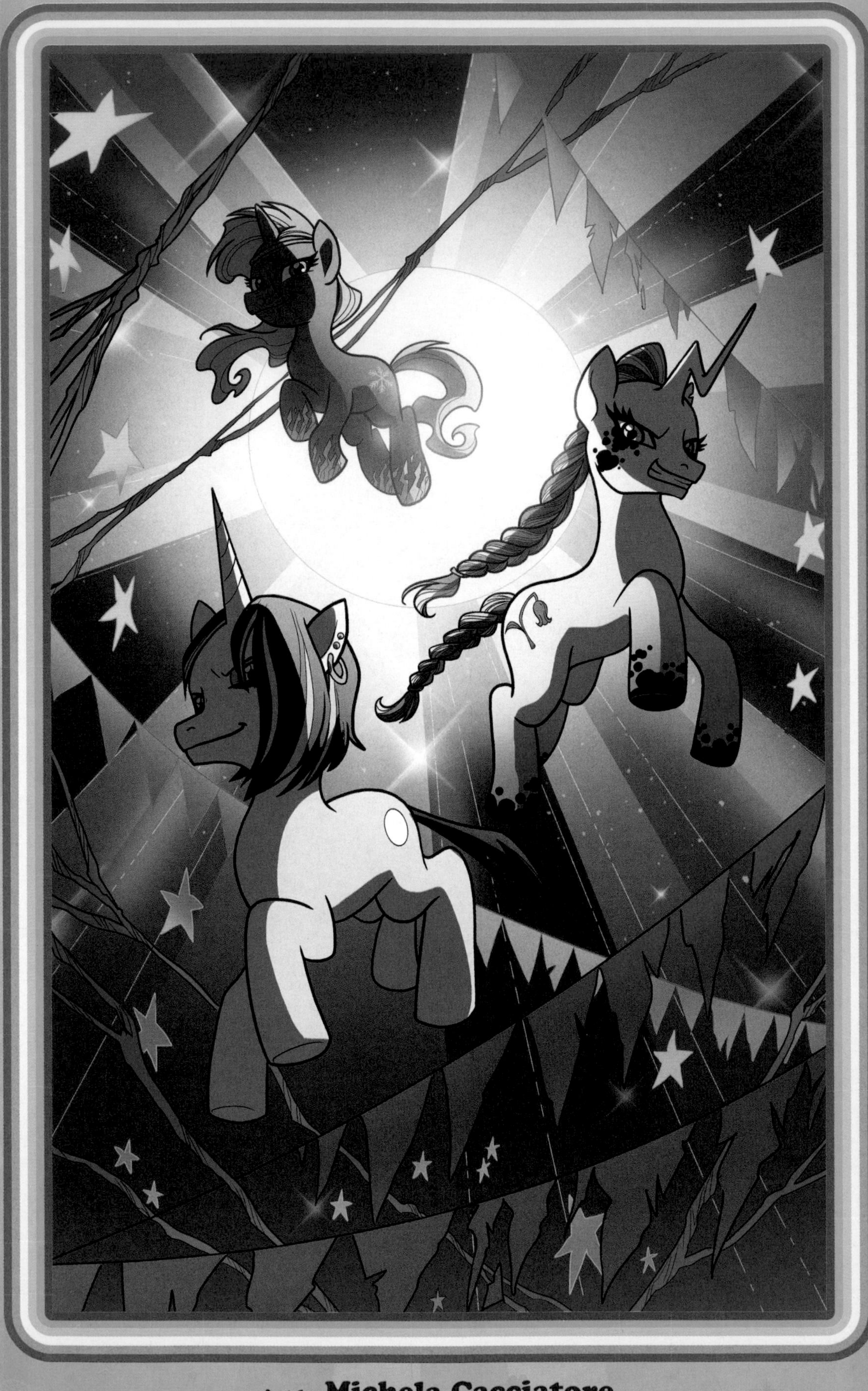

Art by **Michela Cacciatore**

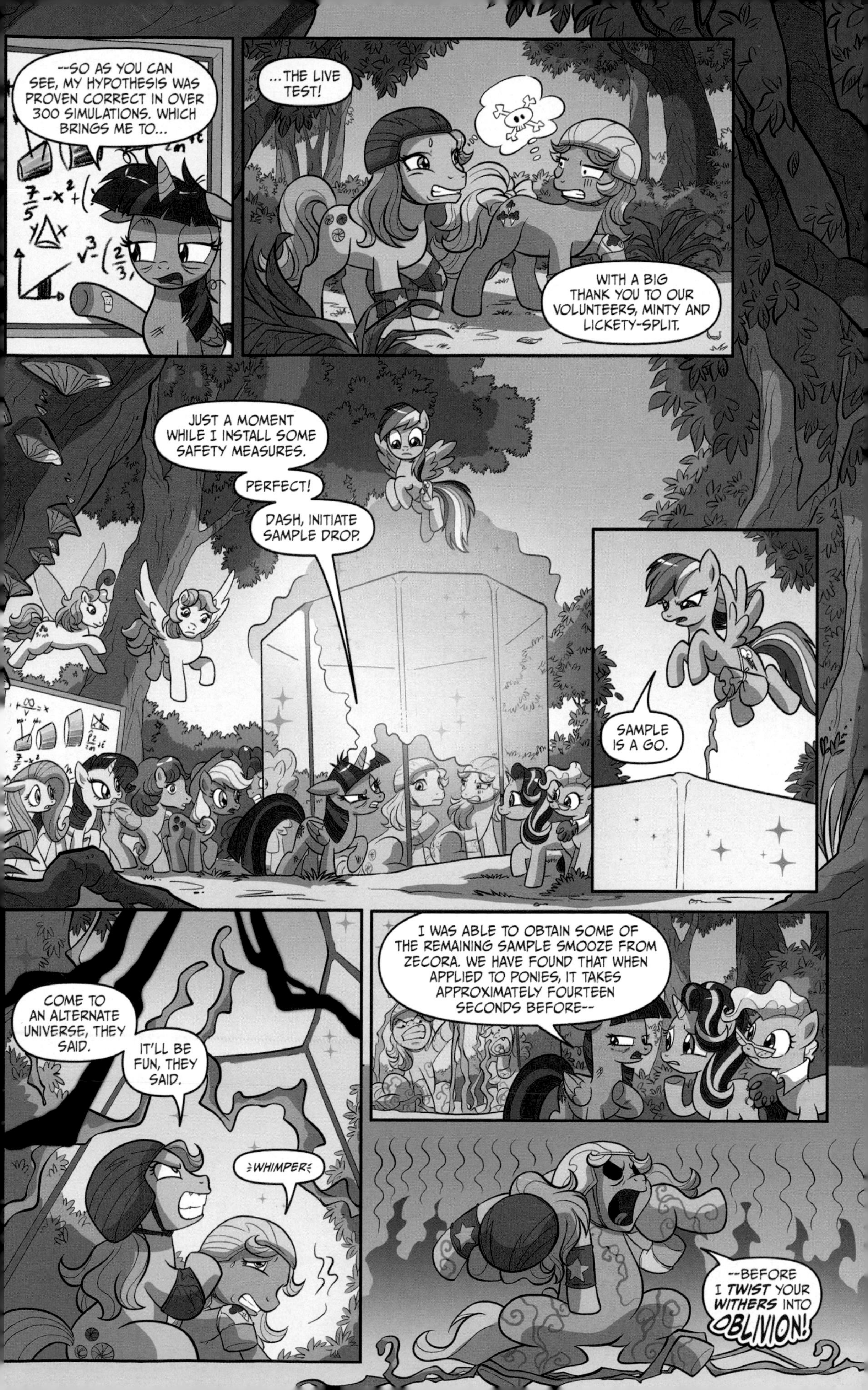
--SO AS YOU CAN SEE, MY HYPOTHESIS WAS PROVEN CORRECT IN OVER 300 SIMULATIONS. WHICH BRINGS ME TO...
...THE LIVE TEST!
WITH A BIG THANK YOU TO OUR VOLUNTEERS, MINTY AND LICKETY-SPLIT.
JUST A MOMENT WHILE I INSTALL SOME SAFETY MEASURES.
PERFECT!
DASH, INITIATE SAMPLE DROP.
SAMPLE IS A GO.
COME TO AN ALTERNATE UNIVERSE, THEY SAID.
IT'LL BE FUN, THEY SAID.
WHIMPER
I WAS ABLE TO OBTAIN SOME OF THE REMAINING SAMPLE SMOOZE FROM ZECORA. WE HAVE FOUND THAT WHEN APPLIED TO PONIES, IT TAKES APPROXIMATELY FOURTEEN SECONDS BEFORE--
--BEFORE I TWIST YOUR WITHERS INTO OBLIVION!

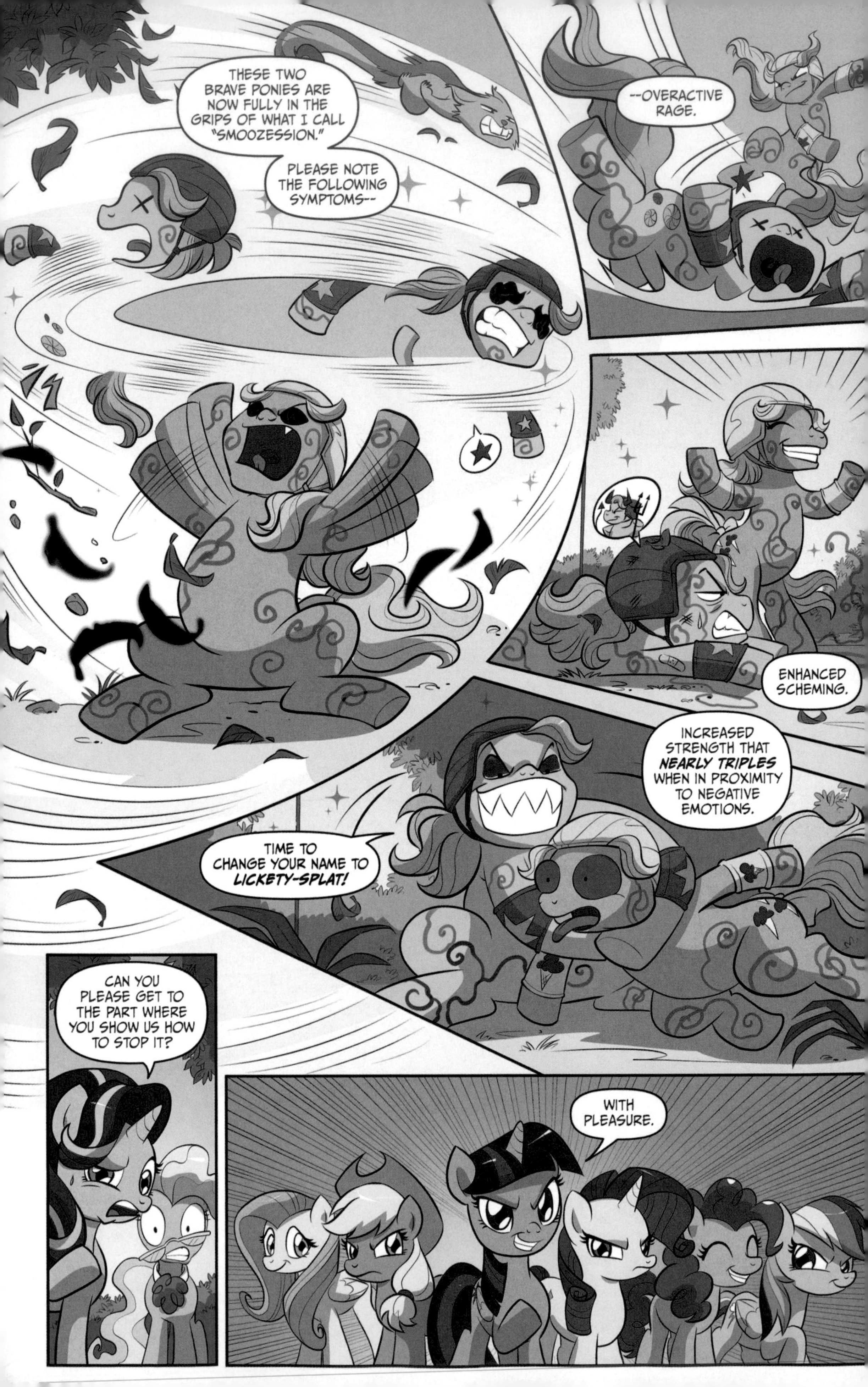

THESE TWO BRAVE PONIES ARE NOW FULLY IN THE GRIPS OF WHAT I CALL "SMOOZESSION."
PLEASE NOTE THE FOLLOWING SYMPTOMS--
--OVERACTIVE RAGE.
ENHANCED SCHEMING.
INCREASED STRENGTH THAT NEARLY TRIPLES WHEN IN PROXIMITY TO NEGATIVE EMOTIONS.
TIME TO CHANGE YOUR NAME TO LICKETY-SPLAT!
CAN YOU PLEASE GET TO THE PART WHERE YOU SHOW US HOW TO STOP IT?
WITH PLEASURE.

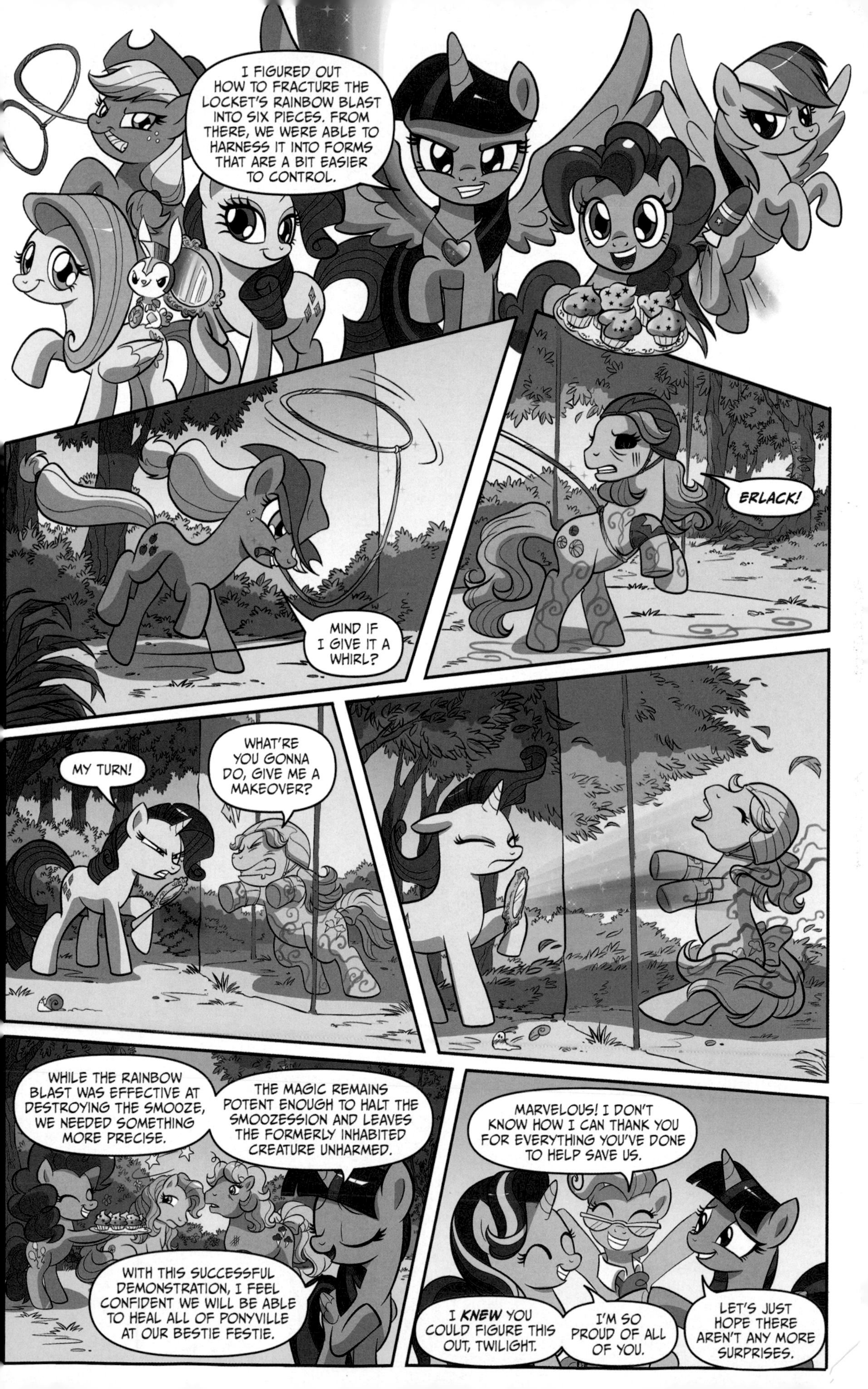

I FIGURED OUT HOW TO FRACTURE THE LOCKET'S RAINBOW BLAST INTO SIX PIECES. FROM THERE, WE WERE ABLE TO HARNESS IT INTO FORMS THAT ARE A BIT EASIER TO CONTROL.
MIND IF I GIVE IT A WHIRL?
ERLACK!
MY TURN!
WHAT'RE YOU GONNA DO, GIVE ME A MAKEOVER?
WHILE THE RAINBOW BLAST WAS EFFECTIVE AT DESTROYING THE SMOOZE, WE NEEDED SOMETHING MORE PRECISE.
THE MAGIC REMAINS POTENT ENOUGH TO HALT THE SMOOZESSION AND LEAVES THE FORMERLY INHABITED CREATURE UNHARMED.
WITH THIS SUCCESSFUL DEMONSTRATION, I FEEL CONFIDENT WE WILL BE ABLE TO HEAL ALL OF PONYVILLE AT OUR BESTIE FESTIE.
MARVELOUS! I DON'T KNOW HOW I CAN THANK YOU FOR EVERYTHING YOU'VE DONE TO HELP SAVE US.
I KNEW YOU COULD FIGURE THIS OUT, TWILIGHT.
I'M SO PROUD OF ALL OF YOU.
LET'S JUST HOPE THERE AREN'T ANY MORE SURPRISES.

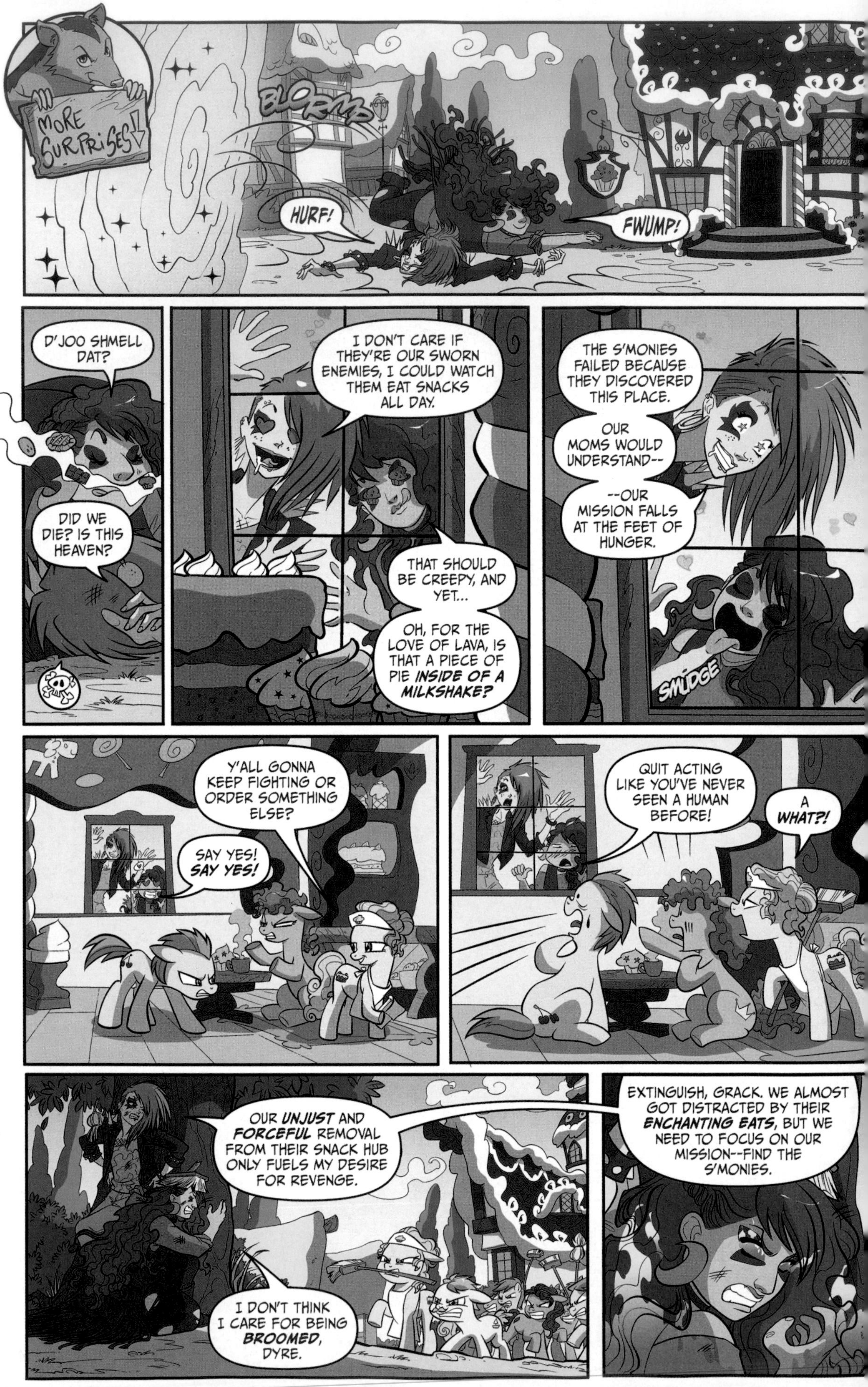
MORE SURPRISES!
BLORMP
HURF!
FWUMP!
D'JOO SHMELL DAT?
DID WE DIE? IS THIS HEAVEN?
I DON'T CARE IF THEY'RE OUR SWORN ENEMIES, I COULD WATCH THEM EAT SNACKS ALL DAY.
THAT SHOULD BE CREEPY, AND YET...
OH, FOR THE LOVE OF LAVA, IS THAT A PIECE OF PIE INSIDE OF A MILKSHAKE?
THE S'MONIES FAILED BECAUSE THEY DISCOVERED THIS PLACE.
OUR MOMS WOULD UNDERSTAND--
--OUR MISSION FALLS AT THE FEET OF HUNGER.
SMUDGE
Y'ALL GONNA KEEP FIGHTING OR ORDER SOMETHING ELSE?
SAY YES! SAY YES!
QUIT ACTING LIKE YOU'VE NEVER SEEN A HUMAN BEFORE!
A WHAT?!
OUR UNJUST AND FORCEFUL REMOVAL FROM THEIR SNACK HUB ONLY FUELS MY DESIRE FOR REVENGE.
I DON'T THINK I CARE FOR BEING BROOMED, DYRE.
EXTINGUISH, GRACK. WE ALMOST GOT DISTRACTED BY THEIR ENCHANTING EATS, BUT WE NEED TO FOCUS ON OUR MISSION--FIND THE S'MONIES.

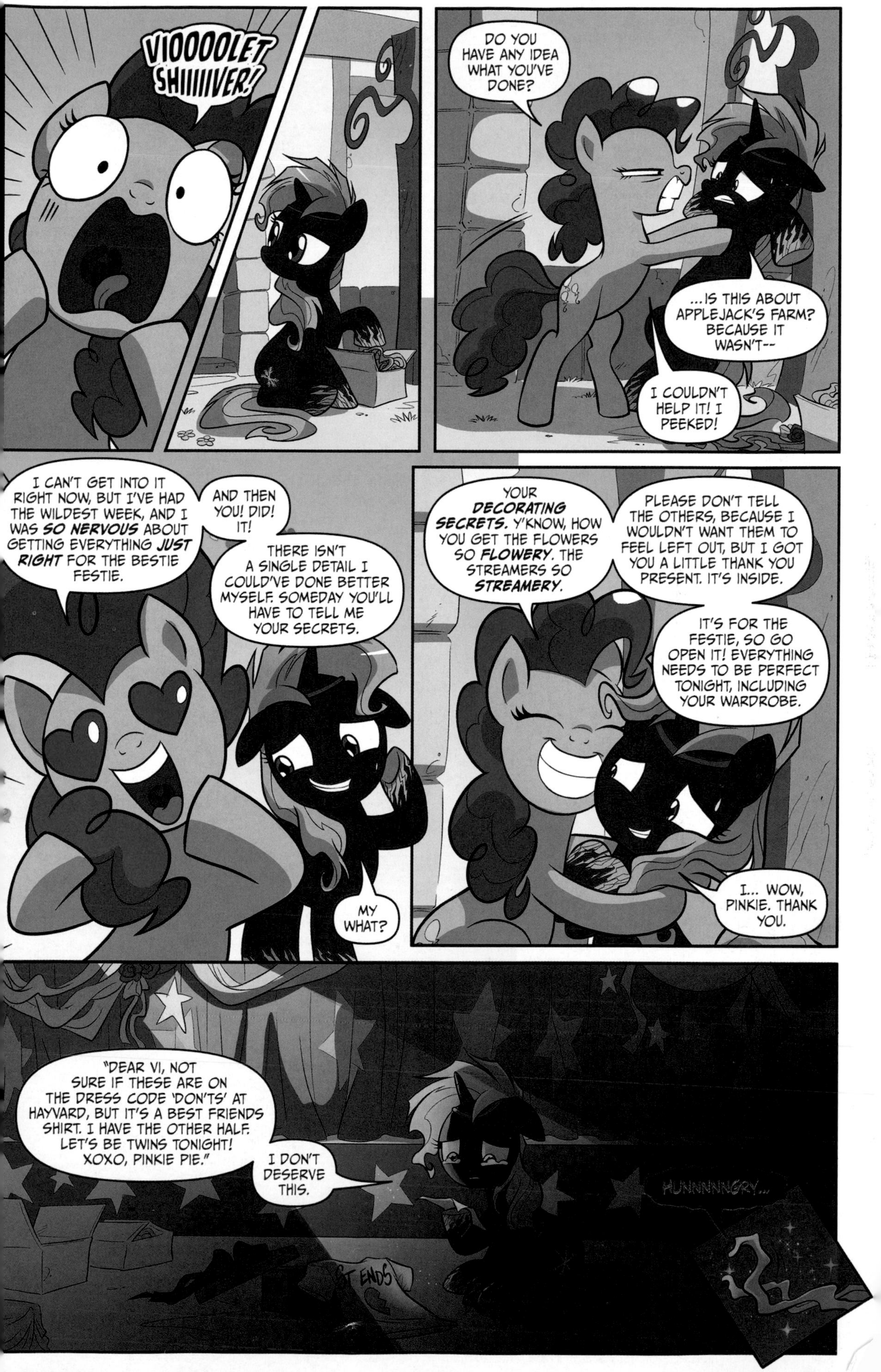

VIOOOOLET SHIIIIIVER!
DO YOU HAVE ANY IDEA WHAT YOU'VE DONE?
...IS THIS ABOUT APPLEJACK'S FARM? BECAUSE IT WASN'T--
I COULDN'T HELP IT! I PEEKED!
I CAN'T GET INTO IT RIGHT NOW, BUT I'VE HAD THE WILDEST WEEK, AND I WAS SO NERVOUS ABOUT GETTING EVERYTHING JUST RIGHT FOR THE BESTIE FESTIE.
AND THEN YOU! DID! IT!
THERE ISN'T A SINGLE DETAIL I COULD'VE DONE BETTER MYSELF. SOMEDAY YOU'LL HAVE TO TELL ME YOUR SECRETS.
MY WHAT?
YOUR DECORATING SECRETS. Y'KNOW, HOW YOU GET THE FLOWERS SO FLOWERY. THE STREAMERS SO STREAMERY.
PLEASE DON'T TELL THE OTHERS, BECAUSE I WOULDN'T WANT THEM TO FEEL LEFT OUT, BUT I GOT YOU A LITTLE THANK YOU PRESENT. IT'S INSIDE.
IT'S FOR THE FESTIE, SO GO OPEN IT! EVERYTHING NEEDS TO BE PERFECT TONIGHT, INCLUDING YOUR WARDROBE.
I... WOW, PINKIE. THANK YOU.
"DEAR VI, NOT SURE IF THESE ARE ON THE DRESS CODE 'DON'TS' AT HAYVARD, BUT IT'S A BEST FRIENDS SHIRT. I HAVE THE OTHER HALF. LET'S BE TWINS TONIGHT! XOXO, PINKIE PIE."
I DON'T DESERVE THIS.
HUNNNNNGRY...

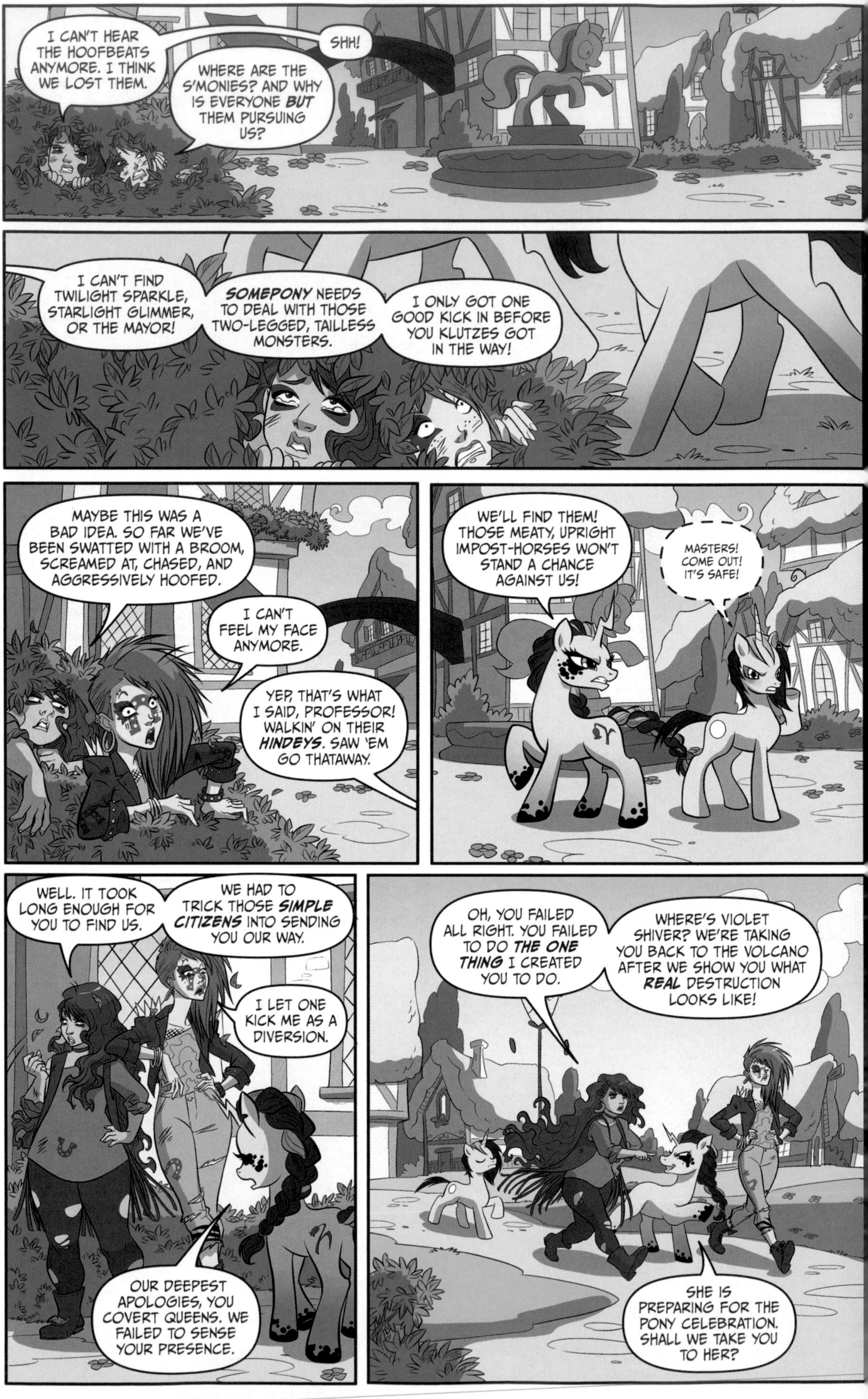
I CAN'T HEAR THE HOOFBEATS ANYMORE. I THINK WE LOST THEM.
SHH!
WHERE ARE THE S'MONIES? AND WHY IS EVERYONE BUT THEM PURSUING US?
I CAN'T FIND TWILIGHT SPARKLE, STARLIGHT GLIMMER, OR THE MAYOR!
SOMEPONY NEEDS TO DEAL WITH THOSE TWO-LEGGED, TAILLESS MONSTERS.
I ONLY GOT ONE GOOD KICK IN BEFORE YOU KLUTZES GOT IN THE WAY!
MAYBE THIS WAS A BAD IDEA. SO FAR WE'VE BEEN SWATTED WITH A BROOM, SCREAMED AT, CHASED, AND AGGRESSIVELY HOOFED.
I CAN'T FEEL MY FACE ANYMORE.
YEP, THAT'S WHAT I SAID, PROFESSOR! WALKIN' ON THEIR HINDEYS. SAW 'EM GO THATAWAY.
WE'LL FIND THEM! THOSE MEATY, UPRIGHT IMPOST-HORSES WON'T STAND A CHANCE AGAINST US!
MASTERS! COME OUT! IT'S SAFE!
WELL. IT TOOK LONG ENOUGH FOR YOU TO FIND US.
WE HAD TO TRICK THOSE SIMPLE CITIZENS INTO SENDING YOU OUR WAY.
I LET ONE KICK ME AS A DIVERSION.
OUR DEEPEST APOLOGIES, YOU COVERT QUEENS. WE FAILED TO SENSE YOUR PRESENCE.
OH, YOU FAILED ALL RIGHT. YOU FAILED TO DO THE ONE THING I CREATED YOU TO DO.
WHERE'S VIOLET SHIVER? WE'RE TAKING YOU BACK TO THE VOLCANO AFTER WE SHOW YOU WHAT REAL DESTRUCTION LOOKS LIKE!
SHE IS PREPARING FOR THE PONY CELEBRATION. SHALL WE TAKE YOU TO HER?

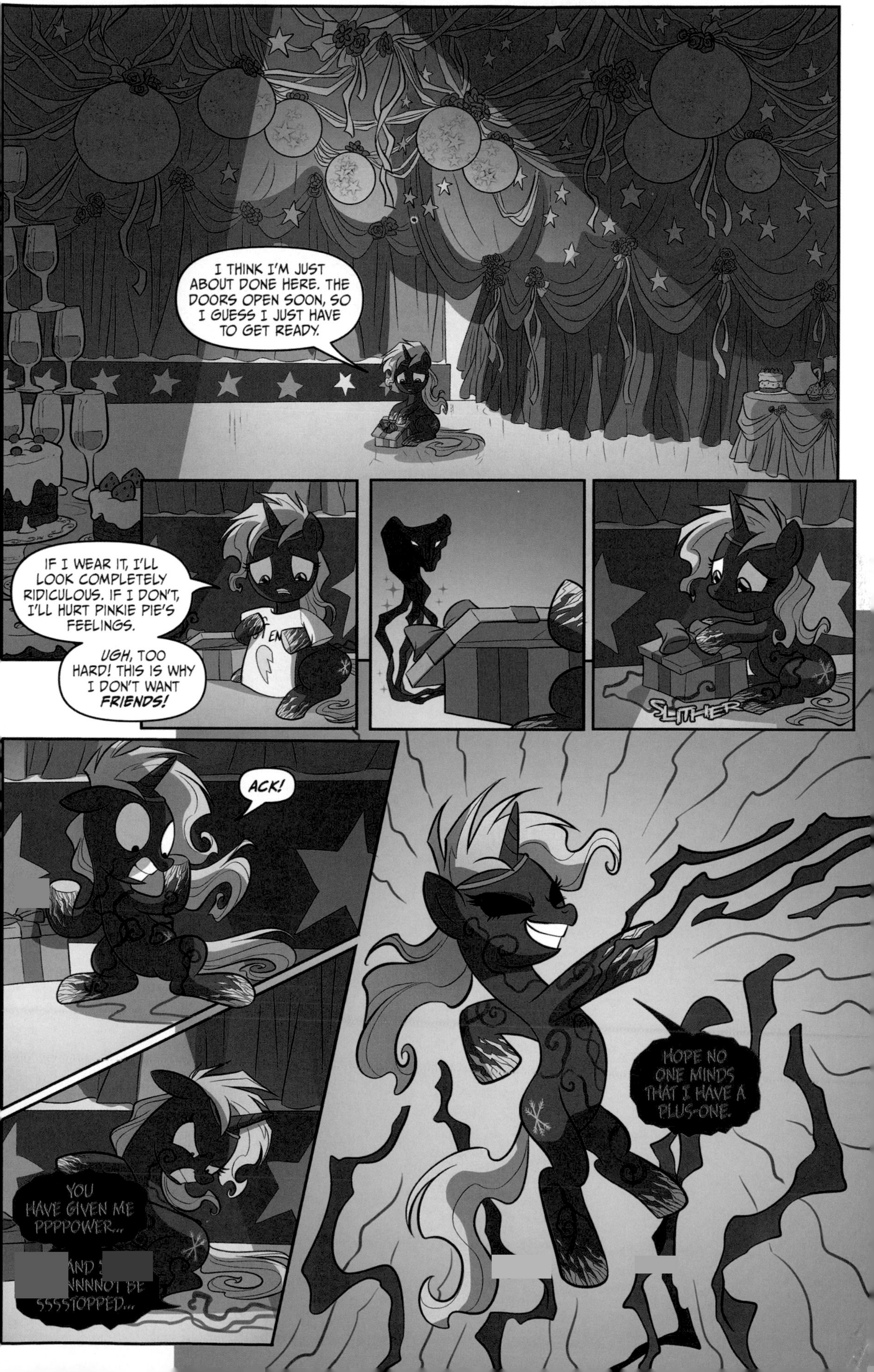
I THINK I'M JUST ABOUT DONE HERE. THE DOORS OPEN SOON, SO I GUESS I JUST HAVE TO GET READY.
IF I WEAR IT, I'LL LOOK COMPLETELY RIDICULOUS. IF I DON'T, I'LL HURT PINKIE PIE'S FEELINGS.
UGH, TOO HARD! THIS IS WHY I DON'T WANT ***FRIENDS!***
SLITHER
ACK!
YOU HAVE GIVEN ME PPPPOWER...
AND
NNNNOT BE SSSSSTOPPED...
HOPE NO ONE MINDS THAT I HAVE A PLUS-ONE.

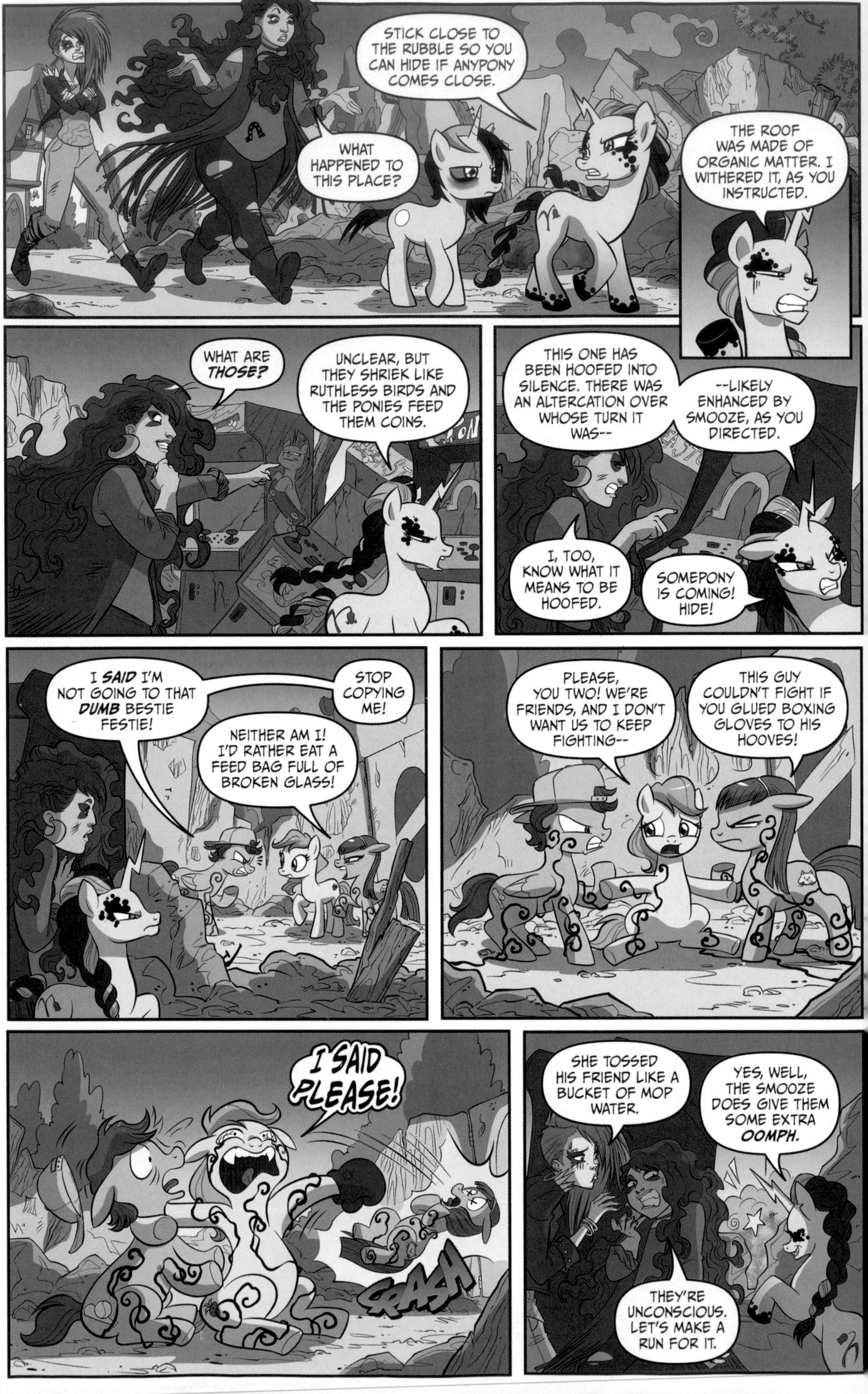
STICK CLOSE TO THE RUBBLE SO YOU CAN HIDE IF ANYPONY COMES CLOSE.
WHAT HAPPENED TO THIS PLACE?
THE ROOF WAS MADE OF ORGANIC MATTER. I WITHERED IT, AS YOU INSTRUCTED.
WHAT ARE *THOSE?*
UNCLEAR, BUT THEY SHRIEK LIKE RUTHLESS BIRDS AND THE PONIES FEED THEM COINS.
THIS ONE HAS BEEN HOOFED INTO SILENCE. THERE WAS AN ALTERCATION OVER WHOSE TURN IT WAS--
--LIKELY ENHANCED BY SMOOZE, AS YOU DIRECTED.
I, TOO, KNOW WHAT IT MEANS TO BE HOOFED.
SOMEPONY IS COMING! HIDE!
I ***SAID*** I'M NOT GOING TO THAT ***DUMB*** BESTIE FESTIE!
STOP COPYING ME!
NEITHER AM I! I'D RATHER EAT A FEED BAG FULL OF BROKEN GLASS!
PLEASE, YOU TWO! WE'RE FRIENDS, AND I DON'T WANT US TO KEEP FIGHTING--
THIS GUY COULDN'T FIGHT IF YOU GLUED BOXING GLOVES TO HIS HOOVES!
I SAID PLEASE!
CRASH
SHE TOSSED HIS FRIEND LIKE A BUCKET OF MOP WATER.
YES, WELL, THE SMOOZE DOES GIVE THEM SOME EXTRA ***OOMPH.***
THEY'RE UNCONSCIOUS. LET'S MAKE A RUN FOR IT.

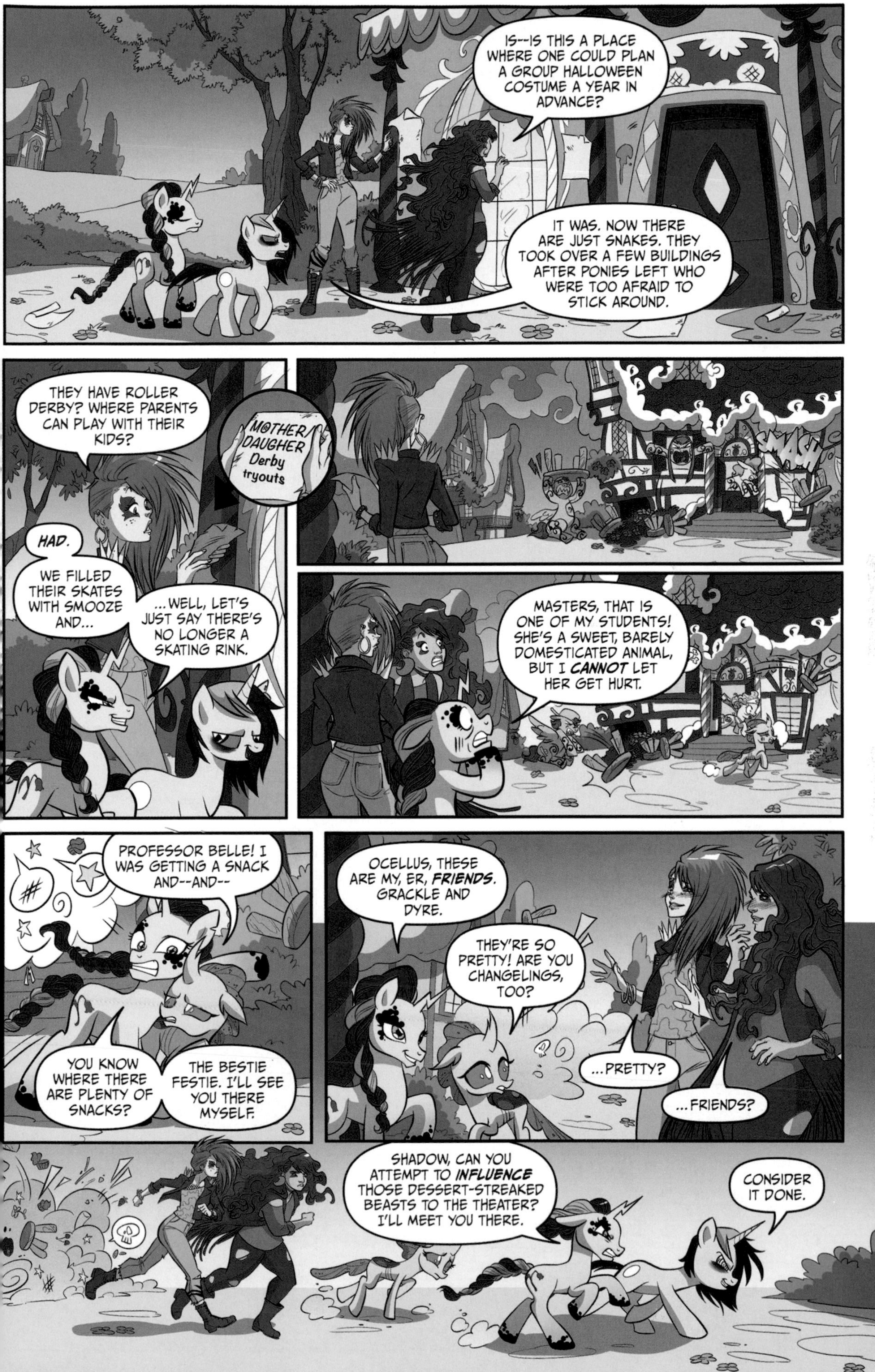

IS--IS THIS A PLACE WHERE ONE COULD PLAN A GROUP HALLOWEEN COSTUME A YEAR IN ADVANCE?
IT WAS. NOW THERE ARE JUST SNAKES. THEY TOOK OVER A FEW BUILDINGS AFTER PONIES LEFT WHO WERE TOO AFRAID TO STICK AROUND.
THEY HAVE ROLLER DERBY? WHERE PARENTS CAN PLAY WITH THEIR KIDS?
MOTHER/DAUGHER Derby tryouts
HAD.
WE FILLED THEIR SKATES WITH SMOOZE AND...
...WELL, LET'S JUST SAY THERE'S NO LONGER A SKATING RINK.
SMASH
MASTERS, THAT IS ONE OF MY STUDENTS! SHE'S A SWEET, BARELY DOMESTICATED ANIMAL, BUT I ***CANNOT*** LET HER GET HURT.
PROFESSOR BELLE! I WAS GETTING A SNACK AND--AND--
YOU KNOW WHERE THERE ARE PLENTY OF SNACKS?
THE BESTIE FESTIE. I'LL SEE YOU THERE MYSELF.
OCELLUS, THESE ARE MY, ER, ***FRIENDS***. GRACKLE AND DYRE.
THEY'RE SO PRETTY! ARE YOU CHANGELINGS, TOO?
...PRETTY?
...FRIENDS?
SHADOW, CAN YOU ATTEMPT TO ***INFLUENCE*** THOSE DESSERT-STREAKED BEASTS TO THE THEATER? I'LL MEET YOU THERE.
CONSIDER IT DONE.

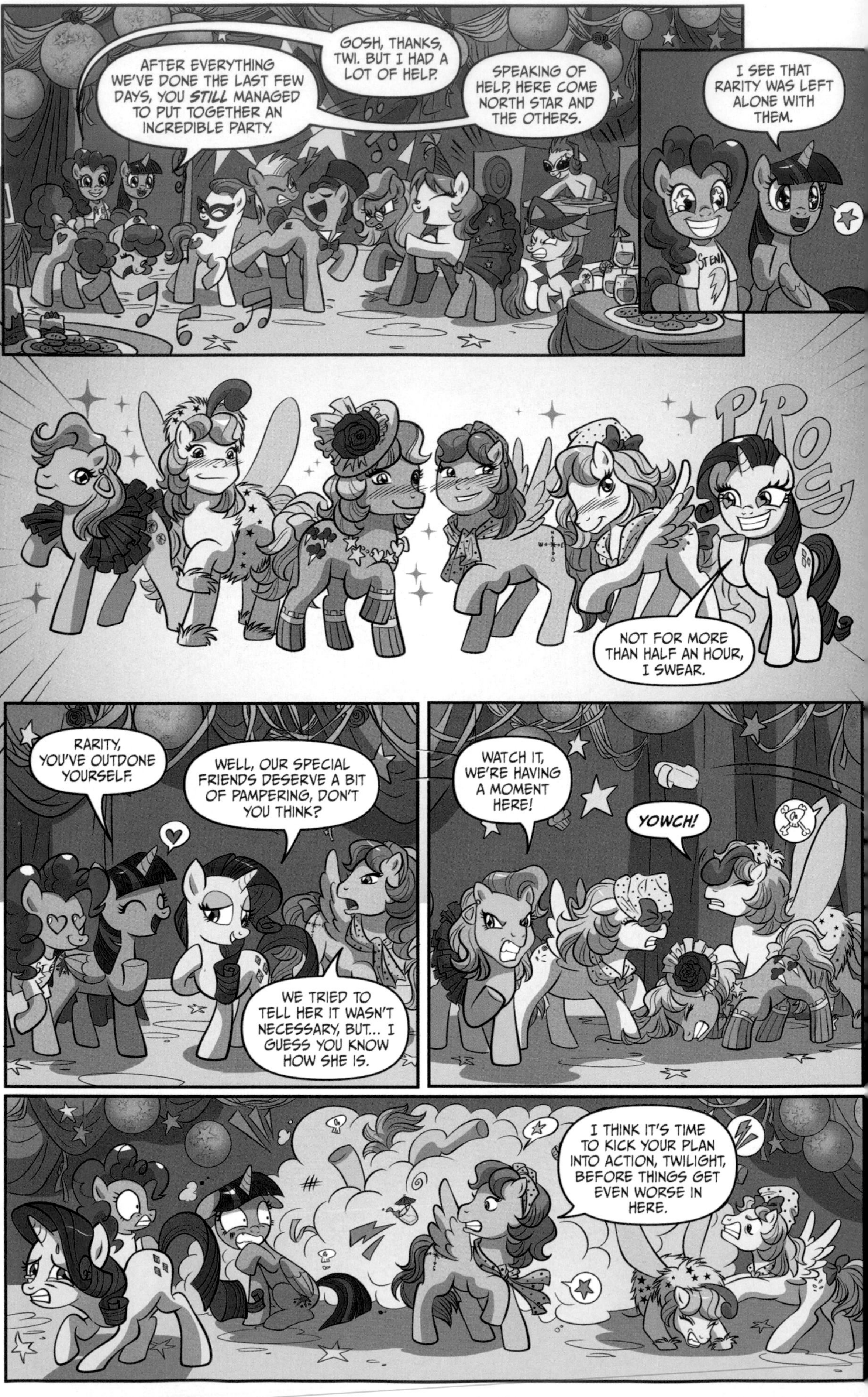

AFTER EVERYTHING WE'VE DONE THE LAST FEW DAYS, YOU STILL MANAGED TO PUT TOGETHER AN INCREDIBLE PARTY.
GOSH, THANKS, TWI. BUT I HAD A LOT OF HELP.
SPEAKING OF HELP, HERE COME NORTH STAR AND THE OTHERS.
I SEE THAT RARITY WAS LEFT ALONE WITH THEM.
PROUD
NOT FOR MORE THAN HALF AN HOUR, I SWEAR.
RARITY, YOU'VE OUTDONE YOURSELF.
WELL, OUR SPECIAL FRIENDS DESERVE A BIT OF PAMPERING, DON'T YOU THINK?
WE TRIED TO TELL HER IT WASN'T NECESSARY, BUT... I GUESS YOU KNOW HOW SHE IS.
WATCH IT, WE'RE HAVING A MOMENT HERE!
YOWCH!
I THINK IT'S TIME TO KICK YOUR PLAN INTO ACTION, TWILIGHT, BEFORE THINGS GET EVEN WORSE IN HERE.

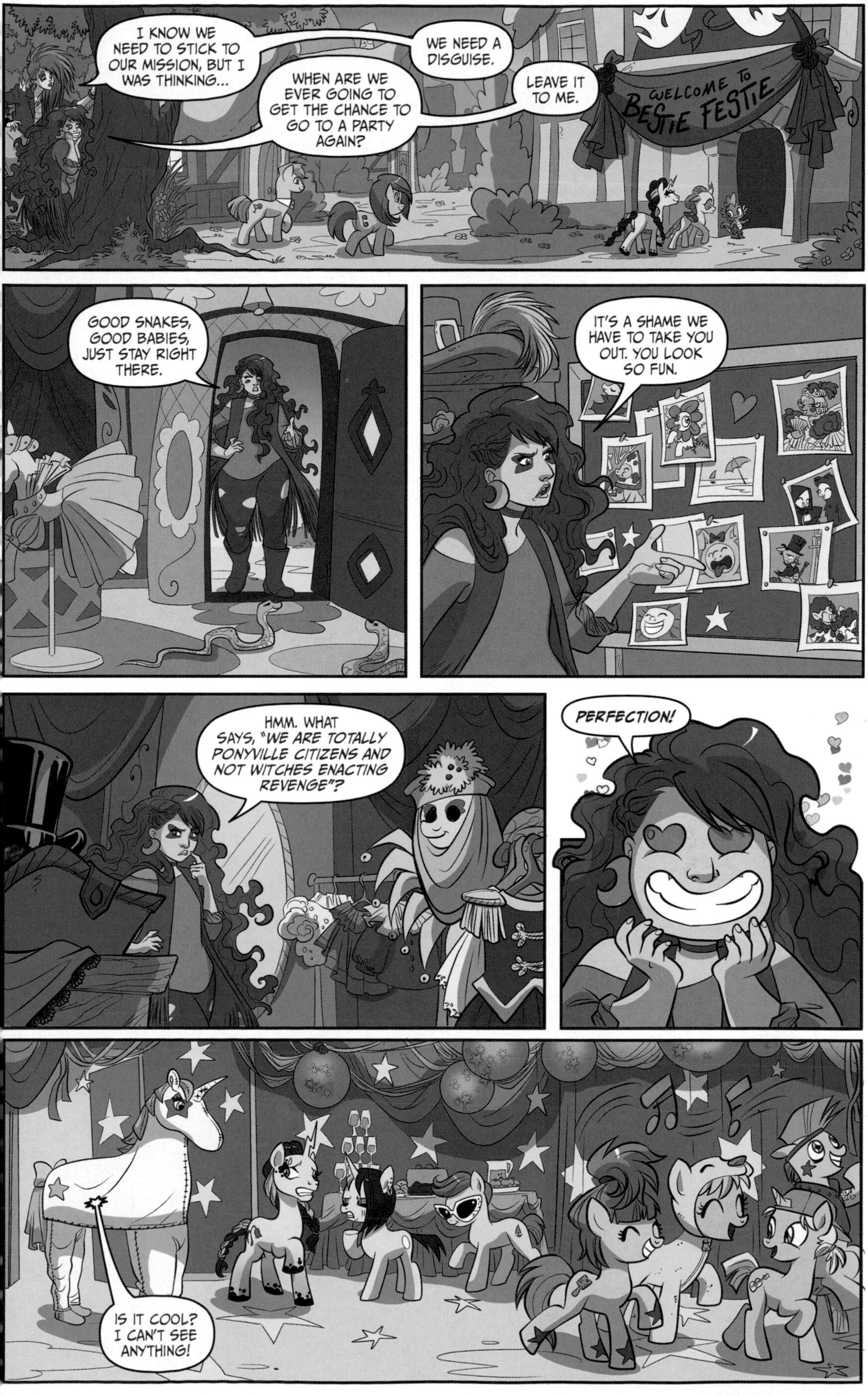
I KNOW WE NEED TO STICK TO OUR MISSION, BUT I WAS THINKING...
WHEN ARE WE EVER GOING TO GET THE CHANCE TO GO TO A PARTY AGAIN?
WE NEED A DISGUISE.
LEAVE IT TO ME.
WELCOME TO BESTIE FESTIE
GOOD SNAKES, GOOD BABIES, JUST STAY RIGHT THERE.
IT'S A SHAME WE HAVE TO TAKE YOU OUT. YOU LOOK SO FUN.
HMM. WHAT SAYS, "WE ARE TOTALLY PONYVILLE CITIZENS AND NOT WITCHES ENACTING REVENGE"?
PERFECTION!
IS IT COOL? I CAN'T SEE ANYTHING!

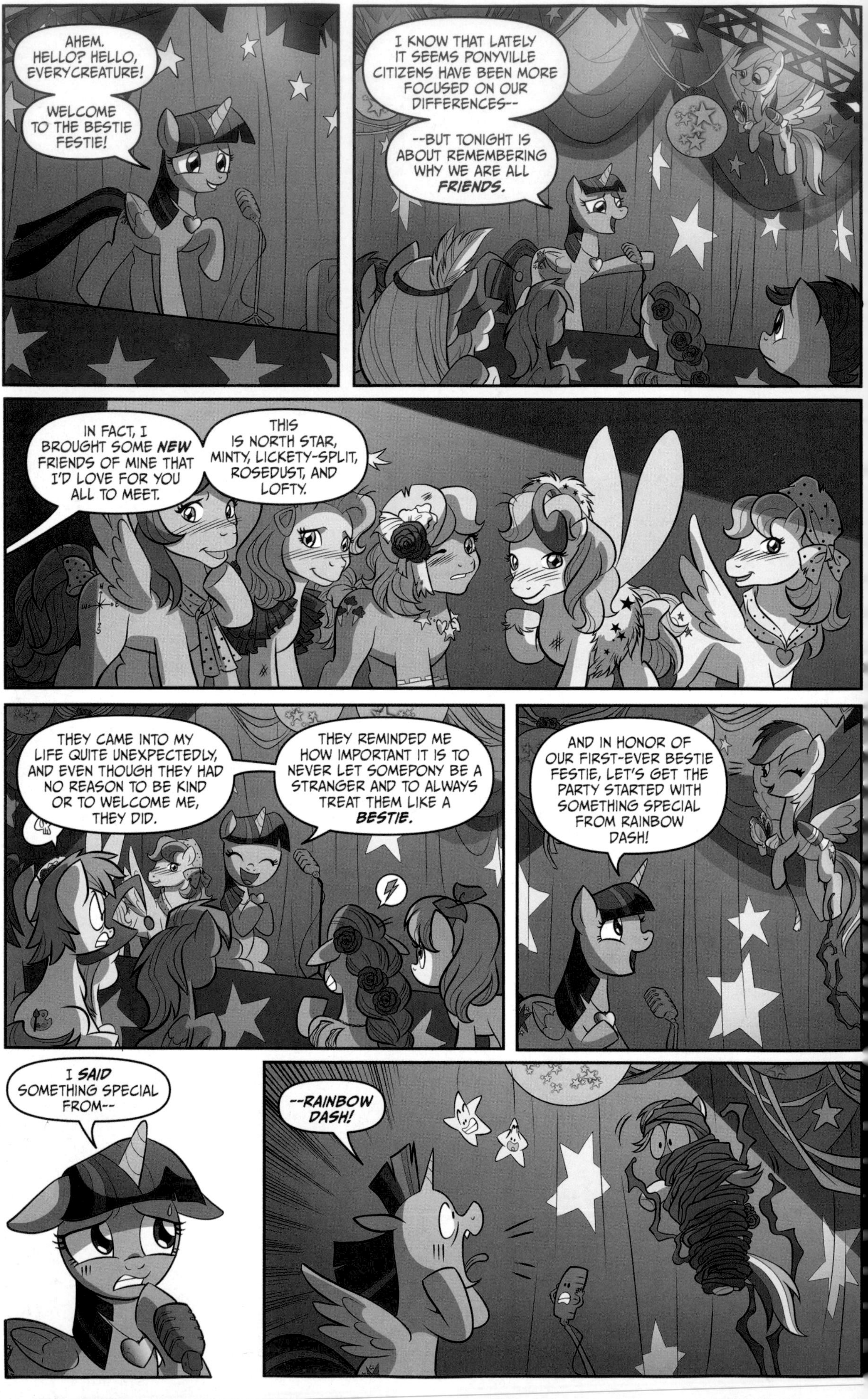
AHEM. HELLO? HELLO, EVERYCREATURE!
WELCOME TO THE BESTIE FESTIE!
I KNOW THAT LATELY IT SEEMS PONYVILLE CITIZENS HAVE BEEN MORE FOCUSED ON OUR DIFFERENCES--
--BUT TONIGHT IS ABOUT REMEMBERING WHY WE ARE ALL FRIENDS.
IN FACT, I BROUGHT SOME NEW FRIENDS OF MINE THAT I'D LOVE FOR YOU ALL TO MEET.
THIS IS NORTH STAR, MINTY, LICKETY-SPLIT, ROSEDUST, AND LOFTY.
THEY CAME INTO MY LIFE QUITE UNEXPECTEDLY, AND EVEN THOUGH THEY HAD NO REASON TO BE KIND OR TO WELCOME ME, THEY DID.
THEY REMINDED ME HOW IMPORTANT IT IS TO NEVER LET SOMEPONY BE A STRANGER AND TO ALWAYS TREAT THEM LIKE A BESTIE.
AND IN HONOR OF OUR FIRST-EVER BESTIE FESTIE, LET'S GET THE PARTY STARTED WITH SOMETHING SPECIAL FROM RAINBOW DASH!
I SAID SOMETHING SPECIAL FROM--
--RAINBOW DASH!

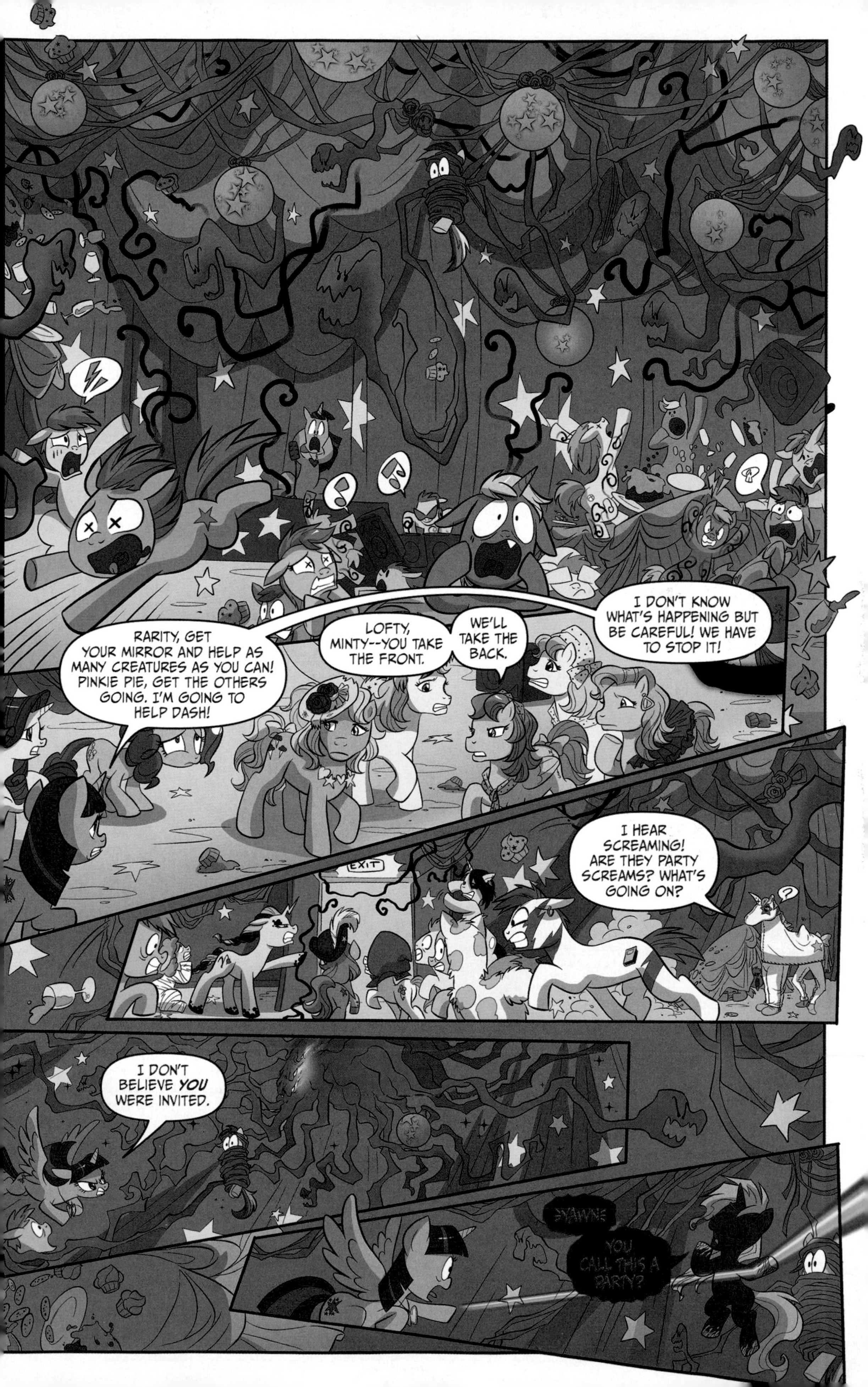
RARITY, GET YOUR MIRROR AND HELP AS MANY CREATURES AS YOU CAN! PINKIE PIE, GET THE OTHERS GOING. I'M GOING TO HELP DASH!
LOFTY, MINTY--YOU TAKE THE FRONT.
WE'LL TAKE THE BACK.
I DON'T KNOW WHAT'S HAPPENING BUT BE CAREFUL! WE HAVE TO STOP IT!
EXIT
I HEAR SCREAMING! ARE THEY PARTY SCREAMS? WHAT'S GOING ON?
I DON'T BELIEVE *YOU* WERE INVITED.
YAWN
YOU CALL THIS A PARTY?

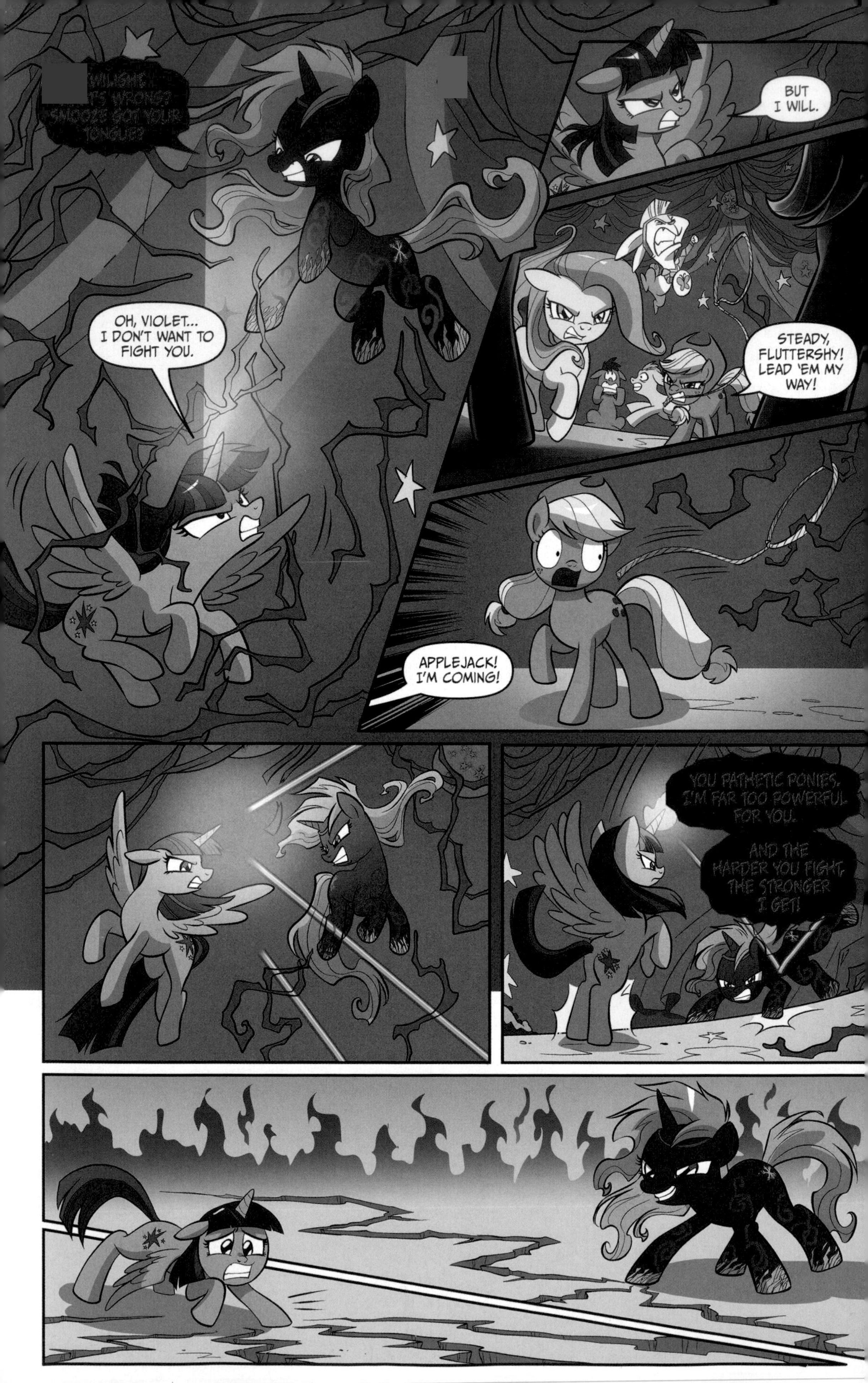
[redacted]WILIGHT. [redacted]T'S WRONG? SMOOZE GOT YOUR TONGUE?
OH, VIOLET... I DON'T WANT TO FIGHT YOU.
BUT I WILL.
STEADY, FLUTTERSHY! LEAD 'EM MY WAY!
APPLEJACK! I'M COMING!
YOU PATHETIC PONIES. I'M FAR TOO POWERFUL FOR YOU.
AND THE HARDER YOU FIGHT, THE STRONGER I GET!

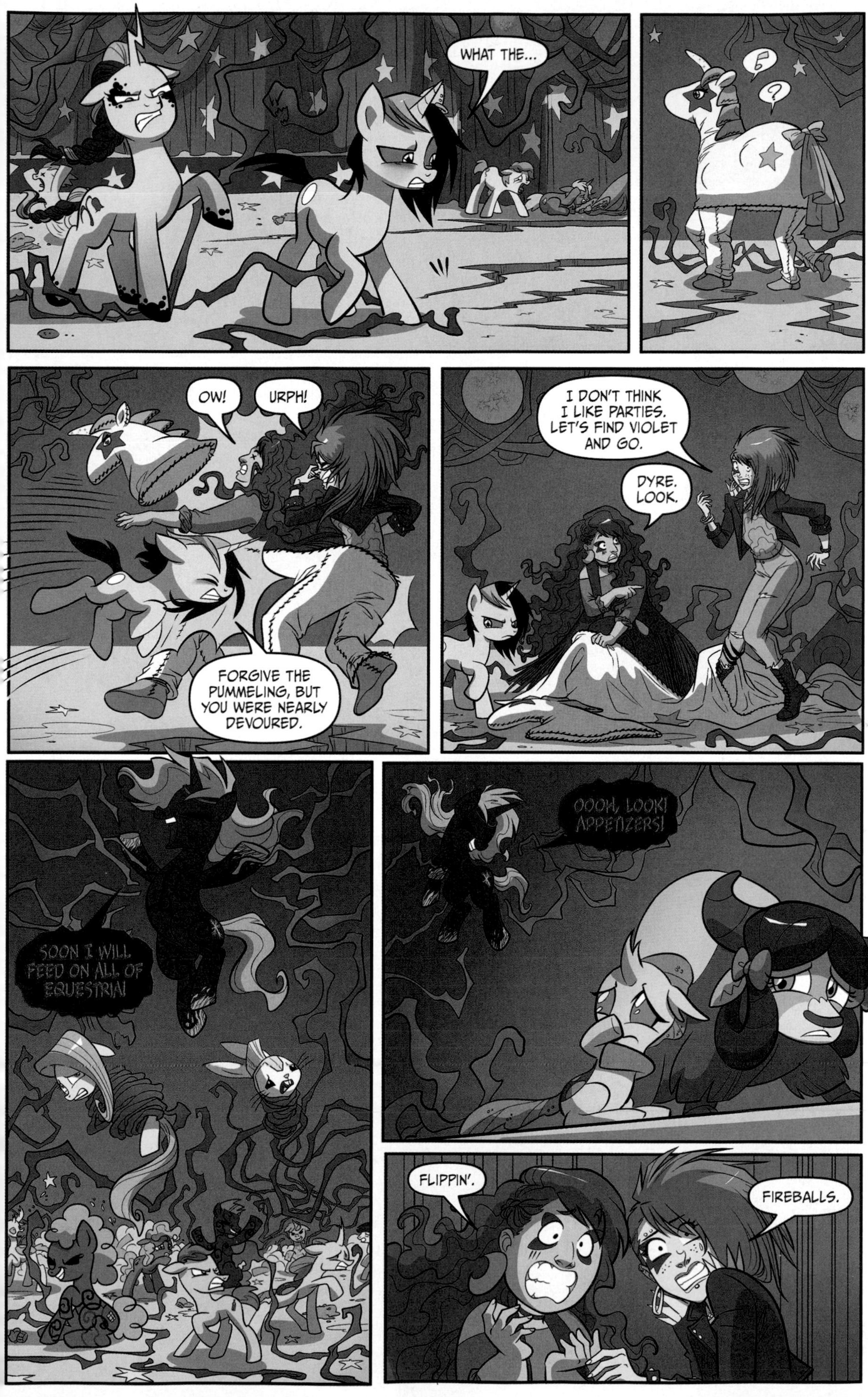
WHAT THE...
OW!
URPH!
FORGIVE THE PUMMELING, BUT YOU WERE NEARLY DEVOURED.
I DON'T THINK I LIKE PARTIES. LET'S FIND VIOLET AND GO.
DYRE. LOOK.
SOON I WILL FEED ON ALL OF EQUESTRIA!
OOOH, LOOK! APPETIZERS!
FLIPPIN'.
FIREBALLS.

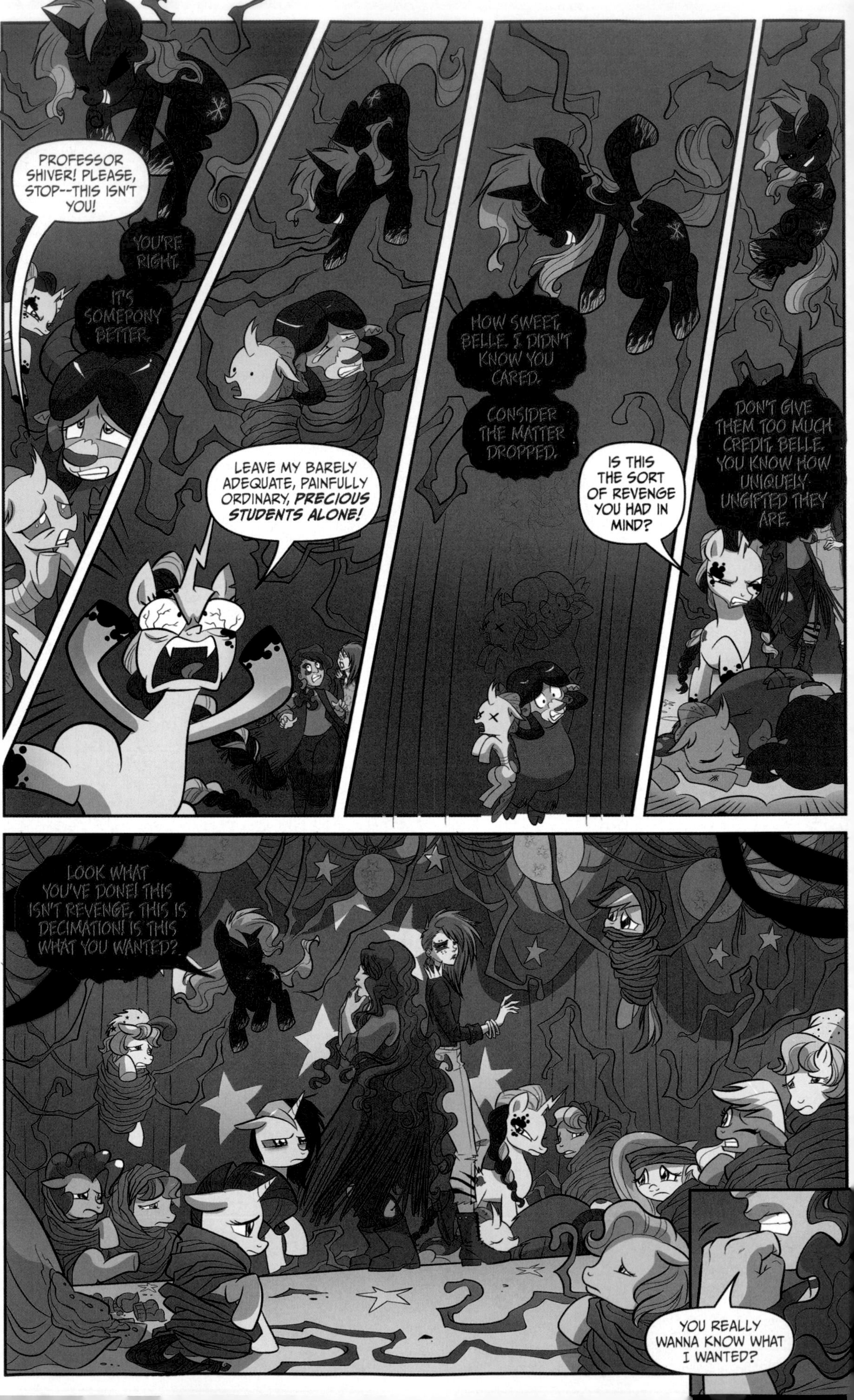
PROFESSOR SHIVER! PLEASE, STOP--THIS ISN'T YOU!
YOU'RE RIGHT.
IT'S SOMEPONY BETTER.
LEAVE MY BARELY ADEQUATE, PAINFULLY ORDINARY, PRECIOUS STUDENTS ALONE!
HOW SWEET, BELLE. I DIDN'T KNOW YOU CARED.
CONSIDER THE MATTER DROPPED.
IS THIS THE SORT OF REVENGE YOU HAD IN MIND?
DON'T GIVE THEM TOO MUCH CREDIT, BELLE. YOU KNOW HOW UNIQUELY UNGIFTED THEY ARE.
LOOK WHAT YOU'VE DONE! THIS ISN'T REVENGE, THIS IS DECIMATION! IS THIS WHAT YOU WANTED?
YOU REALLY WANNA KNOW WHAT I WANTED?

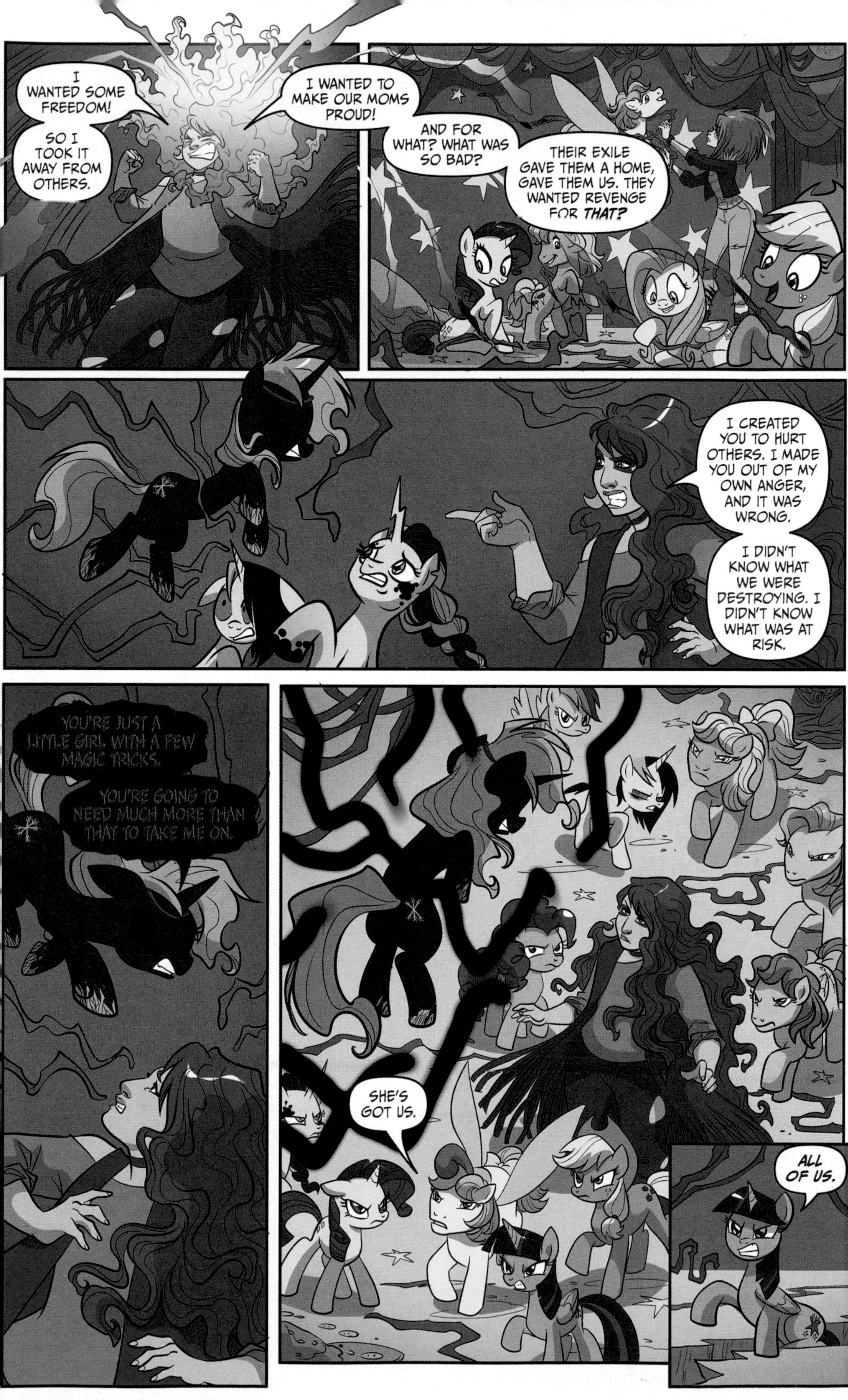
I WANTED SOME FREEDOM!
SO I TOOK IT AWAY FROM OTHERS.
I WANTED TO MAKE OUR MOMS PROUD!
AND FOR WHAT? WHAT WAS SO BAD?
THEIR EXILE GAVE THEM A HOME, GAVE THEM US. THEY WANTED REVENGE FOR *THAT?*
I CREATED YOU TO HURT OTHERS. I MADE YOU OUT OF MY OWN ANGER, AND IT WAS WRONG.
I DIDN'T KNOW WHAT WE WERE DESTROYING. I DIDN'T KNOW WHAT WAS AT RISK.
YOU'RE JUST A LITTLE GIRL WITH A FEW MAGIC TRICKS.
YOU'RE GOING TO NEED MUCH MORE THAN THAT TO TAKE ME ON.
SHE'S GOT US.
ALL OF US.

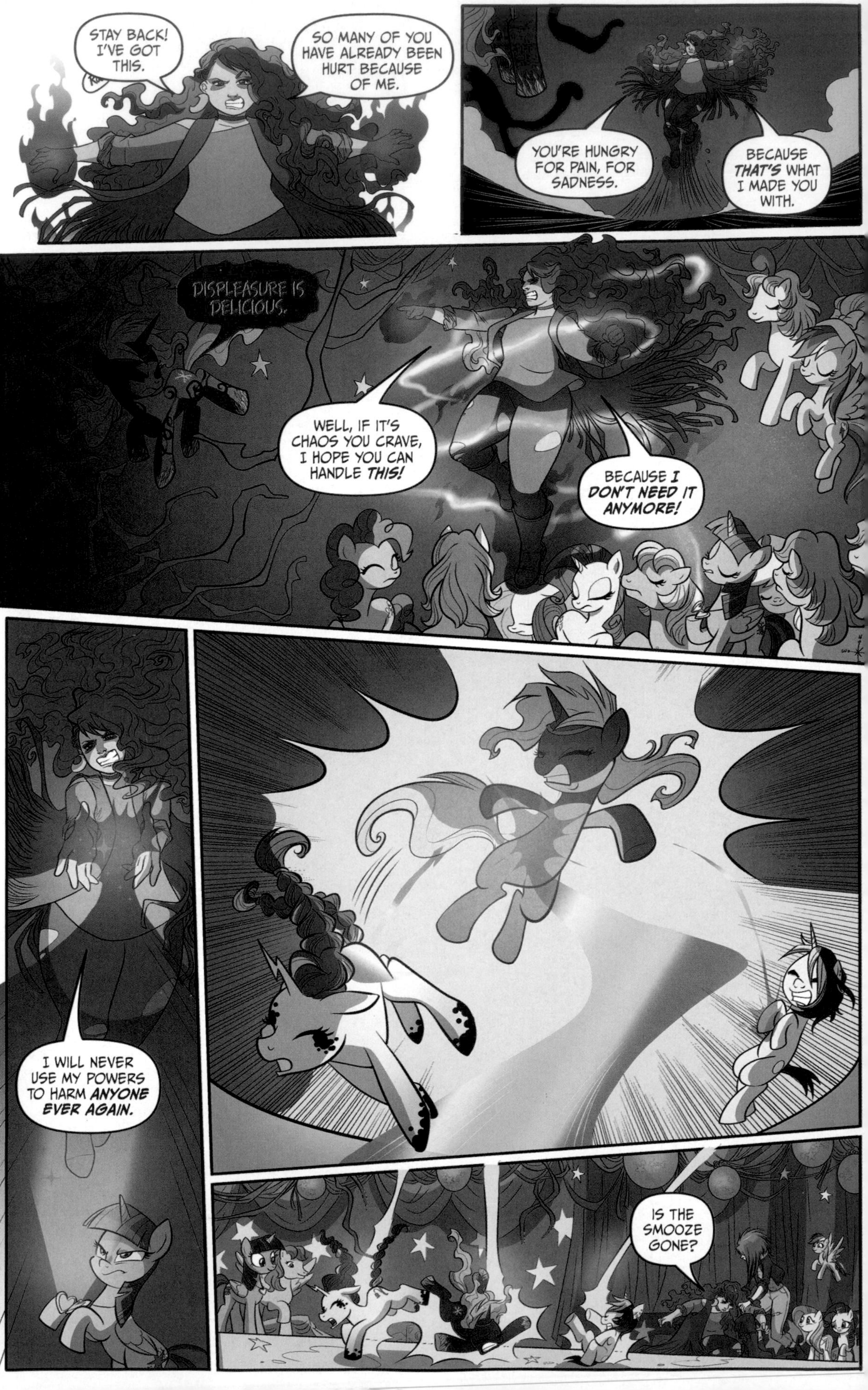
STAY BACK! I'VE GOT THIS.
SO MANY OF YOU HAVE ALREADY BEEN HURT BECAUSE OF ME.
YOU'RE HUNGRY FOR PAIN, FOR SADNESS.
BECAUSE THAT'S WHAT I MADE YOU WITH.
DISPLEASURE IS DELICIOUS.
WELL, IF IT'S CHAOS YOU CRAVE, I HOPE YOU CAN HANDLE THIS!
BECAUSE I DON'T NEED IT ANYMORE!
I WILL NEVER USE MY POWERS TO HARM ANYONE EVER AGAIN.
IS THE SMOOZE GONE?

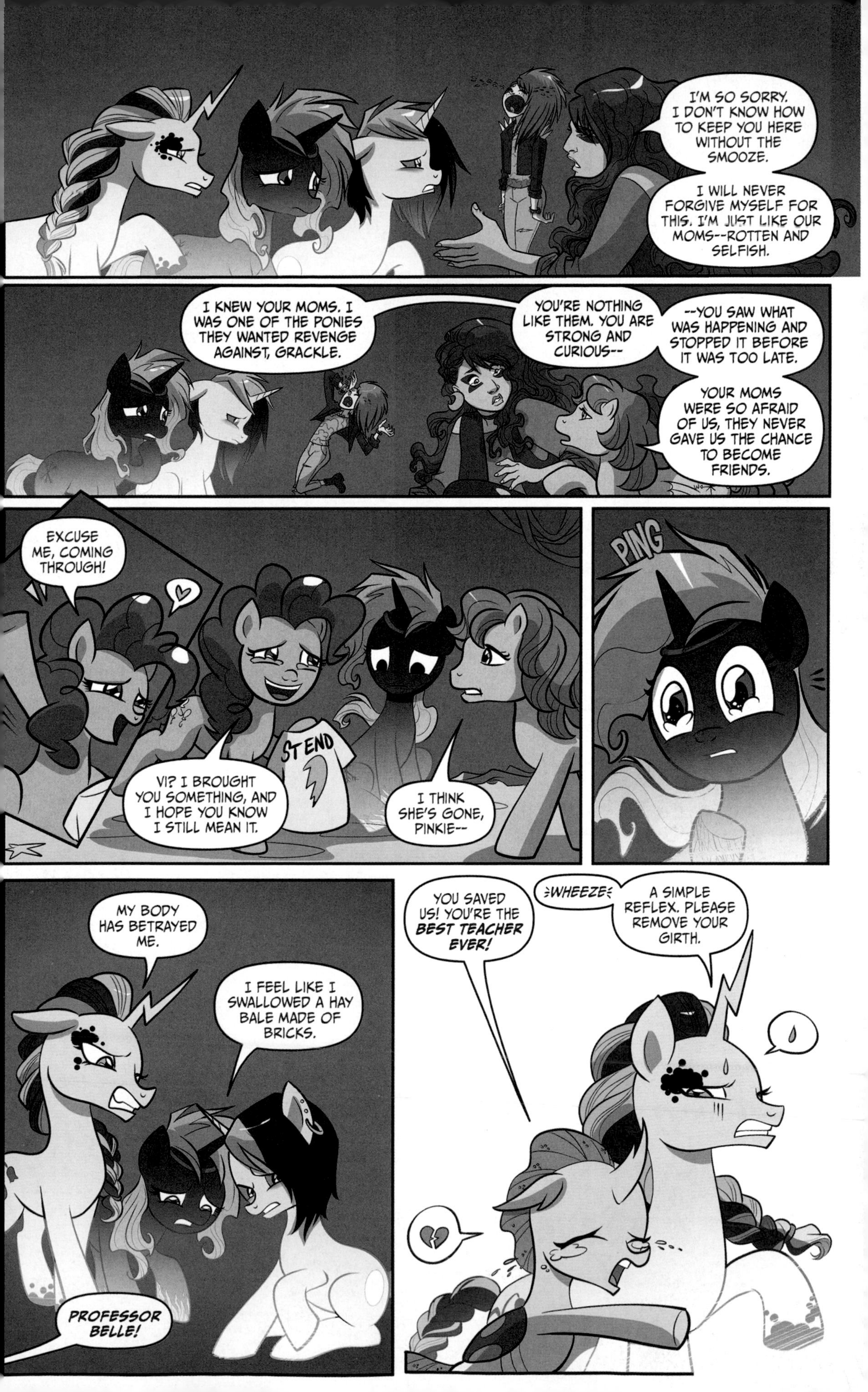
I'M SO SORRY. I DON'T KNOW HOW TO KEEP YOU HERE WITHOUT THE SMOOZE.
I WILL NEVER FORGIVE MYSELF FOR THIS. I'M JUST LIKE OUR MOMS--ROTTEN AND SELFISH.
I KNEW YOUR MOMS. I WAS ONE OF THE PONIES THEY WANTED REVENGE AGAINST, GRACKLE.
YOU'RE NOTHING LIKE THEM. YOU ARE STRONG AND CURIOUS--
--YOU SAW WHAT WAS HAPPENING AND STOPPED IT BEFORE IT WAS TOO LATE.
YOUR MOMS WERE SO AFRAID OF US, THEY NEVER GAVE US THE CHANCE TO BECOME FRIENDS.
EXCUSE ME, COMING THROUGH!
VI? I BROUGHT YOU SOMETHING, AND I HOPE YOU KNOW I STILL MEAN IT.
ST END
I THINK SHE'S GONE, PINKIE--
PING
MY BODY HAS BETRAYED ME.
I FEEL LIKE I SWALLOWED A HAY BALE MADE OF BRICKS.
PROFESSOR BELLE!
YOU SAVED US! YOU'RE THE BEST TEACHER EVER!
WHEEZE
A SIMPLE REFLEX. PLEASE REMOVE YOUR GIRTH.

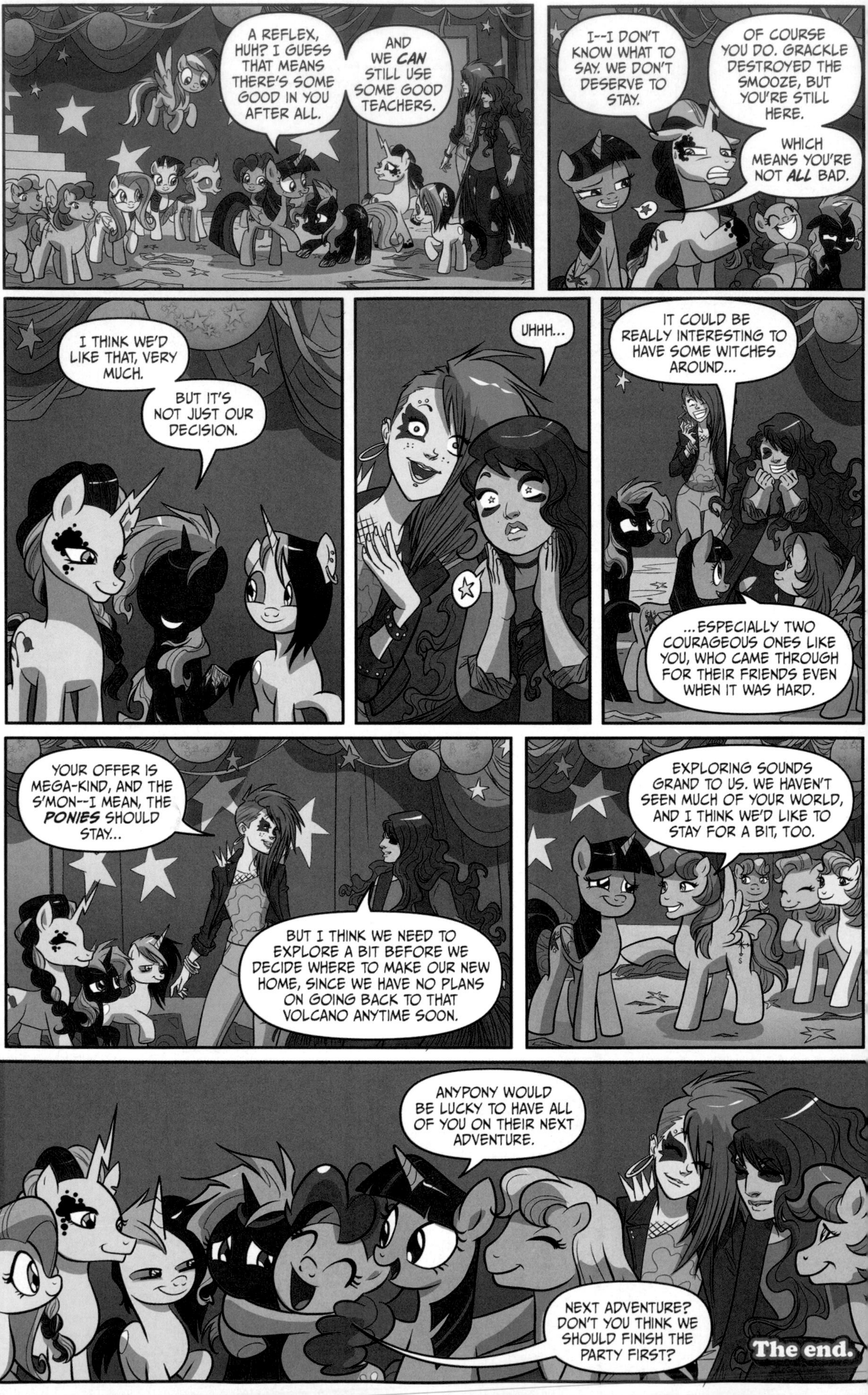
A REFLEX, HUH? I GUESS THAT MEANS THERE'S SOME GOOD IN YOU AFTER ALL.
AND WE *CAN* STILL USE SOME GOOD TEACHERS.
I--I DON'T KNOW WHAT TO SAY. WE DON'T DESERVE TO STAY.
OF COURSE YOU DO. GRACKLE DESTROYED THE SMOOZE, BUT YOU'RE STILL HERE.
WHICH MEANS YOU'RE NOT *ALL* BAD.
I THINK WE'D LIKE THAT, VERY MUCH.
BUT IT'S NOT JUST OUR DECISION.
UHHH...
IT COULD BE REALLY INTERESTING TO HAVE SOME WITCHES AROUND...
...ESPECIALLY TWO COURAGEOUS ONES LIKE YOU, WHO CAME THROUGH FOR THEIR FRIENDS EVEN WHEN IT WAS HARD.
YOUR OFFER IS MEGA-KIND, AND THE S'MON--I MEAN, THE ***PONIES*** SHOULD STAY...
BUT I THINK WE NEED TO EXPLORE A BIT BEFORE WE DECIDE WHERE TO MAKE OUR NEW HOME, SINCE WE HAVE NO PLANS ON GOING BACK TO THAT VOLCANO ANYTIME SOON.
EXPLORING SOUNDS GRAND TO US. WE HAVEN'T SEEN MUCH OF YOUR WORLD, AND I THINK WE'D LIKE TO STAY FOR A BIT, TOO.
ANYPONY WOULD BE LUCKY TO HAVE ALL OF YOU ON THEIR NEXT ADVENTURE.
NEXT ADVENTURE? DON'T YOU THINK WE SHOULD FINISH THE PARTY FIRST?
The end.

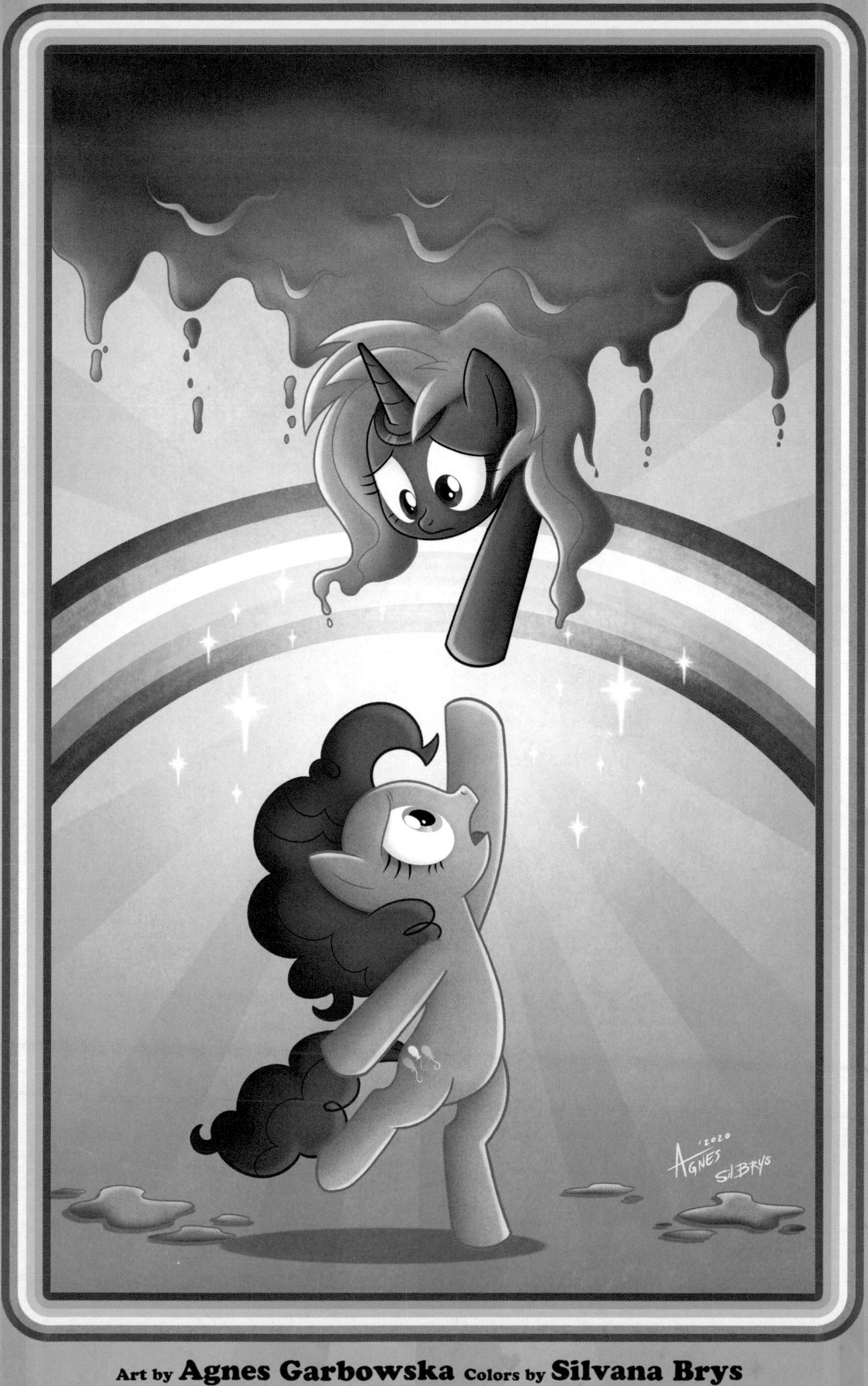
'2020
AGNES
SILBRYS
Art by **Agnes Garbowska** Colors by **Silvana Brys**

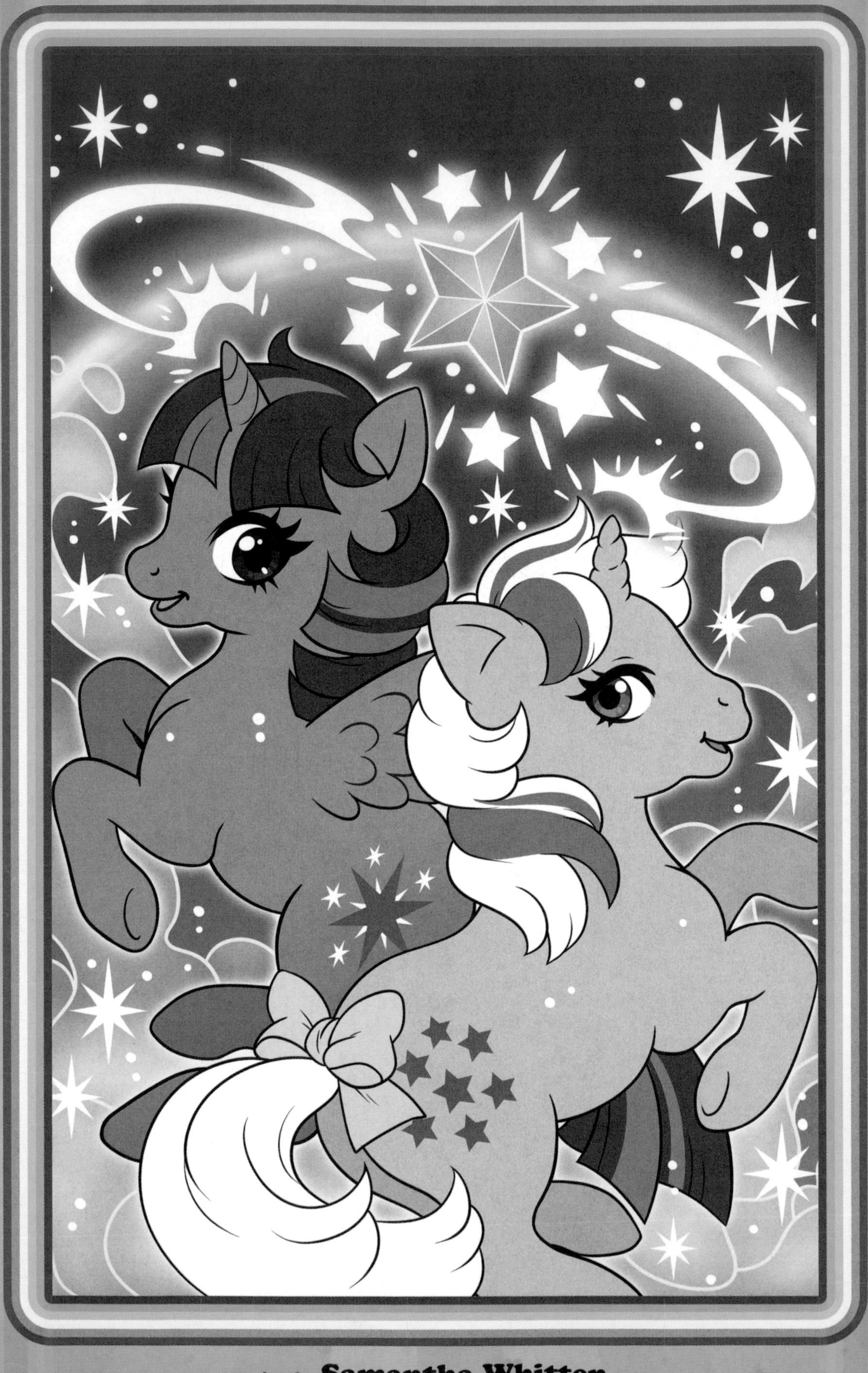

Art by **Samantha Whitten**

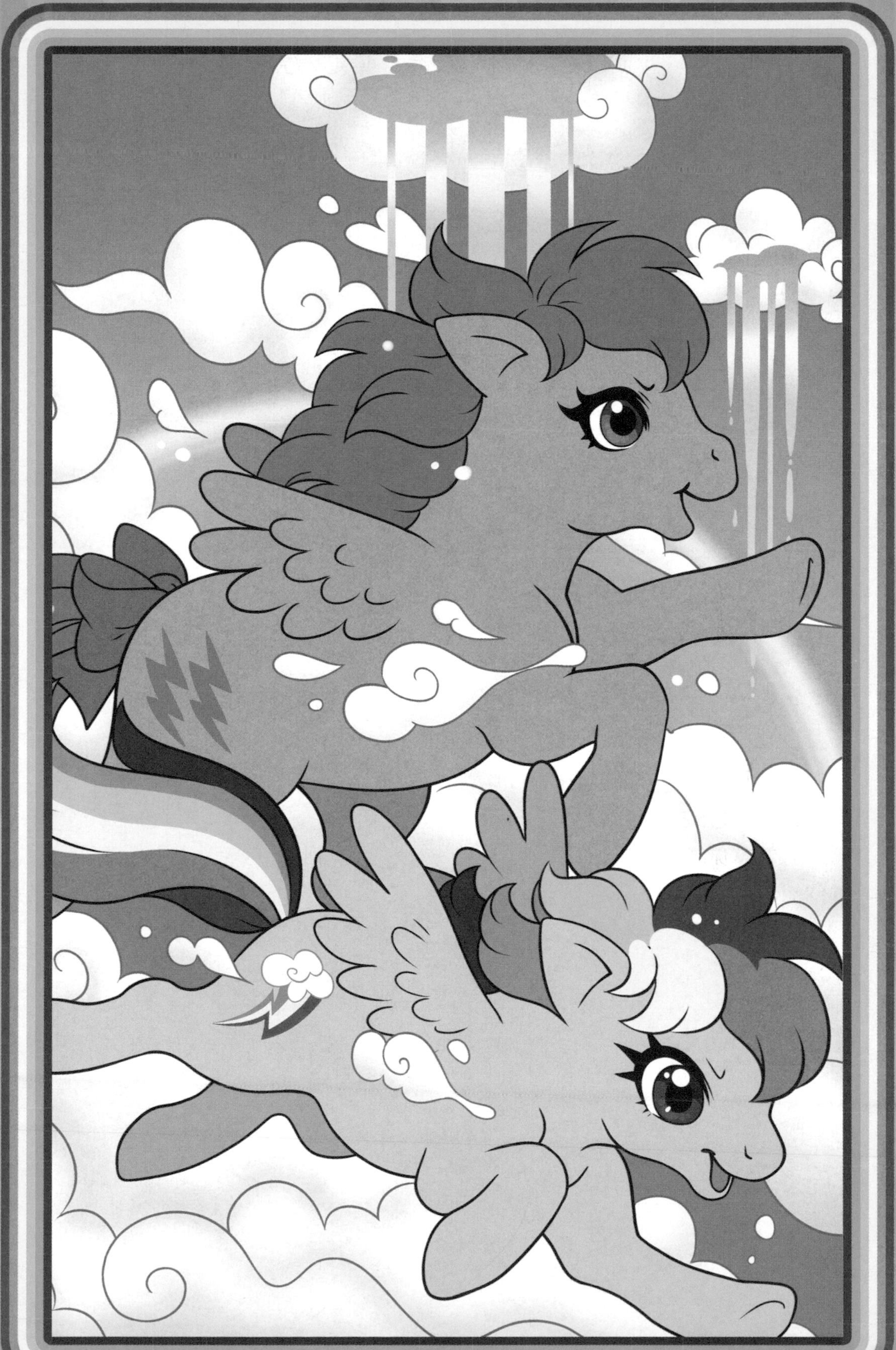

Art by **Samantha Whitten**

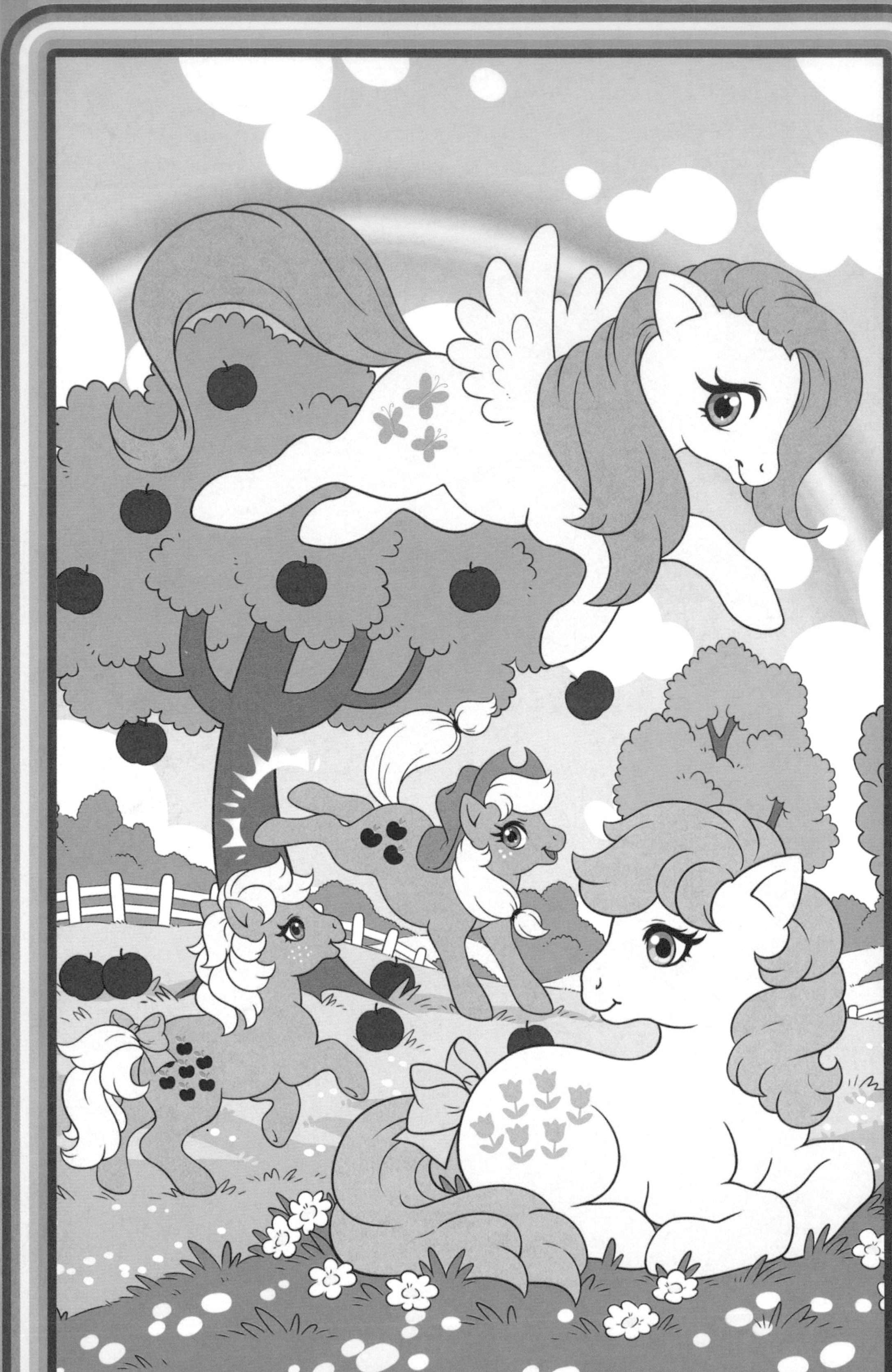

Art by **Samantha Whitten**

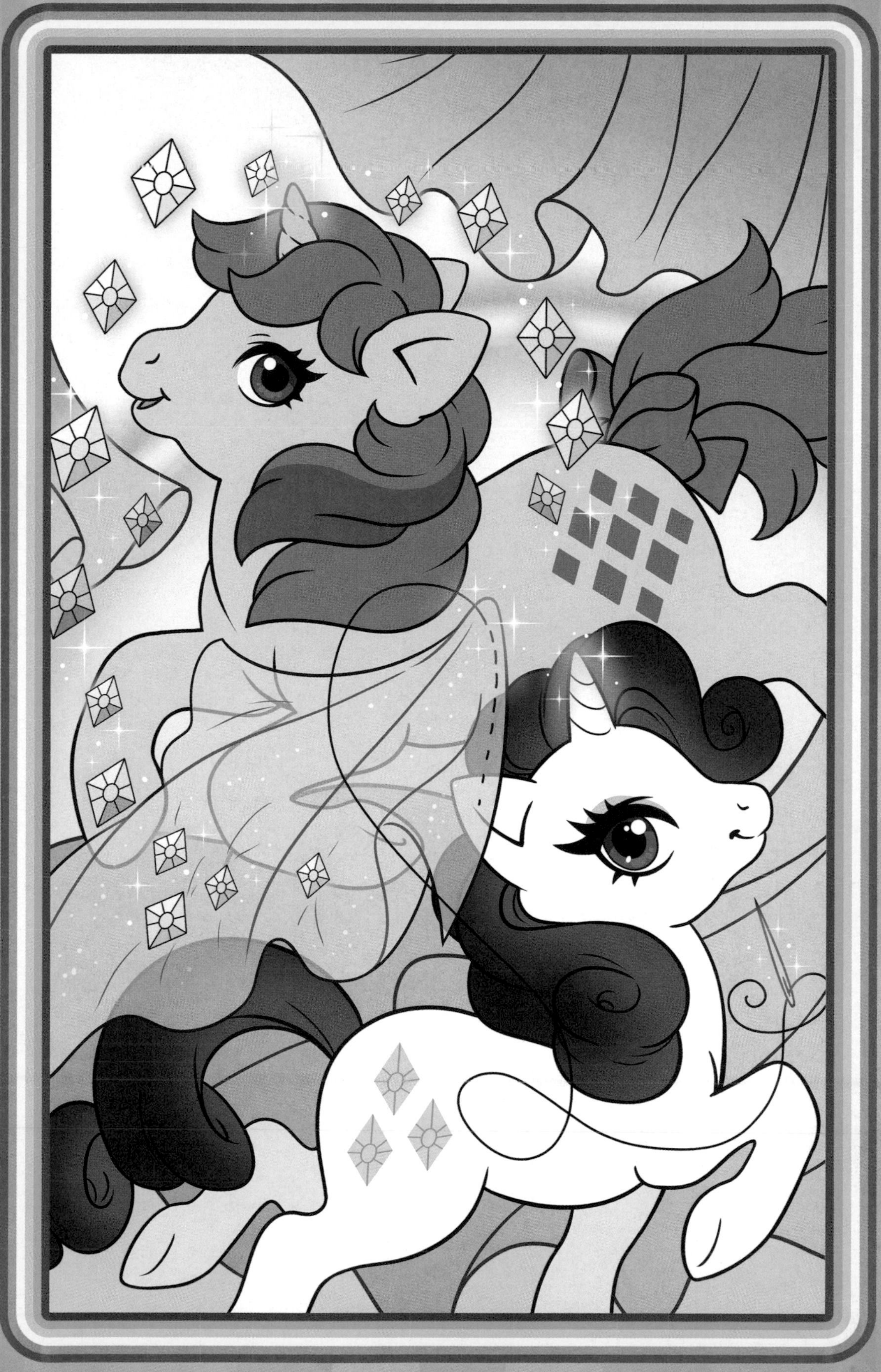

Art by **Samantha Whitten**

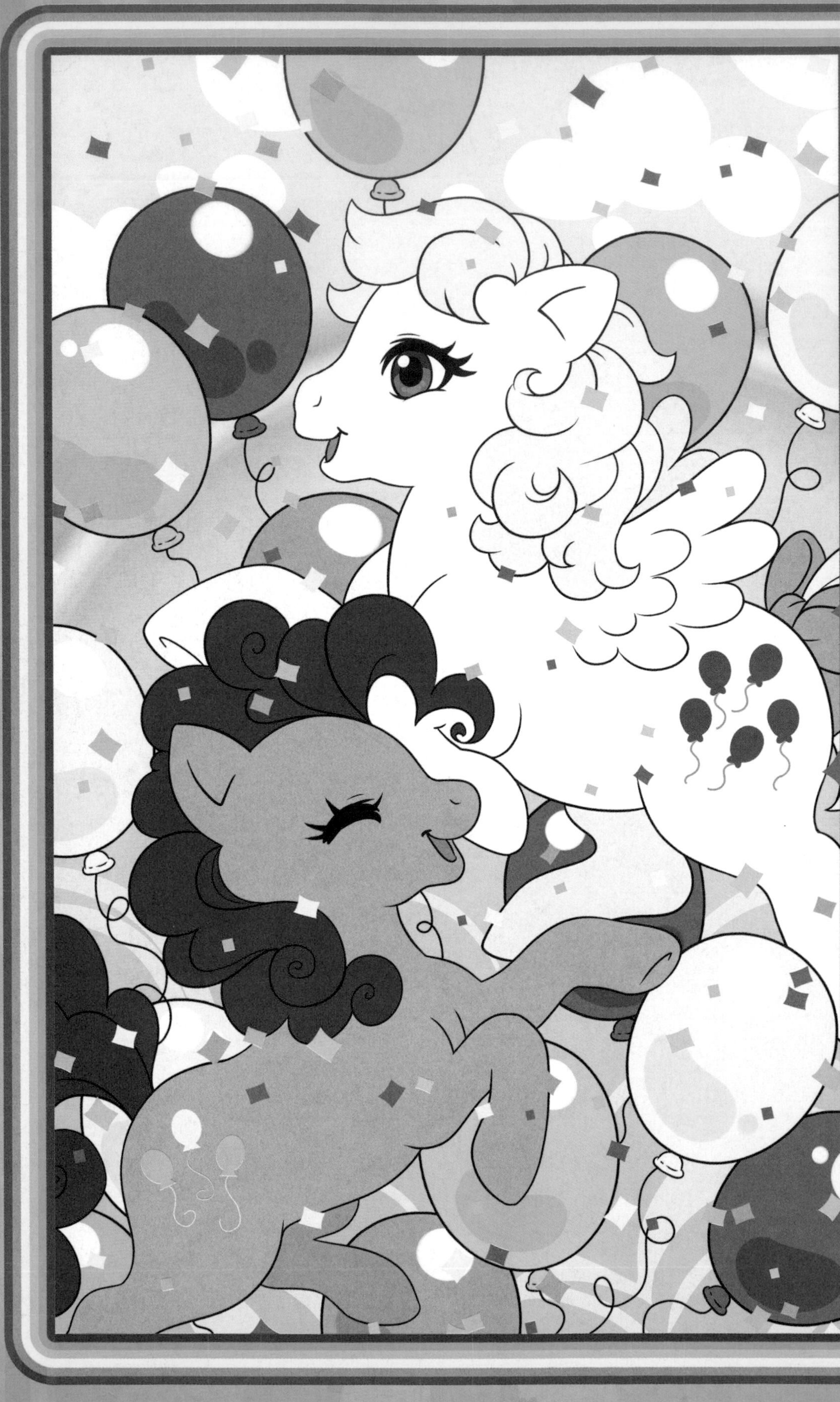

Art by **Samantha Whitten**

GENERATIONS

my LiTTLE PONY

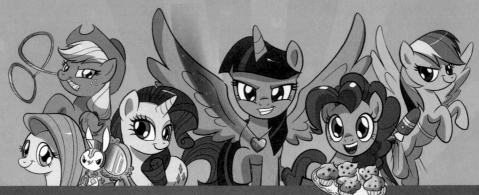

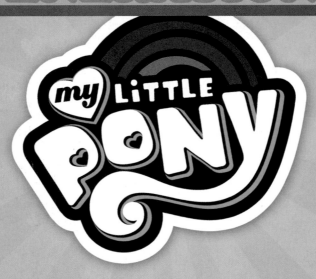